The Oak Island Book Club

THE
OAK ISLAND
BOOK CLUB

CAMERON KENT

PLOT HOUND BOOKS

Winston-Salem

PLOT HOUND BOOKS
Press 53, LLC
PO Box 30314
Winston-Salem, NC 27130

First Edition

Cover design by Kevin Morgan Watson

Library of Congress Control Number
2023950664

ISBN 978-1-950413-73-7

This story is dedicated to all of you who love reading as much as I do. To all of you who dive into a good book for pleasure, enlightenment, or escape. To all of you who started your reading journey with a flashlight under the covers and still love the crackle of the spine of a new book or the distinct aroma of an old one. To all of you who find meaning, value, and purpose in the written word. You are my kindred spirits.

THE
OAK ISLAND
BOOK CLUB

CHAPTER ONE

"Oh, I just want what we all want: a comfortable
couch, a nice beverage, a weekend of no distractions
and a book that will stop time, lift me out of my
quotidian existence and alter my thinking forever."

— Elizabeth Gilbert

A rattlesnake in the mailbox. *A slight nudge on a subway platform. A hitman with reasonable rates.* These were just some of the ways Nicole Shepherd imagined she could kill her husband without going to prison. She was drenched in self-loathing for even allowing such dark thoughts to seep into her brain, but her intense hatred of Lee Wayne Shepherd was far stronger than any shame she might feel over her morbid musings. The murderous plots that swirled inside her would soon come rushing back because she was about to receive the worst news possible following her husband's emergency heart surgery. He'd survived.

Nicole nervously tapped her foot to no particular rhythm as she sat in the waiting room at New Hanover Regional Medical Center in Wilmington, North Carolina. She occasionally glanced at the pages of her book but was easily distracted whenever there was any sound or movement in the crowded room. A visual survey of the anxiety-ridden faces seated around her made Nicole feel certain that she was the only one among them who was secretly praying for a terrible outcome. She checked her watch. It was 1:30 in the afternoon. The three hours she'd been waiting felt like ten. She took that as a good sign that there might be complications.

Nicole could have easily hesitated several minutes before calling an ambulance when Lee Wayne Shepherd collapsed in a cold sweat on their kitchen floor that morning, or never even called 9-1-1 at all. As much suffering as this man had rained down on her, there would have been some macabre satisfaction in watching him doubled over in pain and slipping away. Nature would take its course on his weak heart and her nightmare would be over. She could finally stop entertaining dark thoughts about ways she could assist in his demise. But she hadn't waited, not even for a moment. For better or worse, mostly worse, she was still the good wife. She'd gotten him to the hospital and his life was no longer in her hands.

"Mrs. Shepherd?" called out the handsome young doctor in green scrubs as he entered the waiting room. He tugged his surgical mask down below his chin and motioned Nicole to a corner for more privacy.

Nicole bookmarked her used paperback copy of Lisa Genova's *Still Alice* and clutched it in her hand as she rose gracefully to her feet and smoothed back her shoulder-length blonde hair. Her legs buckled slightly as she crossed the room to join the doctor. She was unable to absorb another word after hearing the doctor say "I have good news for you."

It punched the air out of her like a cheap shot from a boxer. The two short breaths she sucked in without exhaling in between were not of apparent relief. They were of bitter disappointment, born out of long-simmering contempt for the man she'd married. She despised Lee Wayne Shepherd with the same bile-inducing hatred usually reserved for ancient warring clans, but it was an animus she kept hidden through polite Southern manners and heavy makeup, primarily out of fear of reprisal.

She had been so ready to play the role of the newly minted widow, having repeatedly rehearsed her anguished speech upon hearing the "bad news." Her performance was going to be magnificent and memorable. The hospital staff would witness grief and suffering as never before. It would require several sets of strong arms just to steady her from the emotional blow that her husband was dearly departed. It was all going to feel so liberating. She had fully anticipated that the next chapter of her life was going to start right there in that hospital waiting room, followed shortly by a funeral service next to a deep hole in the cold, unforgiving ground, but Lee Wayne's dark heart had not cooperated with the scenario she'd envisioned for so long. Along with her dignity and dreams, it was just one more thing Lee Wayne had stolen from her.

She carried not an ounce of guilt for feeling relieved, exhilarated even, by the notion of her husband's death. She had earned it. She deserved it. His failing heart had given her hope that his time had come and hers was about to begin, but Lee Wayne had foiled her ardent prayers. His return from death's door meant that her renaissance would have to wait.

"When—" she started to say, wanting to finish the sentence with *is that cretin finally going to die?* but sensing the inappropriateness of complete honesty in this situation, she instead peeped "— may I see him?" Her voice was gentle, with a slight accent that was Southern but not country.

"He's recovering in a Step Down Unit. It's one level below intensive care," replied the doctor. "I'll get a nurse to take you back there."

Nicole's eyes filled with a film of tears. The doctor took her free hand and held it gently in both of his. "Try not to worry. We had a few complications, but he'll be okay." She nodded silently, but couldn't have disagreed more. It would only have been okay if the hands she was now touching hadn't been so skillful.

She could feel the dark, soul-stealing anger she had stored up over the years starting to seep out of her as she rapidly tapped her book against the side of her thigh. Nicole no longer had dreams. She only had flashbacks. As always, she fought to keep her true feelings hidden from public view. She knew the consequences if she didn't and she had the scars to prove it.

Ping. Ping. Ping. It sounded like someone was driving railroad spikes just outside his bedroom window, or perhaps directly into his skull. Drew Endicott swore once under his breath, then twice above it. He used every curse word he knew and then invented a few more. He was only partially awake but still fully in bed with a blistering hangover from a pint of bourbon and not an ounce of desire to do anything about it.

Drew massaged his temples with the heels of his hands. His swollen eyes were slammed shut, a common occurrence after the nights when he couldn't stand the pain of missing his wife and daughter. Regrettably, those nights were coming with more frequency. He'd convinced himself he could stop drinking any time he wanted to. He just didn't want to. His bed and the bottle next to it were his safe harbor during those unbearable times, and his resentment was growing that some noisemaking agent outside his window had barged into his muted refuge. He groaned and rolled over to the side of the mattress mashed up against the far wall and opened one eye, poking his finger through the blackout curtains to peer outside. Sunlight bounced off the pallor of his puffy and unshaven face.

In the backyard adjacent to his, just beyond the rusted chain-link fence that separated the two houses, an elderly Asian woman was attempting to pound a metal pole into the ground with a stone. She was barely taller than the five-foot pole she was vainly trying to hammer into the baked earth. Her progress with each blow on the metal pole was minimal, but she banged on, undeterred.

"Perfect," Drew said with a derisive shake of his head. "Early risers," he muttered to himself through two deep breaths. "Just what I'm looking for in a new neighbor." He often talked to himself these days, because there was nobody else who would listen.

Drew rolled back over and looked at his nightstand. A half-empty fifth of Woodford Reserve Kentucky bourbon obscured the numbers on the alarm clock. Actually, it was just a clock. He hadn't set the alarm in nearly two years. Not since the morning he'd gotten up early to put on a black suit. He propped himself up on both elbows to get a clearer look at the digital numbers on the clock. He blinked hard and leaned closer to the dial. It was one-thirty in the afternoon. "Oh," he whispered as if apologizing to the elderly woman for complaining about her pinging.

Drew rubbed his crusted eyes with his thumb and forefinger and swung his legs onto the floor. He finally stood, shakily, ready to start what was left of Friday. He didn't intend to seize the day but merely survive it. Judging by the dirty clothes scattered across his bedroom, it was abundantly clear that he honestly didn't care much about anything right now.

The book he'd been reading had tumbled onto the carpet next to his bed. The gooseneck book light was still dimly lit from the night before. He switched it off and carefully placed the book back on his nightstand. It was William Faulkner's *As I Lay Dying*. Drew had read somewhere that Faulkner had written the book between the hours of midnight and four in the morning, so he figured that was also the best time to read it. Might as well. He was always awake at that hour anyway. He'd been easily absorbed in Faulkner's description of Cash Bundren building the coffin for his own mother. He was happy to add Cash's pain to his own.

Drew sipped the last warm drops from the tumbler of burnt whiskey from the hard night before and returned the glass to the nightstand, the veneer of which was stained with whitish circles from various beverages. Coffee would be the next liquid to pass his lips. Hot and black and plentiful.

Drew saw himself in the full-length mirror attached to the back of the bedroom door. The flesh on his stomach looked like a blob of dough that had been laid out to make buttermilk biscuits. His sallow, stubbly face was obvious evidence of a life turned inward. On most days, normalcy seemed like a vestige from a lost world. He was only alive on the outside. Over the last two years, everything within him had withered away, like an old oak tree that was hollow and rotting on the inside, filled with nothingness and ready to topple over in the next stiff wind. Drew's natural instinct for creativity and achievement had been extinguished. He no longer wanted to thrive. Some days he wasn't even sure if he wanted to live. Life felt like he was constantly walking upstream in swift water. Trudging along, but just barely staying in one place.

His reflection disgusted him to the point where he couldn't look anymore. He immediately decided he would do something about it. He took down the mirror.

His mind drifted back to a time and place he'd been just the day before and the mysterious woman on the beach at Oak Island.

For nearly two years since the drownings, Drew had aggressively avoided human contact, even eye contact, but he suddenly sensed he was ready to make an exception.

The woman stole all of his attention. Her movement was magnetic, powerful enough to pull Drew out of the book he was reading and back into real life. Slowly and gracefully, the striking figure emerged through the winding access between two beach houses. The muscles in her toned legs flexed with each step as she walked through the deep, toasted sand to seek a suitable spot near the water. She carried a chair in one hand and a beach umbrella in the other, with a canvas tote bag slung over one shoulder.

Drew's eyes followed her as she stopped just thirty yards from him, seemingly unaware that he was even there. He should have been disappointed that his solitude was ending. He'd been quite content sharing his secluded space with only Tom Wingo and the other vivid characters in Pat Conroy's *The Prince of Tides*, but now he couldn't keep his eyes on the written words in front of him.

She was deliberate yet fluid as she went through the necessary steps to set up camp. Sliding the tote bag off her shoulder. Unfolding her turquoise chair and carefully placing a towel over the backrest. Pushing her small beach umbrella into the sand and raising the sunflower yellow awning to cast a circular shadow. Slipping off her lace cover-up to unveil a black, two-piece bathing suit that accentuated the best parts of a well-proportioned figure. Her hair, straight and still naturally buttery blonde, fluttered in the light breeze. Her part was slightly left of center and crooked, like the side profile of a staircase, apparently done with no expectations of running into anyone she might know. Her eyes were hidden by dark, squarish sunglasses that covered most of the top half of her face and added to her mystique.

Drew continued to take her in from a distance, peering silently over the top of his book through tortoiseshell sunglasses. He guessed she was about thirty years old, maybe younger, but certain he was at least five years older. He didn't want to intrude upon her privacy, but he couldn't help it. There was something so intriguing about the new arrival to the beach that he simply couldn't stop watching. He convinced himself that he was merely observing and not spying. After all, he'd made a living through casual surveillance and analysis of strangers, so it was second nature. And he rationalized that he certainly wasn't the first person to 'people watch' on a public beach.

The woman applied a generous mist of sunscreen, delicately rubbing it into her lightly tanned skin. She turned slowly in both directions, carefully scanning the area as if to assess her new surroundings and the creatures who inhabited it. Her eyes never stopped on Drew as her gaze systematically covered the shore like the circulating beam of a lighthouse. Satisfied, she sat down in her chair and adjusted her balance in the soft sand around her. She still hadn't acknowledged his presence, nor changed her stoic expression. Under the protection of the umbrella, she finally removed her sunglasses and slipped them into her tote bag. She removed a paperback book, winged it open on her knees, and started reading.

Despite his best efforts to mind his own business, Drew felt compelled to study her. He strained his eyes to see the title of the book she was reading, wondering if it were something with depth and meaning or merely beach tripe. She'd occasionally look up from the pages and out to sea, to some distant place beyond the horizon, perhaps trying to understand how the words she was reading fit into her own life.

Drew attempted to refocus on Conroy's poetic prose but kept reading the same paragraph over and over without fully soaking in the magic of the printed words. He raised his chin to again drink in the woman in the turquoise chair. What was most striking was her elegant posture, even while reading. He sensed it was innate, not learned in some etiquette class. His overall impression was that he found her unrelentingly interesting.

Drew angled his chair so that his back was to the woman, out of his direct line of sight, and for a few minutes, they both disappeared into the pages of their books.

The serenity of the moment was dashed when her cell phone rang. She glanced at the screen, then chuffed and shook her head when she realized who was violating her tranquility. She marked her place in her book and took the call. She spoke briefly in a hushed tone, inaudible over the wind and surf, then quickly stood and walked back toward the house.

Glancing sideways, Drew could sense she was distressed, as if she'd just received bad news, or was simply in no mood to talk to the person on the other end. He had that same look on his own face whenever his mother called.

He watched her enter the beach house nearest to them and close the sliding glass door behind her. Through the large panes, he could see her pacing in short circles and raking her fingers through her hair, clearly on a rapid journey to wit's end.

The house itself looked like something you'd see in an architectural magazine but seemed out of place for the North

Carolina coast. It had a gambrel roof and cedar shingles that had weathered to gray in the salt air. The roofline, deck, and sash windows were trimmed in bright white. The house would have blended in effortlessly in Nantucket, but was out of touch with the other beach houses around it, like someone who'd worn a coat and tie to a bluegrass concert. However, at the end of the day, it was a gorgeous residence. Warm and inviting, impressive without opulence, and handsomely maintained. *She must be rich*, he thought. The woman had been gone for nearly twenty minutes when the tide began to encroach upon her encampment. A large wave pushed its foamy waters right to the brink of her chair, then melted into the warm sand.

Before the next wave came lapping, Drew leaped from his beach chair and hurried over to her belongings. He quickly scooped up her chair and canvas bag and carried them to higher ground. He made a return trip for the umbrella and easily pushed it back upright into the sand. He started to walk away but suddenly turned back. He flipped over the paperback book on her chair to see what she was reading. It was Elizabeth Gilbert's *Eat, Pray, Love,* her memoir about finding one's true self in the midst of crisis. The bookmark was near the end. He was impressed.

He moved his own chair to escape the rising tide and sat back down. He read two paragraphs of *The Prince of Tides* but then marked his place and gazed out over the unending expanse of water. He pondered the paradox that was spread in front of him. There was something therapeutic about the ocean, but all he could feel at this moment was its inherent danger. The unharnessed power of the waves and undertow was no match for humans. He was mesmerized by its majesty but at the same time saddened by its cruel role in his own life. How could something so captivatingly beautiful steal the two things he loved most in this world? The waves came crashing in threes: regrets, remorse, and reliving a life of missed opportunities. Would he ever stop blaming himself for what happened? Could he ever forgive himself? He gazed out over the water, looking for answers. As always, none came.

The incessant pinging of metal on metal from next door brought Drew back to the present. "Christ almighty," he muttered.

He lumbered down the hallway in his boxer shorts, weaving

past a stack of unopened moving boxes and stirring up nests of dust that had gathered along the baseboards. He twisted his neck back and forth to loosen the rigid muscles, and silently prayed to whatever deity was in charge of providing coffee. And aspirin.

As his coffee dripped, Drew's mind again flashed back to the mysterious woman on Oak Island and the tiny glimmer of hope their brief encounter had sparked somewhere deep inside of him. For two years it had seemed unlikely to ever be rekindled, but today felt different. He wondered where the woman he'd seen on the beach was at this very moment. What she was doing. What she was reading. Why she'd been so upset. Most of all, if he would ever see her again.

Nicole entered the Cardiac Step Down Unit and saw her husband stretched out on a hospital bed. She studied his pale hands before she looked at his face. Lee Wayne had always looked older than his forty-four years, and today he looked closer to sixty-five. His florid flesh was pierced with tubes and wires of various colors that nourished and monitored him in his near-lifeless state. His hands were motionless. These were the same pernicious hands that had come down with force and menace on her soft flesh too many times to count. The same hands that had sent her fleeing to the ice maker, the makeup counter, the neighbor's house, and even to the Emergency Room at this very hospital, now lay limply at his side. Impotent and worthless, much like the rest of Lee Wayne Shepherd. She pitied him as much as she loathed him. He had no self-worth and thus sought to destroy hers. He tended to blame alcohol dependence and an overbearing father for the strands of cruelty woven into his DNA, but there was no excusing it. And there had been no escaping it. She'd been trapped from the moment she'd married him. His heart attack had been her final chance to flee his despotic kingdom, but he had somehow survived. A singular thought crept into the darkest edges of her mind; *if only I'd waited to call the paramedics.*

The jagged, bouncing lines on his heart monitor taunted her with their rhythm as if beeping with glee over each steady heartbeat. It was her first empirical evidence that Lee Wayne even had a heart at all. Her own pulse was racing to the point where she could feel the throbbing in her neck. She narrowed her eyes and willed the electronic pulse on the monitor to suddenly flat line, but her desperate desire was no match for modern medicine and the cold-blooded vinegar of Lee Wayne's constitution.

When Lee Wayne was ready to be discharged, she'd have to give him a ride home from the hospital. *A left turn into oncoming traffic with the passenger seat airbag turned off. A sudden lurch of the car in the garage as he was crossing in front.* She shook her head to stem the flow of evil plots. She forced her mind to wander back to Oak Island and the stranger on the beach she'd seen just the day before.

She felt her stomach sink and her throat tighten when she realized that someone had encroached upon her secret corner of the universe. What Nicole loved most about this sequestered section of the Oak Island oceanfront was that it was virtually uninhabited during the weekdays. There was no parking for tourists among the beachfront houses so it was as close to a private beach as she would ever experience. Despite this unwanted invasion, she vowed to overcome the disruption into her purposeful social reclusion.

Intentionally ignoring the intruder, she walked slowly and deliberately past the dunes to her favorite spot, the line of beach demarcation where the shelf of dry sand separates from the wet. She could sense that the man seated thirty yards away was watching her as she set up her turquoise chair and yellow umbrella. He was polite in his voyeurism, doing his best to hide his gaze behind his tortoiseshell sunglasses, but she could sense he was studying her. She removed her lace cover-up to reveal the black bikini she'd bought with cash the night before. Her husband would never have permitted her to wear something so brazen in public, but he was currently in Las Vegas and would never know of her sins.

Nicole wasn't boastful of her body, but certainly not ashamed of it. She worked at it. Hard. Other than the grocery store, the gym was one of the only places her controlling husband allowed her to go by herself. She wasn't sure if she exercised because she wanted to stem the gradual shifting of body parts that naturally occurs with aging, or if it was because she wanted to avoid

Lee Wayne Shepherd's piercing barbs about her figure. For whatever reason, she always felt better after working out. For a woman who had just turned thirty-two, Nicole could pass for much younger and since this was one of the few times in her married life that her flesh wasn't marred by purplish bruises, she intended to take advantage of it.

She sprayed on a liberal dose of sunscreen, ensuring that the tan lines from the immodest bathing suit wouldn't betray her when she returned home.

Nicole took a moment to gaze out over the broad basin of blue water. There was something rejuvenating about soaking it in with all of her senses. It brought her peace, but mostly it gave her hope. Beginning with the Vikings, and then Christopher Columbus, the sea had always beckoned the hopeful. Always wondering what awaited them beyond their limited field of vision, and forever optimistic they'd find what they were seeking, even if they didn't yet know exactly what that was. The incessant yearning for a happier life was what constantly called Nicole to the water's edge. She was drawn to that mystical wondering, that optimism, that unending hope that there was something better waiting for her on the other side of the horizon.

As she scanned her surroundings, she intentionally avoided eye contact with the man in the beach chair adjacent to her. She noticed he was reading, or at least pretending to, but beyond that, she made no more mental notes. She removed her sunglasses and slipped them into her bag, then sat down and settled in to read. She pulled out her copy of *Eat, Pray, Love* and reattached herself to Gilbert's soul-searching journey through Italy, India, and Indonesia. Occasionally she'd look up and stare out at the sea, feeling calmed by its sound and movement.

The spell was broken when her phone rang. She glanced at the screen and saw it was Lee Wayne on the other end of the line. Her initial instinct was always to ignore him, but she inevitably took his calls, fearing his wrath if she didn't. *What could he possibly want?* she asked herself. On his last business trip, he'd called to berate her for not packing his slippers. *You should know how much I detest having my bare feet on the carpet of strange hotel rooms!* was the gist of the stinging admonishment. As if it were ultimately *her* responsibility to determine what did and did not get packed in her husband's luggage. He always sounded like a spoiled child calling his mother from summer camp about some missing electronic toy. Eventually, his criticisms would pivot from just missing slippers or whatever else annoyed him at the moment to a comprehensive laundry list of her shortcomings. She knew that if she simply hung up he would call back, repeatedly and incessantly, until she answered. And if she didn't, her flesh would pay for it later when he returned home. So she always just stood there and took it, like a prisoner of war being tortured by the enemy for information, when there was none to give.

"I'm coming home early," squawked Lee Wayne's angry voice over the phone.

Her heart sank. If he was cutting his Las Vegas trip short, that meant her time at the beach was going to be abbreviated as well because he always demanded that she be there to pick him up at the airport. "Why? What's wrong?" she asked, not truly caring.

"I don't feel well. Must have been something you fed me before I left."

It's always somehow my fault Nicole thought. His illness had *nothing* to do with stale air on an airplane or copious free drinks in a casino. It *must* have been her cooking.

"I'm flying back tomorrow," Lee Wayne said. "I land in Raleigh at 4:40. Don't be late picking me up. You know how you are."

Just the thought of his early return brought tears to Nicole's eyes. Every hour at Oak Island was precious to her and Lee Wayne was stealing them. She couldn't stave off the simmering contempt she felt for this man. "Sure," she peeped.

Mercifully, Lee Wayne ended the call. Maybe some tumbling dice or some toothsome Vegas waitress was beckoning him. She didn't know. She didn't care. For the next fifteen minutes, Nicole stood trembling behind the sliding glass doors and looked out over the ocean in hopes it would calm her after her husband's verbal onslaught. She dabbed her teary eyes, swollen and red from crying. As she watched the crashing waves, Nicole noticed the leading edges of the foamy waters were creeping closer to her beach chair. She wanted to run out and rescue her belongings but realized she'd left her sunglasses in her bag. She was too embarrassed to show her puffy eyes and tear-stained face in public, even if it was only in front of just one stranger who she would certainly never see again. Now distressed that the saltwater would ruin her book, she reached for the door handle, but a sudden motion on the beach stopped her from sliding it open.

The stranger who'd been sitting next to her sprang out of his chair and darted across the sand to her belongings. In one swift and athletic motion, he snatched her beach chair and canvas bag from the threat of the incoming tide and moved them out of harm's way. He quickly made a return trip for her umbrella and planted it next to her chair, exactly as it had been before, only twenty yards further away from the water's edge.

She noticed that just as he started to walk away, the man turned back and took a quick glance at the book she'd been reading. She couldn't see his complete expression, but a gentle nod of his head indicated that he approved. She studied him as he returned to his portion of the beach. *Thoughtful, quick-thinking, and apparently honest*, she thought. She was impressed.

She watched the man relocate his own belongings closer to the dunes, then sit down and resume reading. After just a few moments, he raised his head and gazed out at the horizon, where there was nothing to see except churning water. Again, she couldn't see his face, but he seemed to be lost in thought. After several minutes of searching, he tilted back his head and apparently drifted off to sleep.

Nicole retreated to her bedroom and fell facedown into the pillows, expelling every tear that was left inside her. She thought back to the scene in *Eat, Pray, Love* where Elizabeth Gilbert had collapsed on the bathroom floor at the depths of her marital crisis and sobbed, praying for help. It suddenly arrived with great clarity in the form of a calming silence from a divine agent. Nicole had lived that same anguished scene in every room of her house, falling to her knees again and again in a cascade of bitter tears, yet God had still not spoken to her. She didn't know if she had the strength to keep waiting. Nicole recalled a line from the book that had touched her: *There's a crack (or cracks) in everyone . . . that's how the light of God gets in.* Nicole was cracked and broken, like a porcelain doll that had fallen off a bookshelf, but the darkness inside her remained untouched.

Nicole snapped back to the present when a young nurse with a jet-black ponytail and rubber clogs pushed her way through the curtain and into the small recovery room. She held a clipboard in one hand and moved like she was running late. "I'm Ana," she said, more business than sympathetic, as she quickly checked the numbers on a monitor next to Lee Wayne's bed. "I'll be watching over your husband for the next few hours."

"What all did they do to him?" Nicole asked.

"Well, let's see," began Ana, as she checked the patient's chart on the clipboard she was holding. There was a long pause as she read the chart, scrunching the lines on her forehead as she flipped back and forth between the pages. "Huh. That's odd. Seems as though I can't tell you."

She frowned. "What? Why not?" Nicole asked.

"You're not on the list."

"What list?"

"The list of who we can and can't talk to about his medical condition. HIPAA regulations. It's to ensure patient privacy. I'm sorry, ma'am, but you're not authorized to receive his health information."

Nicole blinked with confusion. "But that's my *husband*."

"I realize that," Ana said. "But it's a federal law. I could lose my job."

Nicole narrowed her eyes, clearly not comprehending. "But I'm his *wife*! If anybody should be on the list, it's *me*!"

Ana tilted her head and nodded, nervously flipping the pages on her clipboard. "One would think. I'm sorry."

"There has to be some mistake," protested Nicole, involuntarily putting her palm on top of her head in bafflement.

"I will check into it," offered the nurse. "Again, I'm sorry."

Ana departed as abruptly as she'd entered. Nicole wanted desperately to follow her, her head still reeling over the confusing exchange she'd just had over her husband's medical information.

Nicole sat down in the vinyl-padded chair and pounded the thin wooden arm one time with her closed fist. The medical machines continued their monotonous watch over their patient. She noted the irony of pain medicine dripping into the veins of a husband who'd caused so much pain himself. If only they would all stop. She wanted to escape from his beeping bedside and just keep running. Anywhere. Not just to survive, but to maybe even thrive. She couldn't bear the thought of one more night spent sitting across the dinner table and absorbing the innate ugliness of the man she'd married.

Nicole shifted in her chair, fighting the sudden and insane impulse to yank away Lee Wayne's oxygen tube and every other lifesaving device that sustained him. It was so tempting. Just one swift snatch of wires and hoses and it would all be over. Nicole remembered one of her foster mothers telling her after she'd threatened to kill the bully who sat behind her in third grade, "Honey, you just ain't the murderin' type." *Maybe she was right*, Nicole thought. But then again, maybe she wasn't.

She wondered where the man she'd seen on the beach was at this very moment. What he was doing. What he was reading. Why he stared out at the ocean with such purpose. More importantly, if she would ever see him again.

CHAPTER TWO

"Before you sleep, read something that is exquisite,
and worth remembering."

— Erasmus

Half-dressed and half-caffeinated, Drew could still hear the incessant *ping ping ping* outside his window. The sound exacerbated his constant state of irritability like water dripping from a broken faucet in the middle of the night. He peered through the kitchen window again at the tiny Asian woman, still laboring to drive the same metal pole into the unrelenting earth.

"Are ya kiddin' me?" he said to her, even though she couldn't possibly hear him. "Still with the rock? Really?" He couldn't stand his previous neighbors with their two incessantly barking Weimaraners and serenity smothering motorcycles, but these new tenants with their constant pinging might be worse.

Drew had lived in this rental house for close to two years but it was still mostly unfurnished and devoid of any color or warmth. No artwork on the walls, no rugs on the cold, hardwood floors. The kitchen had a card table with one chair, both relics of a secondhand store. His bedroom was furnished with only a nightstand and a reading lamp next to a single mattress and box spring. He had a guest room that nobody had ever used. His only surrender to comfort was a reclining chair in the living room, with a cheap floor lamp, where he could read on the nights when he couldn't sleep. A strip of silver duct tape covered one of the chair's arms to keep the stuffing inside. He found himself there frequently, usually when the bourbon had failed to do its job.

Two stacks of hardcover books filled one corner of the living room as if waiting to be returned to the shelves at a library. His collection was continually expanding because he'd never been able to get rid of any book he'd enjoyed. Just from the way he held them, you could tell that each one was like an old friend, just waiting to be revisited. The names on their spines ranged from Alcott to Zafón, Baldacci to Bronte, with Hemingway, Flaubert, Steinbeck, Shakespeare, Conroy, and Grisham interspersed among the titles. It was all the literary genius of the last four centuries assembled in a neat pile like a "Top 100" list come to life. Everyone except Stephen King, for in Drew's opinion, even if the writing was brilliant, nobody over the age of thirty wanted to go to bed scared.

His refrigerator contained the three food groups of male depression: beer, mustard, and assorted leftovers from takeout and delivery. Drew had no idea if his oven even worked.

Sadly, he had chosen to live this way, in a house that appeared to have been raided by repo men or looters. Not so much living as merely existing. He just couldn't bring himself to stay in his former home, the one in the upscale neighborhood with more gables than Hawthorne could have imagined. Not after what had happened. Not with all those memories. Not with all those ghosts. The only thing Drew missed from that house after he'd sold it was his library. Built-ins of dark wood, lined with nearly every book he'd ever read. Hundreds of volumes with spines of chestnut brown and Venetian red, everything from signed first editions to rare finds in antiquarian bookstores to paperbacks grabbed off the rack at an airport, all gathered in one spot like a treasure trove of literary genius. He simply couldn't bring himself to let them go. Most of the books were disrespectfully packed away in boxes now, harboring their splendid stories and brilliant revelations in the darkness of a storage unit. He missed them.

Drew shook his head in cynical disbelief as he looked out the window and watched the old woman continue to strike blow after blow with the rock without making any visible progress. He heaved an exhausted breath and tossed back the final third of his black coffee. He pulled on a T-shirt, slipped into an old pair of leather moccasins, and headed for the back door.

"What are you doing?" he called to the old woman as he walked across his backyard toward the rusting chain link fence that divided their properties.

She wore baggy black pants with tiny white polka dots, a faded red-and-white floral blouse, and a fraying straw hat that resembled a cross between a sombrero and a beachcomber. She was barefoot in the grass that sorely needed mowing. She briefly glanced his way, then went back to smashing the rock onto the spike.

"More to the point, what are you *trying* to do?" he asked.

She replied without looking at him. "*Wo zhèngzài zuò yīgè huāyuán.*"

"Oh boy," muttered Drew. Whatever language she was using, he didn't speak it. He scratched his head as she continued her futile effort to drive metal into dirt.

"She said she's making a garden."

Drew snapped his head to the left to see a young girl, maybe eleven or twelve, emerging from the house and walking toward them. She was dressed in typical clothing for an American girl and spoke with only a hint of an accent. "She wants to keep out the rabbits."

Drew frowned. "Metal spikes keep out rabbits?"

The girl gave a slight roll of her eyes. "She's building a fence. She doesn't want animals eating her vegetables."

Drew looked at the brown, tangled grass underneath the old woman's bare feet and couldn't imagine that where she currently stood could ever be transformed into a garden. "Well, tell her good luck with that. Any idea how much longer she'll be making a racket with that rock?"

"Until she's done. My grandmother has incredible strength."

Drew watched her pinging and shook his head. "I'm not so sure about that." He shook his head to accentuate his irritation and started to walk away.

"I'm Victoria," she called after him. "We just moved in."

"So I noticed," snapped Drew loudly as he stopped and turned back around to face her, gesturing with an upturned palm to the clangorous scene next to them. The young girl stood rigidly in place, not moving a muscle except to blink twice as her soft brown eyes met Drew's. He looked again at the old woman, unrelenting in her quest to drive the metal stake into the ground. "Could you please just ask her to keep it down? Thank you." He trudged forward, back to his house.

"Maybe she could finish faster if she had some help," Victoria called after him.

Drew answered without turning around. "Then help her, already."

"We don't have the right tools. Obviously."

Drew cursed under his breath and stopped walking. He shook his head in mild anger at himself for not having the good sense to stay in his house. He slumped his shoulders, then reversed course and walked a few steps back toward the girl. Remorse washed over him for having been so abrupt. It wasn't *their* fault he was hungover and irritable. "I'm Drew. I live next door." He pointed to his house. "Obviously." He looked at the young girl's innocent face and began to regret his initial rudeness. "You can borrow some of my tools if you want."

Victoria spoke to her grandmother in Chinese. The grandmother looked at Drew with circumspection, then back to her granddaughter. She gave her approval with one quick nod of her head, then returned to her labor.

Moments later, Drew emerged from his garage with a sledgehammer, the heavy kind that Norse gods might wield. He walked with obvious reluctance to the fence and handed it to Victoria on the other side. "Here."

The weight of the sledgehammer took Victoria's arm to the ground. She lifted it with both arms and studied it as if she'd never seen such a tool. "Thank you. I'll bring it back when we're done." Victoria turned away and lugged the sledge toward her grandmother who was still banging rock against metal and still making no progress.

Drew again started back inside. As he approached his garage, he glanced over his shoulder and saw his two new neighbors both holding the heavy sledge, trying their best to raise it high enough to pound the top of the spike, but failing miserably. "Oh, Christ," he muttered. He exhaled loudly and, against his selfish instincts, turned around and headed back to the fence.

The swinging gate on the fence was chained and padlocked, denying easy access. It took Drew several tries to scale the waist-high fence, the extra weight around his girth holding him back, but he eventually landed on the other side.

"Ask her where she wants the stakes," he asked Victoria with only a slight hint of altruism in his voice.

Victoria conferred with her grandmother, who nodded and

placed twelve metal stakes equidistantly around a square patch of ground that measured about thirty feet on each side.

Handling the sledgehammer like a man who had done it before, Drew pounded a dozen spikes into the ground in a matter of minutes. He was sweating underneath the bright sun of late spring and was shamefully out of breath at the end of it, but the job was done. He looked at the grandmother and motioned with his free hand. "Good?" he asked her. She examined his work, cautiously and deliberately moving from stake to stake and inspecting each one for its depth and sturdiness. She turned to her granddaughter and nodded her approval. "*Hao,*" she said to the girl, not to Drew himself.

"She says it's good," Victoria said with a nod of confirmation.

"Good," Drew said. "Good," he repeated. "Then my work is done." He wiped the sweat off his brow and moved back to the chain link fence, already worried about trying to traverse it.

"Thank you for helping her."

"You're welcome," he said blandly. He craved silence, and it was his once again. He scaled the fence with more effort than before, then disappeared back into his lonely quarters.

Nicole nervously paced in the small confines of the recovery room. She sensed it was bad form to be rooting against the legion of nurses who were making sure they kept Lee Wayne alive. *If they only knew the man behind the curtain*, she thought, nearly aloud, *maybe they wouldn't be quite so attentive.*

She finished the final pages of *Still Alice*, secretly musing about what it would be like to experience the same kind of early-onset Alzheimer's that incrementally erased the memory of Harvard psychologist Alice Howland. Dementia might be a blessing. There was a lot about her life she'd prefer to forget, beginning with why she'd ever married Lee Wayne in the first place. If she gave herself a truthful review, it was probably because she wanted someone to take care of her. How drastically the tables had turned. Marrying a man twelve years her senior had been the first of several terrible miscalculations.

Catching herself loitering in self-pity, Nicole recalled the one and only resolution she'd made this year: to only look forward and never back. This would be a good time to stick to it.

With nobody paying her the least bit of attention, something to which she'd grown accustomed in thirteen years of marriage to Lee Wayne, Nicole slipped out of the Step Down Unit, introspective and invisible.

After forcing down a cup of acrid coffee from the vending machine, she took the elevator up to the Neonatal Intensive Care Unit. The NICU had the same cacophony of beeps and buzzes as the SDU where Lee Wayne was recovering, but the vibe wasn't the same. Here, the wires and tubes were all connected to premature babies, some no bigger than her hand. The preemies were fighting for life, even with no idea of what life could turn out to be.

Nicole was mesmerized by the activity and leaned closer to the glass that provided a window into this special world. Everywhere she looked there were women holding babies, speaking to them in gentle whispers, each with the same demeanor of kindness and caring. They looked into each infant's eyes, cooing and rocking, soothing them with medicine dispensed directly from the heart. Despite the wax and wane of crying, joy radiated from every corner of the room, present in every touch, every lullaby, every loving glance. They were all seeking the same outcome: for these children to survive this world of machines and incubators, and to grow tall and strong in the world beyond the safety of these walls.

Nicole wondered what happened if something went terribly wrong with one of the preemies. Surely they didn't all make it out of here. She smiled ruefully when she realized she was worried about the well-being of dozens of babies she would never meet, but had hardly given a smattering of thought to the man three floors below who was fighting the same fight.

Oddly, the two scenes were interconnected by more than just wires and tubes. Lee Wayne couldn't have children. They had tried for several years but to no avail. Perhaps his inability to breed was at the sunless core of what made him so angry. Testing had shown it was his fault, but he was determined that Nicole should share the blame for his lack of an heir. The ill-fated wives of Henry VIII came to mind.

"What are they doing?" Nicole asked a passing nurse, pointing to the women who were cradling the infants in their arms.

The nurse, a woman in her early forties with a welcoming smile, stopped and stood next to Nicole, pausing to admire the work of the women in the NICU. "They're called cuddlers," she said without prompting.

"Cuddlers?"

"That's right," said the nurse with an affectionate nod. "Human touch is really important to a preemie, so the cuddlers fill in when the parents can't be here. Just holding and rocking a newborn is better than any medicine we could give them."

Nicole continued to fixate on the women clutching the infants. Human touch. She'd forgotten what that felt like. Backhands across the cheek didn't count. "Look at how they care for them," Nicole said as she placed her hand on the glass barrier without realizing it. "They're so connected. Is that something they teach you in nursing school?"

"Oh, they're all volunteers," the nurse said. "And I'm pretty sure that's something you can't learn from a book." The look of admiration spread more widely across her face.

Nicole was surprised. They all seemed so capable in addition to being so loving. She'd certainly never had anyone look at her that way. "How do you volunteer?"

"Application. Fill it out online. Then a background check. If you qualify, you come in for training. But frankly, there's not much training necessary. If you can gently hold a baby, you're pretty much qualified. We can always use help on overnights and weekends. My name's Vera. I'm the head nurse in the NICU. Call me if you have any questions."

"Thanks. I'll look into it."

Vera smiled and continued on her way as Nicole stood and stared through the window. Babies fighting for life, helped along by human touch.

She couldn't help but admire the craftsmanship of their handmade caps, knitted and purled by someone who just wanted to help these tiniest of infants survive these early days of life. They were all so innocent and pure, their entire futures waiting to unfold. Perhaps greatness, perhaps mediocrity, perhaps tragedy. She brushed aside a tear as she wondered if they all had a mother who would be coming back to take them home.

She returned to Lee Wayne's bedside and sat on a hard chair that smelled of antiseptic, listening to Lee Wayne snore in his hospital bed and watching him drool from the corner of his mouth. The only comfort she could muster at this moment was knowing that the second he'd recovered enough to take care of himself, she would again seek refuge in the two places she loved most: the beach and a book.

It was coming up on ten o'clock that night when Drew dragged his index finger through a thick layer of dust on the cover of his laptop computer, which hadn't been opened in two years. For reasons he couldn't explain, this was the night he would lift the lid and turn it on. Maybe it was the physical labor that had sparked his desire to create. Maybe it was from hearing the lively lilt of a young girl's voice that reminded him of his daughter. He sensed something was stirring inside of him. Something better than what had camped out in his gloomy brain for the last two years. He just didn't know why.

Drew sat in the darkness of his living room and stared at the screen as it came to life, the bright light hurting his eyes. He placed his hands lightly on the keyboard and let them rest there. Despite his best intentions, he still felt paralyzed. The blood and sweat of words and phrases and stories which used to flow so freely were now staunched as if God had applied a tourniquet to his creativity. Perhaps it was more punishment. Perhaps he was just lazy. Perhaps he was just washed up. Perhaps he should call Holly Hedrick in New York and beg for forgiveness. *Would she take me back?* he wondered. *Doubtful. I wouldn't take me back. Not after what I did.*

Perhaps he was just scared. Scared he had no more stories in him. Nothing meaningful left to say. For whatever reason, the words wouldn't come. He closed the laptop and waited for the humming noise to die. Back to collecting dust.

The white light of the full moon poured through the picture window on the front of the house, intermittently interrupted by the open slats of plastic vertical blinds, the cheap and noisy kind you find in budget hotel rooms. The brilliant moonlight cast shadows that looked like prison bars on the bare wall behind him.

He wondered about the woman on the beach and let his memory rewind to the first time he'd seen her approaching over the sands of Oak Island. He knew there was much more to her story than she'd revealed, but realized he might never learn more. He only hoped she was happy, perhaps curled up with a good book at that very moment.

Drew cracked the seal on a fresh bottle of fine Kentucky bourbon and drank directly from the neck. He loved the way it burned going down. His only consolation came in knowing that in just a few more weeks, he'd again find refuge in the two forces that tugged at him like the moon pulls the tides: the beach and a book.

CHAPTER THREE

"Why can't people just sit and read books and be nice to each other?"

— David Baldacci

J ust two days after his surgery, Lee Wayne Shepherd was leaving the hospital. Health insurance would no longer tolerate the expense, and the nursing staff could no longer tolerate the patient.

Nicole had finally learned from Lee Wayne that he'd had a coronary stent put in. She was still baffled by why she wasn't on the hospital's list to receive his detailed medical information, but at the end of the day, she really didn't care about his health.

Lee Wayne's recovery from the minor surgery was marked by how much more irascible he became. Barking orders, issuing complaints, and berating staffers for perceived shortcomings. These were all signs that his dark heart was fully functioning again. In less than forty-eight hours, the nurses had exhausted their patience with the same boorish behavior that Nicole had endured for over a decade.

Everyone was elated over his discharge, except for Nicole. She would now take over as his sole healthcare provider at home because Lee Wayne was too cheap to bring in outside help. "Why should I pay for some stranger to do what *you* can do for free?" he argued. Since he controlled every dollar of their finances, she had no rebuttal.

As Lee Wayne signed the paperwork for his release, a nurse held a clipboard in front of Nicole and began explaining the various medications he would need, and how and when to administer them. Lee Wayne looked up from his wheelchair and rapidly flicked his index finger back and forth to summon the nurse to his side. "Better give that information to me. There's no way my wife is going to grasp all of that." Lee Wayne spoke in the lazy accent of Eastern North Carolina, where the words *better* and *information* sounded more like *betta* and *infamation*. He chewed his words like they were vinegar-based barbecue, the creases of his lips always harboring tiny bits of spittle. He impolitely flicked his finger at the nurse again. "Come on."

Taken aback much more by the overt criticism of Nicole than the subtle condescension toward her, the nurse cocked her head slightly and peered over her glasses into Nicole's eyes. Nicole pursed her lips to restrain herself from speaking, then closed her eyes and nodded that it was okay. It was a typically Southern response. Hide your dirty laundry with a warm smile. This was not the time or place to begin a battle that she knew she would lose, verbally now, and physically when she got home. Concerned for Nicole, and clearly irked at Lee Wayne, the nurse reluctantly moved to his side and showed him the schedule of medications on the clipboard.

"I don't want to say my wife is stupid," Lee Wayne said as he perused the list of prescriptions, "but she once confused dishwasher detergent with granulated sugar. Worst cookies you ever tasted. Although, she's had a few other batches that came close. And you should see her try to read a map. Like a monkey tryin' to do arithmetic." He snorted when he laughed at his own joke.

The nurse looked at Nicole with wide-eyed disbelief, as if to ask, *Are you gonna take that?* Nicole swallowed hard and turned away, forcing a forgiving smile despite being near tears. It wasn't the first time he'd humiliated her in public but it still cut deeply. Lee Wayne's personality was pungent, an aura emanating from him like spoiled buttermilk. And in just a few minutes she would be descending an elevator and pushing him down the sterile corridor of the hospital to the car that would take him home, where she would have to soak in that aura all day and all night. Damn those surgeons.

◆ ◆ ◆

Drew tried to incorporate the incessant *bam bam bam* into his mid-morning dream, but his sleep ended before the knocking did. His forehead pulsed with pain as he threw back the rumpled sheet and tossed his feet over onto the floor. He'd been particularly generous with the bourbon the night before and he was now getting a return on his investment of overindulgence. He lumbered to the front door in just his boxer shorts and pressed a bleary eye against the peephole. He could see Victoria's hand reaching up again to knock. The sound reverberated through his addled brain.

"Hang on! Just a minute!" he yelled through the door with irritation. Even the sound of his own voice grated against his aching senses.

He quickly pulled on the jeans and T-shirt he'd tossed on his bedroom floor the night before and returned to the front door. He opened it to find Victoria standing calmly on the front stoop. Not only was he annoyed by the intrusion, he was hungover *and* annoyed.

"Has nobody taught you how to use a doorbell?" he demanded. His voice carried the extra testiness that comes with a slight hangover. "They're quite common these days."

"I did. Nobody answered. I thought nobody was home."

"And yet you didn't leave."

"I remembered that you never go anywhere." He could not argue that. Except for groceries and trips to the liquor store, he remained sequestered in his lonely rental house. "Can I come in?" Victoria asked. She was already inside before Drew could tell her no.

Her eyes widened as she moved past the front hallway and looked at the mostly empty space that was ironically known as the living room. She started firing questions as quickly as they formed in her brain. "What happened to your house? Why is there nothing on the walls? Did you get robbed?" Victoria moved past the living room and into the kitchen.

"Why aren't you in school?" he asked.

"Because it's Saturday. And it's June."

She opened the refrigerator door and scanned the empty shelves. "Why don't you have any food?"

"What are you *doing*?" Drew asked in protest, pushing the door closed. "I'm not giving a tour."

Victoria ignored him and kept exploring, walking down the hallway and peeking into his bedroom. "Why do you live alone?"

Drew's demeanor immediately transformed from disturbed to disconsolate. The change was so rapid and profound that even Victoria stopped her whirlwind exploration and looked at him, silently. He moved his tongue from cheek to cheek inside his mouth and after a moment, spoke in a soft tone. "Did you want something?"

Victoria nodded and walked slowly back to the front hallway. "My grandmother wants to borrow your lawnmower."

"Why?"

"I'm guessing she wants to mow the lawn." Victoria rolled her palms over and gestured upwards to indicate that wasn't the most incisive of questions.

Drew rolled his eyes and cocked his chin skyward to tacitly agree. "Does she know how to use one?"

"Not yet."

"Not yet? Whaddya mean, 'not yet'?"

"I'm going to teach her."

"Oh, so *you* know how to use a lawnmower?" he asked.

"Not yet."

"Again with the 'not yet'?"

Victoria was unbowed. "I watched a video. Seems easy enough."

"It's not."

"It must be. *You* know how to do it."

It sounded like something his mother would say. Drew ignored the dig. "Where's your grandmother now?"

"In her garden."

"Doing what? Wait, don't tell me. She's gardening."

Victoria shook her head. "She's waiting."

"Waiting for what?"

"Waiting for me to come back with your lawnmower."

Drew shook his head and walked into the kitchen. He squinted from the sunlight as he looked out the back window. There was the old woman standing like a scarecrow in the middle of the area marked off with metal poles, staring back at him as if she knew he would come to that very window. He shook his head again and drew in a heavy breath. "Let me put on some shoes," he muttered, without turning around.

Just a few minutes later, it only took Drew one blow with the sledgehammer to smash the rusted padlock on the gate of his chain link fence that marked the boundary line between the two houses. Barrier removed, he wheeled his Toro lawnmower through the open gate and into his new neighbor's backyard. The mower was one of the very few large items he hadn't sent off to storage when he'd moved, always preferring to cut his own grass rather than paying someone else for the privilege.

Victoria and her grandmother stood motionless at a distance as he approached them. "I filled it with gas. Should be plenty for you to finish the job. Just roll it back into my yard when you're done." He looked back and forth at the two faces. "You're sure you can do this?" he asked them.

Victoria nodded. "Yes."

"Just be careful," he said, turning away and heading back to his house. As he glanced over his shoulder, he heard a rapid exchange of Chinese as the two women circled the mower, carefully inspecting it as if it were a meteorite that had just landed in their backyard.

Ten minutes later Drew was backing his Jeep out of his garage. A trip to the liquor store was the only entry on his to-do list. He needed to stock up for his impending trip to the beach.

In his side-view mirror, he caught a glimpse of Victoria. She was slowly and steadily pulling the starter cord out of the mower's housing. Her repeated efforts weren't nearly fast or forceful enough to turn over the cold engine. More Mandarin was chattered between grandmother and granddaughter, this time accompanied by animated hand gestures. Victoria tried pulling the cord again. The mower remained quiet.

"Christ Almighty," muttered Drew as he threw the Jeep into park and shut off the engine.

Moments later, Drew was yanking hard on the mower's starter cord. On just the third attempt, the engine sputtered to life. He motioned Victoria closer with his hand and gave her room to get behind the mower. "Hold this," he instructed above the roar, placing her hands on a thin metal bar that he'd pulled up under the handle. "It's a safety device. If something happens, just let go and the mower will cut off. And always keep your feet back."

Victoria nodded and clamped her hands around the safety bar and settled firmly in behind the mower. The handle was nearly as tall as she was, but she leaned into it and started forward. As she slowly pushed into the long grass, Drew retreated to his Jeep and drove away.

He cranked up both the radio and the air conditioner as he drove down the nondescript street lined with nondescript houses. Each one a brick rancher distinguished only by the unimaginative color of the shutters and the shrubbery under the windows. If you want to reside in a state of depression, location is everything.

Drew returned home an hour later with a large pizza box on the passenger seat and two large liquor bottles in a paper bag on the floorboard below. His driveway circled around to the back of his house so that the garage faced his backyard. It seemed like an odd design at first, but he preferred it this way. He could motor directly into the privacy of his backyard and not have to wave to any of his neighbors upon departure or arrival. The rear entry was especially important because his automatic garage door opener was broken, forcing him to get out of his vehicle and raise or lower the door manually, just as homeowners did before such modern pushbutton conveniences were invented.

When Drew rounded the corner to the garage, he saw his lawnmower parked on his back patio. He stepped out and surveyed the yard next door. Only ten feet of his neighbor's untamed grass had been mowed.

CHAPTER FOUR

"A blessed companion is a book—a book that, fitly
chosen, is a lifelong friend . . . a book that, at a touch,
pours its heart into your own."

— Douglas William Jerrold

"You need to leave him. You need to leave him tomorrow. No, you needed to leave him yesterday," Teri Rudisill said as she refilled Nicole's coffee mug. "You deserve better."

"I just can't. Not right now, anyway," Nicole said. She adjusted her balance on the stool at the island in Teri's kitchen. She held the warm mug in both hands and sipped her coffee.

"You've been sayin' that as long as I've known you," Teri said with a slight shake of her head. She was tall and thin with shoulder-length platinum blonde hair that was wispy on the ends. A slight overbite only added to her natural beauty. Teri warmed up her own coffee. "How much longer you gonna put up with it?"

Teri Rudisill was the best friend Nicole ever had. In fact, she would have been the best friend anyone ever had. It was her honest upbringing in a modest home in rural South Carolina that had provided her with such a core of kindness. Candid without being blunt, decisive without being judgmental, lively without being overbearing. Teri was the embodiment of *keep calm and carry on*. If you walked into her salon and told her you wanted to dye your hair purple, her first unblinking statement would be "What shade, honey?" followed closely by "Ya needin' your nails done to match?" and all with a sweet Southern drawl. Teri's own bright blonde hair came from a bottle, so she spoke from experience when she said "We all have our own way of doin' thangs, now don't we?" Other than Nicole's monthly hair appointments in Teri's salon chair, it wasn't often that they got together in person. Lee Wayne discouraged her from seeing other people. He even checked their phone bill to make sure the two women weren't talking too much for his liking. It was only because Lee Wayne was currently sleeping after a dose of pain medicine that she was there right now. But the times the two women were able to share were rejuvenating for Nicole. It rekindled what little spirit she still had. Teri was a sage, a sounding board, and a shoulder on which to shed tears, both literally and figuratively.

The only subject they never talked about was books. Teri wasn't a reader, other than glossy magazines that focused on the fascinating lives of movie stars and pop singers. Nicole didn't view that as a shortcoming, but she did think it was a shame. How she longed to discuss the books she was reading. It was impossible to have those conversations with Lee Wayne so it would have been nice to share her musings with a trusted friend like Teri. But in the same way that some people don't care for sushi or liver, some people simply aren't readers. Everyone has their own pleasures in life. *Their own way of doing things.*

Nicole had never explicitly told her about the beatings from Lee Wayne, but Teri knew. She'd cut Nicole's hair enough times to feel the lumps on her scalp and see the bruising on the back of her neck. Those didn't happen accidentally. She also knew that Nicole would only talk about it when she was ready, and it was not her place to pry. Her gift to Nicole was hope. "All I know is that if I hadn't divorced Stan, I would never have met Jerry. He's shown me what love is supposed to be. He's given me back my self-esteem, my peace of mind, and all those other things money can't buy. I've never been happier."

"He also gave you a really nice beach house, which money *did* buy," Nicole said with a smile as she took another sip of coffee.

Teri raised her mug in an *I'll drink to that* gesture. "Yes, there is that. Not why I married him, but certainly a nice bonus." She winked as she added extra cream to her mug. "By the way, when are you gonna use it again?"

"Soon, I hope," Nicole said. "Lee Wayne wants to get back to his sailboat this weekend." Nicole's single greatest pleasure in life was sneaking off to Teri's beach house on Oak Island for a night or two on weekends whenever Lee Wayne was off with his buddies at sailing school in Oriental, North Carolina. Why the man couldn't learn to sail at nearby Wrightsville Beach she didn't understand, other than his explanation that *Oriental has the best breezes*, whatever that meant. Not that it really mattered to her. She was simply grateful that he chose to drive nearly three hours away to a place with stiff winds and spotty cell service. Drive to Cape Cod or Costa Rica for all she cared. Just go. "I only wish his sailing lessons lasted weeks instead of just a few days. Maybe he'll meet a nice cocktail waitress in Oriental and want to stay there. Oh my, that sounded awful, didn't it?"

"Sounded like the truth seepin' out to me," chirped Teri with a wink. Remarkably, Nicole had never heard Teri say anything unkind about anyone else other than Lee Wayne. That spoke volumes about both of them. Teri added more cream to her coffee. "You do realize that most serial killers have either the name 'Wayne' or 'Lee' in them? Your husband has *both*. Just sayin'."

Nicole laughed so hard that coffee drooled down her chin. She wiped it off with her sleeve. "That never occurred to me."

"Seriously, darlin' girl, why *don't* you leave him? Why don't you just walk out and be done with it? Women do it all the time."

"Actually, they don't. Believe it or not, most women in my situation end up staying. You just never hear about it."

"Why? Why on earth would you stay?"

"It's just harder to leave than you think. In my case, I don't have any job experience, I don't have any family to go to, and if that weren't enough, Lee Wayne is a lawyer. He'd ruin me in court and we both know it. I'd have to start over with nothing. No money, no place to go. So I stay and try to make the best of it."

Teri shook her head, not fully understanding, but letting it go. "I suppose. At least you still have the key to the beach house. It's yours whenever you want it. Lord knows when we'll ever get back there again. Just change the sheets and wash the towels."

"You're awfully generous."

"I'm just glad someone gets to use it. And I'll be happier when that husband of yours feels good enough to go off sailin' again. The more he's away from you, the happier I am."

"That makes two of us." Nicole could feel a lump growing in her throat as she watched Teri empty the filter from the coffee maker. "Can I tell you something, Teri?" she asked in a quiet voice.

"Why sure, hon," replied Teri, her back to Nicole as she wiped the sink clean. What is it?"

"I love you. That's all. I just love you."

Teri shut off the faucet and turned to face Nicole. She wiped her hands on the back pockets of her jeans as she took two quick steps toward Nicole. They embraced like loving sisters. "I love you too, hon."

"Yes, you do. Like few ever have."

Teri patted Nicole gently on the back as they held their embrace. "It's gonna be okay."

Nicole desperately wanted to believe what she knew wasn't true.

Lee Wayne Shepherd's heart was blacker than the boots of a West Virginia coal miner, but it was getting stronger. For the last two weeks, while he recovered from his surgery, Nicole had been a dutiful nurse. She'd dispensed his meds with extreme care, monitored him for any fever that might indicate an infection, and supplied him with fruit, fiber, and juice to help him regain his strength. If she was being honest with herself, she was not providing her services out of love and concern. Her sole motivation was to get Lee Wayne back to full capacity as quickly as possible so that he could get back to work or sailing or golf or anything else that would get him out of her house. Having him around her all day choked her spirit.

Their home was upscale, the kind of one-story place that people with a fair amount of money buy in a planned development where someone else mows the lawn and trims the bushes. It was well appointed with crown molding and wainscoting, granite countertops, and hardwood floors, but it was not spacious. Just three bedrooms, one of which was taken up by Lee Wayne's office and assorted maps he used for sailing.

The guest room had a dresser and queen-sized bed, although they'd never once had a guest come to visit. Its main purpose was to serve as Nicole's sewing room with fabric and patterns and needles and thread tucked neatly inside the dresser that nobody else would ever use. Bulky and tufted old furniture, more suitable for a London cigar lounge, made the limited living space even more claustrophobic.

In such tight quarters with Lee Wayne, she felt like a candle next to a cracked window, the chilled breeze incessantly trying to snuff out her light and warmth. So far he had not quite managed to fully blacken the wick, but all this time together was taking its toll. The doctor had warned her that her patient might sleep more than usual, or perhaps less. Unfortunately, Lee Wayne had fallen into the latter pattern. Her favorite sound had always been hearing the garage door open as he left for the office. How she longed to hear those springs and rollers jump to life again. More than anything she wanted him to be well enough to travel, leaving her free to spend time at Teri's beach house. Lee Wayne had always assumed that Nicole simply stayed at home while he was gone like any dutiful wife should. She was like Cinderella, knowing she had to rush back home from Oak Island to Belville on Sunday afternoons before her husband returned from the perfect winds of the Pamlico Sound, or else her secret trips to the beach would be revealed and terminated, with a beating to follow. Even so, it was worth the risk.

Lee Wayne was starting to return to some normal activities. He'd resumed smoking, which topped the list of the forbidden, and would drink a beer when he thought Nicole wasn't looking. He'd taken a few walks, as the doctor recommended, but the rest of the time he stayed in bed and watched television or played with his electronic devices. The only guideline to which he strictly adhered was to avoid lifting anything heavier than five pounds. He conveniently used that as his "doctor's excuse" for allowing Nicole to take care of absolutely everything around the house.

In truth, it wasn't a tremendous departure from his healthy state. Even on his best day, Lee Wayne couldn't fix anything, including a sandwich, arguing that those jobs came under Nicole's purview, since he was the sole breadwinner and was thus occupied with far more important matters. Like golf and sailboats. He kept a tiny bell on his nightstand to beckon her when he wanted something as if she were a downstairs maid in his manor house.

As his heart grew stronger, Lee Wayne's tongue grew sharper. "How much longer before dinner?" he asked Nicole with a tinge of impatience as he strolled into the kitchen in his bathrobe. "I'm gettin' kinda hungry."

Nicole puckered the edge of her mouth and shot a blast of air out of the corner of her lips to blow away the strands of hair that had fallen across her left eye. She was simultaneously stirring two pots simmering on the stove and keeping a close eye on the timer for the oven. "Ten more minutes. Maybe fifteen."

Lee Wayne took a hard and unnecessary look at his watch and exhaled through his nose.

"How are you feeling?" she asked.

"Better. Not great, but better."

"Are you still going to try to make it to your sailing lesson tomorrow?"

"I think so," he replied, as if it were some awful burden to bear.

There was an uncomfortable pause before Nicole spoke again. "May I ask you something?" she said.

"What?" he replied with impatience.

"When I was at the hospital, they wouldn't tell me anything about your operation. They said I wasn't on the list of people who were privy to that information. Any idea why?"

A tincture of surprise flickered in Lee Wayne's eyes as if he were caught off guard by her question. He immediately recovered and stonewalled. "I have no idea. Probably an oversight. You know hospitals these days. You're lucky to get the correct limb amputated. But I guess that's a good thing. Keeps us lawyers busy."

"Can you please look into it?" she asked. "I'm your wife. I should be allowed to know."

"Will do," was his cavalier response. "Right now, why don't you worry about my dinner?" He glanced back at Nicole's hand as she stirred the boiling water around some lima beans. He moved a step closer, honing in on the stain on the sleeve of her blouse. It was the brown residue from where she'd wiped her mouth while having coffee with Teri. He clamped his hand around her wrist and raised her arm out into the air. "What's that?" he demanded.

Nicole masked her alarm. "It's just from cooking. Cooking *your* dinner."

He squeezed tighter and pulled her wrist up to his nose. "It's coffee. Isn't it?"

"I don't know," answered Nicole as she tried not to tremble.

"You didn't make me coffee this morning, so where did this come from?"

"I said I don't know. I didn't notice it before. Let me go. Your beans are going to get overcooked." She tried to pull away from Lee Wayne's grasp but he wouldn't release her.

"You were at Teri's today, weren't you? Don't lie to me. I always know when you're lying."

Nicole caved. "I was. For a bit when you were sleeping."

He gripped harder. "What have I told you about seeing her? She's nothing but trouble. I forbid it."

"She's my best friend."

"Not anymore. Find a new one."

After flashing his eyes to reinforce his threat, Lee Wayne finally released his captive. Nicole rubbed her wrist, then resumed stirring. She felt tears charging up through her chest and into her eyes, but she refused to let him see her cry. He might have known when she was lying, but he rarely knew what she was thinking, and right now she was thinking she wanted to hurl a pot of boiling water directly into his face. He ducked his head into the refrigerator and secreted a can of beer into the pocket of his cloth robe, obviously thinking that Nicole was unaware. "I'll be in my room. Bring it to me when it's finally ready."

She nodded with false politeness, wanting him to just go away. But Lee Wayne wasn't done. As he exited the kitchen he stopped and picked up a doll, depicting Father Christmas, from a side table. The doll was eighteen inches tall, dressed in a black velvet robe accented with silver braid down the front. His hat, collar, and sleeves were trimmed in soft fur the color of warm caramel. Saint Nicholas was holding a staff made from the twig of a river birch adorned with tiny pine cones and evergreen branches. His eyes seemed to twinkle behind his wire-rimmed glasses and flowing white beard.

Lee Wayne held the doll by the throat as he turned back to Nicole. "Why do you keep this stupid thing out? Christmas was over six months ago. For that matter, why do we have it at all? It's certainly seen better days."

Mildly panicked, Nicole dropped her spoons onto the counter and rushed to rescue Father Christmas from the clutches of her husband. She snatched the treasure from his hand and retreated, inspecting the doll for any damage.

It had been a Christmas gift from one of her foster mothers when Nicole was just fourteen, the last present she'd given Nicole before she died the following spring. It was the one and only possession that Nicole had carried forward from that day to this. She had no scrapbooks, no jewelry, not even one family heirloom that she'd inherited. Father Christmas was the only constant in her life across all those years, and those twinkling eyes and soft coat had sustained her in her darkest days.

Even now, Father Christmas was the only item in the entire house that was uniquely and entirely hers. Everything else had been selected by some standoffish interior decorator with high prices and questionable taste. The artwork in gaudy gold frames, the oversized urns, and the cement statuary all looked as though they belonged in a Babylonian garden. The furniture was bulky and brown, handed down by Lee Wayne's parents and grandparents. Perhaps it meant something to them, but certainly not to her. Nicole had always felt as though she were living in a furnished model home or was perpetually on vacation at a VRBO surrounded by somebody else's tasteless and sterile belongings. Nothing felt personal or treasured. Nothing evoked memories of a special trip or a lucky find at a roadside antique store or flea market. Nothing in the house had been a thoughtful gift from a close friend or had been handmade by a relative or a child. There was no scribbled artwork on the refrigerator and nothing on their Christmas tree fashioned out of popsicle sticks or Styrofoam balls. Every decorative piece in their drab home was something you could easily order from a catalog and have shipped in two days or less. Everything, that is, except Father Christmas in his majestic velvet coat.

Just looking at her doll brought Nicole joy, which is why she kept him out long after the holidays were over. More than that, he gave her hope. His perpetual smile served as a constant reminder that she could always cling to the expectation that despite her misery, despite living with a noxious hotspur like Lee Wayne Shepherd, the gift of peace in her life might still come. She continued to believe that even in the face of significant evidence to the contrary. Yes, her beloved Father

Christmas had seen better days. He'd also been there for Nicole on her worst ones.

She tucked him safely in a corner of the kitchen counter and resumed stirring her simmering pots. "Ten minutes."

Lee Wayne shook his head and walked away. Nicole heard a beer can crack open as he retreated to his bedroom.

Continuing to fix dinner, her thoughts wandered off to the vengeful recipes in kitchens of good fiction. Minny's fecal chocolate pie in *The Help* came to mind. *If only*, Nicole thought. *Mashed potatoes laced with tiny fish bones. A salad tossed with leaves of deadly nightshade.* She swirled the wooden spoon slowly and deliberately, intentionally overcooking his beans.

CHAPTER FIVE

"I have sought rest everywhere and have only found it
in corners and books."

— Thomas à Kempis

It was just after four o'clock when Drew emerged from the
cramped shower of his motel room, having successfully
washed away the gritty sand he'd amassed while at the
beach.

The Riverside Motel was home for Drew whenever he came
to Southport, North Carolina. Southport was just a short drive
from Oak Island and the place just seemed to suit him. The
one-story building on Bay Street was bright white with pale
green shutters. It wasn't fancy, but it was always clean, and
Drew liked the fact that it was situated right on the Cape Fear
River. Just one step out the back door and he could sit on a
porch swing with a panoramic view of the waterfront and just
forget about life for a while.

Drew looked at himself in the mirror above the bathroom
sink, but only briefly, like someone catching a glimpse of a
bad car accident. He may have dropped a few pounds in the
last two weeks, but it was barely noticeable. He brushed back
his wet, wavy brown hair without regard for style, and after
whisking on his blue jeans, a clean T-shirt, and moccasins, he
was quickly out the door.

Drew would make two stops. First, to the drugstore to
pick up some aloe for his burgeoning sunburn, and then to the

used bookstore. It was his favorite place to visit in Southport, although it was also true that *any* bookstore in *any* town could easily be considered his favorite place to visit.

The end of a strip mall was an unlikely place for a keeper of good literature, but that's where The Book End harbored its treasures. The display in the front window was filled with bestselling authors like Mary Higgins Clark, Lee Child, and Michael Connelly. The light from the store's yellowy-orange neon sign bounced off the alluring book jackets of Larry McMurtry, Vince Flynn, Margaret Atwood, and Harlan Coben, all beckoning the reader to step inside.

The Book End was long and narrow, like a New York bar, with bookshelves lining both walls and a few revolving carousels and stacks in the center aisle. With some 50,000 titles in all genres, it was impossible to leave the store empty-handed.

Besides his well-worn copy of *The Prince of Tides,* Drew had brought two other books with him to Southport. One was Chad Harbach's *The Art of Fielding* which online reviews had described as a beautifully written story of a college baseball team but wasn't really about baseball at all. The other was James Joyce's modernist masterpiece *Ulysses.* He'd started the Irish epic more than once and more than once had abandoned it in favor of lighter fare. This time he was determined to plow through it, even if it was just one sentence at a time. After all, it was considered by many to be the greatest novel ever written, so Drew felt it his duty to cross it off his list.

But today, even with two books stacked on his motel nightstand, Drew was in search of something else to add to his library. He sought a book he'd read before when it first came out in 2006 but suddenly felt the need to revisit. He knew it might be hard to find in a used bookstore, because it was the kind of book that most people hang onto, like a favorite pair of jeans. Once he deciphered the bookstore's system of displaying its wares by category, he found it. An old friend with a familiar cover. It was paperback, but it would have to do. He swiftly pulled it off the shelf and clutched it between his fingers and palm as if someone might try to wrest it away from him.

Drew continued to browse on the off-chance that he might stumble upon something else he might enjoy on some lonely night by a fire or under a book light. Out of morbid curiosity, he wandered over to the section that contained mysteries.

Under the letter "E" he saw an entire row of books with which
he was intimately familiar. Apparently, they had *not* felt like
favorite jeans to the previous owner.

Before he allowed dismay to completely overtake him, he
quickly turned, intending to make his way toward the section
in the rear of the store that contained books about gardening.
He hadn't taken two steps when he stopped cold.

"Oh!" he said reflexively as he looked up at the person
standing in the aisle. It was the mysterious woman from the
beach he'd seen just a few weeks ago. She was wearing white
denim pants and a pale blue blouse with short sleeves that were
rolled up at the end to expose well-defined biceps. She was
taller than he'd remembered, even in flat sandals. "It's you," he
blurted, unfiltered.

The instant he spoke with such familiarity, he realized he
didn't know her at all, other than his brief observations earlier
that month, and he was certain she didn't recognize him.

"Do I know you?" Nicole asked.

"Not really. I think I saw you—" He stopped short, not
wanting to have to explain his behavior on the beach several
weeks prior. "No," Drew said. "I was mistaken. Sorry."
He shook his head and waved two fingers in her direction
apologetically, then pressed closer to the bookshelf to slide
around her. He could feel his cheeks burning with more than
just sunburn.

"What are you reading?" came her voice as Drew neared the
end of the aisle.

He turned back in surprise, not even sure she was talking to
him. "Excuse me?"

She pointed to the paperback clutched in his hand. "Your
book. What is it?"

Drew looked down at the book in his hand as if he were
surprised to see it there. There was no mistaking the book's
iconic cover, with its title *Eat, Pray, Love* written in pasta,
prayer beads, and flower petals. He flipped it over, then back
again in a quick examination, stalling for time. "Oh, this?" he
stammered as he rubbed his unshaven chin. "Just something I
picked up."

"You've not read it?" she asked.

Drew waited fractions of a second before answering. Not
only had he read the book, but he'd also spent a fair amount of

time with Liz Gilbert herself, one of the nicest authors on the planet. He wasn't about to reveal *that*. "Yes, I have read it, but it was some time ago."

"So why are you reading it again?"

Drew drummed his fingers on his thigh, searching for a plausible answer. "It was . . . recommended."

"Recommended?" she asked. "But if you've already read it, then you already knew it was good."

He was starting to wonder about the pointed interrogation from the woman as if she knew the answers to her questions before asking them. "Truth is," he began, knowing full well he wasn't going to tell the entire truth, "is that I just felt like spending time with an old friend." The woman nodded approvingly, seeming to finally accept his answer. He held up the copy of *Eat, Pray, Love* for her inspection. "Have *you* read it?" he asked, trying to pretend as though he didn't already know the answer.

She paused for a half-second. "Yes. Yes, I have." She offered no more. "What else are you adding to your stack today?" she asked.

Drew turned and looked at the bookshelves as if the answer were written there. "I'm not entirely sure. Just treasure hunting. Hoping something catches my eye."

"Well, if you need any recommendations, I have a long list. I'm like a walking Goodreads. What do you like to read?"

He shrugged. "Oh, anything with interesting characters, a unique setting, wonderful prose, plot twists, lots of conflict, and a satisfying resolution. Those are my only requirements."

She chuckled at his sarcasm. "That narrows the field a little."

He nodded with a smile. "How about you? What do you like?"

"Anything Oprah tells me to read. But I'm open to suggestions."

"Oh, now *I* have a long list," he said. Drew thought for a moment. "Have you read any Ken Follett? *Pillars of the Earth?*"

"Yes! One of my favorites! And I read it *before* Oprah discovered it."

"We seem to have the same taste in books," Drew said.

"Apparently."

"I don't know how much time you have for reading, but if you're looking for something you can't put down I would highly recommend *Unbroken* by Lauren Hillenbrand. If you didn't know it was true, you'd swear she made it all up."

"I'll look for it. Thanks," she said.

She didn't turn away, but it seemed to Drew that the conversation was over. "It was good to see you—" he started and stopped, abruptly avoiding the word *again*.

"Nice to meet you," she replied, still staring at him.

"Well . . . goodbye then. Happy hunting." Drew nodded awkwardly and turned around, taking a few more steps toward the gardening section. He glanced over his shoulder and saw that the woman hadn't moved, still standing squarely in the middle of the aisle, almost as if she'd expected him to turn around and resume their conversation. She would have been correct in her assumption. For reasons he couldn't explain, he didn't want to execute his usual 'dodge and go' maneuver when it came to interacting with strangers. He turned back and took several steps closer to her, searching for something noninvasive to say. "I'm not from around here. Can you recommend a good place to eat?" In truth, Drew had been to Southport enough times to know most of the good places to dine, but it seemed like the best way to extend a conversation he inexplicably didn't want to end.

She laughed softly. "How many stars do you require?"

"I like anywhere that accepts a shirt sleeve as a napkin."

She laughed again, a little harder. "In that case, you might try the Yacht Basin Eatery down by the water. Seafood, burgers, cold beer. Five-star food, one-star attitude. I think you'll fit right in."

"Thanks." He paused for a moment, already out of questions. It had been years since he'd had an encounter like this and he was decidedly out of practice. "By the way, my name's Drew," he said with a slight wave of his hand.

"I'm Nicole."

"Pleasure to meet you, Nicole.

"You too. Enjoy your time in Southport."

"I will. I have. I am." He winced and shook his head over his inept response, then smiled warmly and waved goodbye, again with two fingers as if that made everything more casual and benign. As he walked away, Drew wanted to turn around one more time to see if she was still watching him. He resisted the urge.

Moments later, as he sifted through the overwhelming selection of books about gardening, explaining how to grow anything, anywhere, Drew was still feeling something that hadn't stirred within him in close to two years. Civility. It was the first time he'd been the least bit cordial to anyone since the funerals. In the last two years, he'd been more than merely standoffish. He'd intentionally become distant and detached, unapproachable and unsociable. Colleagues and acquaintances had been pushed into a deep pit dug by his own misery. His closest friends now were the characters in the books he read. Really, his *only* friends. It was easier that way. They didn't ask probing and painful questions and he could set them aside whenever he wanted. It was the only way he'd found to cope with his overpowering grief. And guilt. His brief encounter with Nicole had created a small fissure in his wall of withdrawal, like the first crocus pushing up through the crusted snow of late winter. It surprised Drew as much as it frightened him. He'd worked so hard to convince himself that he was happy being sad.

CHAPTER SIX

"I have come to believe that books have souls—why
else would I be so reluctant to throw one away?"

— Susan Orlean, *The Library Book*

Before he left the motel for dinner that night, Drew did
something he hadn't done in three days. He shaved. He
wasn't even sure why, because it was a task he regularly
avoided, especially since he was no longer in the public eye. He
went a step further and put on a collared shirt.

He stepped out into the warm, late-evening air and inhaled
deeply. A dozen black-headed laughing gulls were uniformly
lined up on the rooftop peak of Oliver's restaurant, watching
Drew as he ventured into the black and blue of fading twilight.

Floodlights bounced off the cobalt-blue Southport water
tower on North Howe Street, providing tourists with a friendly
landmark by which to navigate their way home to their quaint
bed-and-breakfasts.

It took only two minutes to drive to the Yacht Basin Eatery
at the end of West Bay Street, a cozy restaurant he'd passed by
numerous times but had never tried. The cover band on the
front deck was thumping out Wilson Pickett's "Mustang Sally"
as Drew made his way to the outdoor dining area in the back.
A few older couples were dancing, uncaring that the rhythm of
their movements didn't sync with the music.

High tables with tan Formica tops and orange chairs
dotted the wooden planks on the back deck, stained by years

of patrons spilling buttered seafood and cold beer. A bar with several taps backed up to a wall covered with metal signs advertising assorted craft breweries. The aroma of steamed shrimp dominated the air.

The night air was balmy and humid. Every eleven seconds, the stalwart beams of the Oak Island Lighthouse from Caswell Beach flashed across the black waters of the Cape Fear River. Drew immediately thought of Tom Sherbourne, the lighthouse keeper in *The Light Between Oceans*, and his unwavering devotion to the constancy of the lifesaving light. It was also a haunting reminder of the persistent perils of the ocean and how quickly it can snatch away human life.

Drew found a table on the back deck and settled in. He realized he was the only patron not wearing either sandals or a "Salt Life" T-shirt, or both.

A spirited young waitress with an olive green tank top and khaki shorts was immediately at his table with two menus. "Anyone joining you?" she asked, flashing a toothy smile.

"Afraid not."

"My name's Wendi," she said brightly in a syrupy down east accent. She had her strawberry blonde hair pulled back in a tight bun that revealed a tiny tattoo of a sunburst behind her left ear. A necklace made of tiny shells and dangling earrings completed her ensemble. "I'll be takin' care of you." She handed him a menu and filled his water glass.

"What's good here?" he asked. That strange sense of civility was percolating again.

Her eyes twinkled. "Everything. The worst thing we got is wonderful."

Even though Drew was certain it was a line she'd used on a thousand customers before him, it still brought a smile to his face. "Including the service?"

Wendi beamed. "*Especially* the service. Can I start you off with somethin' to drink?"

"Bourbon on the rocks. Woodford Reserve, if you have it."

"Comin' right up."

Despite an extensive menu, Drew made his selection quickly. Based on Wendi's review, he didn't think he could go wrong. As he waited for the waitress to return, his eyes scanned the wide array of sailboats and outboards moored to the wooden piers just off the edge of the restaurant. He imagined everyone from presidents to pirates would feel comfortable here. The world around saltwater could be a great equalizer. There was something about T-shirts, shorts, and draft beer that leveled the socioeconomic playing field.

Wendi returned with a fresh bourbon. "Here ya go, hon. Have ya decided?"

"I'll have a dozen steamed clams and a quarter-pound of steamed shrimp. I'll start with a cup of the seafood chowder."

"All good. I'll get it out right away."

"Thank you, Wendi." He raised his glass to toast her. There was that faint hint of civility again, a tinge of politeness, a spark of comity that stirred inside him. It seemed both familiar and foreign, like roller skating for the first time since your childhood. The gentle blending of music, kitchen smells, and salt air provided a blanket of warmth, helped along by the first sip of Kentucky bourbon that burned all the way down. He savored the familiar hints of caramel, honeysuckle, and clove dancing like gypsies across his taste buds. The Kentucky hug awakened all of his senses. He'd read that the state of Kentucky has twice as many barrels of bourbon than people and had often imagined it would be a wonderful place to live.

More relaxed now, Drew swiveled in his chair and soaked in his surroundings. He felt a snap of adrenaline when his eyes touched the far end of the outdoor dining area. Seated alone at a table for two was Nicole. She sipped frugally from a tall glass of white wine as she flipped through the menu, oblivious to the noisy world of laughter and liquid around her. Drew watched her as he nursed his bourbon, wondering if she were truly alone, or expecting company. Realizing there was only one place setting at her table, Drew assumed she was by herself.

Drew stared into the table, nervously rubbing his clasped hands together while trying to make sense of why he would even contemplate going over to speak to her. He quickly glanced at her again, torn between his self-imposed isolationist philosophy and a nagging impulse to talk to her for reasons he couldn't explain. Reluctance finally won out over reckless abandon. He sucked in a deep breath, rose to his feet like a defendant in a courtroom about to hear his fate, and sat back down in another chair with his back to her. Out of sight, out of mind, out of reach. It eliminated the temptation to study her as he had done on the beach.

Wendi arrived with his chowder seconds later. "Your clams

and shrimp should be out shortly," she said as she set the steaming bowl in front of him.

"Thank you," he said, politely. "No hurry. And could you please bring me another bourbon when you get a moment?"

"Comin' right up," Wendi replied as she bounced away.

Drew admired the young girl's enthusiasm. Envied it, really. He wished he could get that excited about anything, much less a drink refill. He dipped his spoon into the creamy concoction and lifted it to his lips, gently blowing on it to cool the first taste. He let the chowder fill his mouth and rest on his tongue, savoring its salty flavor. He closed his eyes as the warmth tumbled down his throat and into his stomach. Next to bourbon, Drew thought that good food was the best remedy for pushing your troubles aside. He filled his spoon and sent another gift from the seas into his open mouth.

"Is this seat taken?" a voice behind him said softly.

Startled, Drew spun his head around, spilling some chowder across his chin. He quickly wiped it away with his sleeve. Nicole was standing in front of him. He was momentarily speechless as he processed the sudden change in environment but finally spoke. "Oh! Hi!"

Nicole gestured with the wine glass in her hand to the chair next to Drew "Well, is it?"

Still seated, Drew looked at the three empty chairs around his table, then back at Nicole. "Uh, no, but...."

"But what?" Nicole asked with a wry smile. She seemed to be enjoying his discomfort.

"I usually dine alone."

"Because you *have* to? Or because you *prefer* to?"

Drew thought for a moment before answering. "Some of both I suppose."

"Well, now you don't *have* to. May I join you?"

Drew grimaced slightly and scratched behind his ear with the nail of his index finger. "I don't know . . ."

"Don't worry. I have no hidden agenda. I don't even want to split dessert. I just thought it would be nice to share some intelligent conversation."

"You might be disappointed," answered Drew.

"Wouldn't be the first time," she quipped.

Drew looked at her with mock suspicion. "What makes you think I'm intelligent?"

She tapped her temple. "You wouldn't have been in a bookstore if you didn't have *something* going on up there."

He cracked the thinnest of smiles and cocked his head slightly from side to side as if to agree with her premise. "Perhaps."

"So...may I pull up a chair?" she asked. "Just conversation?"

Drew finally stood up. "Uh, sure," he said even though he didn't sound sure. He pulled one of the chairs away from the table and politely motioned for her to sit down.

Nicole sat down and took a light sip of her wine. Her eyes made a quick sweep around the restaurant. "I see you found the place," she said.

"It's a small town. Didn't take long." He anxiously looked around for Wendi, hoping she'd arrive soon with his fresh cocktail. Nowhere in sight.

She extended her right hand. "I'm Nicole, by the way," she said as a reminder. "It's Drew, right?"

He gave her hand a single shake. "Yes. Good memory." Drew looked again for his waitress. Wendi was already heading his way but he raised a pointed finger anyway as if she might have forgotten where he was sitting.

Wendi navigated the maze of tables and finally arrived. She handed Drew his cocktail and smiled brightly at Nicole. "I see you've got company!"

"Yeah," Drew said. "Late arrival."

Wendi looked at Nicole. "Would you like to see a menu, ma'am?"

Nicole looked directly at Drew. "I'll just have what he's having. I'm sure he chose wisely."

"He did," Wendi said with a wide smile. "I'll get those plates right out!" She bounded off as if putting in a food order was the most joyous task a person could undertake.

Drew took a light sip of his bourbon, letting it glide across his numbed palate. He looked away, frowned slightly, then focused his attention back on Nicole. "I'm just curious. Why did you come here tonight?"

She gave a shrug of innocence. "I came here because the food's good. That's why I recommended it."

"But you knew I'd be here."

"I didn't know that. It's just a coincidence. Like you said, it's a small town."

Drew didn't fully believe her but had no choice but to accept it as the truth. He raised his glass. "Well then, here's to small towns and big coincidences."

Nicole raised her wine glass and took a small sip. "I have a question for *you*."

"No guarantees I'll answer."

"What made you turn your chair around just now? I know you saw me sitting over there."

"You don't know that."

She ignored his protest. "Did I not make a good first impression?"

He shook his head. "No, no, that's not it at all. As I said, I just like to be alone."

"And you were afraid that if we made eye contact, you'd feel obligated to speak to me?"

Drew nodded. "Something like that. And if I'm being honest, it was also out of respect for your desire for some privacy. I sense that about you."

She nodded. "Okay, I can believe that. I *do* like to be alone sometimes. Obviously not all the time." She swirled her wine in her glass. "And if it makes you feel any better, you passed the test."

"A test? Test of what?"

"To see if you were a gentleman."

"I'm confused," Drew said as he took another draw of his drink.

"If you weren't a true gentleman, you would have come directly over to my table and offered to buy me a drink with the intention of joining me and trying to make a night of it. You would have been persistent to the point of nausea. Instead, you avoided me. You passed."

"By avoiding you?"

"Yes. Subtly, I might add."

Drew chuckled. "Who knew? I should have turned my back on women years ago."

Nicole shared in his laughter. "It wasn't just that."

"Oh? What else?"

"I saw you on the beach a few weeks ago. You rescued my chair from the rising tide."

Drew closed his eyes for two seconds. "You saw that? I didn't think you noticed me."

"I did. And I should say thank you."

Drew mulled over the new information. "You weren't completely honest. When I saw you at the bookstore, you pretended like you'd never seen me before."

"True, but neither were *you*."

"I believe I was," Drew said.

"No. You didn't buy a copy of *Eat, Pray, Love* just because, as you put it, 'you wanted to spend time with an old friend.'"

Drew cringed. "I confess. I did take a quick peek at your beach reading."

"Spying on me, huh?"

"I prefer to think of it as 'taking an interest.'"

"It was prying at best."

Drew nodded. "Okay, I can live with prying. But that's also how I knew you were intelligent, which is the only reason I've allowed you to join me." Drew took in some more bourbon. "So . . . what would you like to intelligently talk about? And I immediately apologize for ending a sentence with a preposition."

Nicole made a *tsk* sound with a click of her tongue and shook her head. "And here I thought *you* were intelligent."

"What do they say? Something about don't judge a book by its cover?"

"That *is* what they say."

Wendi arrived with several heaping plates of steamed clams and shrimp. "There ya go. Enjoy! Holler if you need anything!"

"Thank you, Wendi," Drew called out as she scooted away.

"First-name basis with the wait staff, huh?" Nicole said after Wendi had gone. "I'm impressed. You sure you don't come here often?"

"Like you said, I fit right in." Drew pushed his fork into the soft flesh of a clam and dipped it in the melted butter, allowing the excess to drip off before moving it into his mouth. "To be honest, I'm kind of surprised you're here. It seems a little... I don't know . . . casual for you."

Nicole frowned as she dragged an orangey shrimp through a small bowl of red cocktail sauce. "Why on earth would you say *that*?" She sounded borderline offended.

"I guess it's because of your beach house. It's pretty spectacular. Expensive real estate. I half expected the Kennedy clan to come walking out."

"Oh, *that*," Nicole said. His supposition seemed to make sense. "It's not mine. It's my best friend's. She just lets me borrow it. You know, that 'don't judge a book' thing you were just talking about."

"Oh," Drew said, drawing out the sound. The picture was getting clearer.

Nicole looked up from her meal to gauge his response. "You seem relieved."

Drew took a moment to sort out his feelings. "I suppose maybe I am. Frankly, I'm not that comfortable around rich people."

"You prefer the hoi polloi? The huddled masses?"

Drew moved his head back and forth, searching for the right words to explain himself. "I prefer the genuine. Sometimes money has a way of covering that up. Or eradicating it altogether."

"Sometimes," allowed Nicole. "But not always."

"No. But I've seen it happen."

There was a lengthy pause in their back-and-forth. They filled the silence by filling their stomachs and lowering the levels of their respective drinks. Nicole rekindled the conversation, talking with her mouth slightly full. "So what were *you* reading that morning on the beach?"

"*The Prince of Tides* for about the tenth time. Pat Conroy is my absolute favorite."

"I love him too. *Beach Music* should be required reading."

"The man certainly has a lyrical way with words."

Nicole nodded in agreement. "Doesn't he? Pat Conroy could take three pages to describe a hammock that looks over a Lowcountry marsh and by the end of those three pages, you want to move to South Carolina and buy that hammock."

"I know," agreed Drew. "I miss him. I miss his genius. But reading his books is like spending the day with a dear friend and coming away smarter and more human."

Nicole tilted her head and nodded. "More human. I like that."

"Do you have a favorite author?" he asked.

Nicole nodded enthusiastically. "Definitely F. Scott Fitzgerald. I've read everything he ever wrote, including "Bernice Bobs Her Hair." I've probably read *The Great Gatsby* fifteen times."

Drew scowled. "Why? It's the most overrated book in literary history."

"Why would you say that? Look at any list of the greatest books. It's ranked higher than *Moby Dick* and *War and Peace*."

"Doesn't matter. There's not one likable person in the entire story and the character development totally lacks depth. I know more about my mailman than I do about Daisy Buchanan and I've never actually met my mailman."

"Lack of depth? Seriously? You might not *like* Jay Gatsby but you certainly understand him. We know what makes him tick."

"Yeah, ill-gotten money and lavish parties. If I want to get a glimpse into the lives of a bunch of rich, whiny snobs, I'll watch *The Real Housewives of Beverly Hills*."

Nicole shrugged. "I think it's beautifully written. 'Poor ghosts, breathing dreams like air, drifted fortuitously about' is more of a poem than a sentence. The prose is elegant."

"I completely disagree. I find it tedious. And that line you just quoted doesn't mean anything."

Nicole shook her head. "Sure it does. It means you should dream big and follow your dreams. Not just about living the American dream but also the dream of romantic love. It's a story about a desperate yearning for love."

Drew was getting more animated in both his speech and his hand gestures. "Oh, it's definitely about yearning. Makes me yearn to read a different book. Like the phone book. Anyone who thinks it's a great piece of literature is just being pretentious."

Nicole's shoulders slumped. She looked wounded. "Do you mind if we talk about something else?"

"Why? Because I'm right?" Drew could immediately sense that his attempt at levity fell dismally short.

"Because this doesn't feel like a healthy discussion. It feels more like an argument where there's a winner and a loser. I have enough of that in my life already. I love talking about books, but I don't feel like squabbling over them like I'm in a court of law."

Drew lowered his head as he nodded. "You're right. I'm sorry. I got a little carried away. I guess it's been a while since I've had any intelligent conversation. I hope I didn't ruin the evening."

"No. It's me, not you. I admire your passion. I just don't want to bear the brunt of it."

"Understood." Drew paused as he carefully considered the next words to come out of his mouth. "Can we agree that *Tender is the Night* is F. Scott's greatest work and it's absolutely perfect in every way?"

The edges of Nicole's mouth curled slightly in a warm smile

that signaled a truce. "Yes, if we also agree to ignore the fact that the Nicole character in the book was a bit crazy."

Drew returned a conciliatory smile. "Deal." For the first time, he looked at her left hand. It was lacking any jewelry. "You're not married?"

"Actually, I am," she said softly. She gazed into her wine glass, then took a large gulp.

"You're not wearing a ring."

She looked at her bare hand. "I don't wear it at the beach. I'm afraid I'll lose it in the ocean." That wasn't entirely true. In fact, it wasn't true at all. She removed her diamond ring as often as possible to mentally distance herself from her marriage to Lee Wayne.

Drew nodded, but only slightly. He again sensed a lack of truthfulness in Nicole's explanation. In their brief encounter at the beach, he hadn't seen her even approach the water's edge. He let it go.

"Why did you ask me that?" Nicole said.

Drew shrugged. "I don't know. Just curious."

"You're a very curious person."

"I guess curiosity is better than prying."

Her eyes glanced at Drew's left hand for a split second to see if he was wearing a wedding band. He wasn't. "I'm guessing you're not married?"

Drew chewed on his bottom lip and shook his head. "No." He offered no further explanation.

They took a few bites as several moments of silence passed between them. Again, Nicole filled the void. "So why do you read?" she asked him.

"Oh my," he said with wider eyes. "That's like asking me the meaning of life. Not a question easily answered."

"Try."

"Well, I suppose it's for a myriad of reasons. I find it relaxing, I find it entertaining, and it helps to satisfy my inquisitive nature about the world and the human condition. And if I'm being perfectly honest, I think reading makes me a more interesting person."

Nicole tilted her head and looked him over with a squint like a farmer about to buy a horse. "I'll be the judge of that," she said with an impish grin.

"I'm serious," Drew continued. "I think readers are inherently more interesting and complex people. Books are thought-provoking, and they stir your emotions, and the good ones force you to ponder the meaning of your own life. I think that's why people join book clubs. It's so they can talk about what they've just read and try to glean some deeper meaning or insights from the stories and characters that might apply to their own lives. If nothing else, reading improves your vocabulary. I think all of that adds some texture to your life."

"Seems as though you've thought about this."

"A little. But that's the first time I've ever said it out loud. So what about you? Why do *you* read?"

"One word . . . escape. My books take me away from the real world, and I love every minute I'm gone."

"I would agree. I think escapism is a big part of it." Drew took a sip of bourbon and leaned back a little in his chair. "So let me ask you, are you escaping *from* something or running *toward* something?"

"Some of both." She didn't elaborate.

They consumed the next hour by talking about their favorite books and authors while eating their seafood and refilling their drink glasses. The names of Ayn Rand, John Updike, and Sue Monk Kidd were bandied about. *To Kill a Mockingbird, My Antonia,* and *Same Kind of Different As Me* brought nods of approval and recollections of favorite characters and passages. One topic merged seamlessly into the next, and laughter was light and free as they shared their mutual appetite for the well-crafted sentence and story. There were no detours into the personal dossiers of *where are you from originally? Where did you go to school? Where do you work?* They both seemed to prefer it that way.

The literary discussion continued on through a dessert course of two generous wedges of pie. Hers, key lime. His, bourbon pecan. The time passed so quickly that they didn't realize that most of the dining deck was now empty.

Wendi arrived with the bill. "Is this one check, or two?"

Drew looked over at Nicole before reaching for the black folder in Wendi's hand. "Would it be all right if I paid for dinner? It's the least I can do for all that prying."

Nicole smiled warmly and nodded her approval. "That would be nice. And thank you."

Drew looked at the bill, then pulled several large bills from his wallet and handed the cash to Wendi. It was significantly more than the total. "We're good. Thank you for taking such excellent care of us."

Wendi beamed over the generous gratuity. "It was my pleasure. I hope y'all come back."

Minutes later, as they walked to their cars in the parking lot while remaining a respectful distance apart, Drew suddenly focused on Nicole, as if something had just occurred to him.

"May I ask your last name?" he said.

"There you go, prying again."

"Can't help it. It's my curious nature."

"Why should you know *my* last name when I don't know yours?"

"Fair enough. Mine is Endicott. Drew Endicott."

"Shepherd. Nicole Shepherd." She shook his hand as if meeting for the first time.

"It was nice sharing a meal with you, Nicole Shepherd. And some highly intelligent conversation."

"I agree. And thank you for dinner, Drew Endicott."

They walked on in silence until Drew stopped and pointed to his Jeep. "This is me." He dug his hands into his pockets and looked at his feet as if he were a teenager at the end of his very first date. "So I guess this is goodbye."

She smiled with pursed lips and arched her eyebrows. "I suppose so." They maintained their safe distance.

For reasons he couldn't explain, Drew was suddenly struck with a spontaneous burst of courage, the kind required to jump off a tall rock into a dark lake against your natural instincts. He blurted out his thoughts before common sense prevailed. "I don't imagine you'd like to keep in touch somehow? Talk about what we're reading?" His bold words lingered in the night air just long enough for reluctance to creep in.

After a moment's hesitation, she shook her head. "Probably not a good idea." She held up her left hand and tapped her ring finger even though it was bare.

It stung, like a first date rebuffing a goodnight kiss. It was the first time he'd reached out in any human way since the funerals and he immediately regretted having done so. "I understand." He backed away several steps. "Well then, I'll see that you get safely into your car and then I'll be off. Thanks for a memorable evening. Best one in a long time."

Nicole's eyes were suddenly diverted to the distinctive license plate on Drew's Grand Cherokee. It read: THE END. She pointed to it with an expression somewhere between confusion and amusement. "What's *that* supposed to mean?"

Drew followed her finger to the rear bumper of his Jeep. "Oh, that?" he murmured with slight embarrassment. "Several things, I guess. The end of the car. The end of every book. End as in Endicott. It was supposed to be clever. Next time I'll stick with random letters and numbers."

"No, I like it," Nicole said. Once again, Drew wasn't sure about the veracity of her words. "Don't go changin'."

"We'll see. Well, goodnight, Nicole."

"Goodnight, Drew," she echoed. It might have been his imagination, but he seemed to detect the faintest inkling of wistful melancholy as if she were genuinely sorry to be parting ways. He dismissed it as wishful thinking.

Drew watched Nicole climb into her car, a dark, German luxury sedan. He kept his eyes fixed on her taillights as they faded into the darkness of the winding road that would take her back to her house on Oak Island. He remained in the same position long after she'd disappeared, not wanting to write THE END to the beautiful short story he'd just experienced. He loved the way he felt at this moment and wanted to savor it. It was something between excitement and fear, but mostly it was a feeling of imbalance. More than anything, Drew was feeling a measure of pride for even having engaged with a stranger, however briefly. This was the first time since the funerals that he'd even had a meaningful conversation. Eight seasons had come and gone since the last time he'd ventured that far from his dark corner. It felt liberating. It also felt terrifying. For so long, he'd been aggressive in his isolation. He didn't just want to *be* alone, he wanted to be *left* alone. For a time, Drew had envied a man named Christopher Knight, the subject of a book he'd read called *The Stranger in the Woods* by Michael Finkel. Knight had lived as a hermit in the deep woods of Maine, foregoing human contact for twenty-seven years. No talking, no touching, no tethers. *Lucky*, Drew had thought at the time.

As the Oak Island Lighthouse kept up its steady rhythm, penetrating the night sky, Drew could almost feel some light re-entering the cracks in his being. He sensed a slight pause in his life, a wavering, perhaps even a change of direction. He wondered if she might be feeling the same.

Nicole stood on the deck of her seaside sanctuary and watched the moon drape its beams across the calmer night waters. She dreaded tomorrow, knowing she was leaving the eternal peace of this house and returning to the suffocating life at home. She felt some of the moonlight shine into the darker parts of her mind, the places she didn't dare visit. The places where resentment and rage and revenge had planted seeds and were steadily growing. She listened again for hope.

CHAPTER SEVEN

"Books didn't make me wallow in darkness, darkness made me wallow in books."

— Jackson Pearce

Drew woke up earlier than usual and quickly drank two cups of industrial coffee from the tiny coffeemaker that came with his room at the Riverside Motel in Southport. He packed up his few belongings, settled up his bill at the front desk, then drove a few blocks to a coffee shop for a fast breakfast of two cranberry muffins, a small brick of hash browns, and another coffee. If he had even a small hangover, it would soon be exorcised by the rush of caffeine and carbohydrates.

After a drive of just fifteen minutes from Southport to Oak Island, he was parked near the same section of beach where he'd first encountered Nicole two weeks before. He unloaded his beach chair and a small canvas bag that contained only a bottle of water, a hardcover edition of Tara Westover's gripping memoir *Educated,* and a bottle of sunscreen. He'd already decided to use the beach access walkway several houses down from the house where Nicole was staying. He'd driven by and seen her car in the driveway, so he assumed she was there. He was hoping to see her again but wanted to make it appear accidental. Camping out in the same spot as the first time their paths had crossed a few weeks ago might appear to be the actions of a stalker. A hundred yards down the beach he could still see her yellow beach umbrella going up, but he wouldn't appear to be overly eager. The best scenario would be that Nicole emerged from her house and went for a walk, passing by him on her way. He convinced himself it would be almost coincidental.

After lathering his face and legs with milky sunblock, Drew settled into his beach chair and opened his book. For every three paragraphs he read, he made another visual check down the beach to see if any sunflower yellow umbrellas had bloomed in the sand. Nothing.

The caffeine was wearing off, and the midday sun was wearing him down. Drew rested the open book over his knee and stared out at the wide expanse of water. The night before had been a fitful battle of infrequent sleep, mostly from wondering if he'd see Nicole again. Now the beams of sunlight pressed him toward napping, but the unrelenting crashing of the waves wouldn't allow it. With the power of an undertow, the waves dragged Drew back to another time and place. The worst place he'd ever been and was destined to revisit for eternity.

TWO YEARS EARLIER

Drew looked up and saw the line of people snaked out the door of Manhattan's legendary Strand Book Store. His pen hand was red and pulsing from signing his autograph hundreds of times over, but he was happy to bear the inconvenience of it. Every book that was winged open on the table in front of him meant more money in his pocket, more accolades, and more fans who would buy his next book and the next one after that. He'd gotten to the point where he could churn out a new book every six months and he knew it would sell, regardless of literary merit. The thinnest of plot lines and most hackneyed of characters and dialogue were no deterrent to a spot on the bestseller list. These hordes of readers were all here to gobble up the latest potboiler from the fertile mind of J. Andrew Endicott and he was going to cash in at every opportunity.

He'd arranged several meetings in New York and this book signing despite knowing that his wife had already planned a vacation to the beach on the very days he had scheduled himself to be away. The oceanfront cottage in Oak Island, North Carolina, had been rented, local restaurants scouted out on the internet, and new beach toys purchased for his young daughter, so she could construct the perfect sandcastle. But none of that had mattered in the self-important universe of J. Andrew Endicott. *The iron is hot!* he kept reminding himself. No speech, no workshop, no book signing was ever turned down, as the sales and frequent flier miles piled up. Birthdays and other special occasions were often celebrated via FaceTime or a phone call. Sometimes just a text was all he'd managed between meetings. Besides, he told himself, he was doing this for *them*. And he would be there for the last four days of the beach trip. That should be a gracious plenty for someone as busy as he was.

Even on the days he was home at his sizable estate outside of Raleigh, he was sequestered in the detached carriage house he used as an office, crafting new plot twists and catchy titles. No sooner had he typed THE END than he was on a plane out of Raleigh and having dinner with his New York agent, Holly Hedrick.

They'd joined forces when they were both infants in the literary world. She was a junior agent at a boutique literary agency on Fifth Avenue and he'd just left his position as a bright young writer at a large ad agency. He'd taken several years to finish his first novel, a legal thriller. As Drew had no formal training, the writing was a little rough around the edges, but the bones of the story were solid, and the legal detail interspersed throughout the book gave it a solid feel of authenticity. While other agents had rejected his manuscript, Holly had seen his potential. With an MFA from Swarthmore, she was actually a better writer than Drew was, but she happily preferred a role that combined editing with commerce. She'd spent countless hours getting Drew's pile of prose into the best shape possible, and through nothing short of grit and grind, she'd landed him a publishing deal with one of the major houses.

From there, their relationship flourished and was mutually beneficial. He'd made millions from sales and movie rights. On the strength of his name, Holly had risen to the rank of senior agent, and moved to a much nicer apartment on the Upper West Side, an easy walk to Lincoln Center. But despite her relative fame and fortune in the literary world, she'd chosen to remain at the same boutique agency. She still had a love of discovering and nurturing unknown talents and transferring their thoughts and ideas to the printed page for the masses to consume and enjoy. She felt it kept her grounded and reminded her that it was the message and not the money that was truly important. She would always believe that a good book could change lives, and not just those of author and agent.

Thus, it was with overwhelming surprise that Holly received a dispassionate email from Drew informing her that he was leaving her for one of the mega-agencies. *It's just business* was the theme of the message. *No hard feelings.* After seven productive and profitable years together, it was the last correspondence they'd had.

None of that unpleasantness was on Drew's mind as he continued to chat and sign, chat and sign, chat and sign. The assistant manager at the bookstore wheeled in three more boxes of his latest offering, *Tears of the Sycamore.* If he were being honest, it wasn't his best work. He'd struggled with the ending but facing a looming deadline from his publisher, he'd lashed a few thoughts together and hoped it would float. He did, at one point, remember telling himself *Holly would never let this manuscript go out like this.*

The line of autograph seekers was still crowding the bookstore when the life of J. Andrew Endicott was about to change forever. His cell phone buzzed inside the breast pocket of his blue blazer. He'd forgotten to switch it off as was his custom at book signings. He reached into his jacket to end the interruption but stopped when he saw the incoming number that popped up on the screen. It wasn't frequent, but it was still familiar. Drew knew his brother, Eric, would only call if it were vitally important, like something wrong with their mother. He glanced again at the long line of fans and was reluctant to suspend the activity, but something told him to take the call.

"Excuse me for just a moment," Drew said to the next person in line with their book pressed forward. He moved away from the signing table and sought refuge behind a shelf of self-help books. He pressed the phone to one ear and cupped his free hand around the other to drown out the ambient noise. "Hey, Eric. What's wrong?" After hearing only one sentence from his brother, Drew's legs buckled and he fell hard against the shelf behind him. His hand, already fatigued from so many autographs, now shook uncontrollably as he tried to hold the phone to his head and absorb the unimaginable news coming across the line. "I'm in New York. I'll be there as soon as I can," he choked out in a whisper. He ended the call and braced himself against the bookshelves as he stumbled back to the autograph table as if it were suddenly pitch dark. It was the last thing he remembered doing that day, as the shock washed over him like a summer thunderstorm.

Drew snapped out of the trance that had taken him back to that book signing two years ago. *If I had to do it all over again* was the haunting mantra that he recited over and over in the recesses of his brain. He understood on some level that this was why he was lured to the ocean. It was his voluntary punishment. For J. Andrew Endicott, the din of the pounding surf was the scream of the Harpies carried on the wind, swooping down to snatch his guilty soul. The unceasing waves relentlessly demanded contrition, while he begged for the forgiveness that had yet to come.

After four hours of waiting for a woman with a yellow beach umbrella who never arrived, Drew finally packed up and headed back to reality. He really didn't know why he was going home. It wasn't as if there was a job or a deadline waiting for him back in Wilmington. It just seemed like he'd punished himself enough.

Minutes later, when he climbed into the front seat of his Jeep, he noticed a piece of paper tucked under the windshield wiper. *How did I get a ticket?* was his first thought. *This is all-day parking!* He was already mentally composing his indignant letter to the Oak Island Police Department as he scrambled out of the vehicle and snatched the paper off the windshield.

The note stopped him cold. It wasn't a parking ticket. It was simply a phone number, scripted by a woman's gentle hand. He knew immediately to whom it belonged. Drew quickly scanned the area all around him, like someone who'd just heard voices in a cornfield. He was alone. He looked at the note again, then tucked it into his shirt pocket and floated back inside his SUV. That ridiculous vanity plate on his back bumper had finally been good for something.

The phone rang at least seven times before Nicole answered.

"Hello?" she asked as if she didn't already know who was calling.

"It's Drew." There was a long silence, to the point where Drew looked at the screen on his phone to see if he was still connected. "Nicole? Hello?"

On the other end of the phone line was a woman sitting on the edge of her bed with a packed suitcase next to her feet. She was bent over, eyes closed, and lightly massaging her forehead. She was the picture of a woman not sure what she was doing, or more disconcerting, *why* she was doing it. Nicole brought in a deep breath. "Listen . . . um . . . I was going to grab a quick bite to eat before I drove home. I wondered if maybe... you had time to join me." Nicole shook her head, surprised by her nervousness.

"I'd love to," Drew answered softly. "When and where?"

"There's a place on the river in Southport called the Frying Pan. How about 3:00?"

Drew checked his watch. "That sounds great. I'm coming straight from the beach, so you might not want to sit too close to me."

"Not a problem. See you at three."

"Look forward to it. Bye, Nicole."

"Bye."

Nicole turned off her cell phone and tossed it onto the bed. She caught her reflection in the bedroom mirror and held her own gaze for a moment. She closed her eyes and shook her head as if asking herself, *what am I doing?*

By 3:15, Nicole and Drew had settled into a heaping plate of calamari as they sat across from each other at a picnic table on the restaurant's upper deck. They'd already exchanged the necessary pleasantries about the weather and the view after ordering their drinks.

Nicole's nervousness was shrinking away as the calming effects of a mango margarita went swimming into her brain. She leaned forward and spoke softly. "May I make a confession?"

"Certainly. Good for the soul."

"I was watching you today."

"You were? When?"

"While you were sitting on the beach this morning."

"I wasn't anywhere near your house."

"So I noticed. Good effort trying to be coy."

Drew nodded slightly and grazed the top row of his teeth with his tongue. "Well then. It appears as though we *both* have something to confess. That's a little embarrassing."

"Not as embarrassing as me watching you through binoculars."

"Seriously? That's borderline stalking."

"I blame you for sitting so far away."

Drew laughed, then turned more serious. "So why were you watching me?"

"Just curious."

"Curious about what?"

She paused before responding. "Why do you stare out at the water when there's nothing to see? I've watched you do it several times. You just get lost. I'm curious as to why."

Drew turned his head and looked at the river. His mind traveled at quicksilver speed back to New York, to book signings, to heart-stabbing phone calls, to funerals. None of which he was ready to share. He took a long sip from his bourbon, then shrugged slightly. "I guess I just enjoy looking at the water."

"I don't believe you."

Drew nodded. "You shouldn't." Drew swirled his drink as he looked back at the river, then back to Nicole. "May I ask *you* a question?"

"You can ask, but not sure I'll answer."

"Fair enough. Why did you leave your number on my windshield?"

Nicole lowered her head and sipped her drink through the tiny straw. She answered without looking up. "I don't honestly know."

"There must have been some reason. Some impulse."

She nodded with hesitance. She knew the answer. "I suppose I just wanted—" She shook her head and tapped her fingers on the picnic table, stopping short of openly confessing that she simply wanted a few minutes in the company of a man who wasn't condescending, hypercritical, or prone to violence. But that was certainly too much to reveal right now. She finally looked up. "I can't really say."

Drew intuitively understood the ambiguity of Nicole's response. He didn't pursue it. They both had wrenching stories to share, but it would have to be at another time and in another place.

As if declaring intermission on the weighty subtext of their conversation, Drew snatched the menu off the table and examined the contents. "Let's see what else we might want."

An hour later, after a plate of grouper nuggets and a lively conversation about their favorite mystery authors, they exchanged amiable goodbyes in the parking lot.

"Thank you for meeting me," offered Nicole.

"Thank you for asking."

She nodded, searching for the right words. "Well then . . . I guess this is it."

"I guess so," Drew said. "Good luck with everything."

"You too." Nicole swallowed hard. "Goodbye, Drew."

"Bye, Nicole."

From a respectful distance, their eyes silently clung to each other for a few extra seconds. The spell ended with a mechanical wave of their hands and it was off to their separate cars and separate lives.

CHAPTER EIGHT

"A person who won't read has no advantage over
one who can't."

— Mark Twain

Not only had Lee Wayne's appetite for food increased
as he recovered from surgery, but so had his appetite
for sex. Not lovemaking; just sex. Nicole hated it but
believed it to be part of her marital duties, so she just accepted
it. She also knew she'd be knocked about if she didn't. It was
usually after he stumbled in from a late evening of bad golf and
good drinking. He smelled like sweat, Seagrams, and sunblock.
Lie there and just take it, she told herself.

Lee Wayne's primal urges were always heightened after he
returned from his sailing trips. Maybe something about the
wind in his face. That was what Nicole knew was in store for
her when she returned from her weekend at the beach. *It'll be
over soon.*

After satisfying himself, Lee Wayne looked her up and down
like a used car as she climbed out of bed and put on her robe.
"Maybe you need to cut back on your portions, babe. You're
lookin' a little thick in the middle. And you know they make
a cream for those bags under your eyes. Or maybe you should
think about a little nip and tuck."

She turned away to deflect his verbal brickbat, but it hurt
her to her core. She was actually quite trim for her age, and
on some level she knew that, but disparaging remarks from

your spouse about your physical image cut deeply. It was just one of his ways of emotionally controlling her. Lee Wayne fully understood that it was the bruises you couldn't see, the ones on the inside, that inflicted the sharpest pain.

Nicole left the bedroom and moved to the living room couch, where she'd been sleeping for the last two years. She explained the sleeping arrangement by complaining about his snoring. Even the adjacent spare bedroom was too close to the plangent noise that emanated from his nasal passages, and on more than one occasion, he'd locked her inside the guest room as punishment for some perceived transgression.

But for Nicole, not sharing his bed had become about much more than just her husband's snoring. Simply brushing up against him in the middle of the night made her skin crawl. Plus, she could read as late into the night as she pleased with nobody complaining about a book light or the rustling of pages. All things considered, Nicole decided that even though it was less than comfortable, the couch was an infinitely better alternative. Still, it made her angry that she couldn't sleep on a real mattress. *Maybe if I wasn't forced to sleep on the couch I wouldn't have these bags under my eyes*, she thought. Lee Wayne had no issues with Nicole's nocturnal discomfort, proving he could be cruel even while sleeping.

Sometimes, if he were feeling charitable, Lee Wayne would leave money on her dresser after sex. Whether it was a reward or a payoff, she didn't care. It was demeaning. Ironically, it had become the means by which she'd found the escape that books alone wouldn't provide. Nicole used the cash to secretly buy a second phone. Nothing fancy, just enough basic features to allow her to surf the internet, send emails and texts, and make private phone calls without fear of Lee Wayne investigating her search history or phone records, which he routinely did. Her husband's guilty money had been plenty enough to cover the monthly payments.

Nicole hid the secret phone in a hollowed-out volume of Dostoevsky's *Crime and Punishment* which she knew Lee Wayne would never touch. The closest he'd come to reading a book in their years together was the TV Guide. As was her nightly ritual, the moment she heard the snoring commence from the bedroom down the hall, she opened the book and brought the forbidden phone to life. The warm glow of the light was stimulating, almost in an erotic sense. Even though what she was doing wasn't illegal, she still knew it was wrong. But not wrong enough to keep her from doing it.

Occasionally, she'd text back and forth with Teri if her friend were still awake. Usually, she'd check her platforms of social media to see what the outside world was doing while she was trapped inside the walls of "Lee Wayne Manor." Ironically, she found comfort in discovering people who seemed to be as unhappy and dissatisfied with their lives as she was and had finally gotten divorced.

Sometimes she would even venture into the verboten world of a dating site, just to see what else was out there. She was amazed at how many attractive men there were around her same age, all looking for love. Despite the temporary titillation, it brought her as she swiped through the photos, the exercise inevitably brought on a wave of sadness. Even if she were ever to get free of Lee Wayne, she was damaged goods. She had convinced herself that true love, the kind you read about in great novels, would never fall at the feet of Nicole Shepherd.

But none of that was assaulting her thoughts right now. Her pulse had quickened to a pace she hadn't felt in years. To her great surprise, she had a text message waiting for her and she immediately knew who'd sent it.

> Hi, Nicole,
> Hope you're doing well. I finished Prince of Tides
> and moved on to The Alchemist. Have you read it?
> Paulo Coelho is brilliant! Just wanted to thank you
> again for all the conversation. It remains highly
> memorable Regards, Drew

Nicole read the text two more times to discern its full meaning. It was brief and respectful, borderline sanitized, but the last sentence was also slightly suggestive of something more than just two strangers talking about their mutual love of reading. Perhaps there was no deeper meaning to be extracted by reading between the lines, but she couldn't help but feel Drew's outreach to her had one underlying quality: potential.

After several minutes of composing a response in her head, Nicole replied.

Good to hear from you. I finished Eat, Pray, Love. Definitely in my top 10 of all time. Next in my stack is The Paris Wife by Paula McLain. You mentioned the other night how much you love Hemingway, so you might enjoy it if you haven't already read it. I will look for The Alchemist the next time I'm in the bookstore. You never know what you might find there! Keep in touch. Nicole

She agonized over the last sentence, to the point where she had typed it, deleted it, typed it again, and repeated the process one more time. She even debated the use of an exclamation point, lest it seem too forward. She wanted her response to be ambiguous, to tiptoe along the fine line between friendly and polite so that it could be taken either way. *Keep in touch* was her subtle way of conveying that she was happy to hear from him and would enjoy further discussion about their reading lists, all contained within a three-word valediction.

After more hesitation, she finally pressed the SEND button, and off it went. No turning back. She didn't know why she'd done it, or why she'd left her phone number on his windshield in the first place, but the excitement overrode all reason. She craved stimulating conversation, electronically or otherwise, and this was a new avenue she intended to explore.

Nicole waited several minutes for a reply, just staring at the luminescent screen in the darkened living room, but none came. *Maybe he's just reading a good book,* she told herself.

Drew switched off the reading lamp in his living room and stared at the phone in his hand. "What am I doing?" he asked himself out loud. He tried his best not to overthink it. It was just two people talking about books, nothing more. Still, it made him happier than it should have. In a momentary burst of rational thought, he turned off his cell phone before the bourbon sent a text that he might later regret.

CHAPTER NINE

"Books are not made for furniture, but there is nothing
else that so beautifully furnishes a house."

— Henry Ward Beecher

How he loathed their time together. As the elevator slowly ascended to the third floor of his mother's nursing home, Drew's entire life seemed to flash before his eyes, but only the worst parts. He replayed hours of tapes in his head in fast-forward, of the mental abuse Gloria Endicott had spilled out onto her family. Slights, criticisms, and emotional explosions from her hair-trigger temper. All part of the scrapbook of her life, recorded and stored in the minds of those closest to her.

Even now, even with the strength Drew had attained by time and distance from his childhood, combined with truly being loved by someone as an adult, his encounters with his mother grated on every ganglion in his nervous system. His synapses crackled in his brain like party favors popping off after dessert at an English manor house. Drew always steeled himself with a short prayer before entering her room, bracing for the passive-aggressive assault that lay in wait. Nearly every sentence in their strained discourse began with a verbal pinprick, loaded phrases such as *you should* or *don't you think?* soon to be followed by a judgmental salvo like *I'm surprised you don't*, or *one might think you would*, and then she'd fill in the blank with some critical observation she'd made.

In private conversations with friends, Drew had taken to calling his mother The Great Martini, not just in homage to Pat Conroy, but because of the copious amounts of vodka she could consume on most nights of the week. No matter how many times the vodka itself had been filtered, it provided no filter for Gloria Endicott when it came to speaking her mind. If Gloria had limited skills of tact and compassion in sobriety, they were washed away entirely with the introduction of inebriation. When the time came for her funeral, someone would be certain to say something like *You always knew where you stood with Gloria Endicott*, or *Gloria loved to tell it like it was. She was a straight talker.* All code for *Gloria Endicott said whatever the hell she felt like saying anytime and anyplace to anyone.* And her passage into the land of straight-talking wasn't by using the passport of old age, a common excuse. Hers was the product of innate meanness. Of a pure selfishness that made her not just the center of the universe, but one that demanded perfection in everyone. Except her.

Never had this been illustrated in a worse fashion than after the deaths of Emilie and Maddie. She blamed Drew for not being there, even more than he blamed himself if that were possible. She blamed Emilie's maternal judgment for going into the ocean in the first place and she blamed Maddie for not being a stronger swimmer. She did not see fit to blame God or Dame Fortune or even the cosmos for creating the storm or the waves or the riptides that swept his wife and daughter helplessly away. It was unquestionably somebody's fault here on earth, of that she was certain. There was always somebody to blame for everything. Just never her. Gloria could easily see the speck in your eye, but not the log in her own. More like a forest.

Other than the gift of life, and a fraction of his college tuition, Gloria's great bequest to her son was an insatiable love of reading fine literature. Jack London, Robert Louis Stevenson, Zane Grey, E.B. White, C.S. Lewis, and Laura Ingalls Wilder were as familiar to him as a young boy as the starting lineup of the Atlanta Braves. As he matured, he'd read the words of Charles Dickens, Herman Melville, and Ray Bradbury by flashlight under a blanket long after bedtime. As an adult, he would tackle James Joyce, F. Scott Fitzgerald, Ernest Hemingway, and Leo Tolstoy, marveling at how they invented characters and plots and constructed rich sentences to bind them all together.

As a storyteller herself, Gloria demonstrated an amazing deftness in the art of hyperbole and exaggeration and outright lying. She'd grown up dirt poor in Valdosta, Georgia, the only child of a single mother with boyfriends too many to count. She'd used books as a means to not only escape the overbearing life of living in a dusty trailer park but to educate herself in hopes of moving up to a higher station in life. With fiction as her foundation, telling lies at school about her home life had become as easy as breathing. For all her friends and teachers knew, Gloria had the happiest of childhoods, with two parents and a cozy farmhouse in the country bordered by a bold stream where she frolicked every day with all of her wonderful pets.

The lifestyle of falsehood continued into adulthood, albeit more subtly. If Gloria had spent ten minutes picking up a few loose stones in the backyard, her story later had her hauling cement for three hours. She was highly skilled at turning the ordinary into the fantastical, all of which came in handy in the early childhood development of a writer of fiction. Artful lying had been Gloria's greatest gift to future novelist J. Andrew Endicott. A gift tied with ribbons of barbed wire, but nonetheless, a gift.

For years he had fought her, taken her bait whenever it was offered, only to suffer the consequences. But now he better understood her and the complexities of her abrasive personality. It was only after years of pondering the disconnect between mother and son that Drew realized that congeniality was not a birthright. The ability to be consistently pleasant wasn't something with which you were blessed upon arrival on earth, like a melodious singing voice or well-placed dimples. It was acquired, like the ability to bake or to sew, or the taste for fine Scotch whisky. If nobody taught you how to be amiable, or admonished you when you weren't, then it was a skill you wouldn't possess and couldn't employ except in small doses. This was the case with Gloria Endicott. She had never been offered any lessons in being pleasant, nor had anyone placed a corrective brace on the growth of her unfiltered manners to offset her lack of innate kindness.

But the most maddening part was that you could not defend yourself, no matter how firmly attached you were to the correct side of right and wrong. Gloria's deductions were not rational, and therefore neither were her responses. It only mattered to Gloria how an issue affected her, and everything else was irrelevant. If you dared to disagree, you were subject to at least several minutes of screaming, then hours, days, weeks, months—and in a few instances, years—of the silent treatment. She hadn't spoken to Drew's younger brother, Eric, for over a decade and probably wouldn't ever again. It was over something to do with tomato plants, as best as Drew could recall. Too much sun? Not enough water? Drew couldn't remember. He hadn't been there for the initial blowup, but in the case of *he said/she said*, Drew firmly believed the *he said* version.

Along with the inability to be pleasant, Gloria had never been blessed with the power to apologize. She would rationalize her bad behavior in some way to always make it the other person's fault. Conveniently forgetting past misdeeds or rearranging the facts so that history was rewritten in her favor were among her employed techniques. Whether or not she was conscious of what she was doing or if it was just how she survived was unclear. All that really mattered was that this was how Gloria Endicott had lived her life. Her miserable, tragic life.

Why did he visit? Because he was the good son. Or at least the dutiful one. And because nobody else would. She'd been divorced for over thirty years, she didn't speak to any blood relatives, and what few friends she'd made along the way were either dead or dead to her. She'd burned more bridges than a retreating army, and Drew was her only remaining connection to the rational mainland. But if he had been conscripted as her caregiver through default, then he was going to fulfill that duty, even if the cost was a portion of his own sanity.

All of this history of histrionics swirled through Drew's head as he stepped out of the elevator and walked down the corridor of the assisted living center where his mother now resided. It was the best senior facility within a hundred miles and met all of her needs. It also assuaged her son's guilt over having "tucked her away," as she liked to describe it.

Gloria split her time between her bed and the turquoise settee underneath the only window in her two-room apartment. She occasionally watched television, but most of her time was spent either reading or sleeping. At age seventy-one, she insisted she was too weary to do much else. She rarely got dressed anymore, preferring to live out her days in a silk robe. Her once long, naturally blonde hair had turned completely gray, and years of menthol cigarettes and bottom-shelf vodka had left trails of time across her face and vocal cords.

She was in bed staring blankly at the ceiling when Drew entered. "Hello, Mother," he said as sweetly as possible without crossing the line into saccharine.

"So," she began, in the raspy voice of a former smoker. "You're late."

Drew nodded as he bent over to give her a cursory kiss on the forehead. "Yes," he acknowledged, while at the same time wondering why being on time mattered to anyone who spent all day in the timeless vacuum of a nursing home. He held his tongue. "Traffic," was all he said.

"You should allow for that. It's getting worse, you know. They should do something about the bottlenecks."

Again, he wondered, *what do bottlenecks matter to someone who hasn't driven a car in five years?* Again, he held his tongue. "Yeah, they really should." He'd found that simply repeating what she'd just said in an agreeable tone was the easiest way to avoid conflict. Conflict was inevitable, but he could at least stave it off until the next visit.

"You've gained weight," she said.

Drew nodded politely. "Yes. A few pounds."

"More than a few, seems to me."

"Yes, more than a few." He forced a smile and patted his midsection.

"You should get more exercise."

"You're right. I really should."

There was a long awkward pause as her verbal harpoons continued to miss their mark. She tried again.

"When did you stop shaving?" she asked.

Drew rubbed the wiry stubble on his face as he searched for a plausible reason besides abject laziness. "I didn't get around to it today. I knew I was coming to visit you and I didn't want to be late."

"And yet you were."

The other peacekeeping maneuver that seemed to work with Drew's mother was diversion, especially if it involved a gift of some sort. He'd been saving the tactic for later if needed, but it was already time to deploy it.

"Oh, I almost forgot," he said, as he reached into a cloth grocery tote. He pulled out a leather-bound volume of *A Rose for Emily*, only forty pages thick. "I found this at an antique store in Chapel Hill. Not a first edition, but it's a beautiful book."

Gloria took the book from Drew's hand and examined the front cover, then the spine. She did not seem impressed or enthused. She opened the book to the title page, scanned the words, then snapped it shut. She brushed her fingers across the worn, brown leather as she spoke. "You do know this story is about the funeral of a crazy woman, don't you?"

Drew *did* know that, but that wasn't why he'd purchased the book. At least not consciously. Again, he deflected. "I'd forgotten that. I just know how much you love Faulkner. You always considered him to be our greatest Southern writer. I thought you would enjoy having it on your shelf."

"I suppose," Gloria said, setting the book aside. "So," she began again. "What are *you* working on these days?"

Drew shuffled his feet and looked around the room. He wasn't about to tell his mother that the most productive thing he'd done all week was tighten the knobs on his kitchen cabinets and drive some metal stakes into the ground in his neighbor's garden plot. "I've been ruminating on a few ideas. Still fleshing them out, but I'm ready to pick one and run with it." It was a complete fabrication. He hadn't written a single word in nearly two years. Hadn't even had a decent idea for a new novel. It just wasn't in him right now, and, in his mind, for good reason. The ghosts simply wouldn't allow it.

"Are these more thrillers, or are you going to write something more substantive this time?" Gloria asked.

It was a sweeping castigation of his life's work. To be fair, novelist J. Andrew Endicott was not in the same league as the John Grishams or the Danielle Steels of the literary world, but he certainly had his following. Fourteen novels to date, over ten million books sold worldwide, and occasional residence on The New York Times Best Sellers list. He was not famous by modern standards, and because of the dishonesty of someone he'd trusted he was no longer wealthy, but every book club in America knew his name. He specialized in mystery and suspense, with a touch of romance thrown in for good measure. He was a success in everyone's eyes, except Gloria's. By invoking the word 'substantive' she had summarily dismissed every word he'd ever penned.

"It pays the bills," he stated through a weak smile, then added, "all of them." He could see her notorious temper simmering in her eyes as she realized she'd been knocked off her high horse in their verbal jousting.

"Well, whatever you decide to write next, I hope it has a more plausible conclusion than *Tears of the Sycamore*. The ending was horrible."

Drew could feel the air in the room turning combustible. It was just like Gloria Endicott to criticize that which cannot be changed. Not that he wanted to change anything about that book. *Tears of the Sycamore* had been one of his best sellers and a finalist for several literary awards for fiction. The reviews were glowing. Except for his mother's. He cocked his head back and forth and raised his eyebrows. "We shall see."

Mercifully, lunchtime was approaching. Feeling as though he'd fulfilled his filial duties for the week, Drew gave his mother a perfunctory kiss on the forehead and wished her well. Neither one uttered the phrase "I love you."

He escaped into the hallway and drew in a pair of cleansing breaths. He'd survived another visit with The Great Martini.

"Hi, Mr. Endicott, hello Mr. Endicott, how are you today Mr. Endicott?" came the chorus of greetings from the staff members who treated him like a celebrity. He merely waved to acknowledge them, not wishing to engage them verbally as he made his way back to the front door. *They* all apparently liked the way his books ended.

Nicole held up a fan of paint samples in the natural light of the early afternoon. She felt the living room needed freshening up with a bit more color than the light gray that currently covered the walls. She remained undecided between Lenox Tan and Shaker Beige as she cocked her head and squinted, trying to imagine the new paint in broad strokes.

"What the hell are you doing?" ripped Lee Wayne's caustic voice through the quiet. He'd barged into the room without warning.

Startled, Nicole required a moment to gather herself and respond. "I'm thinking about repainting the living room. Maybe a light tan."

"Why would you do that? What's on there now is just fine."

"I thought maybe an earth tone might warm up the room a little."

"Earth tone?" mocked Lee Wayne. "Where'd you get *that*? Sounds like something you'd hear on one of those stupid home improvement shows. Who's watching that crap, anyway?"

"Lots of people. They're full of good ideas for fixing up your house."

"Not *my* house. And let's not forget, this *is* my house. I pay for it, my name's on the mortgage, and I'm sure as hell not gonna be shelling out my money for some alcoholic painter who overcharges us so he can go down to the liquor store and drink himself into oblivion."

If Nicole wanted to rebut any of Lee Wayne's bluster, she wouldn't know where to begin. Instead, she did her best to sound sympathetic. "Why are you angry all the time?"

Lee Wayne pulled his neck back and scoffed. "What are you talking about? I'm not angry all the time. Why would you say something so ridiculous?"

"It just seems that everything I do or say makes you mad."

"Well then, stop doing and saying things that make me mad!" Lee Wayne plopped down in a wingchair and snapped open the newspaper.

Nicole pushed on, undeterred. "Where does it come from, Lee Wayne? What has happened in your life that's made you so bitter?"

He answered without taking his eyes off the paper. "You have *clearly* been watching too much television. Maybe I need to limit your viewing hours."

"I'm serious. There has to be some underlying reason as to why you're constantly angry about anything and everything."

He momentarily lowered the paper. "Stop trying to invent problems, Nicole. Ask any of my friends... they all think I'm great. If there's an issue, it's in your head." He resumed reading.

Nicole waited a moment before talking. She sat down on the edge of the couch and spoke softly. "Would you consider going to marriage counseling?"

Lee Wayne peered over the top of the newspaper. "Now why the hell would I do *that*?"

"I think it might be helpful for both of us."

"I don't need counseling, Nicole. I'm perfectly fine. But maybe *you* should consider it. After all, you're the one with the checkered past." He glared at her for several seconds, widening his eyes and arching his eyebrows for greater emphasis. He purposefully lifted the paper to firmly establish a barrier between them.

His words cut her to the quick. She could never seem to escape a past that had been beyond her control, and now she felt trapped in a world with no future. It had taken considerable courage for her to even raise the possibility of marriage counseling, trying to launch a tiny lifeboat on a rapidly sinking relationship, but the olive branch she's extended had been snatched by a man with deep-rooted emotional problems and thrown into a dustbin of denial. Deflated beyond repair, Nicole stood up from the couch and dragged herself from the room. As she retreated, the paint samples, which only moments ago had held such bright promise, fell from her loosened fingers and fluttered into the trashcan.

CHAPTER TEN

"Once you have read a book you care about, some
part of it is always with you."

— Louis L'Amour

I forgot to tell you that this mower is self-propelled," Drew
said. "If you squeeze this handle and hold it down, the front
wheels push themselves."

Victoria frowned as she stood ankle-deep in the thick grass
of her backyard. She alternated her stare between Drew and
the mower.

He continued, apologetically. "I know, I know. *Now* you
tell me. I'm sorry."

"Would have been nice to know. That thing is heavy."

"Don't worry, I'll make it up to you." He yanked hard
on the starter cord and the mower sputtered and roared. He
squeezed the two metal bars connected to the handle and spun
the mower around as Victoria and her grandmother observed
from just a few steps away. He nodded over the blast of the
engine as if to say *I've got this* and started pushing the rotating
blades through the untamed grass. Mindless manual labor
was a welcome relief after the emotional gymnastics he'd just
performed for his mother.

After mowing just a few rows, his forehead was already
covered in beads of moisture like a glass pitcher of summer
lemonade. The offspring from the marriage of Kentucky corn
and barley he'd consumed the night before was racing from his

pores. He could also feel the afternoon sun slapping his skin, which was still red and sore from his weekend in Southport.

By this time, the grandmother had disappeared. Victoria had edged closer, now walking stride for stride next to him in the freshly mown strip of lawn.

"Can I try?" she yelled above the whirring engine.

With only a moment of hesitation, he nodded her over. He placed her tiny hands around the handle and motioned her to push forward. Drew stood back and observed, grateful for a respite from his profuse perspiring. Although tentative, Victoria moved along nicely until she came to the upslope at the back of the yard. Her slight frame was simply no match for the terrain, and despite her best efforts, the heavy mower wouldn't advance, even with the self-propelled feature engaged. She bent her knees, closed her eyes, and continued her futile battle like Sisyphus pushing a massive stone. Suddenly the mower began to move up the steep slope as if the hands of God had rushed in to assist her. She opened her eyes to realize that Drew had run up behind her and was helping send the mower forward. Together, him standing behind her, they pushed the Toro to the top of the slope. He helped her spin it around and gently aided in the descent, but once on the flat he let go, and she continued to blaze a 28-inch trail across the jungle of a backyard. Drew stood back and watched his new apprentice at work. For the next half-hour, he would help her navigate the up-and-down of the rear slope, then leave her alone until his muscle was needed again. He surprised himself by feeling an emotion he hadn't experienced in a very long time: a sense of pride. He wasn't sure if it was because the lawn looked immeasurably better with a fresh cut, or that he'd taught a young girl a new skill. Whatever it was, it was undeniably there.

"Nice job," he told Victoria, as he kicked some loose blades of grass off the deck of the cooling mower. "You might have a future in lawn care."

"It was kinda fun," Victoria said with a smile. "My hands are tingling." She shook them by her sides to calm the buzzing in her fingers.

"Well, if you thought it was that much fun, you can come over and mow *my* yard. Have all the fun you want."

"Maybe I will."

"And maybe next week I'll teach you how to rake leaves. Talk about *fun*." Drew laughed out loud. Not a full-throated laugh, but nonetheless an audible expression of happiness. He surprised himself.

"I've never seen you smile before," Victoria said, matter-of-factly.

"Yeah, well, what can I say? Yardwork amuses me."

"You look better with a happy face."

"Thanks. Don't get used to it."

Victoria's grandmother emerged from her house carrying a brown paper bag. The nostalgic aroma of freshly mown grass was immediately overwhelmed by the smell of Chinese food. Victoria and her grandmother exchanged several rapid sentences in Mandarin and then Victoria took the bag of food and transferred it over to Drew.

"My grandmother made you dinner."

"Really? For mowing her lawn?"

"No, because she feels sorry for you. I told her you only have mustard to eat."

"Great," Drew said with a tinge of embarrassment. He took the bag of food and held it to his nose. He nodded his approval. "How do you say 'thank you' in Chinese?" he asked her.

"*Xièie*," Victoria replied.

"Set-see-ya?" Drew repeated.

Victoria shook her head and spoke more slowly. "*Xièie*."

"See-ay-see-ay?" Drew echoed.

"Close enough."

Drew turned to the grandmother and bowed. "See-ay-see-ay!" he said loudly, pointing to the bag of food.

"She's Chinese, not deaf," Victoria said.

The old woman bowed her head, then quickly turned and disappeared back into the house.

"Does your grandmother have a name?" Drew asked.

"Of course she has a name. Everyone has a name."

"Okay, okay, I hear ya. Ya know, I don't correct your grammar, like when you say '*can* I' instead of '*may* I.'"

"I wish you *would* correct me. It would help me learn."

"I'll make a point to do that, believe me. Conversely, you can stop busting my chops every chance you get. You're worse than my mother."

"But it helps *you* learn."

"I don't need to learn. My level of learning is just where it needs to be. Let's focus on *your* language skills, not mine."

"I would say that at this point, my English is better than your Mandarin."

Victoria had a way of closing down arguments with irrefutable facts. The child had won again. Drew used the back of his hand to wipe the sweat from his brow as he exhaled loudly and tried again. "Okay, can I ask, what is your grandmother's name?"

"Don't you mean, *may* I ask?"

Drew laughed again, harder than the time before. He shook his head in admiration. "Quick learner, you are."

"Thank you," Victoria said. She flashed a victorious grin.

"Just tell me your grandmother's name!" he blurted out in jest.

"We call her Húdié."

"Hoo-dee-yeh?" echoed Drew.

"Yes. It means butterfly."

Drew's face registered his surprise and amusement. "Butterfly? Really? I was thinking more along the lines of 'Crouching Tiger.'"

Victoria frowned and shook her head disapprovingly. "You shouldn't make fun of your elders. It's disrespectful."

Drew's discourteous grin immediately vanished. She was right. Again. He was growing weary of being taken to task by a child. "How old are you? Forty? Fifty?"

"I just turned thirteen in April."

"I don't believe you. I'm starting to think that's your sister, not your grandmother." He shook his head in disbelief over Victoria's innate wisdom. "I just realized I don't know your last name. What is it?"

"Hai."

"Pronounced like 'hi'?"

Victoria shrugged. "Close enough."

Drew opened the grocery bag and peered inside, letting his nose draw in the strong aroma of the Chinese food. "Smells wonderful. What is this?"

She shook her head. "You don't want to know."

Nicole struggled to get comfortable on the living room couch that doubled as her bed. It had become a symbol of the unsatisfying life she led, riddled with things undone. Her time on earth to this point had been a bucket list that had no checkmarks next to any of the entries. Her lack of accomplishment and adventure reminded her of the laments of Megan Hipwell, a pathetic character from *The Girl on the Train* by Paula Hawkins. She'd dreamed of riding motorbikes from Paris to the French Riviera, from Seattle to Los Angeles on the Pacific coast, from Buenos Aires to Caracas, but they were all trips she never took. "*Maybe if I'd done all that I wouldn't have ended up here, not knowing what to do next.*"

She shoved another pillow behind her neck and adjusted the gooseneck on her book light to illuminate the pages of *The Alchemist,* which she'd purchased earlier that day. It was a quick read, and as the clock neared three, she was nearly finished. She could relate to Santiago's decision to leave the life he'd always known and go in search of the treasure of his dreams. It was her dream as well, to unearth a new life, but she didn't have the faintest notion as to where to begin the quest. All she knew was that she wanted to dream and seek and discover like the young boy from Andalusia. She stared at the ceiling and replayed the sentence from *Eat, Pray, Love* that had permeated her consciousness and wouldn't go away: *The only thing more unthinkable than leaving was staying; the only thing more impossible than staying was leaving.* It summarized the trap of a marriage she had with Lee Wayne.

The sudden buzz of the phone she had resting on her stomach jolted her out of half-sleep like an electric shock. She clutched the phone in her trembling hand and saw the green message icon in the main display had a tiny red "1" affixed to it. She touched the screen and sat upright when she saw it was a text from Drew.

> Hi. Couldn't sleep. Up late reading The Paris Wife. Wonderful book. Thanks for the suggestion. Loved spending some time in Parisian cafes with EH and F. Scott, but makes me reconsider Hemingway as a role model. Not the best of husbands. Hope you're doing well Regards, Drew

Nicole read the note three times, smiling a little deeper with each pass. *What she could tell him about terrible husbands*, she thought. She'd take Hemingway over Lee Wayne any day. At least she'd be living in Paris. She tapped out a response.

**You're not the only one up late. I'm near the end
of The Alchemist. Lovely read. Can't put it down.
(obviously!) Glad you liked Paris Wife. What's
next in your stack?**

Nicole secretly hoped that by ending her text with a question, she would receive an immediate response. Drew chimed in moments later.

Not sure. I've read good things about The Light
Between Oceans. Might go search for it tomorrow

She typed her reply quickly but still stopped to fix spelling errors.

**That's been on my list for a while! Maybe we
should read it at the same time? Then discuss at
some point?**

She sat upright on the edge of the couch, nervously awaiting his response. The longer she waited, the more she regretted her suggestion. The screen suddenly filled with his answer.

I love that idea! We could compare notes!

Nicole couldn't tap the letters on her phone fast enough.

Sounds fun. Like a book club?

A book club with just two people? I like it!
You can be president

No thanks. I get drunk with power.

Does our book club have a name?

**How about the Oak Island Book Club? OIBC for
short.**

Perfect! The OIBC! See? It's that kind of genius

that qualifies you to be president. I'm already
feeling the pressure.

**So Light Between Oceans is first on our list? I was
going to suggest The Great Gatsby, but I'm good
with your idea.**

Lol. I deserved that. Oceans it is. I'll find a copy
tomorrow. For now, it's off to sleep. Good to hear
from you

You too. I'm off to sleep as well. Night.

She waited a moment to see if he would respond one more
time, but the conversation was over. She turned off the phone
but held it in her hand for a moment, savoring the messages it
had delivered to her. She placed it back inside the hollow space
of *Crime and Punishment* and quietly returned the secret vault
to the bookshelf.

Her last response to Drew had been a lie. There was no
possible way she was falling asleep anytime soon. She was
invigorated by the clandestine communication in the depths of
night, like a schoolgirl who'd just found a secret note in her
locker. On some level she knew she shouldn't be exchanging
texts with another man in the middle of the night. In the middle
of the day, for that matter. But they were only talking about
books, weren't they?

It would go no further than that, she promised herself.
Her brain was starved for this kind of stimulation and she
convinced herself there was nothing inappropriate about literary
discussion, be it with a man or woman. On another level, she
nearly didn't care about the impropriety of it. It had given her
some direction, like the idealist Santiago in *The Alchemist* and
his quest for riches. It was as if someone had just snapped the
final straightedge piece of a complicated jigsaw puzzle into
place, completing the border and providing a framework from
which to proceed. There was a long journey ahead to put all
the pieces together and complete the picture, but she felt like
this was at least a start. Her racing heartbeat in the quiet of the
night echoed her newfound excitement.

She read two more chapters of *The Alchemist* before clicking off her book light and nestling into the worn springs of the living room couch. The fact that the curious and courageous Santiago in the book she was reading was a tender of sheep was not lost on a woman whose last name was Shepherd.

CHAPTER ELEVEN

"Books are lighthouses erected in the great sea of time."

— E.P. Whipple

What? What do you want?" Drew asked as he stepped through the door, squinting from the bright sunshine. Victoria stood on his front porch again. She made no apologies for banging on his door like she had a search warrant. "My grandmother wants to know if you own a shovel."

"A shovel?"

"Yes. You use it to dig dirt."

"I know what a shovel is."

"Do you have one?"

"Yes. I have one. Please report back to your grandmother that I indeed own a shovel. Anything else?"

Victoria thought for a moment before responding, like a chess player who'd just lost a valuable piece due to lack of attention. She surrendered with grace. "May she *borrow* your shovel?"

"Oh, she wants to *borrow* my shovel, does she? Why didn't you just say so?" They both fought off a wry smile. "And why does Madame Butterfly want to borrow my shovel?"

"She wants to prepare the soil in her garden. And the actual Madame Butterfly was Japanese."

Victoria had just reclaimed the high ground in their ongoing war of words. Drew offered no reply other than to smile and drum his hands on his thighs as he marveled at her. "Yes, she can—" he stopped and started again. "She *may* borrow it."

Minutes later Drew watched from his kitchen window as

Húdié stood in her garden and attempted to push the rounded point of the shovel into the hard ground. She wasn't wearing gloves and her feet were covered only by what appeared to be silk slippers, but she fought on, undeterred. "Oh, Jesus," he muttered. He checked his watch. He scooped up his car keys and headed for his garage.

Less than an hour later, Drew returned home with a garden tiller he'd rented from the local hardware store. An hour after that, Húdié's garden plot was blackened over with rich, loose soil cut into long furrows.

"Tell her it's ready for planting," Drew said to Victoria as he pointed to the freshly tilled land. He was soaked in summer sweat but feeling quite accomplished.

Húdié was faintly smiling and nodding her approval at the change in the landscape. "I think she can tell," answered her granddaughter.

The chatter of the sewing machine was like a loud greeting from an old friend. It had been months since Nicole had guided fabric through needle and bobbin and the gentle vibrations of the machine sent waves of joy through her. She loved the feeling of cloth in her fingers, pushing it through the feed dog at the perfect tension to create something beautiful and lasting. Learning to sew had been a gift from one of her foster mothers, and, at one point in her fanciful youth, Nicole had imagined this might be her life's work. Not just seamstress, but creator of hemlines and Haute Couture. *Funny how loose stitches unravel and dreams get derailed by mere chance,* she thought. *One wrong turn. . . .*

She was so engrossed in the pleasures of watching the sheer cotton transform into a tunic that she never heard Lee Wayne come up behind her.

"What the hell are you doing?" he barked above the clicking of the needle.

She turned with a start. "I'm doing a little sewing, that's all."

"Well, you'll have to do it when I'm not here. I can't hear the TV with you playing with that thing."

"I'm sorry. I'll finish it later." She pulled the garment off of the needle plate and whisked it into the sewing basket at her feet.

Lee Wayne snorted. "What the hell is it, anyway?"

"It's nothing."

"Then you shouldn't be wasting your time on nothing. Don't you have enough clothes already?"

"Yes. I'm sorry I disturbed you," she replied without looking at him.

Lee Wayne shook his head in disgust and walked away. "You should probably be thinking about dinner," he called back over his shoulder.

Nicole balled her fists to keep from screaming. She wondered without shame if you could taste arsenic in meatloaf. Maybe if you used enough onions. *The only thing more unthinkable than leaving was staying.*

After serving Lee Wayne a dinner of meatloaf and mashed potatoes, arsenic-free, Nicole bided her time until the snoring bellowed from the bedroom.

She pulled out the secret phone being guarded by Dostoevsky and brought it to life. No messages. Her mind fractured into a kaleidoscope of wild thoughts. *Maybe he changed his mind. Maybe he's busy. Maybe he's at a work thing. Maybe he's on a date.* Amidst all the conjecture, she realized she didn't know what Drew did for a living. The subject didn't come up during dinner. *So much I don't know about him,* she thought. *Maybe it's better that way. Safer. Less complicated. Less involved.*

After checking her phone for messages two more times, Nicole finally sagged into the couch and clicked on the table lamp next to her. She opened her paperback copy of M.L. Stedman's *The Light Between Oceans,* which she vaguely recalled had been in a large box of books she'd purchased at a yard sale a few years ago. Why she hadn't gotten around to it before now, she didn't know. Until she started reading.

The story was about a young husband and wife who were stationed on Point Partageuse, a remote island off the coast of Western Australia, so that he could tend to the lighthouse there.

The lead female character, Isabel Sherbourne, had already lost three babies to miscarriage. Nicole knew that pain. All the excitement, all the anticipation, all the dreams of paint colors for nurseries and suitable names, suddenly dashed with a spotting of blood. And now, Nicole was unable to bear children because of her choice of mates. An impotent husband who somehow blamed her for their inability to procreate. At least

Isabel Sherbourne had a husband who loved her.

Nicole kept reading to the point in the story where a boat with a baby inside had washed up on the shores of the island home of Tom and Isabel Sherbourne. The infant would fulfill all of Isabel's maternal instincts. She would finally be able to mother a child, even if it was not from her own womb.

The story pushed Nicole into retrospection, wondering how her own birth mother could have not felt the same motherly instincts as Isabel. How could she abandon an infant daughter when there were so many women like Izzy Sherbourne who were willing to do *anything* to experience that bond? Nicole was only 105 pages in, but she already knew this book was going to be life-changing. She slid her bookmark between the pages and eased her head against two pillows. Staring at the blank ceiling, Nicole made up her mind about what tomorrow would bring. She would call first thing in the morning.

The writing was magnificent. Each sentence was so well constructed, with characters you cared about and a plot and a setting and lyrical dialogue that left you wanting more. Drew had spent most of the afternoon reading *The Light Between Oceans* after buying it during a run to the liquor store. It was the kind of book he aspired to write if only he knew how. He couldn't stop turning pages, projecting himself into the story as if he were one of the residents of Point Partageuse and had a vested interest in the outcome of their lives. He thought he might be able to finish it that night until suddenly he couldn't read another line. It was because of Lucy, the little girl who had miraculously appeared on Tom and Isabel's beach. Taken away without her father having a chance to say goodbye. Even though it was fiction, and set nearly a hundred years before, the story seemed all too real to Drew. The words on the page stabbed at him until he could stand it no more. He set it aside without even bothering to bookmark his place. It would have to wait. It might even go unfinished.

He poured three fingers of alcohol and drank nearly half of it on the first swallow. He exhaled loudly, smelling the oaky perfume of the bourbon in the air around him. He shot a glance at his dusty laptop. Maybe tomorrow.

Drew carried his drink onto the back deck and looked over at

Húdié's garden, dripping in the moonlight that filtered through the limbs of several large trees. It was vaguely reminiscent of the beam of a lighthouse, warning sailors to change course. He pondered its meaning as he killed off the last drops of his bourbon.

Drew felt the loneliness that always knocked about inside his chest when the sun went down. He pulled his cell phone from his pocket and checked for messages. Nothing. He felt a strong urge to text Nicole but wondered if it might seem too forward. *Something benign*, he thought. *Something about books. Something about the weather. Any lame excuse to connect.*

He tapped out a message, deliberating for nearly a minute on the final adjective.

> Just wanted to say hello. Hope you're reading
> something delightful

Nicole felt the buzz of her phone shoot through the nerves in her fingers. She bolted upright on the couch, feeling a chemical reaction of girlish joy rushing through her.

> **Hi! I am! Light Between Oceans is inspiring! It's**
> **bringing me some much needed clarity. Great**
> **first choice for the Oak Island Book Club!**

The abundance of exclamation points in Nicole's quick response alleviated any fears Drew had about texting her.

> I'm glad! The writing is exquisite. You said it's
> inspiring. Why?

> **I've decided to sign up as a volunteer at the**
> **hospital in Wilmington. The book just seemed to**
> **speak to me.**

> Good books have a way of doing that. Does this
> mean you'll be coming to Wilmington more often?

> **Likely. If they approve me.**

There was a momentary lapse in their texting. Reading between the lines was tricky. Drew wasn't sure how excited he should appear to be over that possibility.

As much as she wanted to, Nicole avoided any inference that they might see each other when she came to town.

After serious deliberation, Drew came back with the most upbeat yet sanitized response he could muster.

> I'm really happy for you!

> **Thank you. I'm making the first call tomorrow. I'll let you know.**

> I like your chances

> **Fingers crossed. Miles to go.**

> Sleep well

> **You too. Really nice to hear from you.**

> I feel the same. Night, Nicole

> **Goodnight, Drew**

Drew immediately felt lighter. More connected to the outside world he'd been ignoring for two years. He sensed that he was taking the first steps away from his crippling grief. Why? Was it simply from his late-night exchanges with a remarkable woman on the other end of a cell phone? Was it the satisfaction of having turned over fresh soil for planting earlier that day? Was it merely the passage of time that was now allowing him to finally look up instead of down? Out instead of in? Did it matter why? *Don't overthink this*, he told himself. *Just embrace it.*

Drew returned to his living room and finished the remainder of *The Light Between Oceans.*

CHAPTER TWELVE

"With freedom, books, flowers, and the moon, who could not be happy?"

— Oscar Wilde

The buzzing of Drew's cell phone vibrated throughout his nightstand. Groggy from a short night of sleep, he rubbed his eyes and checked the screen. It was Nicole. He tossed away the covers and swung his feet onto the floor. Fumbling, he finally pressed enough of the right buttons so that he could answer.

"Hello? Nicole? Hello?" His voice sounded like sandpaper on a sidewalk.

"Good morning!" came her cheery reply over the phone. "Did you just wake up?"

He looked at the clock. Ten-thirty. "No," he lied. "Just finished working out." He shook his head to straighten out the cobwebs. "What's going on?"

"I have an interview at the hospital this afternoon. You know, that volunteer position I mentioned. I'll be coming to Wilmington and wondered if you could recommend a good bookstore for me to visit?"

Drew scratched the top of his head as he tried to decipher what Nicole meant by telling him that. Was she asking to see him without actually asking to see him? Or did she honestly want to find a great bookstore? Both were possible. "Um, sure. I like Old Books on Front Street, I like Pomegranate Books on Park Avenue. It's in a cute little house. Wide selection."

"Which one is closer to the Medical Center?"

Now that sounds more like she just wants a good bookstore, Drew thought. "Probably Pomegranate. Plus they have great coffee."

"Wonderful! I should be there about one o'clock. My interview is at 2:30."

Okay, that sounds more like an invitation, he thought. He wished he'd gotten more sleep so he could more easily navigate the subtext of their conversation. He was very careful about the phrasing of his next sentence. "Uh, ya know, I could actually use a good cup of coffee. Would you mind if I join you? Might be a good time to gather ideas for the book club." He closed his eyes and bit his lower lip as he awaited her response. It seemed to take forever.

"That would be wonderful," she said. "I'll see you then and there."

"Wonderful," Drew said. "I'll see you soon."

"Looking forward to it."

The call ended. Drew rubbed the unruly hair on the crown of his head. "What are you doing, Drew?" he said out loud. "Okay, don't overthink it. It's just coffee."

He looked in his clothes closet. Nothing but empty hangers. He started picking up the various articles of clothing that were littered across his bedroom. Nothing passed the smell test.

He was faced with two choices; either do laundry or go buy some new clothes. He tossed on some jeans and a wrinkled T-shirt and grabbed his car keys.

Two hours later, Drew pulled into the parking lot of Pomegranate Books. It was inside a modest house, painted white with aqua shutters and trim. He was early but Nicole was already there.

He got out of the car and looked at his new black jeans and navy blue linen shirt in the reflection of the window, nodding his approval. He checked again for price tags and hoped Nicole wouldn't notice the wrinkles in a shirt that had been folded on a store shelf until an hour ago.

Nicole greeted him with a cup of coffee in each hand when he walked inside the store. "Hi!"

"Great to see you! Thanks for letting me invite myself."

She handed him a coffee. "I got you a vanilla latte. Hope that's manly enough for you."

"Anything with caffeine will suffice. Thank you. Wanna browse?"

"Love to."

Drew gestured to Nicole to lead the way. They sipped their hot coffees as they sauntered down the Modern Fiction aisle, both cocking their heads sideways to read the spines on the shelves. Their meeting had the distinct undertones of a blind date with each of them pondering how to start the conversation.

"So," Drew began, "what's this hospital interview for? Surgeon? Ambulance driver?"

She laughed. "Close. I'm volunteering to be a cuddler."

"Cuddler? Cuddling whom?"

"You hold babies in the NICU when the parents can't be there. Rock them, coo to them, anything to comfort them. Studies show it makes a huge difference in their development."

"I didn't know such a thing existed. Good for you. Do you have much experience with cuddling?" Drew couldn't hide a wry smile.

"Not with babies, no," Nicole replied. They broke eye contact and attended to their coffees for a few seconds.

"Do you have children?" he asked.

"No. Not yet." She just didn't feel like explaining that "not yet" actually meant never. "You?"

"Um...no. No children." It was true but it wasn't true. He just wasn't ready to explain Maddie's drowning.

They turned the corner to Autobiographies. Drew pulled out a book and flipped it over to the back. "Whenever I see an autobiography, I just read the About the Author blurb on the back. Huge time saver."

Nicole laughed out loud. "My autobiography would be a pamphlet. Quick read."

The next aisle over was Romance. The shelves were loaded with small but thick paperbacks by Nora Roberts, Debbie Macomber, and Jude Deveraux. Most of the covers featured beautiful people in seductive poses with flowery font where the author's name was noticeably larger than the title.

Drew picked up a copy of *Sins of Omission* by Fern Michaels and read the back of the jacket. "I can honestly say I've never read a romance novel. I just have this feeling that they're all the same."

"That's like saying that all rock and roll sounds the same."

Drew gestured to the hundreds of romance novels filling the shelves. "Clearly, millions of readers agree with you. What's the allure?"

Nicole thought for a moment before answering. "I think people want to believe that they can fall in love. Either for the first time or the next time. They want to believe in love at first sight and still feel the excitement, the flutter in their heart, that comes with a new love. They want to experience romance in all forms. The first kiss, flowers and love letters, walking on the beach and holding hands in the moonlight, and whatever comes next. If you're not getting that in real life, then you can live vicariously through romance novels."

"Seems like you've put some thought into this."

Nicole flashed an impish grin. "Maybe."

Drew pulled down another book with a sultry cover and provocative title. "Now, when you say people, you really mean women, don't you?"

"Not necessarily. Men can be romantics too."

"Not usually."

Nicole gave Drew's arm a playful push. "Oh come on, Drew, don't you have a romantic heart?"

Used to, Drew thought. He shook his head. "Not really."

"I don't believe you," Nicole said. "It's bound to be in there somewhere. Just needs to be rediscovered."

"You say rediscovered as if it once existed."

"Tell me I'm wrong?"

Drew shrugged. "Maybe." He went to his fallback position of sipping his latte. "Let's find another aisle. Something less frightening than romance, like horror or medical textbooks."

Nicole chuckled. She understood.

After thirty minutes of browsing, they left Pomegranate Books, each with a book under their arm. Nicole bought *A Prayer for Owen Meany* by John Irving and Drew picked up a copy of Joseph Heller's *Catch-22*. They tossed their empty coffee cups in the wastebasket on the front porch and walked to their cars.

"Good luck with the interview," Drew said. "I like your chances. I can already picture you as 'cuddler of the month.' "

"A girl can dream. What are you doing the rest of the day?"

"I'm working the land." He said it like he was a proud home-steader on forty acres.

"What's that mean?"

"It means I'm helping my neighbor start her garden."

"What's she growing?"

"Don't really know. We don't communicate very well."

"Well, good luck with that. I can already picture you in the Horticultural Society Hall of Fame."

He laughed. "No doubt. Another chapter in my autobiography."

"I don't know, Drew. This gardening thing could turn into a romance novel."

"Unlikely."

"You're nice to help out your neighbor."

"Thanks." He dipped his head with an "aw shucks" shrug. *If she only knew*, he thought. He checked his watch. "You better get going. Parking can be difficult at the hospital."

"Yes. Time to move on." There was an awkward silence as they stood in place. It felt like they were supposed to be a farewell hug or some physical gesture that their meeting was adjourned but neither one wanted to initiate the contact. "Well, I guess that's it. First meeting of the Oak Island Book Club is, shall we say, in the books."

"Not sure we accomplished anything, but highly enjoyable," Drew said.

"I will make sure that's noted in the minutes."

"Let me know how your interview goes."

"I will. By the way, I like your new clothes. My compliments to whoever picked them out."

Drew dug his free hand into the pocket of his new jeans and stared at the gravel next to his shoes. He could feel the heat of embarrassment swirling through his reddening face. "That obvious, huh?"

"You kinda have the new clothes smell. Similar to a new car."

"Yeah, well. I'll pass along your kind words to my haberdasher."

She smiled, then her tone turned more serious. "It was good to see you, Drew."

"You too, Nicole. And thanks for the coffee. Thanks for . . . everything."

"It was nice."

They both climbed into their cars and gave each other one final wave before returning to their real worlds, devoid of flowers, first kisses, and moonlight.

CHAPTER THIRTEEN

"Reading well is one of the great pleasures that solitude
can afford you."

— Harold Bloom

Final question, Mrs. Shepherd. Why do you want to do
this?"

Nicole looked blankly at the hospital administrator,
a woman in her sixties with silvery hair and a tailored suit,
sitting on the other side of the desk. She had leaned forward,
clasping her hands in front of her to convey the importance
of her question. It was a question for which Nicole was not
prepared. She had passed her background clearance and her
physical to be a volunteer in the NICU. She'd provided the
necessary references and immunization records. She'd signed
the confidentiality agreement. That had all been easy, pro
forma. But this final question made her clench her back teeth
and stall for time. She wanted to answer honestly but without
breaking into tears.

She drew in a cleansing breath and puffed it out. She
straightened her posture and looked at the floor, then back to
the woman in front of her, still bracing herself on the desk with
her elbows. "I know what it's like to lose a child. I just don't
want that to happen to anyone else. If I can make a difference
by just holding a baby and rocking it, then that's what I want to
do. Simple as that." She slammed her lips shut to prevent any
anguish from escaping.

The woman broke into a warm smile and leaned back in her office chair. "Then you're the kind of volunteer we're looking for." She stood up and removed her glasses, letting them dangle from a chain around her neck. She extended her hand as Nicole rose from her chair to shake it. "Your training will start Monday. Welcome."

Nicole pressed her free hand hard against her mouth to stifle a cry of joy, but it did nothing to stem the tears that filled her eyes. All she could do was smile and nod. This had been her first job interview, and even though she wouldn't be paid, she already knew it would be the most rewarding thing she'd ever done.

Drew stood with arms folded on the top of the fence that separated the two backyards. His hair was uncombed and his beard had three days of stubble. He'd only been outside for a few minutes but he was already sweating through his T-shirt.

Húdié was in her sun hat and slippers, pushing seedlings into her garden and squeezing a small pile of soil around them with her bare hands. Victoria was one step behind, handing her a new plant as they worked their way up the furrows.

"What are you planting?" Drew called.

"Peppers. Chinese five-color."

"Never heard of 'em," Drew said as he bent down to yank away some weeds at the base of the fence.

"I doubt they've heard of you."

Drew laughed. Some days he was no match. "Why are they called five-color?"

"The peppers first turn purple, then white, then yellow, then orange. When they turn red they're ready to pick."

"I see. Is she using any fertilizer?"

"I don't know."

"Could you ask?"

With a slight roll of her eyes, Victoria bent over and asked her grandmother a question in Mandarin. It brought a lengthy response.

Victoria stood erect again. "She said no."

"Oh, come on! She said a lot more than that!"

Victoria rolled her eyes again, pressing another seedling into the dirty, weathered hands in front of her. "My grandmother says you need to shave. She says you look like hell."

Drew's mouth dropped open as he laughed out loud. "You shouldn't swear."

"And you shouldn't drink so much." Victoria motioned to Drew's shirt, spotted with sweat.

His smile faded as he looked down at the moist cotton. "Noted. Anyway, I came out here to tell you I'm going to be away for a few days. Just wanted you to know."

"I'll feed your cat," Victoria said eagerly. "I need to make some money."

"I don't have a cat."

"I'll feed your fish."

"No fish, either. No pets."

"Then I'll water your plants."

"I don't have any plants."

"No plants?" she said. "Really? That's sad."

"Yes. Yes, it is."

"How about I take in your mail?"

"Okay, you can take in my mail."

"Two dollars a day."

"Two dollars? Let's see, it takes about five minutes, so that comes to about twenty-four dollars an hour. Seems a little steep."

Victoria and her grandmother had reached the end of a row and were now moving back toward Drew. "I usually charge three. You're getting the friends-and-family discount."

"You're watching too much TV. But okay, two dollars it is. I'll be gone two nights."

"Where are you going?" Victoria asked.

"The beach."

The teen stopped moving as her grandmother pressed on. The armor of wit was suddenly gone as the corners of her mouth turned down. She spoke softly and seriously. "I've never been to the beach."

"What? You've never been to the beach? But you live in Wilmington! The ocean is only like four miles from where we're standing!"

She shook her head, almost embarrassed. "Grandmother does not own a car, so I've never been. It looks beautiful in the pictures."

He nodded with genuine empathy. "It is. Most of the time." He stopped short of saying something like *maybe I can take you there someday*, but he could see the expectation in her eyes, hoping for some promise of a journey to a land she'd never seen.

"*Kuài dian! Kuài dian!*" Húdié snapped. She was still bent over but was reaching back for a seedling that never came. Drew could only guess it meant something along the lines of *let's go* or *hurry up* based on Húdié's irritated tone and frenzied gesturing, coupled with the quick lunge forward Victoria made to get a new plant into the old hands.

"I'll come over and get my mail Monday," he said to Victoria as he backed away toward his house.

She nodded without speaking, maintaining a wistful expression on her face, the numb look of dreams unfulfilled.

It was Nicole's favorite hour of the week. Four o'clock on Friday afternoon, when Lee Wayne got home early from work and packed his bag for his sailing lessons. His ensemble for this event always included pale-blue boat shoes from Sperry, overly long white microfiber sailing shorts, and a navy blue and white-striped long-sleeve pullover that would look considerably better on a French waitress or a mime. The only way he could look more ridiculous would be to start wearing a white captain's hat with gold braids and an anchor embroidered on the front, and she was certain that was coming eventually. She didn't care. Four o'clock on Friday meant freedom. In just fifteen more minutes, Lee Wayne would be in his car and driving 125 miles north to Oriental's School of Sailing. Fifteen minutes after that, she would be driving twenty-seven miles south to Oak Island. Worlds apart, until Sunday afternoon.

It was just before sunset when a text popped into Nicole's phone. She'd checked the screen four dozen times in the last hour while she curled up with a book in an overstuffed chair in the living room of Teri's beach house, begging it to register a message.

Nicole-
I'm heading to the beach this weekend. You?
Drew

She typed her answer quickly.

I'm already here!

I'm coming down tomorrow morning. Perhaps we should call a meeting of the Oak Island Book Club?

I will be there. I want to maintain my perfect attendance record.

Did you finish Light Between Oceans?

I'm on the last chapter. Don't want it to end. We must discuss!

Ok. First item on the agenda

What should we read next? Suggestions?

Maya Angelou's I Know Why the Caged Bird Sings?

Excellent choice. I haven't read it since high school.

I'll have to find a copy

So will I. Maybe we can meet at the bookstore in Southport and browse?

Perfect. I should roll in about noon, maybe a little before

By the way... I got the job!

That's awesome! You are already the best cuddler I know!

Nicole paused before typing the next text. It was a question that had been on her mind.

Drew, may I ask, what do you do for a living?

There was a significant pause before he replied.

I'm a man of mystery

Yes you are. Seriously, what's your job?

Right now I'm just a gardener

**I like that. The world needs more flowers. I'll see
you tomorrow. Safe travels.
N**

See you then
D

Nicole sat in the soft light of the fading sun of the Oak Island beach house, still staring at the thread of their messaging. It felt both innocent and illicit at the same time. *It was just two people talking about books, the way people do in book clubs and forums every day, all over the world,* she told herself. *Wasn't it? But do they do it in dark rooms at midnight on secret phones? Probably not. Okay, definitely not.* Nonetheless, she was absolutely going to be inside that bookstore long before noon tomorrow.

CHAPTER FOURTEEN

"Second-hand books are wild books, homeless books;
they have come together in vast flocks of variegated
feather, and have a charm which the domesticated
volumes of the library lack. Besides, in this random
miscellaneous company we may rub against some
complete stranger who will, with luck, turn into the
best friend we have in the world."

— Virginia Woolf, *Street Haunting*

On a balmy Saturday morning, Nicole was already
walking the aisles of *The Book End* used bookstore
in Southport. She was scanning the shelves vertically
from A to M, then back up to N and back down through Z
when Drew arrived. As he quietly approached her, he suddenly
realized he hadn't thought through the actual physical greeting.
Should it be a friendly wave? A handshake? Perhaps a quick
embrace with a soft pat on the back? He felt as nervous as a
teenager on a first date, but couldn't explain why.

Nicole solved his dilemma by striking first. "Hi!" she said
from the end of the aisle, quickly waving her right hand from
just above her waistline.

"Hi," he answered, stopping ten feet in front of her.

"You made good time."

"I had good incentive," said Drew. He allowed his ambiguous
words to hang in the air and let her decide what he meant by them.

"Well," Nicole began as she turned her attention back to
the shelves, "we have lots of good choices for our next book."

"What have you found?" Drew asked. He moved only slightly closer to dampen the volume of their conversation.

"They have several copies of *I Know Why the Caged Bird Sings,* so that's one option." Nicole motioned for Drew to follow her to the next aisle. "I also found an entire section of Jodi Picoult. You like her?"

"Who doesn't? Fourteen million readers can't be wrong."

The Picoult section took up nearly an entire bookshelf. Over two dozen titles from which to choose.

"Which one?" Nicole asked. "There are so many!"

"Let's see," Drew said, leaning in closer to the titles. I've read *My Sister's Keeper* and *Handle with Care.* Maybe you should choose."

Nicole pushed in next to him, hunched over, shoulder to shoulder. A young female clerk with bluish hair and numerous piercings moved behind them, pushing a cart. She chimed in with unsolicited advice. "My favorite Picoult is *Picture Perfect.* One of her early ones. It's about amnesia and Hollywood. I think you'll like it."

"Thank you," Nicole said, with genuine appreciation. She grabbed two copies off the shelf. "Done and done!" she said. "I also noticed they have *The Jungle.* Upton Sinclair. Not sure how I made it this far in life without reading it."

"Another good choice. I'm up for all three if you want."

"Might as well!" Nicole said, with more enthusiasm than Drew had ever seen in her. He watched her flit from aisle to aisle, shelf to shelf, getting two used copies of each book they'd discussed. She took such delight in finding the ones in the best condition and cradling them in the crook of her elbow like she'd just adopted them into her family. Drew took deep pleasure in seeing someone who loved the written word as much as he did.

She handed three books to Drew. "Ready to check out?"

"One second. I want to see if they have any Agatha Christie I haven't read yet. Full disclosure . . . I have a massive crush on Miss Marple. I'm a fool for a jaunty hat and a British accent."

Nicole laughed in surprise. "Isn't she a little old for you?"

"Yes, but I'm catching up." Drew raised his index finger in the air for dramatic emphasis. "*And,* she's single. So I feel like I have a chance."

Drew looked at the genre guides attached to the ceiling and found the row marked Mystery. He crouched slightly and beckoned Nicole with a nod of his head. "Follow me," he whispered in a terrible English accent. "All the clues point this way." Drew stealthily moved down the aisle as if he were a detective unraveling a sordid case. In their brief moments together, she'd never seen this playful side of him and she found it oddly refreshing.

"Excuse me," he said politely to an older woman with glasses and a gray ponytail who was standing in the aisle. He and Nicole eased by in the narrow space.

"No problem," she mumbled with a short glance. She went back to perusing the books on the top shelf. With sudden illumination, she snapped her head around. "Hey!" she called out after him. "I know you!"

Drew kept his attention straight ahead as he knelt down and ran his fingers across the spines of the books wedged on the bottom shelves. "I don't think so," he said with a shake of his head. "I'm not from around here. Sorry." Drew tugged at a paperback copy of Christie's *The Body in the Library* and held it up for Nicole to see. "What do you think? Should I get two?"

The woman in the gray ponytail moved closer, and now she leaned down to get a better look at Drew. "I *knew* it!" she said, with the excitement of a prospector discovering a vein of gold.

Nicole was confused. "Knew *what*?" she asked the woman.

The woman honed in on Drew. "You're J. Andrew Endicott, aren't you? The author!"

Drew tried his best to look perplexed. "I think you're mistaken."

"I'm *not* mistaken," she said with an emphatic shake of her head. "I met you at a book signing in Raleigh. *Tears of the Sycamore*. Very good book, by the way, although I didn't particularly care for the ending."

Drew rolled his eyes at the unsolicited criticism but stuck to his defense. "A lot of people look similar. Like luggage."

Nicole looked confused. "Drew? What's going on here? What's she saying?"

"She's just mixed up." He tried to dismiss her with a wave of his hand.

"Am I?" said the woman as she turned her back and moved over to a shelf behind her. She snatched a hardback from its resting place, flipped it over to the back cover, then held it aloft for Drew and Nicole to inspect like a prosecutor presenting Exhibit A. "*Am* I?" she repeated.

On the back of the book jacket was a glossy photograph of one J. Andrew Endicott, acclaimed author of numerous cozy mysteries. Nicole leaned closer to look at the headshot, then back to Drew. One and the same.

"I apologize," Drew said to the woman. "I didn't mean to be rude. I just try to keep a low profile, especially in bookstores. Don't want to cause a scene. You understand, don't you?"

The woman soaked in his explanation and let it steep for just a moment, then broke into a warm smile. She spoke in the whispered tone of secrets. "I think if I were famous, I would have done the same thing." She rummaged through her purse and pulled out a pen. "Could you just do me one favor and sign this for my sister? Her name is Betsy Shaw."

The woman thrust both pen and book at Drew and waited for him to take it. He quickly went to task, ready to end this encounter. She leaned over to mark his progress. "And if you could date it, that'd be great."

Drew nodded and kept scribbling. He finished the inscription and handed it back to the woman. "I hope Betsy enjoys it."

The woman admired the signature and beamed. "Thank you, Mr. Endicott! She's never going to believe this!"

It was only now that Drew realized Nicole was gone. He'd been so caught off guard by the interruption that he hadn't had the presence of mind to keep track of his surroundings.

"Nicole?" he called out softly, turning the corner of the aisle and making a quick inspection down several other rows of the bookstore. "Nicole?" he said, a little louder.

He turned the corner of another row and caught a glimpse of her exiting the front door. He scrambled after her and caught up to her in the parking lot.

"Nicole, wait!" She kept walking without a response. "Nicole, please!" He finally caught up to her as she approached her car.

"You lied!" she growled, rummaging for her keys in the bottom of her purse.

"I didn't lie," he protested.

"You said you were a gardener."

"I am, in fact, tending to a garden. Helping, anyway."

"You left out some important details. I'm sick and tired of men lying to me."

"What was I supposed to do?" He spoke in a deeper, affected

voice. "Hi, I'm the world-famous author, J. Andrew Endicott. Aren't you impressed?"

She finally looked squarely at him, silent but seething. He held his palms skyward in resignation. "Look, I could see you being upset if I told you I was a famous author and it turns out I *wasn't* . . . I can see *that*. But the other way around? I don't think that's a punishable offense."

"Why didn't you tell me?"

"It's a long story. Doesn't have a happy ending."

"Well, why don't you give it a try?" she said, her anger growing.

"Okay, you really want to know? Two reasons. I didn't want it to influence your opinion of me. People treat you differently when they find out you're a celebrity. I mean, you saw that woman in there."

"Oh, so you think you're a celebrity?" said Nicole, nearly scoffing. "I've barely heard of you."

"Well, maybe not a celebrity, but famous. Well, not really *famous*, but notable in certain circles. Small circles. Niches. I don't know what I'm trying to say."

"You should have told me."

"I'm sorry. I would have, eventually. I wasn't hiding anything. But I hardly know you. I didn't want to reveal everything about myself in the first chapter. It felt . . . pretentious. Again, I'm sorry. I'll tell you anything you want to know."

"Too late. I already don't trust you." She found her keys and unlocked her door. "You know that cheesy license plate of yours? The End? This story just arrived there. Have a nice life, Mr. J. Andrew Endicott." Her words were slow and mocking. She slammed the door, backed out with intention, and sped away. Drew could taste her anger in the dust she left behind. He stood alone in the parking lot and watched her vanish, wondering how it had all gone so badly, so quickly.

Twenty minutes later, her legs draped over the end of the couch in Teri's beach house on Oak Island, Nicole was doing an internet search on her phone. She came across a few old newspaper clippings from the *Wilmington Star News*. The more she read, the sicker she felt.

◆ ◆ ◆

The sun was surrendering to the western horizon in a blaze of glorious color as Drew sat on the beach on Oak Island and drank straight bourbon from a black plastic water bottle. He was wearing a pair of vintage Ray-Ban Wayfarer sunglasses to keep the sun and sand from stinging his eyes. It was a good time and place for self-pity. He wondered how many hours he'd spent looking out over the deep blue, asking questions that didn't have answers. He took another long sip from the bottle.

"Is this seat taken?" Nicole's voice came from behind him. He was numb enough from misery and alcohol that he was only mildly startled by the sudden intrusion. He turned his head slightly to acknowledge her, then gestured to the sand next to him as if to say *help yourself*. He took another drink as she settled down next to him. She was close enough to touch him but kept her arms folded across her knees. She joined him in his purposeful gazing for several minutes. There was ambient noise of wind, waves, and winged wildlife all around them, yet it felt oppressively silent.

"I'm sorry," she began, breaking the silence. Drew's expression didn't change. She continued. "I went home and looked you up on the internet. I didn't know any of that."

Drew shook his head. "Doesn't matter."

"Don't say that. You lost your wife and child. Of course it matters."

Drew didn't respond. He again put the plastic bottle to his mouth and sipped.

She could smell the alcohol in the air. "Is that how you handle all this? You need to drink?"

"I don't drink because I *need* to. I drink because I *want* to. Comfortably numb is my favorite emotion."

"That's not an emotion."

"Okay then, my favorite state of being."

Nicole allowed for another long pause to reset the conversation. "I read through all the newspaper reports, but there weren't many details. Can you tell me what happened?" When Drew didn't answer, Nicole repositioned herself in the sand to face him. "Tell me what happened, Drew. I want to know."

Drew swiveled his head away for a moment and chewed on his bottom lip, then turned back to face Nicole. He slowly pulled the frames of his Wayfarers to the tip of his nose to expose his eyes and also to let her know he was gauging her sincerity. He pushed the sunglasses back into place and leaned back on his elbows, returning his gaze to the churning water. He pulled in a long breath and bit down on the inside of his cheek. The professional storyteller wasn't sure where or how to begin. He looked at Nicole again, then back to the water.

"About two years ago I was in New York, wining and dining with some big-league literary agents. Major players in the book world. They were trying to convince me to spice up my novels a little bit, you know, mix in some sex, a little more adult language, that sorta thing. I'd already made a pretty good living and built a decent following writing my harmless little mysteries, so I wasn't inclined to take their advice. But, I had just signed with them and wanted to be a team player." He paused briefly as he thought about his betrayal of Holly Hedrick. He refocused and continued. "It felt a little like selling my soul, but the dollar figures they were throwing out at me were mind-boggling. 'The next level' was the phrase they kept using. I have to admit, I found it all extremely flattering, which in hindsight, was exactly the reaction they wanted from me.

"But what the newspapers didn't tell you is that when I was eating caviar and signing books for adoring fans in New York, I was supposed to be *here,* on this very beach." Drew sat up and became more animated, almost forgetting that Nicole was next to him. "And somewhere in that ocean, somewhere right in front of where we're sitting right now, Emilie and Maddie were playing in the water. Just playing, like millions of people do every summer all over the world." He gestured angrily at the ocean. "And then, right there, right at that very moment, the cosmos decided to send a riptide. Emilie was an incredibly strong swimmer . . . her passion was scuba diving, so she knew the power of the water and respected it, but there was nothing she could do. It pulled them under and out to sea and that was it. Gone." He snapped his fingers. "Just like that."

He turned and looked intently at Nicole. She could see his eyes glistening behind the dark glasses. "And where was I at the time? Where was Daddy? I was surrounded by strangers in Manhattan, hungover from expensive champagne and drunk with the prospects of millions of dollars for my next book."

He stood up and ran his fingers hard through his hair. "I

should have been here, Nicole! I could have done something! I could have saved them. I could have changed the ending. But instead, I was . . ." His voice trailed off. He broke his gaze from hers, choking back pent-up emotion.

She had no words to ease his pain. All she could think to do was rise to her feet and embrace him. She wrapped her arms around his waist and placed her head against his chest. She could hear and feel the pulse of his heart. Drew dropped his chin onto her shoulder and wept, inaudibly, but with his gut heaving with emotional pain. After several minutes he eased away, pulling off his sunglasses and wiping away the water and salt of his tears. "I'm sorry. Can't help it."

"It's okay," she whispered. Nicole inhaled deeply, bit the corner of her bottom lip, and wrung her hands, all to prepare herself for what she was about to reveal.

"I was almost a mother once," she said, barely audible over the sound of a crashing wave. Drew turned his head to acknowledge the import of her words but said nothing. She continued. "When I was nineteen, I got pregnant. It was a boy from my high school who was leaving town to join the Navy. I never told him. I didn't tell anybody. I didn't know what to do. Do I get an abortion? Do I keep it? Do I give it up for adoption? As it turned out, I never had to make the choice. I miscarried before I was even showing. I think I worried the baby to death."

"I'm sorry," said Drew. He let her breathe and continue.

"I know it's not the same as losing a little girl, but it's the same kind of pain. You've lost something precious that you can't replace, and that sense of loss really never goes away. I get that."

They stood side by side and watched the waves unfold onto the sand, again and again and again. The blue water was turning greenish as the sun faded behind them and twilight moved closer.

Nicole glanced at Drew as he removed his sunglasses, then joined him in staring out to sea. "Why do you do it?" she asked.

"You mean, why do I come here? Why do I return to the scene of the crime?" Drew said.

"Yes. Why do you stare at the ocean? Isn't it torture?"

He nodded. "I want it to be. It's my way of doing penance."

"For guilt?"

"Guilt, remorse . . . shame. All those things. Maybe if I stare at the churning water long enough, absorb its raw power, fathom its enormity, come to terms with its impersonal and unforgiving nature, and realize that I was no match for its strength and fury and anger, then somehow I'll be absolved of my guilt. And so that's what I do." He turned to look at Nicole, who instinctively turned to face him at the same time. "I need closure, Nicole. *That's* why I come here."

"Is it working?"

Drew shook his head. "No. Not yet, anyway. And I'm resigned to the possibility that I might never be fully healed. At this point, I'd just like to be able to move forward. I'm not drowning, but I'm not swimming. I'm just treading water. In motion, but without visible progress. Inert and impassive. Does that make sense?"

"It does, but I have to always remind myself that children come into our lives to bring us joy. That's their purpose in life. And that child who was taken away too soon would never want us to spend the rest of our lives grieving over the loss."

Drew glanced at Nicole briefly, then again at the ocean. Deep down, he knew she was right, but he still couldn't bring himself to fully admit it.

They stood in silence as a pod of dolphins bobbed in and out of the water as if heading home after a long day at work.

Drew looked over at Nicole. "So why do *you* stare at the water?"

"I didn't realize I did."

"You do. I've watched you."

She paused before answering. "I'm not really looking at the water. I'm looking at the horizon. Trying to see what's beyond it. Like some ancient mariner, believing that a fresh wind can take him to places that are better than the one he left behind, but always having doubts, because all he can see is water. He sails through storm after storm, but the view remains the same . . . the edge of the horizon and nothing on the other side."

"You're hoping to find an island? A paradise?"

"It doesn't even have to be paradise. I just want a safe harbor."

Drew smiled broadly. "We certainly do like to speak in metaphors, don't we?"

She laughed. "Maybe we read too much."

"Maybe so," nodded Drew. "Maybe so."

Nicole finally broke the spell. "You could probably use some food. I'm guessing you skipped lunch. I could fix you dinner. It's the least I could do."

"That's all right. But thanks."

"Why not? It makes no sense to both eat alone. Maybe we could continue that intelligent conversation you're always talking about."

"I don't think I'd be very good company."

"Well, I didn't want to have to play this card, but as president of the Oak Island Book Club, I'm calling an emergency meeting. Attendance is mandatory."

"Wait, I thought you didn't want to be president."

"Desperate times call for desperate measures."

"Figures. Desperation is the mother of most of my invitations."

"Come on, Drew. It'll be fun."

"I don't know . . ."

"I'm a pretty good cook. Fresh flounder stuffed with crabmeat tonight. Steamed vegetables, fresh bread with garlic butter. How can you turn that down?"

Nicole's expression was playfully pleading. Drew relented. "That actually sounds mighty tasty." He turned his back on the sea and walked toward the street through the warm sand. She followed alongside. "Let me go back to the motel and get cleaned up," Drew said.

"If you don't mind me asking, why do you stay in that tiny motel? Why not a nice B&B?"

"I like it. It's clean, great location, nice view. Plus, it's cheap."

"But aren't you worth millions?"

Drew laughed out loud, amused by the thought of it. "Used to be. Have to pinch my pennies now."

"Why?"

"My business manager-slash-highway robber stole everything I owned when I wasn't looking. Millions of dollars. I reckon he's on a beach somewhere in Mexico or the Caymans enjoying it all. I guess I deserve it for not paying closer attention. All I had left was my house, so I'm living on the cash I got when I sold it. It was a decent chunk of money, but it won't last forever. Anyway, lesson learned."

"What was the lesson?" Nicole asked. "Don't trust business managers?"

Drew shook his head. "Don't trust *anyone*." He checked his watch. "How about I drop by in an hour? Is that good?"

"Perfect."

"Can I bring anything?"

"Just your appetite."

"I take it with me everywhere I go. See you in a bit." Drew trundled away. He tossed the plastic water bottle into the nearest trashcan.

CHAPTER FIFTEEN

"The first thing my family did when we moved was join the local church. The second was to go to the library and get library cards."

— John Grisham

Drew stood in one place but pivoted in a circle to soak it all in, like a tourist seeing Graceland for the first time. The interior of Nicole's borrowed beach home was devoid of the pervasive kitschy decorations one usually finds in a coastal dwelling. No prints of laughing dolphins, crabs, or sand dollars. No glass hurricane lamps filled with seashells, or touristy wall hangings with trite sayings like *Life's a Beach* or *Seas the Day*. If anything, it looked like a country house you might find in the Blue Ridge Mountains or in the glossy pages of *Southern Living* magazine.

The focal point was an interior chimney rising out of the stone fireplace, boxed in with weathered planks from an old pier. Bulky, exposed beams crisscrossed the high ceilings. The couch, chairs, and ottoman were a warm shade of beige, with blue accent pillows to bring color and depth. Original oil paintings of Parisian café scenes added a few reds, yellows, and greens. The glass coffee table was fashioned from old anchor chains welded rigidly in place to provide the base and legs. A floor lamp hovered over one of the chairs, the perfect setting for someone quietly holding a good book. Drew noticed her copy of *Picture Perfect* was on the side table, already bookmarked close to the middle.

There was no visible television. It was either well hidden or non-existent. There was only a smattering of paperbacks on the built-in shelves next to the fireplace. *That might be the one thing I'd change*, Drew thought. *More books. Definitely more hardcovers.*

The kitchen made you never want to leave. The cabinets were a pale blue with milky glass knobs. The countertops were white granite and pendant lights, the color and texture of blue sea glass, hung over the island in the middle. The hardwood floor was whitewashed, creating an extra brightness in the room even at night.

A full wine fridge was among the invitations into the room. Best of all, the view from the sink was of the ocean, making cooking a good meal and even cleaning up afterward that much more joyful. The home was the chapel of someone with taste and imagination, and enough money to support the vision.

Nicole was putting the finishing touches on dinner as Drew sauntered over and observed. "This is a beautiful home," he told her.

"Thank you. I wish I could take credit for more than just keeping it clean." She dusted the flounder with paprika. "I'm just lucky that Teri lets me borrow it, pretty much anytime."

"Why doesn't she use it?"

"Her husband got transferred to a big construction job in Ohio for the next six months, so she goes to visit him pretty much every weekend."

"We should all have such generous friends."

"The best kind. You'd like her."

"Why?"

"What you see is what you get with Teri. You know that feeling when you think to yourself, that's what I *should* have said? Only it comes to you an hour later? Teri says it right then and there, the first time."

"My kind of woman. So where's home for you?" he asked, waving some of the cooking steam into his nose.

"Little town called Belville. Just outside of Wilmington."

Drew nodded. "Sure, I know Belville."

"Only takes me about forty minutes to get here, door to door." She carried the completed dishes to the table, covered with a blue and white tablecloth. "And you live in Wilmington."

"I do. Just north of the university. How'd you know that?"

"The internet provides a wealth of information."

Drew smiled wryly, sharing her laugh. "Yes, and it's all true." He placed a slice of white cheddar cheese on a cracker from the plate she'd set out. He finished it in one easy bite, doing his best to not chew too loudly. "Can I ask you a somewhat personal question? You don't have to answer if you don't want to."

"I wouldn't have. Go ahead. What do you want to know?"

"If you're married, how do you get to come to the beach every weekend by yourself?"

"My husband has taken up sailing. Maybe a midlife crisis thing, not sure. Most men buy a red sports car, he bought a twenty-two-foot sailboat. He drives up to Oriental most weekends to take it out on the water. And I come here."

"Sounds like a good arrangement," Drew said.

"It works out, as long as it doesn't rain." Nicole didn't elaborate on how happy the arrangement made her, or that Lee Wayne had no idea there even *was* an arrangement.

Nicole lit the lone candle on the table but didn't dim the overhead lights. The flame danced off the bottle of white wine and crystal goblets already in place. Drew stood next to Nicole's chair and waited for her to sit down, helping her guide her seat under the table. He joined her on the other side.

"This looks amazing!" he said, widening his eyes and rubbing his palms together.

"Thank you. It's much more fun to cook for two."

Drew reached over and wrapped his hand around the base of the wine bottle, a dry Chardonnay. "May I?" he asked.

"Please."

He deftly poured, filling just over a third of her glass. He did the same to his glass, then raised it by the stem. "I hereby call the second meeting of the OIBC to order." They clinked glasses, sharing first a smile, then a light and savory sip.

Nicole cocked her head and looked at Drew with circumspection. "I thought it was the president's duty to call the meeting to order."

"You've been usurped. All that power was clearly going to your head."

She laughed, remembering how good it felt. "I must say, for someone who's been through some difficult days, you still have a good sense of humor. Oscar Wilde should possess such wit."

"Oh yeah," Drew said, deadpan. "Have you read *The Picture of Dorian Gray*? It's *hilarious*! Especially the stabbing at the end."

The wine in Nicole's mouth nearly exited her nose in a snort of laughter. "See? That's what I'm talking about! An obscure literary reference otherwise lost on a world of non-readers."

"They don't know what they're missing," Drew said. "Nothing like a good book to stimulate your emotions, one way or the other."

Nicole nodded as she pushed her fork into the flounder and lifted up a small portion of flaky fish and tender crab meat. She was pleased by the taste of her own creation.

Drew took a slightly more generous bite, closing his eyes as he savored it. "Mmmm," he murmured. "Delicious! Where'd you learn to cook?" he asked, guiding another steaming fork to his lips.

"The Hard Knocks Culinary Institute. I worked as a waitress for a few years, and I'd go back in the kitchen and learn a few recipes after hours."

"And you didn't make a career out of waitressing?"

She chuckled. "No, it was just to make money for school."

"Oh? Where'd you go to school?"

"I was at North Carolina State, studying fashion design. But I dropped out after two years."

"Why's that?"

She laughed sardonically. "What was it you said before? Long story, doesn't have a happy ending?"

"Something like that. And what was your response? Why don't you give it a try?"

Nicole replenished her wine, banishing etiquette and filling her glass nearly to the brim. She quickly drank half of it, composing her thoughts. Her eyes were fixed on the flame of the candle. "I grew up in foster care," she began. "Bounced around a lot. Nine foster homes in eleven years. No horror stories, but still, you just always felt untethered. Finally, when I was fourteen, I was taken in by a woman who loved me like her own daughter. She did alterations for a local dry cleaner. She taught me how to sew, and she showed me how to love someone." Nicole paused, her mind lingering back in time. A slight smile lit up her eyes. "She also got me my first library card. Turns out, you can learn a lot from books. Who knew?"

Drew remained silent but engaged. He understood the therapeutic power of listening. They both continued to enjoy the meal. *Eat.* After a long silence, Nicole began again.

"I was lucky enough to land a scholarship to N.C. State. I was going to be the next Donna Karan." Nicole rubbed her index finger around the rim of her wine glass, making it vibrate and hum. She was lost in thought as painful memories overtook her.

Drew waited patiently. He easily recognized the tortuous look of regret. "What happened?" he finally asked.

"One weekend I was going to visit some friends at the beach. I made a wrong turn down a one-way street in Wilmington and got into an accident. Nothing serious, but I had to hire a lawyer. I pulled the name Lee Wayne Shepherd out of the phone book. After my case was over, he asked me out on a date. Drove all the way to campus just to see me. Took me to nice places, spent money on me, introduced me to all his fancy lawyer friends. He was older and worldly, had money, all those things. I grew up poor, and this was like a dream come true. He finally convinced me to drop out of school and marry him. So I did. I was barely twenty. Didn't know any better."

She shook her head slowly, her gaze still riveted on the burning candle. "And then . . . then it all changed. Starting with our wedding day. Wedding night, more specifically. He never treated me the same. It was like he spent all the money in his wallet to win the stuffed animal at the carnival and that was the end of it. He knocked over all the milk bottles, heard all the cheers, then went home with his prize and tossed it in the closet." The light of the candle reflected in the tears forming in Nicole's eyes. She sighed heavily and took another long drink from her wine glass. Drew remained silent, waiting for her to continue at her own pace. "He's just mean. That's the only way to sum it up. Just plain mean."

"So why don't you leave him?"

"You're not the first person to ask me that. I ask myself that all the time."

"And what's your answer?"

"Truthfully? It's because I'm afraid."

"What are you afraid of?"

"That I can't survive on my own. I don't have any money in my name, I don't have any real job skills, and I've got nowhere else to go. No family, no nothing. On top of that, he's a lawyer, and he would ruin me if I left him, I just know it. There are two kinds of people that are dangerous . . . those with nothing to lose, and those with *everything* to lose. Lee Wayne is the latter." Nicole turned her head and looked out the window. She felt hopelessly trapped as if she were living in a darkened room, searching desperately for a door but never able to find one. She found it impossible to explain to people why it was so hard to just walk away. Unless you lived it, you simply couldn't understand.

Nicole turned back and made eye contact with Drew. "The only way out is for him to die." Drew nodded, trying to understand. She shook her head with a wry smile. "Do you know that a few weeks ago, I was secretly hoping against all hope that he would die on the operating table? How awful is that? I have terrible guilt for feeling that way, but it's true. I can't help it. That's how much I detest that man. And it's why I escape to Oak Island as often as possible."

"I'm sorry," Drew said. "You really deserve better."

Nicole shook her head as she stood up and started clearing the dishes. "It's my own fault. We all live in a house of regrets. Some are just more expensive than others."

"I suppose," Drew said, unsure if that were completely true. He picked up the remaining dishes and joined Nicole at the sink.

Nicole looked sideways at Drew as she rinsed off the remains of the meal. "You told me in the parking lot at the bookstore that there were *two* reasons you don't go around telling people who you really are. You never told me the second reason."

"Because you slammed the door in my face before I could say anything else."

Nicole nodded, unable to argue. "I'm here now."

She rinsed the dishes while he carefully tucked them between the spines of the dishwasher. "I don't tell anyone who I am because that's not who I am anymore. J. Andrew Endicott is gone. Drew is all you get now. Take it or leave it."

"You're not going to write anymore?"

"I can't. It's just not in me."

"Why do you say that?"

"When Emilie and Maddie were killed, my creative soul died along with them. I've tried, but I just can't bring pen to paper. The grief is overwhelming most days."

"Are you sure that's the only reason you quit writing?"

"Yes, I'm sure." He bristled slightly. "You ask that as though you don't believe me."

"What's more important is do *you* believe you?"

"Yes. No doubt."

"Fair enough. So what's it going to take to fix that?"

"I don't know. Time, maybe. I don't know that it's fixable."

"Can't you harness all that grief? Channel it into your storytelling?"

"It's not that easy," Drew protested.

Nicole continued, more animated than before. "What if every writer stopped writing because of some personal tragedy? We wouldn't have Hemingway, or Wolfe, or F. Scott Fitzgerald. Was Maya Angelou a gifted writer because she had a happy childhood? Elie Wiesel would have never given us *Night* if he hadn't been in a Nazi concentration camp. Frank McCourt wouldn't have had the material to write *Angela's Ashes* if life had been easy. So much of great writing is born out of pain, Drew! How can you write authentically about the human drama unless you've lived it? It shouldn't ruin you. It should make you a better writer for having survived it."

"I'm not sure I've survived it."

"There are two ways to go. You can wallow in it, or you can take something from it. The choice is yours. Frankly, I don't think option one is working out too well for you."

Drew drummed his fingers on the kitchen counter. He wanted to offer some rebuttal, but he hadn't heard anything that wasn't true.

Nicole turned to face him. Her expression was softer than before. "So what are you going to do, J. Andrew Endicott?" she asked. "What's next?"

Drew puffed air out of one cheek. "I haven't figured that out. Right now, I'm living off the sale of my house, plus the little bit I get from royalties, but that'll all dry up soon enough. Then . . . who knows. Maybe I'll try waiting tables."

"I'm just asking you to think about it. Based on what I've read about you, you're way too talented to just quit."

Drew nodded. "Food for thought." He retrieved their glasses from the dinner table and poured equal shares of the remaining wine, leaving hers on the counter. "So," Drew said after a sip of Chardonnay and a heavy exhalation that signaled a segue. "Our book, *The Light Between Oceans*. Thoughts?"

"I loved it," Nicole said with an enthusiastic nod. "I thought the prose was beautiful and the story was meaningful."

"In what way?"

She narrowed her eyes and pondered the question. "I guess I

could relate to Izzy Sherbourne on lots of levels, starting with her prayer on page one. 'Lead us not into temptation, but deliver us from evil.' I think we all fight that battle every day. I think the book's title and the symbolism of the lighthouse is the theme of the story. The constant war between darkness and light."

Drew nodded but with a slight tilt of his head. "Okay, I'm not disagreeing, but I actually think the theme of the book has everything to do with the name of the island, Janus Rock. Janus, the Roman god with two faces. I think it means that you can look at any situation from two viewpoints, and who's to say which is right and which is wrong? Should Izzy keep a child that she knows isn't rightfully hers? I'm sure readers can see both sides. In the human drama, there are no easy answers."

"She'd had three miscarriages. I can't really fault her."

Drew nodded while jutting his chin back and forth. "Would *you* keep a child that you knew wasn't yours?"

Nicole swallowed hard and looked down into the kitchen sink. Her reply came softly and slowly. "I don't know if I can answer that. I only know that there are few greater blessings than having a child in your life."

Drew sensed he'd struck a nerve and knew enough not to ask any more questions. After a lengthy pause, he raised his wine glass into the air. "Janus is also the god of transitions and new beginnings."

Nicole turned to face him and smiled weakly. She picked up her wine glass and clinked it against his. "To new beginnings."

For the first time, Drew noticed that all the buttons on Nicole's blouse were mismatched. He pointed to them. "I've never seen a shirt quite like that, you know, with all the different buttons. It's really pretty. Unique."

"Thank you," she said, nearly blushing. "Just an idea I had. Didn't take long to put it together."

"Wait . . . you *made* that?"

"Afraid so."

"It's incredible. It looks like something from Saks."

"You're kind. It's really not that difficult."

"I would disagree. The only thing I know how to make where there's fabric involved is my bed. And I'm even forgetting how to do that."

"Would you like to see some more? I've been working on a few things."

Drew checked his watch, although he didn't know why. He certainly wasn't on a schedule. "Absolutely."

Nicole walked into the living room and patted the back of the couch. "Have a seat. Be right back."

Moments later, Nicole returned with a half-dozen hangers hooked over her index finger. One by one, she held up each garment against the front of her body like someone visually trying on clothes in a store mirror. A long-sleeved blouse, an unstructured jacket, a black pencil skirt, a sleeveless dress, and the tunic she'd been creating when Lee Wayne barged in on her. It was more artful than utilitarian. Her patterns were tasteful and trim, her choice of fabrics understated but not dull.

Out of more than just politeness, Drew sat on the edge of the couch and complimented every item she modeled. He made specific observations about each one and asked keen questions to let her know he was genuinely interested. He admired both her talent and her enthusiasm. He could see the pure joy it brought her, almost childlike, as she displayed each creation and described its material, design, and function. She had a fresh buoyancy about her that he hadn't seen before. It showed in her face and in her work. Every thread was rich with craftsmanship and creativity, every seam stitched with passion and purpose. She had a gift for it. This was clearly what she was born to do. If only life hadn't gotten in the way.

The final piece in Nicole's impromptu fashion show was a flowing blouse with an abundance of color, like the inside of an abalone shell. It was made of a fabric resembling rayon, but not as nice.

"What do you think?" she asked Drew, holding the blouse up to her neckline.

"Well," he started. He wasn't sure how honest he should be. "It's different from the others."

"Different? Different in what way?"

Drew's brain was stammering. It felt like a trap. "Well," he mumbled, "it's not as— "

"Not as what?" she probed, looking down at the blouse and frowning.

"I gotta be honest," Drew said as he stood up from the couch. "I don't want to hurt your feelings, but I don't like it as much as the other things you showed me. Sorry."

Nicole didn't look up. Her frown grew more pronounced.

Drew was immediately worried he'd wounded her with his criticism, however gentle. He stood up and tried to backtrack. "It's not that it's not nice. I mean, it has lots of color—"

Nicole's chest suddenly convulsed. He stepped toward her, ready to apologize profusely. Then he noticed she was smiling. Then snickering. Then full-on laughing. "Oh my God!" she blurted between fits. "You should see your face!"

Drew held up his hands, bewildered. "I'm . . . confused."

Nicole held the garish blouse at arm's length. "I bought this at a thrift store. Thought I could use the buttons for something."

Drew smiled with tight lips and pressed his clenched fists against his hips in a playful display of indignation. "Now why did you *do* that? I really thought I'd upset you! Now *I'm* upset!" Her continued laughter at his expense was contagious and he joined her.

"It was a test," replied Nicole.

"Again with the test? What were you testing *this* time?"

"To see if you truly liked my sewing, or if you were just being nice."

"You have quite a few tests for honesty, Nicole."

"Because I have a lot of trust issues. The good news is that you pass them. Most of them, anyway." She winked.

"Well, setting aside the finale of your fashion show, I must say, I'm impressed." Drew picked up their half-empty wine glasses from the coffee table and handed one to Nicole. He raised his goblet in a toast. "She cooks, she sews, she reads. Amazing woman."

She joined him in taking a sip. "Indeed. All part of the 'perfect wife' package. Buy it now. Free shipping."

They both grinned and simultaneously polished off the last swallows of Chardonnay. They looked straight at each other with nothing to say. The silence became increasingly awkward. For the first time since they'd met, something more than pure friendship and a mutual love of books seemed to enter the room. Maybe it was just his imagination. Maybe it was just hers. Whatever it was, they both knew it was forbidden. The silence grew louder.

"Well, I guess this meeting is adjourned," blurted Drew, indelicately ending the delicate moment. "I need to be getting back. Thank you for a lovely evening. Dinner and a show. My lucky night."

Drew started for the door and Nicole followed after him. "I'm glad you came over. I enjoyed it too." They were almost to the door, each unsure about the protocol of how to say goodnight.

"Oh! I almost forgot!" she said, turning back. "Wait one second." She disappeared into a back bedroom, then emerged seconds later with four books in her hands. "After I read up on you, and felt perfectly awful, I went back to the bookstore and bought the three books we chose. Plus one more. Agatha Christie's *The Body in the Library* for you, and J. Andrew Endicott's *Tears of the Sycamore* for me."

Drew chuckled with self-deprecation. "I can tell you right now, you're not gonna like the ending."

She handed him the stack of books, the perfect substitute for either an awkward handshake or a boundary-breaking embrace.

He flipped the books over and back. "Can't wait to dive in. Think I'll start with Picoult. Nothing like a good story about amnesia to make you forget your troubles. I noticed you're already halfway through it."

"I couldn't wait."

"How is it?"

"Very entertaining. Not what I was expecting but, still, good."

He looked at her, more seriously. "When do you have to go back home?"

Her smile faded. "In the morning. Right after coffee." Drew hesitated before speaking again. She could sense he wanted to tell her something. "What?" she asked.

He took his time before answering, conjuring up the right words. "It's not my place to say this, but I hate that you have to go back there."

Her chin quivered slightly. "I know." She exhaled as she dabbed away a tear misting in the corner of her eye. "I know."

He nodded in understanding. "Thank you again. For everything. This was . . . memorable."

"Yes it was. Maybe the kind of night that novelists write about."

Drew smiled warmly. "Without a doubt. Goodnight, Nicole."

"Goodnight, Drew."

He eased out of the door and slipped away into the quiet night, tucking his four books between his palm and wrist.

She gently latched the door, still watching Drew through the glass sidelight as he slowly vanished from view. She sighed heavily, regretful the night had ended. She knew it had to, but she also sensed there was much left unsaid, on both sides of the table.

An hour later, Nicole was curled up in bed, the only light in the room coming from the book light clamped over her copy of Picoult's *Picture Perfect*. Earlier that day she had quickly discovered it was about much more than just Hollywood and amnesia. The main character, Cassie Barrett, was trapped in a violent marriage with a matinee idol movie star, Alex Rivers. She'd lost herself in a cycle of abuse, denial, and promises that he'll change and never hit her again. But he still did.

Nicole was just beginning the last chapter, the part when Cassie calls a news conference and unveils the bruises on her body inflicted by a cruel husband. Nicole folded the book onto her chest and fantasized that she could somehow do the same. Publicly exposing Lee Wayne Shepherd for the brutish bully he was would be the most satisfying conclusion to her own story, but the fear of the repercussions dashed any real notions of carrying out such a bold plan. Nicole had also read *Big Little Lies* by Liane Moriarty. One of the three main characters lived with an abusive husband until her friend pushed him off a balcony and ended it. *If only*, Nicole thought. Fictional characters always seemed to be more courageous than the people who were reading about them.

Nicole was startled out of her vengeful musings when her cell phone buzzed on the nightstand. The display showed a new message. She quickly opened it, her pulse quickening.

> Dear N-
> It was something Tom Sherbourne said in
> The Light Between Oceans. "To have any kind
> of future, you have to give up hope of ever
> changing your past." That's the kind of
> sentence that can change your life. If we
> take nothing else away from this beautiful
> book, let us take that
> Night D

Nicole read the message over and over, committing the quote to memory. She also took great note of the fact that it was the first time Drew had used the word "dear" in his greeting. She turned off her reading light and stared at the dark, regretting her past and wondering if she even had a future. *Numb might become my favorite emotion too,* she mused. But for the first time in years, she felt as though someone had struck a match inside the dark room in which she lived. A tiny, flickering flame that fought valiantly against the cloak of blackness that enveloped her. She wondered how long it would last before being snuffed. She dreaded going home in the morning, more than ever before.

CHAPTER SIXTEEN

"The books we love, they love us back. And just as we
mark our places in the pages, those pages leave their
marks on us."

— Jay Kristoff, *Nevernight*

I know, I know," Drew said into his phone as he walked in
circles in his kitchen. The cheap linoleum of the rental house
squeaked under his feet. "I know it's been a couple of years
since I sent you anything, but as you well know, it's been a
difficult time."

He rolled his eyes as he listened to the barrage of annoying
questions from his New York literary agent, the one he'd
foolishly traded for Holly Hedrick. "All I can tell you is that it's
a work in progress. I just need more time and I'll send you some
pages." Drew listened again, occasionally holding the phone at
arm's length to avoid absorbing it all. To end the call, he finally
lied. "I'd say the first draft is close to being done. Just give me
a few weeks and I'll have something for you."

Drew's attention was snagged by something he saw outside
his kitchen window. It was Victoria coming through the gate
and heading toward his back deck.

"Listen, I gotta run. Need to get back to work on those
pages I promised you. I'll be in touch. Bye now."

He abruptly hung up and opened the back door as Victoria came
bounding up the stairs. She was holding a thin stack of letters.

"Here's your mail. Just bills and ads. Nothing important."

"Well, thank you for going through it for me," Drew said, as he took the envelopes and tossed them onto the kitchen table. His sarcasm was lost on the teenager.

"Do you have my money?" she asked bluntly.

He reached for his wallet. "Yeah. How much?"

She held out her tiny hand. "Four dollars."

"Wait, *four*? I was only gone overnight. The price you quoted was two dollars a day."

"Right. Saturday and Sunday. Two days. Four dollars." She poked her hand a little closer to Drew.

"But they don't deliver mail on Sundays."

"Sometimes they do."

"Did they yesterday?"

"No, but I still had to come over and check your mailbox. I can't take time out of my busy day for free. This is America."

Drew winced with laughter. In a terrible way, she was right. "Okay, okay, four bucks it is." He handed her the cash and Victoria looked at it almost in disbelief as if she'd never seen that much money before. She examined both sides of the bills, then cautiously tucked them into her front pocket.

"How much does a basketball cost?" she asked.

"I don't know. Depends on the quality. I think you can get a pretty good one for about thirty dollars. Why do you ask?"

"I want to play on my school team this coming fall. There's a summer league starting soon. Tryouts are coming up."

"Really? I didn't know you played basketball."

"I don't. Yet."

Drew looked at Victoria from head to toe, less than five feet of her. "Not to burst your bubble, but aren't you a little . . . uh . . . small?"

"My grandmother says 'a straight foot is not afraid of a crooked shoe.' "

Drew's face scrunched. "What does *that* mean?"

Victoria shook her head. "I'm not sure."

"Why basketball?"

"Because at school, if you want to fit in, you have to be a part of something and not just some club that anyone can join. It has to be something you earn."

"Makes sense. Why don't you try out for something like chorus? I've heard you sing. You have a beautiful voice."

"Because all they do in chorus is sing. Sing, sing, sing."

"Well, yeah. That's kinda the point."

"It's not for me. I need more activity."

"What about cheerleading?"

"Why would I want to cheer for someone else when I could have someone else cheering for *me*?"

Drew chuckled from deep in his belly as he marveled at the wisdom of the tiny sprite who stood before him, determined to play basketball. "Are you sure you're only thirteen?"

"Yes. It's the oldest I've ever been."

"I don't believe you. Let me see your driver's license."

"I don't have one. Yet. First I would need a car. How much does a car cost?"

"A lot more than a basketball." Drew pulled a box of cereal from the cupboard and poured a generous amount into a dirty bowl that had been sitting in the sink. He reached into the refrigerator for a carton of milk, smelling the contents before deciding it was safe to use.

Victoria pulled the money Drew had given her halfway out of her pocket, looked at it, then tucked it back in for safekeeping. She spoke softly and earnestly. "After I save up enough money, do you think you could take me to go buy a basketball?"

He stopped what he was doing and turned to look at Victoria, feeling the pleading in her eyes. It was not the first time a little girl had asked him to take her to the store, but it had been over two years since the last time. He walked closer and bent over, hands on his knees, eye level with Victoria. "Tell you what. I think I might have a basketball somewhere that you can have. It's not brand new, but close to it. You can save your money for something else."

An expression of sincere gratitude spread across Victoria's face, something between a smile and tears. She looked at Drew for several precious moments, eye to eye, then suddenly sprang forward and hugged him around the waist, as little girls do. "Thank you," she whispered as if Drew had just promised her a new car and not a used basketball.

He patted her gently on the back. "You're welcome. You better run along now. Grandmother might start to worry."

She squeezed his waist one more time with her arms, then let go. "Do you know when you might be able to get the ball?"

He checked his watch and squinted while he did the math in his head. "I suppose I can get to it today."

Victoria looked up at him with pleading eyes. "Promise?"

"Promise." As the word left his mouth, Drew realized it had been a long time since he'd made a promise. Even longer since he'd kept one. He already knew it was a promise that was going to be difficult to honor.

The rollers on the corrugated metal door rumbled up the vertical tracks of the storage unit. Light poured into the bay for the first time in over six months, exposing dozens of cardboard boxes randomly stacked onto each other.

Drew hesitated for a moment at the front, then heaved a sigh and moved forward. He felt as though it was a world where he didn't belong, like an archaeologist stepping into a sacred Egyptian tomb. He intended to quickly locate the basketball and immediately get out before the pain that lingered within these cinderblock walls could catch up to him. The flaw in his plan was that he had no idea where to begin looking. After Emilie's and Maddie's deaths, and the sale of their house, everything had been put away in storage so hastily that there was no rhyme or reason to their whereabouts. Sporting goods were mixed in with Christmas decorations, and lamps were interspersed with fireplace tools. Nothing was labeled. Most of it should have been given away or even thrown away, but at the time Drew didn't know what to do with a houseful of things that still carried the imprint of his wife and daughter, so he simply boxed up all the painful memories and stored them away to be dealt with at some later time.

Each box he opened not only brought back a stab of anguish, but also guilt. Dance recitals he'd missed because of book signings, soccer games he didn't make because he didn't feel like taking the redeye home, scrapbooks filled with pictures of other people in his life, but not him, because he wasn't there. Other matters in the life of J. Andrew Endicott had always been more important than the events represented in these boxes.

He folded back the flaps of a small box and there, wrapped inside a beach towel, was a rare family photo that actually included him. It had been taken on a vacation to Puerto Rico, back when Drew could afford such things. He was leaning in on one side of Maddie, with Emilie on the other, against the backdrop of the perfect palm trees of Luquillo Beach. The three smiling faces reminded Drew that he was at least capable of being happy. He blew off a thin layer of dust and gingerly returned it to the confines of the pasteboard.

After opening three more boxes, each filled with more haunting memories of Easter baskets and ticket stubs and kitchen gadgets, he found the basketball. The scuffed leather felt good in his hands. He bounced it a few times, the sound echoing off the cold walls of the storage unit. It took his mind racing back to baskets he'd scored in old gymnasiums with waxy floors and on asphalt playgrounds with chains for nets. It might do him some good to hoist up a few jumpers. He closed the box and tucked the ball under his arm, heading back to the front door. He suddenly stopped, backed up a few steps, and revisited a box he'd opened just a few minutes prior. He pulled out the beach photo of himself with Emilie and Maddie and freed it from the heartless darkness of the storage unit.

Hospitals are unique institutions. On one floor there is rejoicing at the birth of a baby, with pictures taken and phone calls going out to loved ones to spread the good news.

On another floor, there is sobbing as a heart monitor has stopped registering a pulse. Wires and tubes are unhooked and unplugged and phone calls go out to deliver the sad news.

On one special floor of that same hospital, both of those scenes in the human drama are played out. In the Neonatal Intensive Care Unit, critically ill newborns are fighting for their lives. No bigger than a baby bottle, they battle for survival using only some primal instinct to stay alive.

They do have help from modern medicine. They're kept warm and protected from germs in Plexiglas isolettes with sensors stuck to their soft skin to monitor their progress or lack thereof. Ventilators and oscillators keep the preemies breathing while their lungs develop, and a cadre of devoted nurses and doctors tend to the babies, while also offering comfort to frightened and weary parents. Feeding tubes keep them nourished, and soft lighting keeps everyone calm.

Just a few weeks ago, Nicole had never been in a NICU, and now she was a trained volunteer entrusted with perhaps the most important job for anyone not wearing a stethoscope. Her job was simply to hold and rock babies when their parents weren't there. As they'd reminded her over and over during her training, human touch was as important to an infant as any drug.

Nicole held a little boy, wrapped in a soft Carolina blue blanket, as she swayed back and forth in the rocking chair. She cooed softly and caressed his wee fingers. The baby clutched her index finger with all the strength he had.

"You doin' okay?" It was the same woman who'd greeted her the day Lee Wayne had his heart surgery. Her warm smile had not changed.

"Yes," Nicole replied. "I'm so glad you suggested this."

"So am I," the nurse answered. "You're a natural. Do you have kids of your own?"

"No," Nicole said with a quick shake of her head. She was going to say *not yet*, but thought better of it. "No," she repeated, quieter this time.

The nurse was intuitive enough to not ask more questions. "The little boy's name is Cody. His mother delivered ten weeks early, so he's got a long road in front of him." She patted Nicole on the shoulder. "But I'm confident he's got the right person to help him through."

"Thank you. I hope I'm good at this."

"You are, honey. You are. Call me if you need me."

"There is one thing," Nicole said.

"What's that?"

"Do the babies keep these blankets when they go home? It seems like it would bring them some reassurance when they're adjusting to a new environment."

The nurse shook her head. "No, but that's a really good idea. Maybe in next year's budget!" she said brightly, then checked her watch and moved on. *God bless nurses*, Nicole thought. What would a NICU or a battlefield be without the comfort they bring?

She took a moment to survey the scene around her. Babies instinctively sucking on feeding tubes, physicians in white lab coats checking charts and conferring and counseling. A young mother, sick with worry, pressing her weary fingers against the glass of the incubator to get as close as possible to her endangered child. There is no bond stronger in the universe than that between mother and child. Nicole wondered how difficult it must be for a mother to give up her baby for adoption. Her own mother must have had a good reason. Must have.

She returned her attention to the precious little hand clinging to hers as if Cody fully understood she was his lifeline. So fragile. So vulnerable. As she cradled him, she realized it was the first time she'd ever held a child this young and how much responsibility she felt to see him get beyond his struggles and thrive. She also wondered who was going to benefit most from their relationship.

CHAPTER SEVENTEEN

"I have always imagined that paradise will be a kind of library."

— Jorge Luis Borges

Drew had barely tossed his car keys on the kitchen table before there was a pounding on the back door. He'd fully expected it but was still a little surprised by how quickly the knock had come upon his return home. He opened the door to a breathless Victoria, who charged into the house, uninvited but welcome.

"Won't you come in?" Drew said, long after she'd already crossed the threshold.

"Did you get my basketball?" She excitedly shifted her weight from one foot to the other.

Drew slapped his head. "Oh! I *knew* there was something I forgot!"

"You didn't forget."

"No, I didn't forget." From behind his back, Drew produced a basketball, nearly new. Monarch-orange leather with black seams and the name Spalding emblazoned on the front in bold, black lettering.

Victoria didn't snatch it from his hands. Instead, she held up her tiny hands, reverently. Drew gently placed the sphere in her fingers. She pulled it closer and rolled it through her palms as she felt its weight and perfect balance. She smelled it, drinking in the aromas of leather, sweat, and gymnasium floors. She bounced it on the kitchen floor, making the pile of dirty dishes in the sink rattle and hum.

"Easy now. Basketball's not an indoor game."

"Yes it is."

"Okay, you're right. Just not *this* indoors."

Victoria clutched her new ball to her chest like a little girl hugging a baby doll. She closed her eyes and rubbed the knobby leather against her cheek. "I love this, Mr. Drew. Thank you."

"You're welcome. Now go enjoy it."

Victoria looked at Drew with eyes full of hope. "So when can you start teaching me how to play basketball?"

"I never said I'd teach you."

"Who else is going to?"

Drew clasped his hand around his forehead and massaged his temples with his thumb and forefinger. He sighed for effect. "Honestly, sometimes I don't know if you're naïve, or you're just playing me. I go back and forth."

"Are you hesitating because you don't know *how* to play basketball?"

"Of course I know how! I have a basketball, don't I?"

"That doesn't mean anything. *I* have a basketball and I don't know how to play."

Drew looked at his waifish neighbor, still clutching her precious new ball. *How can I possibly say no?* he thought. Okay, I'll teach you. But I charge two dollars a day."

She knew he was kidding. "That seems like a lot. Are you worth it?"

"Tell you what, I'll give you the first lesson for free. If you like what you see, I'll have my lawyer draw up a contract for future instruction. You can pay me back when you sign with the WNBA."

"Deal." She stuck her hand out to shake his, grasping just the tips of his weathered fingers.

"Whoa, whoa, whoa," Drew said, shaking his head. "That's not how you shake hands. It's like this." He thrust his hand firmly into hers, making sure that the crease between his thumb and index finger was jammed against hers. He pumped her arm up and down three times. "Shake hands like you mean it. A firm handshake tells people that they need to take you seriously, especially men."

"Why is that so important to men?" she asked in all seriousness. She released his grip, and then shook his hand again, exactly as he'd just taught her.

"Because men are idiots."

"That's what my grandmother says."

"Wise woman." Drew paused momentarily as he formulated his next question. "Victoria, may I ask you something?"

"Sure." She was still shaking his hand, enjoying her new life skill.

"Where are your parents?"

She released his hand and slowly wrapped both of her arms around the basketball. "They're gone."

"Gone? As in moved away?"

"No. Gone as in . . . gone." She looked down at the floor and bit her lower lip.

"May I ask what happened?"

"They were killed in a car accident when I was ten. That's why I live with my grandmother."

"I'm sorry," Drew said, wishing now he hadn't asked.

"So am I," Victoria whispered. "So am I."

"Where did you live before you moved here?"

"In Durham. In an apartment. We moved here so that Grandmother could have a garden again. She bought the house with insurance money, but I'm not quite sure how all that works."

Both of them sat quietly as they searched for a way out of their mutual discomfort. Drew finally broke the silence. "There's a playground about a mile from here. Go put on some basketball clothes and meet me in the driveway. Lesson one begins in fifteen minutes."

She nodded and bolted out the door, bounded down the steps and across his backyard. She tossed the basketball over the fence, then climbed over and chased it down. *She's fairly athletic,* Drew thought as he watched her through the window. *Better than I expected. Maybe I can make a point guard out of her yet.*

Drew saw that the Chinese peppers in Húdié's garden had grown at least five inches and that something akin to lettuce was starting to come up along the far end. A few other plants were just peeking through the tilled soil. He also saw that the four-foot-high chicken wire Húdié had stretched between the metal spikes was now drooping a little in one corner. He made a mental note to fix it for her when he got back from basketball with Victoria. But so far, the makeshift fence was doing its job. No rabbits.

Drew retreated to his room to lace up some old sneakers, passing by his dusty computer. Those pages he'd promised to write would have to wait.

Victoria was already waiting in Drew's driveway when he came down the back stairs dressed in his gym clothes. He couldn't hide his shock when he took stock of what the young girl was wearing. "Whoa!" he blurted out, holding up his hands in surrender. She had on striped leggings, a sweatshirt that was going to burn her alive in the hot sun, and leather-soled shoes with short heels that looked more corrective than comfortable. It reminded Drew of the classic image of a city slicker showing up for his first camping trip.

"What's wrong?" she asked.

Drew moved both hands in front of him in small circles like an artist about to go to work on a blank canvas. "This. All of this. It needs some work." He opened his garage door and motioned her toward the car. "Get in. We've got to make a stop before I let you anywhere near a basketball court."

Still slightly confused, Victoria nonetheless obeyed orders and scrambled around to the passenger door.

Fifteen minutes later, they were at a sporting goods store. Not the big box kind, but a family-owned place in a strip mall. With a little guidance from Drew and the pleasant girl working the floor, Victoria picked out two pairs of nylon gym shorts, a light blue and a dark green T-shirt, and a sturdy pair of all-purpose athletic shoes. They were a little jazzier than what Drew would have chosen, but he could tell by the light beaming off Victoria's face that she loved the way they looked and how empowered they made her feel. *She may not be able to play a lick*, he thought, *but at least she'll look the part.*

Nicole rubbed her hand across every bolt of blanket material in the fabric store. She didn't know exactly what she wanted just by looking, but she would know it when she felt it. It had to be exactly the right weight and softness to swaddle the tiniest of babies.

Her hand pushed up and down a bolt of organic Jersey knit

cotton, buttery yellow with a print of tiny white sheep. *Perfect.* She found some creamy white fleece for the interior. Five yards of each should do it. A roll of white Velcro and her shopping was complete.

Thirty minutes later, Nicole sat at her sewing machine and studied the pattern she'd found online for a baby swaddle wrap. She figured if she cut the dimensions in half it would be just about right for the body of a preemie.

She carefully cut the pieces, her shears gliding through the fabric along perfect lines.

She eased the curved seams under the thread, skillfully depressing the pedal of her sewing machine at just the right speed for the backstitching, loving the feel of the soft Jersey as it slipped through her fingers like warm milk.

As the thread darted in and out of the blanket, Nicole thought about how often she'd imagined making baby clothes for her own child, a child that now was never to be born. She had feared this project might dredge up a deep sadness that had no cure. The wanting of a child was something she knew would never leave her, and sometimes just seeing a young mother pushing a stroller washed melancholy all over her. But she felt none of that as she fashioned these swaddling blankets. The best of her maternal instincts had risen to the surface. If she couldn't bear children of her own because of forces beyond her control, then the next best outcome was to provide loving care for those who could. This was the optimal use of her time and talent. A gift she could share with the struggling infants.

In just minutes the Jersey and fleece were connected as one, with thin strips of Velcro attached to the wings that would keep the blanket snug and secure with a tiny baby inside, warm and safe, like a mother's womb. Nicole held it up and inspected it, even going so far as to nod in quiet approval. One down, nineteen more to go.

What Victoria lacked in talent on the basketball court, she more than made up for in eagerness. She and Drew were at the nearby playground, the kind you would find on the streets of any big city, with weathered blacktop, metal backboards, and chain nets. Like a sea sponge, Victoria soaked in every word of Drew's basic instruction. How to pass a basketball, how to catch one, where to place your fingers when you're getting ready to shoot, and how to launch it toward the rim. She took to all of it readily and earnestly, until it came time for dribbling. Victoria paddled the ball with both hands like an African drum as she moved awkwardly around the court.

"You can't dribble with both hands," he called out to her.

"Yes I can!" she called back, eagerly slapping the ball with alternating hands.

"No, I mean you're not allowed to!" Drew said.

"Why not?" she asked, without stopping.

"The rules say you have to dribble with only one hand," Drew coached. "Like this." He took the ball and deftly dribbled with one hand, weaving back and forth around the court as he switched from left hand to right and back again. He felt fifteen again, bouncing the ball like he was back on the wooden planks of his high school gymnasium. *I still got it,* he allowed himself to think. He sent a bounce pass back to Victoria. "Your turn."

She caught the ball and smacked it up and down on the asphalt with just her right hand. Better, but still not good. She picked up the ball in both hands and ran a few steps toward the basket, then started dribbling again.

Drew shook his head and whistled between his teeth. "Whoa! You can't run without dribbling! Once you stop dribbling, you can't start again. You have to either pass it or shoot it."

Victoria shook her head, the first sign of frustration. "Basketball has a lot of rules."

"So does life. Get used to it." Drew playfully tousled Victoria's black hair. "That's enough for today. I gotta get on home."

"Why? You don't have a job."

"No, but I have things to do."

"Like what?"

Drew realized that *drinking and reading* didn't constitute a viable to-do list, so he changed course. "I just don't want to wear you out on your first day."

"I think *you're* the one who's tired."

"I'm fine. I just have other matters to attend to."

"You ended a sentence with a preposition."

Drew laughed heartily. "What am I gonna do with you?"

"Promise me we can come back here tomorrow."

He nodded. "Deal. Ten o'clock?"

"Deal."

Drew held out his clenched fist as an invitation for a fist bump to seal the arrangement. Victoria just stared.

"What are you doing?" she asked him. "Why are you making a fist?"

Drew shook his head in amusement. "So much to learn, grasshopper. *So* much."

The only light in the dining room came from the gooseneck lamp Nicole had attached to her sewing machine. The only sound in the house was the soft, rhythmic whir of the mechanical needle pulling thread. The sound changed with the maneuvering of the foot pedal. Sometimes slow and deliberate, like a covered wagon clacking over a wooden bridge, then accelerated sound, like a hand mixer in a thin batter. Nicole was lost in the moment as she pieced the swaddling blankets together, imagining how warm and safe the tiny infants in the NICU were going to feel, coddled in the soft fabric. It was the first time in years she'd felt a true sense of purpose, giving of herself, her time, and her talents.

Lee Wayne roared in from the hallway and shattered the perfect moment. "Do ya mind shuttin' off that damn thing? People are tryin' to sleep in here."

Nicole lurched with a stab of adrenaline as she spun around to see Lee Wayne looming in the frame of the archway. She snatched a breath and clutched her breastbone. "I'm sorry. I thought you were asleep."

"I *was*. Until your little sweatshop cranked up."

Nicole hurriedly gathered up the loose pieces of fabric on the table and placed them in a paper shopping bag. "I can do this later. I'm sorry."

Lee Wayne shook his head in disgust as he muttered his way back down the hallway. "I shoulda never let you do this stupid little hospital thing. You've turned our whole house upside down."

In the course of just two sentences, Lee Wayne had twice managed to use the word *little*. To Nicole's ears, that elementary word was as hurtful and insulting as any expletive or skillfully constructed invective he could have hurled at her. It was Lee Wayne's uncultured way of belittling anything she did. To characterize something as "little" was to immediately devalue and dismiss it as childish nonsense, and there was no rebuttal once it had been deemed as such. She felt her nerve endings burning as she packed up her materials and clicked off the sewing lamp. How she loathed that man and his little ways.

Drew was beyond tired when he pulled his legs up off the floor and into his bed. The basketball lesson with Victoria was the most physical activity he'd had in a while. Four Advil hadn't done much to put a dent in the creeping soreness. *Maybe I don't "still got it,"* he mused.

He backed into the three pillows mashed against his headboard and found his bookmarked page of *The Boys in the Boat* by Daniel James Brown. Drew didn't read much non-fiction other than the occasional biography or memoir, but this account of America's eight-oar rowing team at the 1936 Olympics in Berlin was captivating. It had been Drew's recommendation for the Oak Island Book Club, so he was relieved it was a great read. Having spoken to many book clubs in his writing career, he knew there were few greater embarrassments in those circles than suggesting a book to the group that turned out to be tedious and indigestible.

The grit those college boys from the University of Washington displayed in Hitler's Germany was inspiring. Drew tried to extract some metaphorical meaning out of the visual that as the boys rowed onward, they could never see where they were going, only where they'd just been. The past shrank behind them in the distance as they continued to move forward in time and space. With muscles burning, they pressed on in blind faith with only a small voice to guide them, each new stroke more searing than the last as they approached an unseen finish line.

Drew felt just the opposite of the boys in that boat. He was trying to look forward but felt as though he was drifting backward most of the time. At the very best, he was only treading water. And every image of water that formed in his mind as he read the story made him lose focus on the written words. His thoughts were taken painfully back to a beach at Oak Island where water had swept away his future. He placed the open book on his chest and closed his eyes, trying to purge from his mind the thoughts of a wife and daughter screaming for help as they were swept out to sea while he was autographing his novel in a bookstore on Broadway, too far away to hear their cries. He wondered if the haunting images would ever expire and leave him in peace.

Eyes still closed, he felt along his nightstand for his glass. He took a burning sip of bourbon. It soothed him, even though it was significantly less than his usual dosage.

Nicole settled into the folds of the living room couch and cracked open her copy of *The Boys in the Boat*. It wasn't a book she'd normally have chosen to read, but the more pages she turned the more she was glad Drew had suggested it. She kept wondering what it would be like to be a part of a team, something she'd never done. She wondered what it must be like to share that camaraderie, that special bond among warriors. She wondered what it would be like just to have eight friends.

When the snoring began from Lee Wayne's bedroom, her mood brightened. *I might be the only spouse in America who looks forward to the sound of snoring,* she thought. It meant the beast in the bed was finally asleep, which in turn meant a few hours of freedom.

Nicole removed her secret phone from the safe clutches of the hollowed-out book and switched it on. When it came to life, there was a message waiting.

How do you like Boys so far?

It's great! Halfway through.

You're a fast reader. Do you skim?

No. I just read intensely!

How much do you read?

Depends. Two books a week on average.
Sometimes three. Usually more than one at the
same time. You?

**Maybe one a week if I'm lucky.
I need to pick up the pace!**

I'll probably finish this by tomorrow. What should
be our next book? You can decide. It's too much
pressure! And I promise I'll like it, whatever
you choose

Hmmm... decisions, decisions.

See? The pressure is already getting to you

**I'm torn. Part of me wants to read a classic, but
there's another part of me nagging to read
something a little saucier. Maybe a Sandra Brown
or a Jackie Collins. Borderline lascivious.**

How about both?

Explain

We could read a "saucy" classic, like Fanny Hill,
Tropic of Cancer, or Lady Chatterley's Lover

I could go for a little D.H. Lawrence.

Then Chatterley it is! (if I can get through the
embarrassment of going to buy it)

**Forget the buying part... what about the group
discussion at the next meeting of the OIBC?!?**

We'll let you lead that one

When are you coming back to the beach?

I'm thinking about this weekend. You
already there?

**Going on Friday, just as soon as 'Skipper' heads
out of town. That gives us a few days to finish
two books. Can't wait to "Chat"!**

I see what you did there! I'm off to bed.
Tired bones

Me too. sleep well. Night, D.

Goodnight, N

Drew finished the last swallow of his bourbon and reached for the switch on the lamp on his nightstand. Just before the light went out, he took a long look at the new addition to his bedroom wall. The family photo on the beach in Puerto Rico with Emilie and Maddie he'd retrieved from the storage unit. Perhaps he was starting to row forward.

Nicole read one more chapter of *The Boys in the Boat* before turning off her book light. She placed her head on a leftover swatch of the soft Jersey knit she'd bought for the baby blankets. It felt warm and comforting. She closed her eyes and allowed a smile to spread over her weary face. Despite the venom of Lee Wayne, this had been a good day.

CHAPTER EIGHTEEN

"If you have a garden and a library, you have
everything you need."

— Cicero

It was just before ten o'clock the next morning when Drew
bounded down the stairs off his back deck with his car
keys jangling in his hand. Victoria and her grandmother
were both in their garden. Most of the brown soil was now
covered in green as the seeds they'd sown weeks before were
all springing to verdant life, blossoming in a variety of shapes
and sizes.

Victoria was hunched over, pulling weeds and putting them
in a wooden bucket. Húdié had her back to Drew as he approached. She was bent over with her hands clasped behind her
back. As Drew got closer he could hear the old woman whispering something in Mandarin, seemingly to herself.

"I thought we said ten o'clock!" he called out to Victoria.

"Grandmother says I can't play basketball until all the weeds
are gone."

Drew looked skyward in exasperation as if he had something
else on his schedule. "How much longer is that gonna take?"

Victoria snapped back an answer without looking up. "I
don't know. Maybe if I had some help I could get it done
sooner."

Drew had no comeback other than to hop the fence and
start pulling weeds. As he knelt alongside Victoria and dug his

hands into the dirt, tearing out wild violets and chickweed, he couldn't help but notice that Húdié was still carrying on a one-way conversation. "What's she doing?" he whispered to Victoria. He wasn't sure why he'd whispered, since the old woman couldn't understand English.

"She's talking to her plants."

"Why on earth is she doing that?"

"Grandmother says plants are like people. If you talk to them and let them know you care about them, they will grow and thrive."

"Okay. Can't argue that." Drew surveyed the budding plants as he weeded and pointed to a grouping of plants with purplish conical fruit on the end of the stalks that looked like unopened tulips. "I know those are Chinese peppers. What else did she plant?"

Victoria looked across the four corners of the garden and started pointing. "Over there is bitter melon. It's like squash. Grandmother uses it mostly for medicine. Along the back there is daikon. That's a radish. Right now she's talking to the mizuna, which is like spinach. And those little ones behind you are bok choy. It's a kind of cabbage."

Drew noticed the bok choy didn't seem to be flourishing like the rest of the plants. He knelt over them to get a closer look. "They look a little puny. Why aren't they growing like the others?"

"That's because Grandmother says bok choy doesn't listen."

"So . . . what's going on with *you*?" Teri asked as she took tiny snips from the ends of Nicole's wet hair.

Nicole knew it was a question rife with subtext, the kind of question only a therapist or a hairdresser is allowed to ask. Nonetheless, Nicole deflected. "Nothing. How 'bout yourself?"

"Come on now. This is Teri you're talkin' to. Somethin' has clearly added a little sparkle to your step."

Nicole remained coy. "I have no idea what you mean."

"Well, for starters, you've lost a little weight and I can see a little more tone in your arms. I hope Lee Wayne has taken notice."

"Not hardly. However, he *did* notice that I'd bought a different brand of mayonnaise. I got an earful about that."

"But it's more than that. You've been goin' to the beach house just about every weekend lately, which I think is great, but it's a little out of the ordinary for you. And the fact that you're in my shop about two weeks earlier than usual and that you asked for somethin' 'a little different this time' gets me to wonderin'. Ya know?"

Their eyes met in the mirror. Nicole knew that Teri knew. "Well, all I can tell you is that I have joined a book club. We read the same books and discuss them. Sometimes our meetings are at the beach. That's all I can tell you."

Teri beamed, not just for being proven right, but also because she was genuinely joyful that something good was happening to Nicole. "I see. And exactly how many people are in this book club?"

"Let me think . . . including me? That would be . . . two."

"And does this other member have a name?"

"Drew."

"Drew," repeated Teri. "Could be a man or a woman."

"Yes. It is definitely one or the other." Nicole's eyes twinkled, providing a clearer answer than her vague verbal response.

"Okay then," Teri said with delight. "No further questions." Teri pumped the foot pedal on the chair to elevate Nicole just a few more inches. "Now then... let's see what else we can do to get you dolled up for your next book club meeting."

Drew had learned long ago to never underestimate someone who has already firmly made up their mind. You will always lose. He could see the sheer determination in Victoria's eyes to improve and excel at basketball. Her dribbling and shooting had gotten markedly better in just the few lessons he'd given her. He suspected she was practicing on her own.

Even though they didn't look remotely similar, and their personalities were decidedly different, Drew couldn't help but see a little of Maddie in Victoria. His daughter had been all girl, loving dresses, dancing, and drama. Victoria was much more of a tomboy. But they were both fun to be around, each in their own way. They shared a curiosity about the world and a love of learning that made teaching and coaching them a joy for someone like Drew, who felt he had a lot to give if only someone would ask for it. More than anything, they had a burning desire to achieve. Whatever the pursuit, they both had that drive for accomplishment. Not necessarily to be the best, but to at least be proficient. As he watched Victoria labor hard to hoist up long jump shots and then rebounded her frequent misses, Drew pondered how his own drive and ambition to be a bestselling author had eventually derailed him. He also wondered why he no longer possessed the will to do anything but merely exist day to day.

The chain net rattled in celebration as Victoria sank a shot from fifteen feet away. She walked over to Drew, beaming with a sense of great achievement. "I need a nickname," she proclaimed matter-of-factly.

"You do? Why?"

"All the great basketball players have a nickname."

Drew tried to hide his wry smile, not wanting to burst her bubble. Despite her lack of skill and credentials, Drew could not argue her point. Nor did he want to. "You're right. All the great ones do."

"So what should mine be?"

Drew squinted as he cocked his head and gazed into the distance, deep in thought. He stroked the end of his chin with his thumb and forefinger as he mulled over the possibilities. He pondered for some time, wanting her to know he wasn't rushing into it. He finally looked directly at her and nodded his approval at his own idea. "I think we should call you Iron Butterfly."

The young girl's eyes immediately brightened. "Iron Butterfly. I like it!"

Drew didn't mention that Iron Butterfly was also the name of a '60's heavy metal rock band that hit the charts with the rock anthem *In-A-Gadda-Da-Vida*. Better that she believed it was original thought.

Victoria snatched the basketball from Drew's hands and dribbled a few times. "Five seconds left, down by one, the ball goes to Iron Butterfly. Two seconds left, one . . . she shoots!" The ball clanged off the side of the backboard, missing the rim entirely. She chased it down and came running back to Drew. "It's okay," she assured him. "It was just halftime."

He burst out laughing, a robust laugh that started low in his gut and exploded out of his mouth. He couldn't stop laughing. Nor could he remember the last time he couldn't stop laughing.

◆ ◆ ◆

On the drive home from the playground, Victoria drummed her fingers on the basketball in her lap. She suddenly stopped as a worried look spread across her delicate face.

"What's wrong?" Drew asked.

"I am not sure I can play in the summer league. I have no way to get to practice. Unless you drive me."

"How far is it? Can you ride your bike?"

"No."

"Why not?"

"Two reasons. I don't have a bike. And also I don't know how to ride one."

"Those are two good reasons." Drew looked at the clock on the dashboard. "What time do you have to be home?"

"One o'clock. It's my day to fix lunch."

"Come on. I have an idea."

Drew rolled up the corrugated metal door on his storage unit. Coming here didn't seem to be getting any easier, but at least he felt he had a purpose for this visit other than shrouding himself in sentimental grief.

"What's all this stuff?" Victoria asked as she followed him inside.

"Another life," he said, softly.

Drew waded through the columns of stacked boxes until he came to a bicycle leaning against the back wall. It had been Maddie's. The tires were both flat and the chain had fallen off. The red paint was scraped in several places from minor accidents. He lifted it up over his head and set it down in an open space. "Here. Needs a little work, but this is yours to keep."

Her eyes lit up and a broad smile spread from ear to ear. "You're *kidding*!" she squealed, wiggling involuntarily with sheer delight. She didn't notice any of its imperfections. She ran her fingers along the sturdy frame like it was the Holy Grail and angels were singing.

Drew started opening other boxes. "I think there's a helmet in here somewhere."

He dug through some salad plates, a collection of audiobooks on cassette, and some camping gear, still splotched with mud stains from their last outing in the Blue Ridge Mountains. He popped open another box and suddenly clutched for breath. On top were Maddie's ballet slippers. He held them in his hand, feeling their soft, pink leather with his fingers. A hard lump formed in his throat. He didn't remember packing them. Nor could he remember the last time his daughter had worn them, probably because he hadn't been there to see her recital. He'd been having dinner with ambition that night. He closed the box and exhaled loudly, taking a moment to compose himself.

Moments of happiness flitted in and out of Drew's life, randomly and infrequently. A humorous line in a good book or a favorite song on the radio would spark a moment of cheer, but felicity was fleeting. Sadness never seemed to be too far away, always lurking in the shadows, always stepping in at the strangest of times, interrupting his life. He didn't want it to be the central part of his being, but he just couldn't will it away. The sadness of losing people you held close to your heart is like a tattoo that fades over time, but never completely vanishes. You never forget it's there. All it takes is a tiny pair of ballet shoes to send it crashing back into your broken heart.

"You're getting sad again."

Drew snapped out of his mild trance. He'd forgotten Victoria was there. "What?" he asked. His voice was tremulous.

"I can see it on your face. Grandmother says your face is filled with tiny rivers of sadness."

"She does, does she? Maybe she's right."

"Is that why you drink alcohol? Grandmother says it is bad for you."

"She's right again."

"So why do you do it?"

Drew scanned the stacks of cardboard boxes that contained the life he used to know. He shook his head and made a quiet clucking sound with his tongue as he pondered the child's question. "I don't have a good answer."

A few blocks from the storage unit they drove past a small garden center, buzzing with summer gardeners picking out seeds and saplings. With uncharacteristic spontaneity, Drew mashed hard on the brakes and wheeled into the second driveway of the nursery. Technically the exit, but suddenly an alternate entrance.

"Why are we stopping?" Victoria asked.

"I want you to pick me out a plant. A house plant. Anything you want."

Her eyes brightened at the prospects. Drew could sense it was the first time she'd been consulted in such matters.

Victoria took her assignment seriously, moving slowly up and down the aisles filled with a wide variety of flora and fauna. She carefully read the information cards attached to each plant, unwilling to make a hasty decision based on looks alone. Drew stood in the corner, admiring her diligence. She finally settled on a leafy palm tree, about four feet high.

"I like this one," she called over to him. Drew nodded his approval and joined her. Victoria wrapped her bony arms around the black plastic container and carried it to the checkout counter. "It's an Areca palm."

"Why that one?" Drew asked.

"Two reasons. It's from Madagascar and I've always wanted to go there."

"Because of the movie?"

"What movie?" she asked.

"Never mind," Drew said with a chuckle. "What's the second reason?"

"It says it's easy to take care of. I think you need some easy in your life."

Drew nodded. *More than you know*, he thought. Or maybe she did. Drew was never quite sure what was pure innocence or when she might be jerking his chain. Either way, he found it refreshing.

They left the nursery with a bicycle sticking out of an open tailgate and a four-foot palm tree buckled up in the backseat with half of it poking out the side window. Victoria, now wearing the bike helmet, repeatedly turned around to make sure both items were secure and would reach their final destination unscathed. Drew felt a tiny twinge of happiness.

They pulled into his driveway and got out. Victoria carefully removed the palm tree from the backseat, her face lost in the long, feathery fronds as she wrapped her arms around the bottom. She shouted instructions as she carried the plant up the back stairs to his deck. "Make sure to put this in bright, but indirect light," she told Drew. "Too much sun can burn the leaves. And don't overwater it. Keep it moist, but not soggy. You should let the top few inches of soil dry out before you water it again."

"I'll do my best," Drew said. He was amazed her young mind had absorbed so much information from just a little plastic placard stuck in the rich soil of the pot.

He pulled the bicycle out of the trunk and set it on the driveway, popping down the wobbly kickstand to keep it upright. "Give me a couple of days to fix this up and we'll have a bike riding lesson."

Victoria bounded down the stairs. "This is so exciting! My very own bike!"

"Let's hope you still think so after a few skinned knees and elbows."

"How long will it take you to fix it?"

Drew gave the bike a quick inspection. "Let me figure out what she needs to get up and running. Gotta make sure the brakes work and all that."

"Please do it quickly, okay?"

"I will."

"Promise?"

"I promise," he assured her. "You need to get home and fix your grandmother's lunch."

"Oh! I forgot!" The young teen bounded home, still wearing her bike helmet.

As he walked over to lift open the large, white garage door, an idea jumped into Drew's brain. It brought a smile as he thought it through.

He called out to Victoria across the backyard. "Come over to my house at about 8:45 tonight, right when it gets dark," he hollered. "And bring your grandmother."

Somewhere between puzzled and eager, Victoria's eyes lit up. "Why?" she yelled back.

"Can't tell you. It's a secret."

"Do I need to bring anything? Like a covered dish or something?"

Drew laughed out loud. "No! Just come as you are."

"Okay!" She opened the back door of her house and disappeared.

Drew checked the afternoon sky. Lots to do between now and nightfall.

◆   ◆   ◆

Nicole was in a rocking chair in the NICU cradling Cody in her arms when a young woman in her early twenties came in, being pushed in a wheelchair by a hospital volunteer. She looked weak and drained of color. A rectangular section had been shaved out of her dishwater blonde hair and a large, gauze bandage had taken its place. She was wearing blue jeans, a long-sleeved T-shirt with a cartoon racecar on the front, and pool sandals with no socks. She wore sky-blue eye makeup but no lipstick. After a quiet exchange with a nurse, the young woman was wheeled over to Nicole and Cody. Nicole knew right away that this was the baby's birth mother. She stood up with the little boy to greet her as the volunteer gave the two women time alone.

"Hi." The young woman spoke with a thick eastern North Carolina twang. "I'm Lyla. I'm his mama."

"It is *so* nice to finally meet you!" Nicole said, immediately holding the infant out for his mother to take him. "I've been taking good care of him. So has everyone else here."

"Thank you," Lyla whispered as she took her baby into her arms. Her eyes misted over as she gripped his tiny fingers and gazed into his face. "He's beautiful," she said softly, more to herself than to Nicole.

"So this is the first time you've seen him?"

Lyla nodded, still holding her attention on her baby boy. "I guess I been in a coma or somethin' for a few days. That's what they tell me."

"Were you in an accident?" Nicole asked, pointing to the bandage.

"Kinda. I fell down the stairs. I reckon that's why he come so early." She bent over and kissed Cody on the forehead.

Nicole took a longer look at the bandaged forehead. "You all right?"

"Much better, thank you," Lyla said flatly.

Nicole gathered up her purse next to the rocking chair and backed away. "I'll leave you two alone. It was nice to meet you, Lyla."

Lyla nodded without looking up from her precious baby boy.

On the elevator ride down to the parking garage, Nicole started to cry and she wasn't even sure why. She knew it had something to do with handing baby Cody over to his mother, but why exactly that triggered a torrent of tears wasn't clear to her. The nurses had cautioned her during her cuddler training to not get too attached to the babies but even as they were issuing that warning, she hadn't seen how that was possible.

Drew showered quickly and then jumped back in his car. He made several quick stops, including one to the bike shop for the necessary repair parts. It was going to feel good to get his hands greasy again.

CHAPTER NINETEEN

"Books don't offer real escape, but they can stop a mind scratching itself raw."

— David Mitchell, *Cloud Atlas*

Nicole had just finished putting a roasting chicken in the oven when she heard the garage door open. She felt the perpetual pit in her stomach leap to life as the grinding gears signaled Lee Wayne's arrival home from work. Even though she often felt like a prisoner, being home alone was far preferable to his company. She felt guilty for secretly hoping his heart troubles would resurface.

"What the hell have you done to yourself?" were the first punitive words out of his mouth when Lee Wayne trudged up the steps and into the kitchen. He tossed his briefcase on the kitchen table and slowly walked circles around Nicole, studying her hair which was now alive with creamy blonde highlights and considerably shorter than the last time he'd seen her. "What is *this*?" he said.

Nicole smelled alcohol on his breath as he orbited her. She moved out of his reach. "I just thought I'd try something different."

"Did I say you could try something different?"

"I wanted it to be a surprise. I thought you'd like it."

"Well, I don't. I hate it. You'll go back to that little hairdo gal tomorrow and get it fixed. Is that clear?"

Nicole hesitated. She liked her haircut just the way it was.

She cowered next to the counter and stared intently at the four burners on the stove, as her brain calculated the various scenarios of action and reaction.

Lee Wayne's face was reddening as Nicole failed to reply to his command. He grabbed her by the throat, clamping down on her windpipe with his thumb and fingers, digging his nails into her skin. "I *said*, is that clear?"

She still didn't respond. She hated him for barking orders at her and despised herself for always following them. Somewhere, she found the courage and resolve to speak her mind. To speak the truth to the bully. Maybe it came from reading about Cassie Barrett in *Picture Perfect*. Maybe the strength came from Lila Wingo in *The Prince of Tides*, or from Hadley Richardson in Paula McLain's *The Paris Wife*. Nicole didn't know. But she felt it. Inner strength like never before. She sensed that she was at a crossroads, and she was prepared to take the hard road forward. She slowly and proudly raised her chin and stared directly at the ugly, crimson face of Lee Wayne Shepherd. She ran her fingers through her highlighted strands for dramatic effect. "I like my hair just the way it is, thank you. If you don't like it, then don't look at me."

She jerked violently out of his grasp. She turned her back on him and mindlessly wiped the sink with a dishrag. She heard the rushing wind of the blow to her back before she felt it. Two more punches in the back from the irate fists of her husband, then a single blow to her head. She slumped to the floor as a dull, black pain ran through her body. She knew the drill. The bruises he left would go through their kaleidoscope of colors, from blue and purple to red, orange, and yellow, and eventually fade altogether from view. Until the next time. But this time was different. She felt she'd earned them. Even in a crumpled heap, Nicole managed to crack a thin smile. *A propane leak. A firm push above a scenic waterfall. A hairdryer in the bathtub.*

Victoria and her grandmother arrived promptly at 8:45, just after dusk, as if they'd been sitting in their house watching the second hand on the clock go around until it registered the appointed time.

Drew's driveway had been transformed into a tiny outdoor movie theater. A large white bed sheet had been tacked to the garage door. Fifteen feet away on a card table was a DVD player connected to a small projector. Three lawn chairs, the old kind with aluminum frames, green and white plastic webbing, and wooden armrests, were in place to accommodate the audience.

"Have a seat!" Drew beckoned to the arriving crowd.

"What is all this?" Victoria asked, gazing in awe.

"It's movie night. Tonight's showing . . . *Madagascar*! I hope you haven't already seen it."

Victoria's reaction was exactly what Drew had been hoping to see. He watched her eyes light up in wonder and delight as she examined the projector and the makeshift movie screen in front of it. She kept glancing his way as if to say, *you did all this for me?*

Victoria and Húdié exchanged a few questions and answers in Mandarin as Drew ushered them into their seats.

Drew had made a large batch of popcorn and divided it into three bowls, each portion slathered in melted butter. He'd also bought three boxes of Good & Plenty. The sweet licorice bites with the pink-and-white candy coating had always been his favorite movie treat as a young boy, and he was delighted to pass on the legacy.

He turned on the projector and the bedsheet came to life with movement and color. For the next eighty-six minutes, they watched the escapades of Marty the zebra, Alex the lion, Melman the giraffe, Gloria the hippo, and a quartet of cute and cuddly penguins. Drew split his attention between the action on the screen and the reaction from the audience. Victoria was riveted as if she'd never seen a movie before. *Maybe she hasn't,* Drew thought. He was certain that Húdié wasn't understanding a single word of dialogue, but seemed to be enjoying the film as much as Victoria, following her cues to laugh in all the right places.

The three generations sat quietly in the driveway and munched popcorn and candy as they watched the animated characters on the screen. Cicadas sang their scratchy songs and fireflies twinkled around them. There was nothing else going on in the entire world at that moment.

When the movie ended and Drew stood up to turn off the projector, Húdié leaped from her lawn chair and hugged him, her head barely higher than his belt buckle. She looked up at him and nodded once, then touched the bottom of his chin with her index finger and left it there for several seconds. The old woman swallowed hard, then abruptly turned and headed home. She said something in Mandarin to Victoria as she walked away, presumably along the lines of *don't stay out too late*.

Drew remained motionless, soaking in the endorphins the unexpected embrace had released in his body. "What was *that* for?" he asked Victoria.

"She misses her son."

Drew nodded as he watched Húdié disappear into her house. He understood that feeling.

A few hours later, Drew was reading in his living room. He'd made the difficult transition from a computer-animated children's movie to the raw and carnal writing of D.H. Lawrence. *Lady Chatterley's Lover*, the story of a torrid and unlikely affair between an aristocratic woman and her husband's gamekeeper, was the polar opposite of other masterworks of fiction. *War and Peace* and *Atlas Shrugged* were novels most people claimed they'd read when they actually hadn't. Conversely, *Lady Chatterley's Lover* was a book many had read but wouldn't admit they had.

The story was complex and intriguing, but the language was so coarse that Drew was regretting he'd suggested it for the Oak Island Book Club. He wondered how Nicole was reacting to it.

Curled up on her living room couch, Nicole was finding the book to be the guilty pleasure she'd hoped it would be. Constance Chatterley's impotent and ineffectual husband Clifford resonated strongly. Clifford Chatterley reminded her of a similar character in Ken Follett's *Eye of the Needle*; David Rose, a wheelchair-bound husband whose inabilities in the bedroom had driven his wife Lucy to take on a lover, even when she knew he was a German spy.

Both men reminded Nicole of Lee Wayne and the hazards of social isolation. Is that what bitter men do? Force their partners into the arms of other men as a perverse way to assuage their guilt over their manly shortcomings? Maybe in books, but not in real life. Not *her* real life, anyway. Despite his weakness as a man, she knew Lee Wayne Shepherd would eviscerate her if he had even the slightest inkling she had affections for another man. Maybe worse.

Ironically, and imperfectly, the story also reminded Nicole of Drew. Oliver Mellors, the gamekeeper, had his life turned upside down when his wife left him. He only found happiness in solitude in the deep forest. Mellors needed a woman to draw him out of his isolation. Perhaps Drew needed the same.

Despite the gripping plot, the description and language used to describe the intercourse between Oliver Mellors and Constance Chatterley made Nicole blush. "Oh my God," she whispered out loud, more than once. She was grateful she was reading the book in the dark. And alone.

She set aside the ice pack she'd been pressing to her knotted head and reached for her secret phone. She sent Drew a quick text.

This is like reading highly literary pornography.

Drew responded quickly, as if he'd been expecting, or even hoping for a text.

It's not LIKE that. It IS that! I'm sorry! You can pick next time!

Nicole sat up on the couch. Her pulse was racing from the combination of Drew's text and Lawrence's saucy prose.

I'm ALONE and I'm still blushing!

I'll be finding a cold shower shortly

She thought for a moment if she should follow up with something titillating, perhaps borderline sexually inappropriate given the mood, but thought better of it. That was a fork in the road that she knew she wasn't ready to take. Not yet, anyway. Nicole deftly changed the subject.

Will I see you in Southport this weekend?

Yes. Probably get there Saturday morning

Time for coffee?

Yes. I'll need some coffee after reading this.
It's going to keep me up late

**I'll look forward to it. What's next on our reading
list?**

I don't know. After this, I'm thinking we need
something tamer. Like maybe the Bible

I've read it. Saw the movie too.

The book is always better :)

**Have you read Shadow of the Wind? One of my
all-time favorites. I'd happily read it again.**

Great choice! I'll try to find a
copy tomorrow

**I'll do the same. I'm off to sleep. Chatterley and
Friends will have to wait.**

I'm out too. Hope all is well.
Night, N

Night, D.

She clicked off the phone and pressed the ice pack against
her aching scalp. All was *not* well, but she sensed it was about
to get better. Soon. As always, reading would take her mind off
the throbbing pain.

Miles away, Drew closed his book and slid onto his living
room floor. He made it to nineteen pushups before tiring. A
cold shower would do him good.

CHAPTER TWENTY

"Books are mirrors: you only see in them what you
already have inside you."

— Carlos Ruiz Zafón, *The Shadow of the Wind*

When Nicole walked into the NICU early Friday morning for her volunteer shift, Lyla was sitting in her wheelchair next to the incubator that baby Cody called home. It was empty.

"Good morning, Lyla!" Nicole said as brightly as possible. "Where's Cody?"

"The doctor took him for some tests. I'm just waitin'."

Nicole felt alarmed. "Was it something serious?"

"They didn't say."

"Do you know how long it's going to take?"

"They didn't tell me that either. Makes me worry."

Nicole looked at her watch. "You want to grab a cup of coffee while you wait? My treat."

"Sure."

Nicole pushed Lyla's wheelchair into the hallway and over to the elevators, where they would go down to the ground floor to a coffee shop.

Moments later, they sat together at a table in the corner. Nicole with a small vanilla latte and Lyla with a large cup of black coffee.

"So, how are you feeling?" Nicole asked, pointing to Lyla's forehead. "Healing up?"

Lyla shrugged. "Little by little."

"That must have been quite a tumble you took down the stairs."

"Yeah," Lyla mumbled, as she looked into the swirl of her coffee. "Yeah, it sure was."

Something about the tone and the vagueness of Lyla's response seemed irregular to Nicole, but she quickly dismissed it. "There's lots to do when you have a baby coming home."

"I'm findin' that out. You have kids?"

It was Nicole's turn to look down at her coffee. "No. Never blessed with a child."

"Well, I didn't plan on this one, but now that he's here, I'm really excited."

"Is your nursery ready?"

"My daddy is at home right this minute puttin' up the crib. There ain't much room in my trailer for a baby, but I guess we'll manage."

That slight unnerving Nicole had sensed just moments before returned. This time the picture was clearer. She looked up at Lyla, then back down at her coffee. "If you don't mind me asking, Lyla, how did you fall down the stairs if you live in a trailer?"

Lyla hesitated. It was clear she was trying to come up with a plausible explanation. "It was the steps leadin' up to my front door."

Nicole nodded. "I see." There was a long, awkward pause as suspicion as to the true origin of Lyla's injuries hung in the air like the smoke from a distant campfire.

"You know . . ." Nicole delivered her words quietly and carefully. "The first day I met you I noticed some bruises on your neck. The kind of bruises that you don't think anyone will notice, because they usually don't." Nicole took the white napkin on the table in front of her and held it to her own neck. She wiped away a thick layer of concealing makeup, exposing the unmistakable choke marks that could only be caused by a violent hand. "Bruises like these." She paused, then leaned closer to Lyla. "You didn't fall down the stairs, did you?"

Lyla swallowed hard. Her eyes started to glisten with tears. She shook her head as she tried to explain, as much to herself as to Nicole. "He didn't mean to do it. He just went a little crazy. He was just overwhelmed by the baby comin' and all."

"And was it the first time?"

Lyla shook her head. "No."

"And do you think it'll be the last time?"

Lyla again shook her head. "Don't expect so."

"You know there's help if you want it, Lyla. All you have to do is talk to one of the social workers here and they'll find a way to get you out. You need to do that, not just for you, but also for Cody. It's not safe."

Lyla nodded in agreement, then suddenly looked puzzled. "But wait. You—" Lyla pointed to the fresh bruises on Nicole's neck.

"I know," Nicole confessed, cloaked in shame. "I know."

Drew held onto the bicycle as long as he could, but as Victoria picked up speed, it was time to let her go. He sent her off, hoping the helmet clamped onto her head was enough to protect her. She wobbled down the street and nearly toppled over as she made a wide turn in the cul-de-sac, but managed to remain upright. She was grinning from ear to ear as she made her way up a slight incline and back to Drew.

"Keep pedaling!" he called out to her.

Victoria nodded, concentrating mightily on pumping her legs while maintaining control of the handlebars. She made a circle, then another, and another. The more she rode, the steadier she became. Drew stood on the sidewalk and admired his pupil. He felt like Professor Henry Higgins with Liza Doolittle. It had taken two hours of him running alongside her and several near-miss crashes, but by George, she'd finally gotten it.

Victoria was now singing to herself as her tiny legs propelled her in circles around the cul-de-sac. She was not one to be underestimated.

Nicole glanced at the clock on the shelf. It was 3:00. She figured she had another hour to sew and clean up before the sickening bellwether of the garage door opening, signaling the intrusion of Lee Wayne. But it was Friday, and that meant her interface with him would only be brief before he set sail for Oriental and she would be free to flee to Oak Island.

The fabric running underneath the dancing needle of her

sewing machine was a turquoise brocade, medium weight. She was working off her own design for a cocktail dress with a scoop neck and a hemline that would finish just above her knees. She'd seen something similar in a catalog that was selling for nearly three hundred dollars, but Nicole figured she could make it herself for about forty.

She could feel the warmth of pure joy running through her veins as her creation took shape. She didn't know if she had been born to envision designs and transform them into dresses, but she knew she was more than capable of doing it, as capable as anyone who had their name stitched on a designer label. She allowed herself a wandering daydream of her creations gracing the glossy pages of *Vogue* or *Elle* next to other fashion icons. Leggy models swiveling down runways in Paris and Milan, or starlets sauntering across red carpets in Cannes, wearing the latest Nicole Shepherd.

These weren't wild, unattainable fantasies in her mind. These images were dreams she thought she could have realized, had she been given the opportunity, like an obscure musician who rockets to fame when the right person hears his or her songs. But instead of seeking notoriety for her genius, she fashioned together pieces of cloth with thread in the obscurity of a tiny bedroom, worried that someone might find out what she'd been doing with her time. She glanced at the clock again, knowing that sense of joy and those distant dreams would instantly vanish the moment her husband came home.

Her two hours of bliss were gone before she knew it. She'd been happily lost in her sewing when she suddenly heard the garage door open, snapping her back to reality like someone turning on bright lights in a bar at closing time.

She quickly shut down her sewing machine and shoved all evidence of her work into a drawer. She padded quietly into the kitchen and started cleaning a coffee pot that didn't really need cleaning.

"I'm home," announced Lee Wayne as he walked through the door. He entered the kitchen holding a large white shopping bag.

"Oh, hi," she said with mock surprise. "I didn't hear you come in. How was your day?" she asked blandly.

He didn't respond to the question, but instead reached into the shopping bag and removed a full-length fur coat. He held it high in front of her. It was mostly white with random black splotches. "It's snow leopard," he said proudly. He walked behind her and fanned it open. "Here. Try it on."

Nicole's heart sank as she slipped her arms into the sleeves. She detested fur on several levels, especially for humane reasons. The coat was thick and bulky and fell nearly to her ankles. She felt like a cross between an overfed Dalmation and a giant skunk.

Lee Wayne stood back and beamed. "Wow. What a beautiful coat! You like it, don't you?"

Nicole smiled wanly. "It's very nice."

"My office party is coming up and you need to wear this. It'll impress everyone."

Nicole stared at her hand as she reluctantly stroked the fur of one sleeve. "It will make quite the impression. Thank you."

"Well, I gotta go pack." With that, Lee Wayne abruptly left the kitchen.

Nicole closed her eyes and tried to process the whirlwind of what had just happened. She hated the coat and the thought of having to wear it to an office gathering made her ill, never mind that it would be in the middle of summer. She took it off and draped it over a kitchen chair, shaking her head. She closed her eyes and ran the tip of her middle finger down her forehead to the bridge of her nose and back again.

Drew carried the brimming watering can over to Húdié as she surveyed her lush garden. He handed it to her, only allowing a few drops to slosh out of the top during the transition. He was amazed by her strength as she gently gave each of her Chinese pepper plants a rain shower, knowing the line between too much water and not enough. The plants were now nearly a foot high and a foot wide, and most of the peppers were transitioning from milky white to pale yellow.

"Guess what?" came an excited voice from the house. Drew turned his head to see Victoria racing toward him, as animated as he'd ever seen her.

"Let me guess, you've won a Nobel. Or a Pulitzer. No, wait . . . both!"

"No, even better!" She was already next to him, nearly dancing with excitement.

"What's the good news?" Drew asked.

Victoria's hands were gesturing nearly out of control as she delivered the update. "Okay, you know that I'm not a great basketball player."

Drew hadn't wanted to confirm her suspicions. "Go on," was all he said.

"Well, the track coach saw me running up and down the court at basketball practice and she wants me to try out for the Cross Country team in the fall!" Without warning, Victoria flung her arms around Drew's waist and hugged him mightily, pressing her cheek against his torso.

Drew patted her gently on the back, nodding his head. "That's great, Victoria. I mean really great. I'm proud of you."

She pulled back and looked up at him. "And you know the best part?"

"What's that?"

"Now you can teach me how to run!"

He laughed out loud. "What's to teach? You just put one foot in front of the other. The faster you do that, the more ribbons you take home. Simple."

"There's a lot more to it than that. I need you to teach me. I know you know how."

"What makes you think that?"

"I Googled your name. You ran track at the University of Virginia. Half-mile. Second team All-Conference, whatever that means."

"It means I wasn't as fast as the guys on the first team. And that was a long time ago."

"Maybe, but I'm pretty sure it's a lot like riding a bike. And you did a great job teaching me how to ride a bike."

Drew was exceedingly impressed at how this young girl had just converted a trite metaphor into a winning argument. He figured it wasn't by accident. She continued to stare up at him with pleading eyes. He glanced briefly at the heavens, exhaled loudly, then looked back down at the girl still clinging to him. "Fine. We'll start Monday."

"Thank you!" She squealed and hugged him tightly again. "Thank you!" She abruptly pulled back and looked up at him. "Wait, why Monday? Why not start tomorrow?"

"Because I'm going to the beach tomorrow. Which reminds me, I need you to take in my mail and water my plant."

"Watering is an extra fifty cents."

"That works out nicely."

"What do you mean?" she asked.

"Because my running lessons are also fifty cents."

"I didn't agree to that."

Drew shrugged. "You don't expect me to give away my services for free, do you? Like you said, this is America."

Victoria thought long and hard. "Okay, I guess that's fair. But only if you promise I'll be better at running than I am at basketball. I want a money-back guarantee."

"Deal," he said with a wry smile. They fist bumped as if she'd been doing it all of her life.

As Drew returned his attention to the pepper plants, Victoria took on a serious look. "Can I ask you something?"

"You may."

"Why do you go to the beach so much?"

He chuckled slightly. "Why do you ask so many questions?"

"I'm serious. What's at the beach?"

Drew's smile faded. He paused as he mulled over his reply. "I'm not entirely sure," he told her. "I think maybe I'm looking for something."

"Looking for what?"

He shook his head as he dropped to his knees in the dirt of the garden and affixed the lower branches of the pepper plants to the stakes. "I honestly don't know. But I feel like I need to keep looking."

Victoria nodded, deeming that an acceptable answer. "When I searched your name, I also read a newspaper article about your wife and daughter. I'm sorry. I know that made you sad."

Drew nodded. "It did. Still does."

"Google also says you write books," Victoria said.

"Used to. Not anymore."

"Why'd you stop?"

"There are a lot of people asking me that same question."

"So what's the answer?"

"I just don't feel like it."

"Why don't you feel like it?" she asked.

"That's also a very good question. Another one to which I don't have a good answer."

Victoria nodded again. "Perhaps you'll find the answer at the beach."

Drew stood up and swallowed hard. His eyes moistened with the tears of ancient sorrow. He walked over and wrapped his arms around Victoria's tiny neck. "Let's hope," he said, in a voice that sounded less than hopeful.

CHAPTER TWENTY-ONE

"If you don't like to read, then you haven't found the right book."

— J.K. Rowling

The sun was beating down on Southport on Saturday morning and despite a northerly breeze, the oppressive humidity was winning the day. Drew and Nicole had rendezvoused by the Southport water tower. She'd arrived first, having made the short drive over from Oak Island after spending the night at Teri's beach house.

The very first thing Drew did as he approached Nicole was to compliment her new haircut. She made a full spin to show off the back of her head and when she faced him again, he gave her a warm embrace that lingered just a fraction longer than a simple friendly hug. His praise was genuine, as was her appreciation. It was impossible not to compare how the eyes of two different beholders had looked at her.

They decided against coffee and chose instead to get ice cream cones. They captured the slow drips with their tongues as they sat down on a wooden bench in a park by the water overlooking City Pier. They sat in silence until Nicole finally chimed in.

"Okay, I don't think we can avoid it any longer. Are we going to talk about *Lady Chatterley's Lover* or is it just too embarrassing?"

Drew measured his words before giving his review. "I'm going to say that I liked it, but didn't love it. Wasn't crazy about the ending. But I'm still glad I read it."

Nicole nodded. "I agree. It was entertaining. Held my interest, especially in certain parts, except it was hard to get through. I had to keep stopping and looking up all the strange words Lawrence uses like 'pilchard,' 'bounder,' and 'arriviste.' Slowed it down too much."

"You looked up all those obscure words? Why? Most people just skip over them."

Nicole dabbed off her upper lip with the flimsy napkin from the ice cream parlor. "You want to know why I look up the words? I'll tell you why. Because when I was first married to Lee Wayne, he and his smug law school friends used to toss around ten-dollar words in front of me, knowing full well I had no idea what they meant. They'd manage to work in words like 'ersatz' and 'soporific' and 'moribund' into the conversation, words normal people never use. I grew up with people who use words like 'kinfolk' and 'yonder' and 'reckon.' You know, plain speak. If something is laughable, then it's *laughable,* it's not *derisible.* You know what I mean?"

"I reckon I would have to agree," Drew said with a trace of self-amusement.

"The whole purpose of their little game was to make this country girl feel stupid, which it did. So I took to going home and looking up all their fancy words, plus a few more. Pretty soon I had a better vocabulary than they did."

"And that carried over into your reading?"

"Exactly. So now I look up every word I don't know. Try getting through Pat Conroy doing *that.*"

"Perhaps you should hit Lee Wayne with the word 'longanimity.' "

"Exactly," Nicole agreed. "Long-suffering." She took a bite of her ice cream and talked with her mouth full. "What an idiot I married. Correction, *I'm* the idiot for marrying *him.*" She shook her head, pondering mistakes she couldn't undo. "Anyway, back to this book. There are parts that really made me squirm. I can't imagine how that was received back in 1928."

"Not very well," Drew said. "Except for the people who were actually brave enough to read it. The publisher was still getting sued in 1960 for obscenity. Back then, the whole thing made everyone uncomfortable."

"It wasn't just *then*," Nicole added. "Even now, anytime you talk openly about sex it makes people uncomfortable."

"That's because sex is an impossible subject for men," Drew said. He broke eye contact, then gazed out into the distance, the way people do whenever they're discussing something sensitive or embarrassing.

"Why do you say that?" she asked.

"Because women hold all the power."

"I'm not sure I agree."

"Think about it. If men talk about sex too much, we're accused of having a one-track mind, or worse. Our motives are questioned. 'You only want me for sex' is about the worst thing you can say to a man if he truly loves you. It's like a man telling a woman 'you only love me for my money.' In her mind, that's not true at all, but how do you prove that? How do you convince a woman that she's wrong about your intentions? How do you let her know that you want sex because it's just another way to express how much you love her?"

"But that's not true with a lot of men. Maybe even most men. They just want to be physically satisfied."

"I'm not denying that. But what about the man who truly wants to feel an emotional connection through a physical act? It's not as rare as you might think. But getting a woman to understand that is almost impossible. For whatever reason, she'll always have that nagging doubt that all the man wants is a physical release. And so the man keeps his primal desires in check because he doesn't want her to ever think the worst. But the flip side of that is just as bad, maybe worse."

Nicole raised one eyebrow, mulling it over. "What's the flip side?"

"What if the man shows no interest in sex? What signal does *that* send? That I don't find you attractive anymore? I don't desire you anymore? You don't please me anymore? I don't love you anymore? You certainly don't want your partner thinking any of *that*, and so you constantly walk this tightrope between coming on too strong and keeping your distance and hoping for the best. Like I said, women hold all the power. By the way, I speak on behalf of all men when I tell you these things. It's a universal truth that we all agree on. In fact, it's the *only* thing we all agree on."

"You've clearly given this some thought."

"I have lots of time to think. Am I wrong?"

"It's never good to generalize. I would argue that there are plenty of exceptions. The ideal situation would be two people who want sex in equal amounts, at approximately the same time."

"Good luck with that."

Nicole shrugged. "I think it's possible."

He gave her a sideways glance before returning his gaze to the water. "How so?"

"Commitment. Trust. And that only comes with time."

"You don't think a man and woman can trust each other from the beginning?"

"I don't know. I would say it's more difficult for a woman. Especially if she's had a bad experience with sex. Even one. Think about it . . . when you were seventeen, no woman ever came after you for your money. Girls can't say the same thing about the intentions of young boys."

"True. But we're not teenagers anymore."

"But for women, that feeling of mistrust never completely goes away. We're always wondering about intentions until finally, we're not. At the end of the day, it's all about trust."

"Do you think you'll ever get there? To that point of complete trust in a man?"

"Doubtful."

"Why not?"

"I'm damaged goods. Too much water under the bridge. Or over the dam. Whatever it is they say about water."

"And we're back to the aquatic metaphors."

"They seem to apply."

"Well, I'm no expert, but I believe everyone deserves a partner who wants sex because they love you and respect you and want to show you in more ways than just flowers and jewelry and Hallmark cards. I think it's possible."

"Perhaps," Nicole said with a slight shrug.

"Well, at least we've gone from 'doubtful' to 'perhaps' in the last few minutes. Perhaps we should leave it there."

"Perhaps."

Drew stood up and swallowed the remainder of his brittle sugar cone. "Well then, I think we've covered that subject sufficiently. Wanna go read on the beach?"

"Love to," she said as she cleaned the sticky remnants of ice cream from her fingertips. "I'll see you there in half an hour."

"It's a da—" Drew quickly caught himself before the last word escaped his mouth. "It's an *appointment*," he said, with emphasis. His face had reddened slightly.

Nicole smiled. "An appointment it is," she replied.

Drew waved with two fingers and turned to leave. He was dying to see the expression on her face but was too embarrassed to turn back around.

Back in his room at the Riverside Motel, Drew changed into his bathing suit. Before putting on his shirt he dropped to the floor and counted off thirty painful pushups, then rolled over and did fifty sit-ups just for more punishment. Temporarily exhausted, he stood up and checked his shirtless profile in the mirror over the dresser. Better, but still pathetic. At least he was making an effort. He would mark that down as progress.

Forty minutes later, Drew and Nicole were sitting next to the water on the sands of Oak Island. Their beach chairs were in close proximity and angled slightly toward each other, but not so much as to be misconstrued as anything more than convenience for conversation.

They were both holding used copies of *The Aviator's Wife* by Melanie Benjamin. The fictional biography recounted the life of Anne Morrow Lindbergh, wife of Colonel Charles Lindbergh. What at first seemed like her flawless fairytale marriage to the world's most celebrated hero had descended into heartbreak, riddled with catastrophe caused by external forces outside their union and by cruelty from within. Anne Morrow's hopes and dreams had been eclipsed by the overbearing drive of her famous spouse. Despite her own intelligence and capabilities, she had lost her identity in the kingdom of Lucky Lindy. Forever a co-pilot, forever Mrs. Lindbergh, forever a footnote.

Books have a way of speaking to the reader with exactly the right words at precisely the right time in their lives. In the turning of four hundred pages, it is often just one paragraph or even just one sentence that speaks the loudest and bravest and becomes the single takeaway from the long investment of the reader's time. Nicole had reached exactly that point in

The Aviator's Wife. The words leaped off the page. *Dreams may have been the paintings on my walls, but doubts and fears were the bars on my windows*, echoed the voice of Anne Lindbergh. Nicole rested the open book on her knee and let her mind drift back to her cramped sewing room and the unrealized dreams of *Vogue* and *Elle*. *What a waste,* she thought, as she added up the sum total of her life's accomplishments. *I have so much to offer. What a terrible waste.*

"You okay over there?" Drew asked.

It took a moment for his words to penetrate her consciousness. "What?" she said, snapping back to the moment. "Oh, yes. Fine. Just taking a little break."

"You enjoying the book?" he asked.

"Very much. I haven't had to look up a single word. How about you?"

Drew didn't want to answer honestly. He loved the writing, but some of the themes and the parallels to Charles Lindbergh made him uncomfortable. A celebrated husband so wrapped up in his work and fame that he neglected the most important aspects of his life. And a child taken away. It made Drew uneasy to read it. He then drew comparisons to Nicole's life, living with an overbearing husband and no dreams to call her own. "I'm enjoying it," he said in a monotone voice. He marked his place and quickly changed the subject.

"Do you have dreams?"

"Dreams," she repeated. "About what?"

"Things you want to do. Places you want to go."

Nicole laughed. "I'm afraid that ship has sailed, Captain."

"Surely you have some great white whale you'd like to chase."

"That sounds very 'Melvilleian,'" Nicole said.

Drew looked at her with narrowed eyes. "Is 'Melvilleian' even a word?"

She shrugged. "If it's not, it should be. If 'Hemingwayesque' or 'Shakespearean' are valid words, then I think 'Melvilleian' also qualifies."

Drew nodded in agreement. "It fits. So answer the question . . . dreams?"

Nicole set her open book in her lap and took a moment to gather her thoughts, unsure how much she wanted to reveal. She stiffened slightly and shook her head. "No. Not anymore." She returned to her book but Drew could sense that she wasn't reading it unless it was between the lines.

He let the moment pass and drummed his fingers nervously on the arm of his chair. "Any chance you'd like to have dinner tonight? All that talk about Melville put me in the mood for shrimp."

"I'd love to, but I have to get home. Lee Wayne's office party is tonight."

"Oh," Drew said, almost inaudibly. He tried to be nonchalant, but his voice dripped with disappointment. "Didn't know you weren't staying."

"I'm sorry. Wifely duties."

Drew nodded and attempted to return to his book, but nothing was registering. He marked his place and leaned his head back over the chair. "I know it's not really my place, but honest to God, I don't see why you stay with him."

She snickered. "You and everybody else who's ever met him."

"Then why? He's a bully. Why don't you leave?"

"It's just not that easy. Everyone thinks it is, but it's not. If I'm being honest, I'm just too scared to venture out on my own. And maybe I feel sorry for him in some way. I'm all he's got." Nicole wasn't sure she believed that last excuse herself, but it made her sound more noble than feeble.

Drew shook his head. He didn't agree with any of her reasoning but knew it was out of bounds to press the argument. A long silence lingered between them. There was much more each wanted to say, but they were both feeling a certain safety in silence.

Drew turned to look at Nicole. As if on cue, she looked up from her book and met his silent gaze. He felt something rising up inside him that he hadn't experienced in a long time, maybe ever. It was something between wanting and worry, between desire and jealousy, between love and lust. He wasn't sure what it was. He only knew that it was getting stronger.

"I—" he started, without really having formed a sentence in his mind. He felt like he wanted to say something, *needed* to express himself, but couldn't find the right balance between honesty and regret.

"What?" she asked, wondering why he'd cut his sentence short. "What were you going to say?"

Drew shook his head as if confused by his own outburst. "Nothing. It's just that I enjoy our conversations. I hope they're not too personal."

She smiled warmly. "You're fine." She held his gaze for a few more beats, even past the point of feeling awkward. She looked down at her watch and exhaled as a way of putting a punctuation mark on the exchange. "I should be going."

Drew nodded in agreement as they both got up from their chairs.

Nicole collected her belongings, then leaned over for a brief embrace. "I loved sharing. All of it."

"I did too," Drew said. "Best book club meeting I've ever attended."

"I would agree." Nicole smiled, then turned and made her way back across the sand. In a matter of moments, she would be gone.

Drew could only watch her walk away, wondering if it were really true that some things are better left unsaid.

CHAPTER TWENTY-TWO

"Some books leave us free and some books make us free."

— Ralph Waldo Emerson

Nicole studied herself in the full-length mirror. Despite a few encroaching lines in her face caused by matrimony and acrimony, she liked what she saw in her reflection. She'd lost a few pounds in the right places, the muscles in her arms had a better tone, and the summer sun she'd allowed to lightly kiss her skin during her trips to the beach had given her a healthy glow.

The turquoise dress she'd just finished sewing fit perfectly, one of the benefits of having a very close relationship with the seamstress. She smoothed out a slight wrinkle on her left hip. Lovely in the eye of the beholder.

She absolutely detested Lee Wayne's office parties. Nothing but lawyers speaking in legalese about litigation and liability. The only sector of the legal code that currently intrigued her was divorce law. So, if she was going to be forced to endure another "bar exam" as she liked to call it, she was going to look her very best. As she looked at herself in the mirror she felt as though she'd achieved that.

Lee Wayne appeared in the reflection behind her.

"You're not wearing *that* are you?" he asked.

"What's wrong with it?"

Lee Wayne pointed to her scoop neck, which barely revealed

her cleavage. "I'm not gonna have every guy in the room leering at my wife like she's some tramp. Do you intentionally try to humiliate me, Nicole? What were you thinking?"

Nicole tried to hide how wounded she was. "I thought it looked nice."

"You thought wrong. If I see that dress again you better be using it to wash my car. Now go put on something that won't embarrass me. And don't forget to wear the fur coat I bought you."

As he walked away, she now felt more angry than hurt. The thought of stabbing him in the back with sharp shears flashed through the reckless part of her brain. But she was too weary to fight. She would dutifully go to the closet and change.

Lee Wayne was long past over-served when he spotted Nicole from across the hotel ballroom having a conversation near the dessert table with a man he didn't recognize. The laughs they shared between them angered Lee Wayne, enough to where he was determined to put an immediate stop to it. He pushed his way through the party to get to the other side of the ballroom, spilling nearly a third of his vodka tonic in transit.

"Who the hell are *you*?" Lee Wayne growled on approach.

Nicole's heart sank as she saw her husband crash onto the scene. "Lee Wayne—" she whispered loudly, trying to defuse the impending bomb that was whistling their way.

The startled man turned to greet Lee Wayne, a polite party smile still covering his face. "I don't think we've met. I'm Davis from bankruptcy. I'm new." He extended his hand but Lee Wayne ignored it.

"Davis from bankruptcy," repeated Lee Wayne in a mocking tone, nodding his head and sizing up his adversary. He took a drunken sip of his vodka. "Well, you *must* be new."

The smile had left the man's face. "I'm sorry?" Davis turned to look at Nicole and then to the other partygoers nearby who had now turned their attention to the bellicose Lee Wayne Shepherd. "Am I missing something here? Is this a prank on the new guy?"

"You know how I can tell that you're a newbie, Davis from bankruptcy?" Lee Wayne walked over and draped his arm around Nicole's shoulder. Mortified, her head slowly dropped and her eyes bored holes in the floor below her. "Because anybody who's been with the firm any length of time knows better than to hit on my wife."

Davis took a step backward, as his eyes grew wide and he held up his open palms. "Whoa! Wait a second, pal. I wasn't doing any such thing!"

"First of all, I'm not your *pal*, and second of all, I can tell when a guy is hittin' on my wife. I saw all the chit-chat and all the giggling goin' on between you two."

"Lee Wayne—" Nicole said, her eyes still fixed on the floor.

"Shut up!" he barked. "I'll deal with you later."

"Look, I don't know what your problem is, but we were just talking about the desserts, and that's *it*. I didn't say one word that was inappropriate."

"So why all the giggles? What's so funny about dessert?"

Davis hesitated, looking at Nicole for help. She didn't move. "I simply said something about the cheesecake. That it's not really cheese and it's not really cake. And she said, 'yeah, kinda like Grape Nuts.' And that was it, I swear it."

Lee Wayne took his arm off Nicole and started circling Davis like a predator. "You two are just a regular comedy team, aren't you? Like Simon and Garfunkel come back to life."

Nobody corrected him, least of all Davis.

"You know, Davis from bankruptcy, there's nothin' funny about dessert. Nothin' at all. Look what all that cheesecake and ice cream has done to my wife here." Lee Wayne craned his neck to peer down at Nicole's backside "I like to call her Crisco. You know why, Davis? Because she's fat in the can. Get it? Fat in the can? Now *that's* funny!" Lee Wayne slapped Nicole across the rear end and lifted his head to expel a vodka-fueled belly laugh. The gesture brought audible gasps from both the men and women who had circled up to watch the spectacle.

Embarrassed beyond words, all Nicole could think to do was flee. She ran across the ballroom and burst through the nearest exit to escape the madness. She stopped to swallow two deep breaths, then took off her heels and moved as quickly as possible to her car. She was only halfway there when she realized that in her haste to leave she had left her purse and her coat inside the hotel. She didn't care about the coat, but the purse was a problem. No keys, no phone. She stopped running and walked in solemn resignation the rest of the way to the car. She would have to wait there for however long it took for Lee

Wayne to arrive, and for whatever punishment he wanted to dispense.

She put her head on the cold metal of the hood of the car and cried from her chest. *A carbon monoxide leak. An accidental shooting. An insanity defense.*

"Why do you do that to me?" Nicole pleaded as she leaned her head against the side window on the ride home. She looked as wounded as she sounded.

"Do what?" Lee Wayne asked, scrunching his forehead.

"Humiliate me like that! That was *awful* what you did to me in there!"

"I don't know what you're talkin' about."

She whipped her head around to face him. "Are you *serious*? You *really* don't know? You called me 'fat' in front of everyone!"

"You're overreacting. I was just kiddin' around. Can't you take a joke?"

"It's not funny, Lee Wayne! You don't say that about your wife, not even in jest. And *especially* not in public! And you weren't joking. You did it just to be mean. No other reason."

The drunken grin on Lee Wayne's face instantly vanished. Without warning, he reached over with his right hand, grabbed a handful of Nicole's hair, and jerked her closer to him. "Mean? You think I'm mean?"

She was wincing in pain. She grabbed his wrist with both hands to try to ease his grip on her scalp but said nothing.

"Answer me! You think I'm mean? You think a mean person lets you live in a half-million-dollar house and buys you a fur coat and a fancy luxury car?" He yanked on her hair again. "Is that what you think?"

"I think you need help. I think you have problems you can't fix by yourself."

"Oh, so now you think I'm crazy? *You're* the one who's hysterical and you're callin' *me* crazy?" The sudden backhand slap on the side of her temple was just a taste of the justice Lee Wayne intended to mete out once they were home.

Lee Wayne pushed Nicole through the front door and slammed it behind her, sealing off the rest of the sane world. "You embarrassed me tonight!" yelled Lee Wayne through gritted teeth.

Nicole's eyes widened as she shook her head. "I embarrassed *you*? Are you serious?"

"Yes! First with your shameless flirting and then storming out on me! Why do you do this to me, Nicole? Why do you always make me so angry?" Building into a rage, he immediately tore off her clothes and threw her onto the couch. He put his full weight on top of her and had his way with her, as ugly men do. It was brutal and barbaric. Primal urges were unleashed, uncaring about anything other than hormones and physical release. Most of all, it was a raw display of dominance and control.

She submitted, helpless to fight back. Drew was wrong. When it came to sex, women didn't have all the power.

Lee Wayne's appetite for anger had not been sated. He stumbled into the spare bedroom and wrapped his sweaty arms around Nicole's sewing machine. He nearly fell backward as the cord remained plugged into the socket, but he yanked it free and staggered into the hallway. Hoisting the sewing machine up over his head like a weightlifter, Lee Wayne flung the machine as far as he could into the living room. It smashed onto the hardwood floor, cracking plastic and twisting metal before finally sliding to rest against the wall.

The crash snapped Nicole's head around, but she otherwise didn't move. What was done was done. She dropped her head again in quiet resignation.

"That's *my* contribution to the fashion world," Lee Wayne slurred. He looked triumphantly at his misdeed. The tantrum over, Lee Wayne retreated to the bedroom.

Nicole wrapped a blanket around her nearly naked body and walked over to the fractured sewing machine. She picked up its wrecked casing like someone trying to salvage a precious keepsake from the rubble of a tornado. Like so many other things in her life, it was irreparable. She let the broken parts fall slowly to the floor as she dropped to her knees and slumped against the wall. She curled into a ball and softly cried herself to sleep.

Waking after several hours, Nicole raised her bruised head and blinked hard to clear her blurry vision. As if guided by some external force, her eyes immediately caught sight of her St. Nicholas doll standing firm on the table across the room. He had seen the trauma she had just endured. For some odd reason, Nicole was embarrassed that he had to witness that. She stood and walked slowly over to the doll, lifting it off the table and stroking the soft fur of his coat. Despite the wounding he had just watched, Father Christmas was still smiling. He had traveled with Nicole on every painful journey of her life, shared every sadness, including the one tonight, and yet he was still smiling. She clutched the precious doll to her chest. It gave her comfort. It gave her hope. It gave her strength. The kind of strength she was going to need to get through the next ten minutes of the unending misery of her married life.

With a sudden impulse, she returned the doll to the table and turned quickly down the hall into their spare bedroom. First, she put on the handmade turquoise dress she had been forced to abandon a few hours earlier. Second, she flung open the closet door and snatched a small suitcase from the floor.

Moments later, she had barged into the master bedroom where Lee Wayne had passed out in what few articles of clothing he hadn't tossed aside during forced intercourse. Nicole flicked on the light and yanked open the drawers on her dresser. She began filling the suitcase she'd placed at the foot of the bed with clothes. The commotion was enough to wake Lee Wayne from his brooding sleep.

"What the hell are you doing?" he snarled, raising himself onto his elbows.

"I'm leaving you!" she screamed. Nicole had just spoken to Lee Wayne with more force than she ever had in her life. Her reservoir of fear was evaporating. Her anger was fueled by a new inner strength, galvanized by a resolve she didn't know she possessed.

"You wouldn't dare!"

"Watch me! By tomorrow morning I will have a divorce lawyer and I promise you that she will be ruthless, whoever she is."

Lee Wayne started to laugh. Not the laugh of someone finding humor in the situation, but a sardonic roar intended to project superior knowledge and belittle the others in the room, like a mad king watching a serf hopelessly battle a lion. "You can't divorce me," he said in an amused stupor.

"I can, and I will. I don't care about your money and I don't care about this house or anything in it. I am a caged bird no longer." She kept packing with greater intensity.

"And I'm tellin' ya, you can't divorce me," Lee Wayne said in a more menacing tone. He swung his legs onto the floor and stood up, momentarily bracing himself with one hand on the nightstand.

She stopped shoving her belongings in her suitcase and turned to face him. The smug look was still splashed across his face. "And why's that, exactly?"

"Because we're not actually married."

The words hung in the air like the stench of rotting meat. Nicole blinked hard and gave her head a hard shake as she tried to comprehend the bombshell revelation of the drunk wobbling in front of her.

"Say that again?" was all she could think to say.

"I said, we're not actually married."

"What do you mean?"

"I mean we're not legally husband and wife. So you can't divorce me. Sorry." He spit out a single burst of laughter.

Nicole still couldn't grasp what Lee Wayne was presenting to her. "But we *are* married, Lee Wayne. We had a wedding, we had a reception, your friends were there. Are you too drunk to remember all that?"

"Oh, I remember. And a helluva reception it was."

"Then what are you saying?" she asked, her frustration growing.

"I'm sayin' that all that pomp don't amount to anything if you don't have the paper."

"Paper? What paper?"

"The marriage license. I told the magistrate who performed the ceremony that I needed to make a quick copy of the license for insurance purposes, but I never mailed it in. Therefore, this union, or whatever you want to call it, is not official. Not legal. Uncertified." Lee Wayne took a measure of joy in revealing his secret.

Nicole was horrified. "You *forgot* to mail our marriage license?"

"Oh, I didn't forget. I just didn't mail it."

Nicole braced herself against the dresser to steady her wobbling knees. Her eyes burned at him as they narrowed with incomprehension. She lowered her voice to where it almost sounded calm. "Why not, Lee Wayne? Why didn't you mail it?"

"Because of this exact situation."

"What do you mean? What situation?"

"Just in case you ever tried to leave me. I didn't want you to get half my stuff. Especially since you didn't earn it."

Nicole closed her eyes and let her forehead sink into her palm. "Leave you? *Leave you?* Are you *kidding* me? I've suffered under you for years but I stayed with you! I stayed through it all! I don't know anyone else who would have! Not for one day, much less thirteen years! And you think I didn't *earn* it? I have hundreds of cuts and bruises that say I earned every penny."

"As if you had a choice," muttered Lee Wayne. "You have no job skills." He raised his arms to highlight his dominion. "You wouldn't have *any* of this without me. *Never.*"

"You're right, Lee Wayne. I would have never had *any* of this without you." Nicole slammed a few more items into her bulging suitcase and half-zipped it closed, just enough to keep things from falling out. She whisked the suitcase off the bed but suddenly stopped.

"Wait," she said, her mind putting puzzle pieces together. "Is that why I wasn't allowed to see your medical records at the hospital?"

"I'm amazed you figured that out. Did you never notice that your name wasn't on the mortgage, the car titles, the insurance, bank accounts, nothin'? It's like you don't even exist."

Nicole's anger was boiling over to the point of uncontrollable rage. And it was more than just anger. She felt utterly foolish for having been so naïve. She knew she had to leave before her crashing emotions got the better of her. She snatched her keys off the dresser.

"This won't stand," she barked at him. "I'm going down to the courthouse tomorrow morning and straighten this out."

"Good luck. The magistrate who performed our ceremony is dead. So it's like it never happened. And the state of North Carolina doesn't recognize common law marriage, so you're pretty much screwed."

"You won't get away with this."

"I do believe I already have. So feel free to leave me, but you'll walk out of here with no money, no credit, no health insurance, no nothin'. And if you ask me, you're a little too old to be startin' over."

Nicole had no reply. It was all true. His words had intended to hurt her, and they'd found their mark. She fought off the trembling in her body, not wanting to give him the satisfaction of watching her wilt.

"I need to go." She grabbed her suitcase by the handle and burst out of the bedroom. Lee Wayne waved her away as if to say *suit yourself.*

Nicole was heading for the front door when she abruptly stopped. She ran back to the bookshelf and snatched away the hollow copy of *Crime and Punishment,* then rescued Father Christmas from the side table. She clutched them both to her chest and marched out the front door.

As she drove away, Nicole wiped away a wave of blinding tears. She gathered herself enough to dial Teri's number.

Teri answered on the second ring. "Hey, sweetie!"

"I did it," Nicole said. "I left him."

There was a long silence. "Oh, honey, I know that was hard, but I'm so proud of you. Are you okay?"

"I will be."

"Where are you? What are you doing? Do you need a place to stay?"

"I'm driving back to Oak Island and wanted to make sure I could stay at your house."

"Of course, darlin'. Anything you need. What else can I do?"

"That's all. I just need to get away."

"I understand. Just do me a favor and call me when you get there. I just wanna know you got there safely."

"I will. I love you, Teri."

"I love you too, hon. And sweetie? It's all gonna be okay."

"I know. I know. Thanks."

"Make sure you call me. You know I worry."

"I will. Goodnight."

"Night, sweetie."

Nicole hung up. She would cry all the way to Oak Island.

CHAPTER TWENTY-THREE

"Reading is like thinking, like praying, like talking to a
friend, like expressing your ideas, like listening to
other people's ideas, like listening to music, like
looking at the view, like taking a walk on the beach."

— Roberto Bolaño

Nicole blew her nose three times and took a deep breath.
She sat on the edge of the bed in Teri's beach house
as she dialed Drew's number in the dark. Twice she
started to hang up but held on as the phone rang nearly ten
times.

"Hello? Nicole?" Drew asked, sleepily.

"I came back to Oak Island. Would it be out of line to ask
you to come over?"

There was a long pause before Drew answered. "What's
wrong?"

Nicole's voice cracked as she started to talk. "I'm just very
upset right now and I need someone to calm me down."

"I'll be right there. Give me a minute to get all these people
out of my room," he joked.

Nicole laughed through her approaching tears. "Thank you,"
she whispered into the phone, then disconnected. She tossed the
phone onto the bed and fell backward onto the plush mattress.
She stared at the ceiling, wondering how her life had gotten so
jumbled.

◆ ◆ ◆

Twenty minutes later, Drew and Nicole were reclining in chaise lounges on the back deck of the Oak Island beach house, staring up at the canopy of twinkling stars. There was barely enough wind to move a candle flame. She'd poured them both a glass of Pinot Grigio which they sipped quietly, nearly in unison. The rhythm of the waves calmed Nicole as much as just having Drew nearby.

She still hadn't shared with him what was troubling her, and he had the wisdom not to pry. The truth was, she really didn't think she could tell him what had transpired earlier that night between her and Lee Wayne, for two reasons. First, she would look incredibly foolish for having been duped all these years, even though her husband was as dishonest and duplicitous as they come. Second, she was worried that if Drew found out she wasn't legally married, it might somehow alter the dynamic of their relationship. He had become a trusted friend and she cherished the cerebral and Platonic nature of their connection. She didn't want to do anything that might jeopardize that.

She finally broke the silence. "Remember that little poem from Maya Angelou's *I Know Why the Caged Bird Sings*? 'The caged bird sings with a fearful trill, of things unknown, but longed for still, and his tune is heard on the distant hill, for the caged bird sings of freedom.'"

"You memorized it," Drew said, still staring skyward. "Why?"

"Because that's how I feel. Caged up. Trapped. Somewhere inside me, I know I have the ability to spread my wings and fly, but I know I'll never get out of this cage."

"Lee Wayne?" It was all Drew said. It was all he *had* to say.

Nicole nodded, more with resentment than resignation. "I hate him."

"Hate's a strong word."

"So I've been told, but it'll have to do until something stronger comes along. Right now, I can't think of any word stronger than hate, so I'm forced to go with hate. If an emotion worse than hate is invented, then I'll trade up. But for now, it's hate."

Drew chuckled, then stopped himself. "I'm sorry. I don't mean to laugh."

"It's okay. It's all laughable. Or should I say *derisible?*"

They both snorted with laughter. Each took a healthy sip of their wine.

"What exactly does he do that makes you dislike him so much?"

Nicole took another sip of Pinot as she pondered her answer. She couldn't tell him the truth, at least not the ugly truth. She couldn't tell him about the beatings, or the shaming, or the myriad of emotional abuses he concocted. But there was still enough hatred, on enough levels, that she could start small and work her way up. "Once, just for fun, I left a note out next to the fireplace for Santa Claus. Thought it would add a little holiday spirit."

"And?"

"Lee Wayne made some corrections to my grammar with a red pen."

Drew winced and scratched the back of his neck. "Not good."

She continued. "He'd always wear his law school T-shirt to rock concerts as if he thought Springsteen or Elton John would be impressed by his higher education. I couldn't stand that. And he's always rude to waitresses. I hate that too. It's just his petty way of exerting power over someone who's helpless to fight back. It's like living with the Great Santini, except without the military medals. The great irony is that he's a personal injury lawyer. Represents it at work, inflicts it at home."

Drew sat up slightly, his concern deepening. "Has he ever hit you?"

She didn't answer directly, but her eyes darkened as she stared into deep space. No answer was answer enough.

"I don't want to pry, but I suspect there's a lot more going on in your life that you're not telling me. More than just that he's rude to waitresses. I sense a much deeper pain."

"It's not pleasant, so I don't like to talk about it. Not just with you, but with anyone."

"I understand. I'm just saying that when you're ready to talk about it, I'm ready to listen."

Nicole nodded with acceptance. There was a lengthy silence that Drew didn't dare disrupt. He sensed she wanted to say more, and he intentionally created a void in case she wanted to fill it. A muffled yelp escaped her throat as she suddenly started to weep. She tried to dab away the tears from the corner of her eye, but it was futile. The sadness was flowing faster than she could brush it away.

Drew quickly went inside the house and immediately returned with a handful of tissues. Nicole took one and wiped the moisture from her eyes even as she continued to cry. As she brushed the tissue across her left cheekbone she winced, enough for Drew to notice.

Alarmed, Drew knelt down next to her and strained to get a better look at her face in the dim light of the deck. The makeup she'd hastily applied to cover the bruising from Lee Wayne's backhand earlier that night had been wiped away in the facial tissue.

"Oh my God," Drew gasped. He reached up to touch Nicole's face but she instinctively pulled back.

"It's nothing," she declared firmly.

"Don't tell me that. Clearly, it's not."

"I'm fine. I really don't want to talk about it."

Drew stood up, torn as to how to proceed. His primal instinct was to drive directly to Belville and inflict some serious bodily harm on Lee Wayne. Beyond that, he *certainly* wanted to talk about it, but he also wanted to respect her wishes. He was also learning that with Nicole, prolonged silence was often a better prompter of conversation than prying questions. He stretched out on his chaise lounge, folded his hands over his stomach, and waited. If she wanted to open up to him, he would let her do it on her schedule.

After nearly ten minutes of mutely staring at the dark sky, Nicole finally shook her head with simmering anger. "I hate everything about him," she blurted out. "I hate Lee Wayne Shepherd with every muscle in my body. I sometimes lift weights with the idea that it makes my muscles stronger just so I can hate him harder. I *hate* that man," she reiterated with inflamed emphasis. She glanced over at Drew for some reaction, then refocused on the sky above her. "Sorry. That just sorta spilled out."

"It's okay," he replied as gently as he knew how.

"No, no it's not. I think I've said the word 'hate' fifteen times tonight. You must think I'm an awful person."

"I don't. I think you're *married* to an awful person. And I can tell it's been building up. It's good that you let it out. That much hatred can be destructive. It'll eat you up from the inside."

"Too late. I'm empty inside. There's nothing left to destroy."

"I disagree." He rolled halfway over to look directly at her. "There was another line in Maya Angelou's book that I loved. It was something like 'pursue the things you love doing, and then do them so well that people can't take their eyes off you.' Words to that effect."

Nicole tilted her head sideways. Her gaze met his. Their visual connection lasted just slightly longer than it probably should have. She turned back and looked up into the night. "Meaning, you think I should flee my cage and fulfill my destiny? Something like that?"

"Something like that."

"Easier said than done. You're not married to a vindictive lawyer," she muttered. *Actually, neither am I*, she thought. *Maybe he's right. Maybe.*

"Was there ever a time when he was good to you? Must have been if you married him."

"Oh, absolutely. When I first met Lee Wayne, he was like Prince Charming. He was so confident and intelligent and witty and just oozed success. He had this natural charisma, this magnetism about him that was irresistible, like a huge bowl of chocolate ice cream, and I wanted to eat as much as I could before it melted away. He would buy me gifts and take me to concerts and fancy restaurants, places I'd never dreamed of going. He would do these wonderful impulsive things like buy me flowers from a street vendor or hand a homeless guy a twenty-dollar bill. I loved it. One of the things I found most attractive about him is that he would sit and listen to me as if he were mesmerized by my every word. It was this major 'charm offensive' that swept me off my feet. He drew me into his amazing world and I gladly followed." She looked away, biting the inside of her cheek and shaking her head. "Knowing what I know now, he might as well of had the word 'narcissist' tattooed on his forehead. All the signs were there, all the red flags, but I either didn't see them or chose to ignore them. I was young. Naïve, foolish, stupid, whatever you want to call it. I thought he was my golden ticket, but I could not have been more wrong." She turned her eyes back to Drew. "You eat too much chocolate ice cream and eventually you come to hate chocolate ice cream."

"Do you think you could ever reclaim some of that magic? Do you even want to?"

"I don't know. I keep hoping I can change him. Take him back to what he used to be when we were dating. We'll see." She pivoted onto her side as she changed the subject. "Were you a good husband?"

"No," he shot back with a quick shake of his head before the question had even left the air.

"That was fast. You didn't even have to think about it."

"Oh, I've thought about it. I've been asked that question before. A million times over."

"By whom?"

"By *me*. And the answer is always the same. I was a lousy husband."

"Why do you say that?"

"Because it's the sad truth." Drew looked away and stared into the blank space in front of him. "I wasn't terrible. I was kind, I was a good provider. I truly loved her. But I wasn't there for her or my daughter, in mind or body. I was always on a book tour, or at some conference, or sittin' around with my pretentious cronies talking about the next great novel we'd write. Jesus, what a grand waste of time." Drew slowly shook his head from side to side with remorse. He clicked his tongue against his teeth. "I was always out chasing that great white whale." He returned his gaze to the empty sky. "Bottom line, if you asked me what was my wife's favorite kind of ice cream, or her favorite color, or favorite book, I couldn't tell you. That sorta sums it up." He looked back at Nicole. "What's the opposite of a stay-at-home dad? I was a stay-*away* dad. Especially on the one day they needed me most." He laughed sardonically at his own failings. "So, no, I was not a good husband."

The crashing waves filled the brief silence until Nicole spoke. "May I ask you something else?"

"Sure. Why not."

"Why do you come to the beach?"

"You've asked me that before."

"I know. I just wondered if your answer had changed. If it's more than just to torture yourself."

Drew hesitated before answering. "In all honesty? Lately, I come here to see you. To talk about books."

"But you were coming here before you met me. Why?"

Drew waited thirty heartbeats before answering. He scratched his fingers through his hair. "I guess I'm not really sure. I suppose it's to find some answers. Some closure. Don't honestly know. Maybe I'm hoping this is all just a bad dream and that I'll wake up and see them standing there in the sand. Maybe it's just to punish myself for all the mistakes I made so I can start healing. And on some days, the darker ones, I consider finding my own riptide I can wade into the middle of and leave this nightmare behind."

"You don't seriously think about suicide."

"I confess that it occasionally creeps into some of the shadowy corners of my brain. Not as much as it used to, but it's still there. I've imagined what my own funeral might look like. All the nice things that my friends might say about me after I've departed, assuming I have any friends left. One of the sad truths about life is that people always wait until after you're dead to tell you what they think about you. By then it's too late. So yeah, I've thought about it. It tends to be a common trait among novelists."

"Is it just grief or are there other forces at play?"

Drew bobbed his head to the side. "Maybe a little guilt tossed in there too, but mostly grief. It's relentless, like those waves you're hearing right now. The grief just keeps crashing down on top of me, and some of the waves are bigger than others. I keep asking myself, is there ever an end to bereavement? Does it come with an expiration date?"

"It just takes time, Drew. There's no other answer."

Drew nodded in agreement. His rational mind knew that. His heart had not yet reached that understanding. He glanced sideways at Nicole. "What about you?"

"What about me?"

"Have *you* ever thought about suicide?"

She shook her head. "No. *Homicide* a few times, but never suicide."

They both laughed at the macabre joke. Drew let the smile fade away. "Seriously, have you ever thought about murdering Lee Wayne?"

"Not seriously, no. But not unseriously."

"Unseriously? Is that even a word?"

"Not sure, but it works in this case. I will admit, after certain events, I've wished something bad would happen to him. More along the lines of some outside force, some kind of *deus ex machina*, like a lightning bolt or a city bus, something that intervenes on my behalf and takes him away. That way he's gone, but I don't have to do prison time. Although sometimes I think prison might actually be better than living with him."

"Remind me not to cross you," Drew said with a wry smile.

"And remind *me* to say nice things about you before you kill yourself."

Their soft laughter floated away into the salt air. They went quiet, each absorbed in their own thoughts for a few moments as they wrapped themselves in the soft velvet of the humid night. As they gazed at the stars, they shared the same view but with opposite perspectives. Drew looked into the past, while Nicole looked into the future.

"You ever think of books as medicine?" Drew asked. "That the words and actions of characters that someone else invented, and thrust into a story, somehow have healing powers?"

Nicole shrugged. "I suppose I never really thought about it in that way. What made you ask that?"

"I was just thinking. A few years ago I read this book, *The Little Paris Book Shop*, by Nina George. It's essentially the story of a man who runs a bookstore out of a barge on the Seine in Paris. It's more or less a literary apothecary. He dispenses books like medicine to people who are struggling with some aspect of their lives. I think the author was trying to say that if you read the right books, you get the right answers."

"Books as therapy," Nicole said. She tilted her head and nodded. "I can see that."

"There was a sentence in the book I loved. It was advice from one of the bookseller's friends. It said something like 'spend time with people who are friendly and seek to understand you in their own particular way.' I thought that was brilliant advice."

"What made you think of it just now?"

"Because it's been a long time since I did that. Spent time with friendly people."

Nicole exhaled heavily. "I'm not sure I ever have. Just once in my life, I'd like to have a friend who completely understood me. Not just liked me or enjoyed my company, but *really* understood what makes me tick."

"What about Teri?"

"I love her, but we're just different. Life seems to come easy to her, so I tend to keep my problems to myself."

Drew paused for a few thoughtful moments before answering. "I believe you'll find that person. Just keep looking."

The silence returned as they both wandered away again into their private thoughts. Drew finally stood to leave. "I should be getting back. I'm heading home in the morning. You feel better?"

"Much. Thanks for coming over. I needed it."

"It was good for me too."

Nicole stood and smoothed back her hair as she faced Drew. "So, what's our book club's next read?" she asked.

"I was thinking about *The Bell Jar*. Sylvia Plath."

Nicole grimaced. "A book about suicide? Seriously? Let's find something else."

"Good thinking." He paused for the briefest of moments, not sure what to do next. It seemed like an appropriate moment to embrace, even if it were just a friendly hug, but he feared how long it might last and where it might lead. He slid open the glass door and stepped into the house. "Goodnight, Nicole."

"Goodnight, Drew."

He nodded and vanished, gently closing the door behind him. She stood in place and heard the front door shut, then the ignition turning on his car, and finally the sound of four wheels rolling away into the night. *Why didn't I marry someone like him?* she thought, as she stretched back out on the chaise lounge and scanned the skies. She wondered again why she hadn't confessed to Drew that she'd left Lee Wayne.

Drew couldn't sleep when he returned to the Riverside Motel, and he didn't know why. To relax his mind, he read *The Aviator's Wife* deep into the night. It was page 333 that spoke to him in the quiet. *Jealousy is a terrible thing*, Anne Morrow Lindbergh wrote. *It keeps you up at night, it demands tremendous energy in order to remain alive, and you have to feed it, nurture it — and by so wanting, you have to acknowledge that you are a bitter, petty person. It changes you. It changes the way you view the world.*

Drew rested the open book on his chest. *Oh my God*, he thought. *I'm jealous! I'm jealous of Lee Wayne Shepherd!* Drew got out of bed and paced the floor, pushing his sweaty hair back with his fingers as he tried to come to grips with his epiphanic insight. *I'm not jealous of the man himself,* Drew thought, shaking off the thought. *He's abusive, he's a bully, he's weak and uninteresting. I despise him, even though I've never met him. No, I'm jealous because he has the one thing that I desire. Nicole.* The thought of it was unsettling. Drew had never remembered feeling jealous before. He'd always believed it was the lowly domain of the bitter and petty, just as Anne Lindbergh had stated. So maybe it wasn't true jealousy. Maybe it was something else. But what? What raw emotion had him pacing the floor in a tiny motel room at two o'clock in the morning? He stepped outside and gazed up at the waxing moon, searching for answers. He had no way of knowing that at that very moment, twelve miles away, the other half of the Oak Island Book Club was doing exactly the same thing.

CHAPTER TWENTY-FOUR

"Books are the quietest and most constant of friends;
they are the most accessible and wisest of counselors,
and the most patient of teachers."

— Charles William Eliot

D rew's legs felt heavy the next day as he ran through the neighborhood streets with Victoria. His heaving lungs, burning at their core, and the fountain of perspiration from his brow reminded him of just how far he had allowed himself to physically decline. He glanced over at Victoria, who appeared as though she could run all day, even in the heat of early summer. He pointed to the next intersection. "Maybe we should turn here and head for home," he said with great effort.

"Why?" she asked.

"You look tired," Drew said between gulps of air.

She cocked her head and examined him. "You look awful."

Drew rolled his eyes with a *yeah, well* expression, more or less agreeing with her assessment of his current condition. When they entered the intersection Drew made a hard right, heading back to their houses. Victoria reluctantly followed.

When they arrived home, Húdié was on her knees in the garden carefully uprooting plants that looked like pale white carrots and placing them in the wooden basket next to her.

"What are those again?" Drew asked. Sweat dripped from his brow.

"That's daikon," Victoria answered.

"That's right. You said it's like a white radish?"

"Exactly. Grandmother calls it *bailuobo*."

Recognizing the word, Húdié turned and handed Drew one she had just picked, brushing off some of the dirt still clinging to the skin. "*Chi, chi*," she told him as she repeatedly moved her fingers toward her mouth.

Drew looked at the radish with skepticism, rolling it around in his fingers.

"She wants you to eat it," Victoria said.

"I know she does. I'm just not sure that's a good idea."

"*Chi!*" repeated Húdié, still gesturing.

Victoria nodded in accordance. "Grandmother will be insulted if you don't eat it. It is a gift from her garden."

With both of them staring at him with eager anticipation, Drew realized he didn't have much choice in the matter. He cleaned a little more dirt off the daikon, then nodded to Húdié and took a bite. It had the approximate texture of a raw McIntosh apple, crisp but not tough. Drew's eyes widened slightly as he chewed. He found the daikon to be slightly bitter, with a prickly astringency that triggered small bumps on his tongue. Húdié and Victoria were watching his reaction intently. Drew swallowed a few times, rocking his head back and forth as he formulated his review. He wanted to be honest without being insulting.

"It's . . . uh . . . wow. What can I say? I would describe it as, uh . . . tangy. Pungent is another word that comes to mind." *Vile might be more apt*, Drew thought, but he swallowed those words along with the rest of the radish.

Húdié whispered something to Victoria, who translated. "She wants to know if you like it."

"Do I like it? Uh . . . I would have to say . . . yes." He held up the daikon and nodded his approval. A full smile blossomed across the old woman's weathered face. Drew looked at Victoria and motioned his head toward Húdié. "Tell her it's the best daikon I have ever eaten."

Victoria passed along Drew's praise in Mandarin, then translated Húdié's response. "Grandmother says food brings people together."

Drew looked at the daikon and moved his head in a circular motion, something between an agreeable nod and a respectful shake. *This sure doesn't*, he thought. *This makes me want to stay away.*

Húdié gathered up a handful of the white radishes and placed them in a small basket which she handed to Drew with a slight bow of her head. She mumbled a few words in Chinese and gestured to Victoria to relay the message.

"Grandmother also says they will help you lose weight and that you could stand to drop a few."

Drew cocked his head slightly and let loose a wry smile. "How diplomatic of her."

Húdié passed along another message to Victoria. "And Grandmother says if you cook it and make it into a soup it will help a hangover."

Drew laughed out loud. "She said that, did she?"

"Yes," Victoria said. "Also, what's a hangover?" she asked.

"It's a curse. Something aspirin companies invented. That's all you need to know." Drew looked at his full basket. "I better get going. I have lots of daikon to attend to. Tell your grandmother 'thank you' for my gift."

Drew turned to Húdié and bowed slightly. "*Xièie,*" he told her, gesturing to the daikon in his hand. She crinkled her face into a smile and clasped her hands together in front of her chest, pleased with the exchange.

Drew looked back at Victoria. "And you might want to remind her that even though it's her garden, if you stop and think about it, I did all the work getting it ready. Tell her that."

Victoria and Húdié exchanged a few sentences in Mandarin. Victoria reported back to Drew. "She says she knows." The old woman broke into a toothy smile. Drew couldn't help but laugh. With every joint, muscle, and tendon in his lower body starting to bark at him, Drew hobbled home.

A few minutes later, standing at his kitchen counter, Drew rinsed the dirt off another daikon radish and took a bite. He washed it down with several gulps of cold tap water. It was definitely an acquired taste, but he might get used to it over time. He'd managed to do it with single malt Scotch, so he knew he had it in him.

Without much forethought, he moved a bottle of bourbon from the countertop to an upper cabinet and quietly closed the door. Out of sight.

◆ ◆ ◆

It was later that night, after a sensible meal of grilled chicken on a bed of baby spinach, that Drew had settled into his easy chair with a worn paperback edition of Michael Shaara's *Killer Angels*. Most of his body was feeling the effects of running for the first time in years but a couple of Advil had taken the edge off. Noticeably missing from the scene in his living room was the cocktail glass that was usually sweating with condensation on the side table. It had been replaced by a plastic bottle of water.

Drew had visited Gettysburg on a field trip in elementary school but couldn't remember anything about it except a few songs they sang on the bus ride there and home. Now, after reading Shaara's Pulitzer Prize-winning account of the epic Civil War battle, he yearned to go back and meet all the ghosts of history that now roam the quiet fields and forests of southern Pennsylvania. He hadn't mentioned to Nicole he was reading it, only because he wasn't sure how she felt about bloody battle scenes. In hindsight, he wished he had, so they could be enjoying it together.

It was the recurring theme of "moving forward" that made the greatest impression on Drew as he read the detailed accounts of brutal victories and defeats. He couldn't help but marvel at the courage it must have taken for the soldiers at Gettysburg, many of them just teenagers, to charge headlong through the choking smoke of rifle and cannon fire to risk life and limb for a cause in which they believed, even if many of them were fighting for the wrong side of history.

It reminded him of another book he'd read years ago, *The Bedford Boys*, by Alex Kershaw, the story of nineteen young men from the same small town in southern Virginia who had all died on a beach in Normandy during the first bloody minutes of D-Day. Farm boys jumping off Higgins boats into the roiling waters of the English Channel and charging across foreign sands under blistering German gunfire, intrepidly moving forward while their brothers fell around them.

Drew propped the open book on his knee and stared at the ceiling. The image of young soldiers bursting out of the woods and across the open fields of Gettysburg reminded him in many ways of *The Boys in the Boat*. They were all pressing on into the unseen and unknown. Drew again considered the moldering state of his own inert existence, treading water in a stagnant pool. It was like driving across the middle of Texas. You try to move forward but the scenery never changes and it never feels like you're making any progress.

Drew gave himself a modicum of credit for at least taking a few small steps forward in recent weeks, but in the quiet hours of the night, when self-appraisal is the most honest, he knew he was still languishing in his misery. He closed his eyes and prayed something would jolt him out of the doldrums and push him to move forward, like rowers, like soldiers, like anyone with a purpose and an unburdened heart.

His phone *dinged*. A warm smile covered his face when he read the text.

> **Can't sleep. I need a good book to help slow down my brain. What's next for the OIBC?**

Drew debated whether or not to tell her about *Killer Angels*, but decided it was too late. It felt like watching a recorded episode of a television show without telling your spouse.

> How about Love in the Time of Cholera?
> Gabriel Garcia Marquez?

> **I've heard it's astonishing, but I can't remember what it's about.**

Drew thought carefully before typing his response, not wanting to add too much subtext.

> I think it's about two people who spend years looking for their soul mate

There was a long pause before Nicole's response chimed in.

> **Sounds intriguing. I'll swing by tomorrow and look for a copy.**

> I'll do the same. You still in Oak Island?

Yes. And I will admit it's a bit lonely here tonight.

She debated whether or not to tell him about her separation
from Lee Wayne. A large part of her wanted him to know, if
for no other reason than to show someone in this world she'd
found the strength to finally break free. On the other hand, she
knew that revealing the truth would further complicate their
already undefined relationship and she wasn't sure she was
ready for that. And dropping a bombshell like that in a text, or
even over the phone, was unfair.

Drew pinged in.

> **Know the feeling. Perhaps that's why we're
> not sleeping?**

It seemed to Drew that it was an inordinately long pause
before she came back to him. Maybe just his imagination.

> **Perhaps.**

> **I'll sign off and give you a fighting chance.
> Goodnight, N**

> **Night, D. And remember... the best pillow is
> peace of mind.**

Drew silently agreed, but left it there. If only he could find
peace again.

He marked his place in *Killer Angels* and set it on the side
table, then ambled off to his lonely bedroom.

Miles apart, in separate beds and separate worlds, Nicole
and Drew both fought for sleep, but their active minds
overrode their weary bodies. They were discovering that it was
impossible to doze off when you're trying to decide what you're
going to do with the rest of your life.

CHAPTER TWENTY-FIVE

"What a blessing it is to love books."

— Elizabeth von Arnim, *The Solitary Summer*

The first light of day had yet to burn off the dew from the lawns as Drew and Victoria ran at a brisk pace through their neighborhood. The lightness in their legs and their unlabored breathing were clear indicators that their level of aerobic fitness was improving after just a week of running, especially his. The soreness in his hips and legs had subsided and his knees no longer felt like rusty door hinges.

As they entered an intersection, Victoria motioned forward with her hand to indicate they should take on more miles before making the turn for home. Drew grinned at her eagerness and nodded his approval, even picking up the pace a little. *Moving forward*, he thought to himself.

This has to be more than just luck, Nicole thought. A tiny shop that sells sewing machines just five minutes from Teri's beach house. *This has "meant to be" written all over it*, she thought.

Oak Island Sewing Machines was in a modest house on a wooded lot at the end of 4th[h] Street. It was part retail shop and part museum, filled with new and used machines from every era, including high-end models that could stitch sailcloth, if that was what you needed.

"Anything I can help you with today?" An older man looked up from the sewing machine he was repairing under a bright light on his workbench. "My name's Sal," he said in a friendly voice that carried the accent of a New York transplant.

His name fit him so perfectly that Nicole might have guessed it without knowing. He had the white hair and short beard of someone in his early seventies, and glasses that he wore near the tip of his nose.

"I'm Nicole. I need a new sewing machine."

"The old one finally give out on ya?" He wiped his hands on a small towel as he moved out from behind his work-bench.

"You could say that."

"I also do repairs. Maybe I could save you some money."

Nicole smirked, but only to herself. "I would say it's beyond repair."

"What are you looking for?" Sal asked, moving closer to the tables filled with various models on display.

"I'm not exactly sure. May I just poke around?"

"Take your time. It's a very personal decision, so let's make sure you get the right one."

"Thank you," Nicole said. It felt comforting to be treated nicely for a change when it came to her passion.

After perusing the selections for close to half an hour, Nicole finally settled on the one that suited her needs. It was a heavy-duty Singer with thirty-two built-in stitches, automatic needle threader, and capable of over a thousand stitches a minute. The sturdy metal frame looked like it would last forever. That is unless someone pitched it across the room.

"How about this one?" she asked.

Sal nodded his hearty approval as he walked over to Nicole. "This is one of my best sellers. You're gonna love it. Comes with everything except its own tailor." Sal carried it to the counter and carefully set it down. He perched his glasses on the tip of his nose and checked the price tag. "With tax, it'll come to $198.22."

"You take a credit card?" Nicole pulled her card from her purse and handed it over.

"Sure do." Sal slid the card into his reader and waited. The message on the screen made him furrow his brow. "Hmmm," he mumbled. "That's odd." He tried to run the card again.

"What's wrong?" Nicole asked as she leaned over to get a closer look.

"It's saying 'card declined.' Let me try again. I've been having some trouble with this machine."

Even though Sal was determined to get the card to register, Nicole knew immediately what was happening. In fact, she'd expected it, just not this soon. Lee Wayne had canceled her credit cards. She was equally angry and embarrassed. "Must be something on my end. I'm so sorry to have wasted your time." She took her card back from Sal and returned it to her purse. She kept her head down to hide the tears of humiliation that were pooling in her eyes.

"I can take a check," Sal said brightly.

"I don't have a checkbook," Nicole said, growing more embarrassed by the second. She rummaged through the billfold in her purse. "I only have cash. Forty-two dollars, to be exact."

Sal's New York street smarts provided him with a good grasp of the situation. He could intuit Nicole's pain and discomposure. "Tell ya what," he began, as he moved out from behind the counter, "I've got a nice Singer 6234 over here that's been refurbished. Not quite as many bells and whistles as the other one, but she gets the job done. I can let you have it for, let's say, twenty-five bucks. That includes tax. It's my early bird special," he said with a twinkle in his eye.

Nicole looked at the sewing machine. A little scuffed in places, but still in good shape. She also noticed the price tag of seventy-five dollars. "You're undercharging me. By quite a bit."

"It's fine. My job is to make sure these babies find a good home, and I'm quite sure that's where this one will end up."

Nicole swallowed back tears, deeply touched by his kindness. "At least let me give you forty-two dollars."

Sal held up his hand as he shook his head. "Nope. Twenty-five it is, and that's my final offer. You can spend the rest on fabric." He flashed an impish grin as he picked up the Singer 6234 and walked toward the door. "Cash and carry. You give me the cash, and I'll carry it out to the car for you!"

Moments later, Sal had loaded the sewing machine into the passenger seat of Nicole's car and even fastened the seatbelt around it. "You take good care of her," he said to Nicole, giving the stalwart Singer a gentle pat and then closing the door.

Nicole nodded as she handed him the money, then hugged him mightily. "I will," she whispered. "And thank you."

Sal gently patted her on the back. "And take care of yourself, too."

Nicole was unable to say anything more. She let go of Sal, brushed aside a tear from her smiling eyes, then climbed in the car and slowly drove away. She glanced over at the sewing machine and gently stroked its housing. *Meant to be*, she thought.

Nicole reached through her car window and slid her plastic card into the flashing slot of the ATM machine. She pressed the keypad to enter her PIN number, then selected an amount to withdraw. The message that popped up on the screen seemed as though it were scolding her: *You have insufficient funds for the amount requested. Your balance is $00.00. Would You Like Another Transaction?* She stared at the screen for several seconds until it dawned on her what had happened. Obviously, Lee Wayne had drained the money from their joint account and put it in a place where she didn't have access. Her chin dropped to her chest. She ran her trembling fingers across her forehead and into her hair. His meanness knew no bounds.

She retrieved her worthless card and drove off, her chin quivering from a mixture of fresh worry and enduring anger. The daunting realization was growing of how difficult it was going to be to strike out on her own without any money. The small amount of cash she'd squirreled away over the years was quickly running out.

Nicole glanced at the sewing machine in the passenger seat and found comfort. She gripped the steering wheel a little tighter, determined to find a way.

CHAPTER TWENTY-SIX

"What really knocks me out is a book that, when
you're all done reading it, you wish the author that
wrote it was a terrific friend of yours and you could
call him up on the phone whenever you felt like it.
That doesn't happen much, though."

— J.D Salinger

The blender on Drew's kitchen counter was filled with various ingredients for a healthy shake, a radical departure from the cinnamon rolls or frozen sausage biscuits he'd been eating every morning for the last few months. He'd just dumped in a handful of frozen blueberries when his phone rang. The call was from a familiar number.

"Hi, Nicole!" he said, standing up a little straighter.

"Hi," she replied, one hand on her phone and the other holding the steering wheel. "I'm driving up to Wilmington this morning. I'm filling in on a shift at the NICU. Do you think we can have lunch before I go back?"

"I'm sorry, but I can't. I have to visit my mother."

"Oh. I see," Nicole replied flatly.

Drew could hear the deflation in her voice. "That's not a lame excuse. I'd *love* to have lunch with you, but I honestly have plans to visit my mother."

There was a long pause. "What time?" she asked.

"One o'clock."

"I'm finished at the NICU at 12:30. Would it be okay if I go with you?"

"You don't want to do that. Trust me, it'll ruin your day. My mother can give aspirin a headache."

"I'd really like to meet her. Please? Might help me figure you out."

"I'm not sure I approve of that plan. I'd like to remain a man of mystery."

Nicole pressed on. "Where should I meet you?"

Drew exhaled slightly in surrender. "How about I pick you up at the hospital. Main entrance, say around 12:45?"

"It's a date," Nicole said with a refreshed amount of cheer in her voice. "I finally get to meet the parents!"

Drew just laughed, unable to offer a comeback. "I'll see you at 12:45."

"See you then."

Drew disconnected and smiled. He couldn't remember the last time he'd been on a date. *Not that this was a date*, he reminded himself. Nonetheless, it still brought him joy. He dropped in a few chunks of daikon from Húdié's garden and topped off the blender jar with a handful of fresh kale. "Kale?" he muttered to himself. "Really? Who eats kale?" He snapped on the lid and turned it on, watching the blades churn up a green gloppy mess. "Apparently *I* do." Drew shook his head in disbelief that this was something he was about to ingest. Then again, with a visit to his mother in the offing, it might not be the worst thing he had to stomach that day.

Nicole lightly brushed the tip of her index finger against Cody's tiny chin. The human touch in just the right place always brought a smile to his face and subsequently to hers. Maybe it was her imagination but it seemed to her that she always had a uniquely calming effect on the baby boy. As she glanced around the NICU she saw that other infants were bawling despite their cuddler's best efforts to soothe them. She couldn't help but wonder what kind of mother she might have been, had she been given the proper chance. Based on her semi-maternal bond with Cody, she imagined she would have done well.

She looked at the clock above the nurses' station. Two hours with a precious child had flown by.

♦   ♦   ♦

As they drove away from the hospital, Drew gave a sideways glance over to Nicole in the passenger seat. "This is your last chance to bail. I can drop you off at a nice coffee shop and pick you up after the carnage."

"You shouldn't be so pessimistic."

"I'm just realistic. Years of evidence to support me."

Nicole turned her gaze to the side window, lost for a moment in the blur of trees, traffic, and telephone poles in her peripheral vision. She spoke in a subdued tone. "You know, Drew, you really ought to be grateful that you even have a mother."

Drew glanced over at Nicole, trying to gauge the depth of her meaning from the pensive look on her face. She continued, unsmiling. "You've always known who she was and where she was and what she was doing. Not everybody is given that privilege. You may have your differences, but at least you know."

Drew opened his mouth to respond, most likely with a sniping comment about his mother's disposition, but immediately thought better of it. He looked straight ahead as the car moved forward down the road. "You're right," he said, quietly.

Gloria Endicott was sleeping in her crimson silk robe when Drew and Nicole entered her room. His gentle knock on the door had not roused her, so he lightly shook her elbow. "Mother?"

She awoke with a start but actually smiled when she saw who was standing at the edge of her bed. "Hello, Drew," she said weakly. "I'm glad you could make it." She turned and glanced at the clock on her nightstand, but made no mention of the time. Gloria looked much worse than the last time he'd seen her, which was only a week ago. Her skin was pale and her eyes were sunken, ringed by chestnut brown circles. "Was there traffic?" she asked.

Drew knew that question was code for *why are you late?* and so he pretended it didn't register. He'd brought an arrangement of Peruvian lilies for this exact moment, and he placed the vase on her nightstand. "Thought you might enjoy these. Probably need a little more water."

Gloria gave the flowers a quick examination and nodded her approval. For the first time, she noticed that Nicole was in the room. She sat up straighter and smoothed back her hair, turning on a practiced smile. "And who might *you* be?" she asked Nicole, extending her right hand to be taken.

"I'm Nicole Shepherd," she said, reaching for Gloria's hand and shaking it lightly. "I'm a friend of Drew's."

"Oh," Gloria said. Her rehearsed charm escalated. "Of course! He's told me a lot about you."

At least two of the people in the room knew that wasn't true, but it seemed easier to move forward rather than correct Gloria's claim. Drew had heard his mother tell so many white lies in social settings that he wasn't sure if this was another case of deliberate misinformation or if Gloria was remembering something that never actually happened.

"That's nice to hear," Nicole said, glancing over at Drew and smiling with a warm twinkle in her eyes. She was saving the day and Drew already knew he wouldn't be able to thank her enough once they left this room.

"You know that my son is an author," she said to Nicole.

"Yes ma'am. He's very humble about it."

"Have you read his latest, *Tears of the Sycamore*?" she asked.

"No, not yet." She shot another quick glance at Drew. "But I hear it's very good."

Gloria sat up even straighter before responding. *Here it comes*, Drew thought. *We're done with civility for the duration.* Gloria surprised him. "Oh, it is! Extremely complex characters. Similar to something Hemingway or Faulkner would create. You really have to read it several times to appreciate the intricacies of the relationships."

Drew was shocked by what had come out of his mother's mouth. He'd never heard her lavish any sort of praise on him, especially when it came to his talents as a writer. *Was it part of a charm offensive on Nicole? Or was it possibly genuine admiration for his work?* Given their history, only the first theory seemed plausible. But perhaps he was wrong. Perhaps she was softening. Perhaps she knew something about her future she wasn't sharing.

The rest of the conversation focused on undemanding topics. The weather, the new mall being built, the rising price of gasoline, or anything else to avoid a lull. Most of the threads of discussion ended with Gloria complaining that nobody was doing anything about the situation, especially the humidity.

Drew tapped the top of his wristwatch within Nicole's line of sight, indicating it was time to get going. "We should probably take off, Mother. It's getting about time for your lunch, I suppose."

"The food here is terrible," Gloria said with a dismissive flip of her hand. She turned to Nicole. "Honestly, you would think that for all the money I spend in this place they could make me a decent corned beef sandwich."

"It was nice to meet you, Mrs. Endicott," Nicole said.

"So nice to meet you," answered Gloria. "Drew could use a few more friends like you."

"Goodbye, Mother," Drew said as he stepped forward to the bed. "I'll be back soon."

Gloria beckoned him closer with the wave of two fingers. She reached up and touched the side of his face, a gesture he had never experienced before. "You know, Drew… you're a good boy. I love you." She said it almost as if she wanted it to be the last thing he ever heard her say. To Drew, it felt something akin to an apology, like putting a pretty bow made of satin ribbon on a box full of broken glass.

"I love you too, Mother." He bent over and gently kissed the top of her cheekbone. If this was truly goodbye, then he wanted to wrap it up with his own pretty bow.

Drew and Nicole sipped iced tea and ate pimento cheese sandwiches on grainy toast at an outdoor café with chairs made of curved bamboo, the same kind you'd find at a Parisian bistro. It was the perfect atmosphere for a debriefing on the last few hours.

"I know you don't believe me, but I genuinely enjoyed getting to meet your mother. I found her quite charming."

"She can be, in spurts."

"Those last few moments were touching."

"I think it's a sure sign that her mind is slipping."

"She's proud of you, you know."

"It's hard to tell. She's rather frugal with praise. Growing up, I don't ever recall her telling me or my brother anything affirming."

"Some parents just don't know how to do that."

"Then they shouldn't be parents. Seriously, how hard is it to tell your kid 'good game' or 'nice job on the finger painting'?"

Nicole couldn't disagree. "Why doesn't your brother ever visit?" she asked.

Drew swallowed a sip of his tea before answering. "He's not equipped to handle the situation."

"Why not?"

"He has a temper. Not a terrible one, but a temper nonetheless. He inherited it from her. Put them in the same room for any length of time and it's incendiary."

"You don't have that problem?"

Drew shook his head. "I got lucky. The temper gene apparently skipped me."

"You don't have a temper?"

"No. Not at all."

"Why not?"

"I don't need one."

"You don't get mad?"

"Oh, I get mad, just like everyone else. I just don't feel the need to erupt. I can express my displeasure in a normal speaking voice."

"So you *never* lose your temper," she stated.

He looked squarely at her for emphasis. "No. Never."

Nicole scrunched her face, disbelieving. "Why not? That *has* to be a conscious decision."

He rattled the ice cubes in his tea as he assembled his thoughts. "Because I've seen what a temper can do. I've seen it ruin family vacations, Christmas dinners, game nights . . . you name it and a bad temper can ruin it."

"Marriages?" she added.

"Especially marriages," Drew said. "I'm just thankful that a hair-trigger temper wasn't among the gifts she passed down to me."

"What gifts *did* she give you?"

"Oh, she gave me lots of things . . . heartburn, ulcers, self-esteem issues. The list goes on."

"I'm serious. Surely you can think of one gift she gave you."

Drew thought for a moment, bobbing his head from side to side as he tried to conjure up a response that might satisfy her. "She gave me a brother. I'm grateful for that."

"Okay. What else?"

Drew gripped the sweating glass of iced tea more tightly and looked straight ahead as if the answer were somewhere in the busy street. Nicole looked at him intently but didn't speak, letting the wheels in his mind backtrack to distant memories. She could sense the writer's active brain was percolating.

After nearly two minutes of sitting in silence, Drew finally spoke. "She gave me the gift of reading. My mother gave me books and the love of words and sentences and stories and characters, and the ability to lie in my bed at night and escape to far-off places I've never visited or that don't even exist in the real world, but I got to go there in the pages of a book. She gave me the love of the written word, from Seuss to Shakespeare, from the Hardy Boys to Hawthorne. She taught me to love public libraries and bookstores and musty antique stores where I might discover a precious first edition bound in red leather. I wouldn't have been a reader without her, I *certainly* wouldn't have been a writer, and as it turns out, I probably wouldn't have met you, because I wouldn't have had anything interesting to say. So *that's* what my mother gave me, and for all of that, I will be forever grateful."

Drew turned to face Nicole, who was beaming through watery eyes as if that were the most touching thing she'd ever heard. He wasn't sure which part of what he'd said had moved her nearly to tears, but he hoped it was the reference to meeting her.

A half-hour after lunch, Drew pulled past the rolling gate of the storage facility and parked in front of his unit.

"This might take a few minutes," he said to Nicole as he stepped out of the car. "I could probably use some help."

"I'll be glad to," she called after him, as she exited the passenger side. "Plus, it'll give me yet another peek into the mysterious world of reclusive novelist J. Andrew Endicott. Kinda like poking around in J.D. Salinger's attic."

He rolled up the front door and stepped into the labyrinth of cardboard boxes. "It's in here somewhere."

Drew pushed a few boxes aside as he searched for an electric fan that Victoria had requested. Apparently, Húdié was being stingy with the air conditioning, and the girl needed some relief from the sweltering heat of mid-July.

He wished more than ever that there was some order or method to the way he'd stored away this part of his life, some manifest that pointed him to exactly the right box. Because of his haste to move out of the house he'd shared with Emilie, each visit to the storage unit had become more of a treasure hunt than a simple errand.

"Any idea where to begin?" Nicole asked, trying to help.

"Not really. I guess we just start opening boxes."

Nicole obligingly began unfolding the overlapping flaps of the unmarked cardboard boxes, revealing random collections of Christmas decorations, camping gear, and sports trophies. She noticed that Drew had suddenly stopped opening cartons and was hovering over one box in particular. She twisted her way over to him and saw that the box was filled with scrapbooks. Plastic sheets protecting pictures, a moment in his personal history permanently preserved.

Drew set one of the scrapbooks on a short stack of boxes and flipped through the crackling pages. Nicole eased up behind him and looked over his shoulder as he studied the photos, daring to press her hip against his in the narrow confines.

"You aren't in any of these pictures," she observed. "Is that because you were always the one taking the pictures?"

"No, it's because most of the time I wasn't there. While they were down at Disney World, I was out in Hollywood."

Drew continued to turn the pages of Emilie and Maddie posing for pictures, usually arm-in-arm with glowing smiles.

"They look happy," offered Nicole.

Drew gently glided his fingers over the various snapshots of his wife and daughter. "Scrapbooks are funny that way," he said in a soft voice. "They only show you pictures of the good times. Nobody ever takes a picture during a fight or right after they've gotten bad news. It's only ever happy people in happy places. Maybe that's a good thing. Unless you're like me and you're not in any of the pictures. See? Like I told you before. Lousy husband."

Nicole moved to Drew's side so she could see his face and better gauge his reaction to the pages unfolding in front of him. "Is this hard for you? Sifting through fragments of your other life?"

"A little. But I always know what I'm in for when I come here." He smirked, trying to lighten the somber mood. "Kinda like getting ready for a root canal."

Nicole remained serious. "Is it getting any better? Easier?"

Drew mindlessly thumbed through the pages of the scrap-book. "It's funny. You think it's the greeting-card days that are going to be the worst. Birthdays, anniversaries, holidays. But they're not. You can brace yourself for all that because you know it's coming. No, it's the little things, the day-to-day events that take you by surprise. A song on the radio, a whiff of perfume in an elevator, a little girl riding a bike. All that pain comes rushing back without warning, and there's no way to protect yourself from it. You want to go on living, you want to look to the future, but life keeps reminding you of the past. It just won't go away." Drew gave his head a shake. "No, it's not getting easier. I doubt it ever will."

He turned to meet her gaze, their faces only inches apart. If this were a first date, this would be the moment that he would lean forward and give her a romantic and respectful kiss. If this were a second date, this would be when he would push into her and kiss her with passion and intimacy. But this was neither of those. This was merely two friends in close proximity and nothing more. *Or was it?* His mind raced. *Is this one of those rare moments in life that I need to seize?* Drew thought. She hadn't moved an inch. He could feel her warm breath on his flushed cheeks. *What is she thinking right now?* he wondered. *Does she want me to do something? Is she expecting me to do something? I shouldn't. She's still with someone else.* The moment lingered on the brink of uncomfortable.

Is he going to kiss me? wondered Nicole. *He seems like he wants to. Or is it my imagination? Am I ready for this? I haven't been kissed by another man in years. But is this improper? Don't I still belong to another man?*

What finally stopped Drew from leaning closer and brushing her lips with his was the scrapbook in his hand. Despite whatever chemistry there might be fomenting between them, whatever urges he wanted to pursue, this didn't seem to be the proper time or place. Kissing another woman while holding pictures of his late wife and daughter seemed disrespectful at best, wicked at worst.

Drew broke the spell. He abruptly pulled away and gently placed the photo albums back into the box that held them. "It's getting late. We need to find that fan before a teenager dies of heat stroke. Plus, you probably want to get on your way. I've kept you for too long." Drew waded through more boxes to another corner of the unit.

"I'm not in a hurry," she gently countered.

"Maybe in here," Drew said as he unearthed the contents of yet another container. "Here we go!" he exclaimed proudly as he extracted a small plastic fan from the bottom of the box. He held it aloft like a trophy. "Three speeds, oscillating is optional. Victoria can rest easy in the comfort of moving air."

Nicole could easily sense that the sudden playfulness in Drew's voice was a signal that the emotional drawbridge he'd lowered for her a few moments ago had been raised. The castle was again safe, its thick walls impenetrable.

"It appears that you have found what you're looking for," Nicole said, making her way back to the front of the storage unit and leaving Drew to wonder exactly what she meant by that.

The first few minutes of the drive back to the hospital parking lot were relatively quiet. The radio played in the background, loud enough to fill the void but not loud enough to hear the words.

Nicole glanced over at Drew several times to gauge his mood. He seemed lost in thought, his mind perhaps still back in the archives of the storage unit. "What's your opinion about nostalgia?" she asked him, seemingly randomly.

Drew blinked his way out of a mild trance and swiveled his head at Nicole, then back to the road. "What? You're asking me about nostalgia?"

"Yes. What do you think about it?"

"That's the oddest of questions."

"Perhaps. Even so, your thoughts?"

"I honestly never thought about it. Why are you asking?"

"I just find it to be the most interesting of all the emotions."

"Better than 'numb,' I'll give you that. Where are you going with this, Nicole?"

"Nostalgia is the only feeling humans have where you're both happy and sad at the same time. You think about something, maybe some event in your past like a special vacation or summer camp, that brought you joy in your life, but now it's gone. When you think back on it, you're smiling over the fond memories, but then tears form in your eyes because you miss it so much. Nostalgia. Nothing quite like it."

"Is this just a random musing?" Drew asked. He glanced over at Nicole for two seconds longer than a driver should. "Or is there a point you're hoping to make?"

"The point is, it's okay to be both happy and sad at the same time when you think back in time. You don't have to choose. That's the eternal gift of nostalgia."

Drew moved his head from side to side, trying to determine what he made of Nicole's assertion. He asked another question, keeping his eyes fixed on the road. "You said this happens when you think about some*thing* in your life. Does that also apply to some*one?*" Only now did he look at her.

Drew hustled around the back of his Jeep to open the passenger door for Nicole after pulling up next to her car in the hospital parking lot. Unaccustomed to chivalry, Nicole was already out of the car and had shut the door behind her by the time he arrived.

"Thanks for letting me tag along today," she told him.

"There will be more jewels in your crown for putting yourself through all that," Drew said.

"I actually enjoyed it. All of it. Who knows, in a few years from now, I might even be nostalgic about it."

Drew laughed. "You're somethin' else, Nicole Shepherd. Someone should be writing books about *you*."

It was her turn to laugh. "Ha! Nobody's *that* good!" She bit the corner of her bottom lip as she amended her statement with a twinkle in her eye. "Well, *almost* nobody."

Drew nervously dug his hands into his pockets and took two small steps backward. "Thanks again for coming. I didn't realize how important it was to have you there."

"Anytime."

"You heading back to Oak Island?"

"Yes." She glanced at her watch. "Hopefully I beat rush hour."

"You've gotten to spend a lot of time there lately."

"Uh, yeah. Lee Wayne's been out of town. Frees me up." She felt horrible about lying, or at least not telling Drew the entire unfiltered truth, but a hospital parking lot didn't seem to be the right place for such a serious revelation. She should have done it a half-hour ago in the car. Or the night it first happened. Would there ever be a right time?

Drew took his hands back out of his pockets and patted his thighs. "Well, I guess this meeting of the OIBC is adjourned." He stepped closer and spread open his arms to indicate he was coming in for a friendly goodbye hug. He wrapped his arms around her and she did the same. They both gripped tighter. Standing in the narrow space between his door and hers, they held each other for much longer than just a casual goodbye. It felt more like hello.

CHAPTER TWENTY-SEVEN

"The best books . . . are those that tell you what you know already."

— George Orwell, *1984*

The last few moments of his third set of thirty-five pushups had been a struggle, but Drew had triumphed over his aching arms and shoulders. He rolled over onto his back and reveled in the seeping perspiration he'd generated from a brisk run and a rash of sit-ups and now pushups.

A quick check of the bathroom scale confirmed that he'd lost a few more unwanted pounds this week. He made the bold move of pulling the mirror out of the closet. It was time to return it to the wall.

The sudden pounding on his back door interrupted his mission. He was not the least bit surprised to see Victoria standing on his back deck. He pulled the door open and looked her up and down. "You again?" he said, trying to sound annoyed.

"I need help," she told him but without any urgency in her voice.

"What's wrong?"

"I have to write a book report on *Gulliver's Travels.*"

"Great book. A classic. What's the problem?"

"My teacher wants us to report on the hidden meaning of the book. I have no idea what she's talking about."

"She wants you to figure out what the author was really trying to say. What's the symbolism? The imagery? Metaphors, allegories, analogy, things like that."

"Okay, now I have no idea what *you're* talking about."

Drew pulled the door open wider and beckoned her inside. "Have a seat. Class is in session."

Victoria hopped up on a kitchen stool, prepared to soak in every word.

"Your teacher wants you to figure out beyond just an entertaining adventure, what's the author trying to *tell* you? What's the lesson you take away?"

"I don't know."

"Okay, think back to the movie *Madagascar*. What was going on with those characters that might pertain to your own life?"

Victoria mulled it over, going over the plot in her head. "That they're friends, and that your true friends will help you in time of need. Like us."

"Yes. Like us."

"You're my best friend," Victoria said.

"I am?"

"Yes. And I hope you know that I would help you any time you needed it."

Drew smiled and bobbed his head. "That's good to know."

"And that Alex the lion was just pretending to be strong and brave, which he was able to do as long as he was still in a cage in a zoo, but once he got out into the real world he discovered he wasn't so tough at all."

"Very good. Now you're getting it."

"Is that why some people never leave their house? They're afraid that people will find out they're fake?"

Drew looked at the little girl and scratched his head. She had no idea how wise she was. "Maybe so. Maybe so." His mind drifted away for just a moment as he considered the realities of his own cage. He shook his head to clear it. "So anyway, back to Gulliver. There's a lot going on there besides Lilliputians tying down a giant. Jonathan Swift was making fun of the English government."

"How?"

"He wanted people to question its authority. Basically, should physical size and power determine who gets to tell everyone else what to do? Or can lots of little people, working together, control the giant?"

Victoria was scribbling notes as fast as she could. "I got it!" she cheered as she wrote. "So he's using the characters in the book to entertain us, but he's really talking about something else."

"Exactly. It's one of the reasons why people love to read. To see if there's some life lesson hidden in the pages that they can uncover and apply to their own lives."

"Is that why you read so much?"

"That's one of the reasons, yes."

"Is that why you wrote books?"

"I think so. But I don't think most of my readers got much out of it."

"So why don't you write anymore?"

"You asked me that before."

"And you didn't answer."

"It's complicated, Victoria. I think maybe it's because I just don't have any more words to give. I'm like an aging rock star who wrote a lot of great songs when he was young, but just can't seem to come up with another hit. You just dry up."

"Or maybe there's another reason?"

Drew nodded ruefully. "Maybe."

Victoria jumped off the stool and scooped up her notes. "Thanks for the help. I can take it from here."

"I feel certain you can." Drew gave her a little wave as she headed out the door. He rubbed hard on his chin. His discussion with Victoria was going to nag at him long after she'd skipped out of his kitchen.

Nicole was propped up on the bed in Teri's beach house reading *Love in the Time of Cholera*. She could easily relate to the lovesickness that Florentino felt for Fermina. The emotional and physical agony of being apart. Florentino was so sick with worry that he was nearly diagnosed with cholera. The feeling of longing for something or someone is one of the most difficult human conditions. It's like a gnawing hunger when you have no idea when or if another meal is coming. At least with death, there is a finality. Longing is open-ended, with no outer limits, no boundary, no finish line. You just wait for whatever may or may not come. It can be torturous and crippling. But it can also be worth it.

It had taken her much of the summer to admit to herself how strong her feelings were for Drew. She had fought the impropriety that accompanied those emotions, but she couldn't deny them. She'd never met a man quite like him, not even close. Intelligent, humble, funny. More than anything, he was kind. She couldn't imagine him raising his voice, much less his hand. By his own admission, he needed healing, but he didn't need fixing.

Nicole powered up her secret phone and started tapping.

What do you think of Cholera?

Drew responded right away as if he'd been waiting for her text.

I'd prefer to avoid it. That and tuberculosis

The book, smart boy. The book.

Oh. That. Loving it!

Me too. Brilliant prose. What's your takeaway so far?

That pursuing wealth degrades your spirit. Perhaps I already knew that

As do I. Fermina married a wealthy man but still wasn't happy because she didn't have love.

Seems like a simple formula for happiness

So why doesn't everyone follow it?

My other takeaway was that you should never give up. It's never too late to live the life you envision

It took Florentino and Fermina 51 years to finally find love. Gives me hope that I can do the same.

Drew wasn't sure how to respond. He couldn't tell if they were still talking theoretically about love and life in the fictional context of the book, or if Nicole had dipped a toe into the unspoken complexity of their own relationship.

How long are you staying at the beach?

The change of topic felt abrupt and Nicole wondered if she'd somehow crossed a line that Drew wasn't ready to step over. It was impossible to tell in a text.

I'm going back tomorrow morning... I'm volunteering at the NICU. You coming back soon?

Staying here this weekend. My neighbor is running in her first 5-K race and I'd like to be there

Should I be jealous?

Insanely

I'll try to control my emotions.

Please do... what have we said about tempers?

Good point.

Don't worry. She's just the girl next door

That doesn't help me.

She's 13! Her name is Victoria. I've been coaching her a little bit

Maybe you should have led with that. Would have saved me a little angst!

Sorry!

Nicole knew she was about to take a giant leap. She hesitated, letting her finger hover over the phone before finally pushing the button.

I'll miss you this weekend. The Book Club meetings aren't the same without you.

To Nicole's great relief, Drew's response was immediate.

I'll miss you too

Drew paused before sending an addendum to his last text but finally sent it her way.

A lot

:) Night, D.

Goodnight, N. Sleep softly

I will. A little reading first.

I'll join you

See you there. Sweet dreams.

Nicole turned off her phone and clutched it to her chest as if it contained precious letters. In many ways, it did. She set her bookmarked copy of *Love in the Time of Cholera* on her nightstand and picked up an adjacent book, *Tears of the Sycamore*. She flipped it over and stared at the picture of Drew on the back of the jacket. There was that longing feeling again. Her growing affections for Drew were slowly sneaking up on an area that was beyond fondness and closer to love. Her conscience seemed to be looking the other way.

Nicole's other phone chimed with the announcement of an incoming message. It was at least the thirtieth manic message she'd received that night, all from the same familiar number. All thirty had gone unanswered.

CHAPTER TWENTY-EIGHT

"A book must be the axe for the frozen sea inside us."

— Franz Kafka

Nicole was running a few minutes late for her volunteer shift at the hospital. The drive up from Oak Island which normally took her fifty minutes had taken a little over an hour because of an accident during Wilmington's morning rush hour. It was five minutes after eight o'clock when Nicole breezed into the NICU and started toward the incubator that protected baby Cody from the contagions of the outside world. Her heart was light, having looked so forward to holding him again and feeling his warm skin against her cheek. She'd worried before signing up to volunteer that such close contact with an infant might prove to be painful, dredging up the deeply rooted raw emotions of never having had a child of her own, but it had turned out to be quite the opposite. Her time with Cody had been therapeutic, reminding her that even though she'd never given birth herself, she still had gifts within her that she could share with a child who needed her maternal touch. Her time in the NICU was saving two lives.

Before Nicole could reach Cody's station, Vera, the head nurse, intercepted her.

"Nicole—" she began, pursing her lips before continuing. "We did everything we could do. I'm so sorry." She didn't have to say another word. The sudden shock of what had happened to her precious baby boy was like a blinding white light, nearly incapacitating. Nicole's knees buckled slightly and Vera clasped her arm. Regaining her balance, Nicole pulled gently away from the nurse's steadying grasp. Tears flowed quickly into her eyes, blurring her vision as she walked slowly to the empty incubator. He was gone. Just a few weeks into his life and he was gone. Despite all of her cuddling, all of her cooing, all of her caring, baby Cody was gone.

She stroked the metallic edges of the incubator. She looked at the swaddling blanket she'd made for Cody that wasn't going home with him. She recalled again, with great clarity, the admonition in training to not get emotionally attached, and she now fully understood why this had been such wise counsel. But how could she not? How could she not feel a terrible sense of loss over a child that she had held and nurtured and protected and that she felt *certain* was going to survive simply because he was the recipient of so much love? How could she not feel as though her heart was being ripped out of her chest?

Nicole fought hard to squelch her mounting tears. She leaned against the edge of a table and stared into the nothingness, her senses going numb. The head nurse came over and held her closely, trying to offer unspoken reassurance. Nicole knew everyone else in the room was watching her. They'd no doubt experienced the same shock of losing an infant in their care. But she believed her loss was different. Deeper than most. She had felt this kind of death before. She knew more about the severed bonds of mother and child than anyone else on the premises, or at least she believed that to be true at this moment. It was greater pain than any woman should have to bear and she wasn't sure if she could ever overcome it. The images in Nicole's addled mind were spilling on top of each other, rapidly moving and shifting like the dark clouds of a summer thunderstorm, harbingers of the destructive winds and rains that were descending on her. She thought of a difficult day when she was just a teenager, and a drop of her urine revealed a plus sign on a home pregnancy kit. She thought of her unknown mother who'd given her up for adoption and then vanished.

She turned her head and looked intently at Cody's empty incubator, but suddenly through a different prism. Something reminded Nicole that this wasn't just about her. As devastated as she was, she couldn't begin to imagine what Lyla must be feeling over losing her baby. But perhaps it was the best outcome after all. Perhaps leaving a world where he might battle infirmity his entire childhood and into adulthood if he lived that long, was the better path for Cody. He was free of his Plexiglas prison, free of tubes and monitors and nurses with needles. He was no longer the caged bird. He could fly. He could soar. He could sing.

Finally regaining control of her jagged emotions, Nicole stood and nodded to Vera that she had recovered enough to function.

Vera stood squarely in front of Nicole and softly placed her hands on the side of Nicole's shoulders. "Honey, I know you're heartbroken right now, but you have to understand that this happens to all of us up here on this floor. We do our best, but sometimes the outcomes aren't what we hope for. We've all been through it and you'll get through it too." Nicole dipped her head and nodded, sniffing into the back of her wrist. "Look at me," Vera said. Nicole raised her glistening eyes and met Vera's gaze. "You *do* want to come back, don't you?"

Nicole gave a slight nod. "I do," she said in a voice that was barely audible. "I really do."

Vera smiled warmly. "I'm glad to hear that. We need you here. These babies need you here." Vera leaned in and gave Nicole a reassuring hug, patting her on the back. "Go home and do something that brings you joy. We'll see you back here when you're ready."

Nicole nodded as the embrace ended. She forced herself to push one foot in front of the other and find her way to the exit of the NICU. Despite what had happened, she already knew she'd come back.

It wasn't the first time that Drew had noticed Húdié was moving just a little slower than usual. It seemed as though it required more effort now for her to lift a shovel or bend over to pull weeds in her garden. Her breath came shorter, and her tiny legs no longer moved with the same tilt and lilt as they had just a few weeks prior. Drew wiped his sweaty brow and he trimmed away some grass that was encroaching on the garden and decided Húdié's sluggishness was nothing more than a function of the wilting summer heat.

He started to walk over to the far corner of the yard to see if Victoria needed a break from mowing the lawn. He already knew she would turn down his offer for relief, always wanting to prove herself, but he thought he should at least make the gesture to ease his conscience. His cell phone buzzed in his back pocket. He looked at the incoming number but didn't recognize it. He decided to let it go to voicemail and slipped it back into his shorts.

It immediately rang again. Now curious, Drew picked up. "Hello?" he mumbled, more of a question than a greeting. All he heard from the other end was the faint sound of someone rapidly breathing through their nose. "Hello?" he said again, louder this time, and with a hint of irritation. The breathing continued. He was about to disconnect when he heard his name.

"Drew?" the voice on the other end whispered.

"Nicole? Is that you?"

"Yes. I'm calling you from a payphone."

"Why? Where are you? What's wrong?"

"I'm fine, I really am. Are you coming down to Southport today?" she asked, her voice cracking.

"I hadn't planned on it, but I certainly can. Why? What's going on? You don't sound good."

"It's too much to explain over the phone. Is there any way you could meet me at Oak Island?" she asked, almost apologetically. "I just need someone to talk to."

"Of course." He checked the time on his phone. "I can be there in an hour."

"Thank you."

She hung up, leaving Drew standing in the yard staring at his phone with a thousand more questions than answers.

He ran over to Victoria and gestured for her to turn off the mower. "I have to go. Please tell your grandmother I'll finish the edging when I get back this afternoon."

Victoria could see the alarm in his eyes. "Of course. What's wrong?"

"I don't really know." He jammed his work gloves into his back pocket and ran home.

Drew pulled into the driveway of Teri's beach house, sand spitting out from behind his wheels.

He charged up the staircase just as Nicole came out of the

front door with tears streaming down her reddened face. He whisked her up in his arms and pulled her tightly to him. He had no idea what was troubling her but instinctively knew that this was exactly what she needed at this moment. He didn't speak and he didn't let go. He just held her, letting her soak in the therapeutic goodness of human contact.

"I don't know how much more I can take," whispered Nicole. "I'm so tired of crying."

Twenty minutes later they were walking down the beach, the sun directly overhead, pressing their bare feet into the soft, wet sand near the water's edge. Nicole had tearfully recounted the death of Cody, stopping numerous times to force back rising tears. Drew simply listened, giving her time and space to vent her swirling emotions. There was healing power in the simple transaction of listening.

Nicole suddenly sat down cross-legged on the sand as if to signal the next few moments would require their full attention. Drew eased down next to her, stretching his less-than-limber legs out in front of him.

Nicole picked up a tiny stick of driftwood and scratched a few lines and circles in the sand as she leaned over and rested her elbows on her knees. Again, Drew remained silent as he allowed her to collect her thoughts.

"You know what's funny about all this?" she said. "I often wonder how much better my life would have been if I hadn't had that miscarriage when I was a teenager and had gone ahead and had a baby out of wedlock."

"How so?"

"I would have never gotten involved with Lee Wayne. He would have had zero interest in an unwed mother or raising some other man's child. Ironic, since he never got to raise his own. I wouldn't live in a nice house and drive a fancy car, but I'd have been happy. I just know it. And at the end of the day, I'd rather be happy in a Ford pickup than miserable in a Mercedes."

She tossed the driftwood forward into the sea. "You're the only person I've ever told that I lost a baby. I don't know why I never told anyone else, other than it's just so painful."

"So why did you tell me?"

"Because I feel I can be totally honest with you, which is strange because if you think about it, we really don't know each other that well."

"I'm glad you trusted me enough to tell me. I know that wasn't easy."

"I just didn't want to start off with any barriers between us."

"I agree." Drew squinted as he looked at the crashing waves. He wondered what she meant when she said *start off*. Perhaps nothing.

She looked away, trying to figure out what to say next, or more importantly, how to say it. "There's something else you need to know."

It worried Drew that she wouldn't make eye contact. He spoke as gently as possible, his intuition telling him that she was on the verge of changing her mind about talking. "I'm listening."

She waited several more moments, steeling herself, before spinning back around to face him. "I left Lee Wayne."

Drew was unable to fully mask his reaction to the startling news. He didn't want to appear overly happy, fighting off outward indications that he was pleasantly surprised, like someone who'd just drawn the perfect card to complete a winning hand at poker. "When?" he asked her.

"Five days ago. I'm sorry I didn't tell you sooner."

"Why?" he asked, as benignly as possible. "I mean, I guess I know *why*, but why *now*? What changed?"

Nicole didn't want to offer any details. "Let's just say I couldn't take it anymore."

"So what are you going to do?"

Nicole brushed away a single tear of worry from the corner of her eye. "I'm not entirely sure. I'm going to stay at Teri's house until I can figure it out. She's the only other person who knows."

"Are you scared?"

She nodded slowly as she pondered her immediate future. "Beyond scared. I know he'll come after me, one way or the other."

"Is there anything I can do?" Drew asked.

"No. Just keep me in your prayers."

"Of course. But what else can I do to help?"

"I can't ask you to do anything. This is my problem. I got myself into this mess and I've got to figure out a way to get myself out. But thanks."

Drew touched her once on the shoulder, lightly. "I'm here if you need me."

"I know. I know. And I'm sorry I didn't tell you earlier."

"Why didn't you?"

"I don't know. Lots of reasons. Didn't want to burden you, for one." She brushed away another tear. "Mostly because it's embarrassing. No matter how bad your relationship is, there's still a sense of failure when you end it. You wonder what you could have done differently to prevent it from falling apart."

"Maybe there's nothing you could have done," Drew said. "Maybe it's simply not your fault, other than choosing the wrong person."

"I suppose. Lesson learned. But my embarrassment goes way beyond that."

"How so?"

"Well, as it turns out, we weren't actually legally married."

Drew's face reflected his utter confusion. "*What?* What do you mean?"

"Lee Wayne purposefully neglected to send in our official paperwork. It was all just a sham."

Drew mashed his fingers against the top of his forehead and closed his eyes. "I'm confused. How is that even possible?"

"He intentionally held on to the marriage license. It was his slimy version of a prenup."

"Oh my God!" Drew said as he shook his head and looked skyward. "I can't believe that's even legal!"

"You must think I'm incredibly stupid." She looked away and bit the top of her lip in embarrassment.

"Nicole, look at me." She turned back to meet his eyes. "I don't think that for a second. The *only* thing I think is that you deserve better."

Nicole nodded. Somewhere deep inside her, underneath a few layers of guilt and shame and regret, she agreed.

"So does this mean you're free of him?" he asked.

"I guess. I'm not sure."

"What's next?"

"I don't really know. I can't live in Teri's house forever, so I suppose I need to start looking for a job. Again, I'm sorry I didn't tell you sooner. It just all makes me look so foolish."

Drew cleared his throat as an audible segue to what he was about to say. "In the spirit of truth-telling, I wasn't completely honest before when I told you I didn't know why I can't write anymore."

"What do you mean? You lied?"

"Didn't lie. Just didn't admit the whole truth."

"Why not?"

"Mostly because I have a hard time admitting it to myself. And honestly, I only recently figured it out."

"So what's the truth? Why *can't* you write, Drew?"

"The truth is, I don't want to write anything because I don't want people to read anything I have to say."

Nicole furrowed her brow. "I'm confused. Isn't that the point of being a published author?"

"You have to understand that when you're an author, readers soak up your words, your thoughts, your insights, and perceptions. They take them to heart, like somebody who latches onto a specific Bible verse and it becomes their mantra or the cornerstone on which they make all their important life decisions. They read one sentence in one book and they cling to it like a life preserver. I don't want that responsibility."

Nicole shook her head. "I think you're exaggerating."

"Am I? *Am* I, Nicole? Then tell me this . . . why, after reading *Black Beauty* or *My Friend Flicka*, did every kid want to go out and buy a horse? Why did millions of people never go back into the ocean after they read *Jaws*? How many people finished Steinbeck's *Travels with Charley*, or Kerouac's *On the Road*, or Least Heat-Moon's *Blue Highways*, and got in their vans and drove across the country? How many of us read *The Sun Also Rises* and daydreamed about running with the bulls in Pamplona? How many people read Cheryl Strayed's *Wild* and decided right then and there that they wanted to go hike the entire Pacific Crest Trail? Not just *wanted* to, but *needed* to! Books have *immense* power, Nicole. They move people to action. They change lives."

Nicole placed her hand on Drew's knee and spoke in a compassionate voice. "But isn't that what's *supposed* to happen, Drew? Isn't that *why* writers write? To inspire others? To motivate them? To move them to some action? To make them view the world through a different prism so they can grow and change? Isn't that why you pour out your heart onto paper?"

He shrugged slightly. "Maybe for some writers, but consider the source. I have absolutely no right to tell people how to live their lives when my own life is such a mess! It's not fair to them. It's . . . it's . . . fraudulent."

She pulled her hand away. "That's a pitiful excuse not to write."

Drew was taken aback by her bluntness. "What? Why?"

"How many authors do you know who led exemplary lives? Who weren't somehow touched by tragedy, or scandal, or mental illness? Was Hemingway perfect? F. Scott? Norman Mailer? Oscar Wilde? Poe? Do you think your beloved Pat Conroy led an easy life? Of course not! But that didn't stop them from expressing themselves! Some of the best advice in the world on how to live a happy life comes from the pens of people who didn't heed it."

Drew hung his head and stared at the sand, soaking in Nicole's words. He felt off-balance as if her words had triggered some emotional vertigo within him that wouldn't stop spinning.

Nicole continued but at a lower volume. "I think you're just looking for an excuse. So far I've heard you give about seven different reasons why you can't write and I'm not buyin' any of them."

"Oh yeah? Well, since you seem to know me better than I know myself, then *you* tell *me*! What's keeping me from writing?"

"One word. Fear."

"Fear? Fear of what?"

"Fear of failing."

Drew resisted the urge to immediately rebut. He gazed out at the horizon. "I'm listening."

"You feel like you've failed as a husband. You feel like you failed as a father. You feel like a failure as a good son. You failed the agent who made you famous. You failed to keep an eye on your money. In your mind, writing books is the only real success you've had in your life and now you're afraid you can't even do *that*, so you don't even *attempt* to write just to avoid failing. But *that's* the failure, Drew! Not even trying is failing."

Drew widened his eyes and pulled in a long, slow breath. "Wow. You don't pull any punches, do you?"

"You need someone to be honest with you."

"After all this honesty, I think I need therapy."

She took his hand gently in hers and caressed his bare knuckles with her thumb. "The truth is, I've read some of your books lately."

"You're kidding! Which ones?"

"*December Dance* and *Tears of the Sycamore*."

"Let me guess. You hated the ending."

She laughed. "Actually, I rather liked it."

"*You're* the one."

"I thought it was the only way it *could* end. But that's not my point. The point is, you're a *very* talented writer. You have a gift to tell stories with words and descriptions that can melt chocolate. And you're just wasting it."

"I don't know about all that."

"I do. And consider the source, Drew. I'm an expert on giving up and wasting talent. So take my advice and find a way to get back to your passion. Go write a book that moves people and changes their lives for the better."

Drew exhaled loudly, not totally convinced even by sound logic. "Maybe."

"You know I'm right." She poked him in his chest with her index finger. "And I also know you have a lot more stories inside you that people want to hear."

Drew chuckled softly. "True. I have enough grief stored up to write a trilogy. I'll call the first installment *Seaweed and Sadness.*"

It took a moment, but they simultaneously broke into a wide smile. Nicole reached over and patted the top of Drew's hand. "So you'll think about it?" she asked.

"I'll think about it." He dipped his head and scratched the top of his scalp.

"Promise?"

"I promise to think about it." Drew was eager to change the subject. "Now that we have *that* settled, what's our next book?"

"I have two possibilities."

"I'm open to suggestion. What are they?"

"The first one is called *A Gentleman in Moscow,* by Amor Towles. Seems like every book club in America has read it."

"What's it about?" he asked.

"I've only read the synopsis, but I think it's the story of a Russian aristocrat who's sentenced to house arrest at a hotel near the Kremlin after the Russian Revolution."

"That doesn't sound all that harsh of a punishment, considering what the Bolsheviks did to most of the aristocracy. I could read that. What else are you thinking?"

"How about *The Nightingale?*" she suggested. "It's by Kristin Hannah."

Drew nodded. "Yeah, I met her once. She's really good. Remind me what it's about?"

Nicole spread her hands apart like a sleight of hand magician for dramatic effect. "Love and betrayal during World War Two, set against the backdrop of the French Resistance."

"I'll read anything that involves romance in Paris." Drew cast a sideways glance at Nicole. "Have you ever been to Paris?"

"Not yet," she said ruefully. "Only in books."

"Oh, you really need to go. You haven't lived until you've kissed someone underneath the Eiffel Tower." Drew immediately regretted saying that. He hadn't meant anything significant by it, no more than if he'd said *you haven't lived until you've had a beignet at Café Du Monde in the French Quarter of New Orleans,* but the simple declaration had inferred much more than he'd intended. He could tell it inflicted a stab of pain in Nicole. Not only had she never been to Paris and perhaps never would, she'd never truly been romanced.

"Then I guess I haven't lived," was all she said as she abruptly scrambled to her feet and resumed walking.

Drew jumped up and caught up with her. He shoved his hands into his pockets and looked down at the virgin sand in front of his feet. He looked out at the ocean, then over to Nicole, who continued to look straight ahead.

"There's still time," he said.

She glanced at him, holding his gaze for a few seconds, then refocused on the path ahead. They walked on in uneasy silence.

Drew's return to Wilmington in the early afternoon was filled with regrets for things both said and unsaid in the few hours he'd shared with Nicole. He'd spent most of their time together doing a good job of consoling her, only to stick a dagger in her back with the offhand comment about romance in Paris.

The only panacea he could think of to ease the clawing in his stomach was a trip to *Old Books on Front Street,* an iconic Wilmington bookstore just a block from the Cape Fear River. Used books, rare editions, and out-of-print copies, all surrounded by the blissful aroma of worn pages and leather spines. Each visit was like a treasure hunt with no map. Hopefully, *The Nightingale* was in stock. Hopefully, they had it in hardcover. Hopefully, she'd still want to read it with him.

CHAPTER TWENTY-NINE

"I have never known any distress that an hour's
reading did not relieve."

— Montesquieu

Nicole had reapplied her mascara before walking into
the alterations shop on Long Beach Road in Southport.
She had arrived unannounced, looking for a job. It
would be the first of seven awkward conversations she would
have that day that began with an introduction and a listing
of her qualifications and ended in rejection and apologies for
wasting their time.

It was deflating and embarrassing. Sewing was Nicole's only
marketable job skill, but apparently, nobody in Southport or
Oak Island currently needed it.

The late afternoon sun of July was losing its steam as Drew
and Victoria worked side by side in the garden, pulling the few
weeds that had dared to pop up amongst the vegetables. The
pasty pallor in his face had been replaced with a deepening tan.

Húdié's garden was covered over by a rolling carpet of green
leaves and sturdy stalks. Many of the Chinese peppers were
now tiger orange in color. Soon enough, they would complete
their five-color journey into bright red, mature enough to be
separated from the plants that had nurtured them, but for now,
they weren't quite ripe.

Victoria's question came out of nowhere. "What do boys want?" she asked.

"What?" Drew's head snapped around. He'd heard the question clearly but was taken off guard and ill-equipped to answer it. And certainly not with the universal truth of what most boys *really* want. "What do you mean, 'what do boys want?'" he repeated, more out of stalling for time than seeking clarification.

"What do boys want in a girl? Do they want pretty? Do they want funny? Do they want smart? Do they want sexy?"

"First of all, *please* don't use that word. You're only thirteen, for cryin' out loud. Save that word for when you're at least twenty-one. Fifty-one, if you can wait that long."

"You didn't answer my question."

"Well," Drew started, grasping for answers. "Intelligent is a good place to start. A sense of humor is also very attractive. A good heart is a must."

"What about pretty?" she asked.

Drew cocked his head back and forth, unsure how to field that one. "Pretty doesn't hurt either, but it's certainly not the most important thing." He finally stopped and gathered his thoughts. He imagined himself having this same conversation with his own daughter. What would he have told a thirteen-year-old Maddie Endicott if she'd asked him, *what do boys want?* As if by divine intervention, the answer came to him with amazing clarity. "You're working the wrong end of the problem," he told Victoria.

"What do you mean?"

"Don't focus on what boys want in *you*. Think about what *you* want in a boy."

Victoria mulled it through her young mind for a moment. "But I don't know what I want. I'm new at all this."

"Everybody is new to it at some point."

"So what *do* I want?"

Drew dropped to one knee to face Victoria at eye level. His words flowed smoothly and gently. "You want somebody who's first and foremost respectful. That's the most important quality. After that, you want someone who's kind. Someone who's curious about the world and can carry on a decent conversation while looking you in the eye. You want a boy who takes care of himself. You want a boy who's nice to his mother and has manners and is good around children and dogs. You want a boy who looks at you like you're the only girl in the room. And it wouldn't hurt to hang out with someone who reads a good book now and then. *That's* what you should want."

"Wow," murmured Victoria. "That's setting the bar kinda high."

"Which is where it should be for an amazing young lady like you. That's the kind of boy you deserve. So don't settle for anything less."

"Still, I'd like to look pretty. There's nothing wrong with that, is there?"

"I suppose not if it doesn't dominate everything else."

"Your wife was pretty, wasn't she?"

Drew smiled and looked away wistfully. "Emilie was the most intelligent, most caring person I've ever known. She was witty, she was talented, she was well-read, all the qualities I admire. And yes, in my eyes, I thought she was the most beautiful woman I'd ever seen." He looked back at Victoria, the tears of nostalgia clouding his vision. "But beauty was just a bonus. I truly loved her for what she was on the inside. That part never fades with time."

Victoria let his words hang in the air for a moment, then she spontaneously leaped forward to hug him, resting her chin on his sturdy shoulder. "I hope I find a boy like you," she whispered.

Drew smiled and swallowed hard. "I hope you find one better."

"Grandmother says boys will only break your heart."

"She may be on to something there."

Victoria looked up at Drew with earnest eyes. "Have you ever had your heart broken?"

Drew smiled and nodded. "Sure. We all have. It's part of life."

"How did you get over it?"

Drew hesitated before answering. He wasn't just remembering the heartache of teenage breakups or college romances that ended abruptly. The image of Emilie's funeral entered his mental vision and remained there, moving in slow motion. "Time," he finally said. "That's the only cure. You have to survive a lot of painful memories and just hope someone new comes into your life who can get you moving forward again. Giving your heart to someone comes at a price, but don't let anybody ever tell you that it's not worth it."

Victoria bobbed her head in agreement, then scrunched her face. "What about makeup?"

"What about it?"

"I'd like to wear some, but I don't know how."

"Well, sweetie, I'm afraid that's above my level of expertise." He thought for a moment. "However, I do know someone who might be able to help."

Victoria's face brightened. "Who?"

"A friend. I'll talk to her. In the meantime, why don't you check out a book called *Little Women* by Louisa May Alcott. Packed with information."

"What's it about?"

"Can't tell you. You have to read it. But you're going to love meeting a girl named Jo March. Full of spunk, like you. I have a copy of it somewhere in storage. I'll dig it out for you. Now run along before your grandmother gets angry."

"I'm not afraid of her."

"No, but *I* am."

CHAPTER THIRTY

"In the case of good books, the point is not to see
how many of them you can get through, but rather
how many can get through to you."

— Mortimer J. Adler

Both members of the Oak Island Book Club were absorbed in the printed words under their book lights. They both felt it. The stories were speaking to them, clearly and profoundly, like never before in their reading lives. It was as if the characters had escaped the written pages and taken up residence inside their brains, constantly whispering insights and admonitions into their consciousness.

Nicole turned page after page of *The Nightingale*, doing nothing else between her dinner and the approach of midnight. She was completely absorbed in the lives of two French sisters, Vianne Mauriac and Isabelle Rossignol, and their radically different approaches to dealing with the Germans who'd taken over their country and their lives during World War Two. Their suffering under the Nazis seemed to help put Nicole's own misery into perspective. If they could survive the Gestapo, then perhaps she could survive Lee Wayne.

She identified most closely with Vianne, who would do anything to protect the lives of the children in her care, including submitting to rape by Von Richter, the Nazi officer who'd billeted in her home.

Nicole rested her copy of *The Nightingale* across her breastbone as she considered how the story related to her own life. Vianne had already had a hand in the murder of one German soldier. Perhaps that was the only way to get rid of unwanted men in your house.

It was just after midnight when a text chimed in from Drew's phone.

You reading Nightingale?

Despite what had transpired between them earlier in the day, Nicole was pleasantly surprised to hear from him.

Loving it.

Drew's pulse quickened when Nicole's response bounced back.

Same here. Mesmerized

What page are you on?

277. You?

370. Been reading all night. Can't put it down.

Me too. This book is powerful

I'll say. If I had a yellow highlighter I'd have marked up half the pages by now. Kristin Hannah weaves a great story.

Favorite part so far?

I'm just inspired by the two sisters, for different reasons. Hannah wrote this on page 194 about Isabelle. "Someone told her she couldn't do something, she did it. Every barrier she turned into a gate." It really spoke to me. That's exactly what I needed to hear. It's what I need to do.

We all have our barriers, don't we?

Yes. It just seems some are more insurmountable than others.

It feels that way some days. You okay otherwise? You had a very difficult day

Still pretty teary, but sleep will help. Heading there soon.

I'm here if you need me

I know. I appreciate it. Truly.

There was a brief pause before she texted again.

I'm sorry about the awkward moments earlier today. It's just been a terrible day and I know I overreacted about Paris. I know you didn't mean to hurt me. It just hit me the wrong way at the wrong time. Please forgive me.

I'm the one who needs to apologize. It was insensitive, especially given the day you've had

Let's move on. Deal?

Deal. May I ask you something way off topic?

Sure.

How much do you know about makeup?

Why, are you thinking about an extreme makeover?

Clearly I could use one, but no. Victoria is asking a lot of questions about hair and eyeshadow and other things that are way above my pay grade. I need a woman's input

**I can help. Any chance you could bring her
to Teri's salon tomorrow? She's the real expert.**

I'm pretty sure I can do that

**It's called Fieldstone. It's on Hanover
Street in Belville. I'll drive up in the
morning. Meet me around 11?**

I'll make it happen. Thank you!

**Thank you, for everything today. I needed
a broad shoulder today and you dropped
everything to be there. Very grateful.**

Sleep softly. See you tomorrow

Night, D.

Night, N

Drew turned off his phone and finished another chapter of *The Nightingale*, then rubbed his weary eyes with his thumb and forefinger and switched off his book light. He sat in his living room, in the peaceful stillness of the dark. For the first time in a long time, he felt as though he wasn't completely alone.

Nicole found her place again in *The Nightingale* and was instantly transported back to the desperate days when the Nazis occupied France, where the women in Hannah's book were forced to make compromises and sacrifices beyond what they could have ever imagined, just to stay alive. Disheartening for Nicole to read about what they endured, but inspiring to watch them prevail. Her peace was shattered when her other phone *buzzed* on the nightstand. She checked it and rolled her eyes in dismay. Another message from Lee Wayne, the most recent of forty-seven texts that had all gone unanswered. *Why won't he just leave me alone?*

CHAPTER THIRTY-ONE

"We read to know we're not alone."

— William Nicholson, *Shadowlands*

Tiny snippets of Victoria's black hair were dotting the floor of Fieldstone Salon. Teri had artfully trimmed and layered Victoria's plain haircut into a stylish new look. With just a different haircut, Drew couldn't help but notice how much older she looked. As Teri and Nicole applied just a minimum of cosmetics, the little girl's budding maturity became even more pronounced.

"Now the secret to eyeliner is that less is more," Teri said as she applied makeup to Victoria's eyes with the steady skill of a surgeon.

In less than an hour, Victoria had transformed from a chrysalis to a young butterfly. Even the tiniest bit of makeup had a dramatic effect on her overall look. Drew could tell from the way Victoria beamed as she sat in the chair and tilted her head back and forth in the mirror that she could sense she'd taken a large step toward womanhood.

"*Thank you,*" Drew mouthed to Nicole. She returned a warm smile, happy to have helped. Drew had to believe that this might be a welcome distraction from the trauma of yesterday in the NICU.

Teri spun her chair around so that Victoria faced the salon. "Okay, y'all squish together for a picture," she commanded as she waved her arms in and out to usher Drew and Nicole to either side of Victoria.

As they crouched over and leaned in for the photo, Drew could see their reflection in a large mirror on the other side of the salon. The composition of the picture, a man and woman flanking a young girl, was more than just a little similar to the photo of himself with Maddie and Emilie on the beach in Puerto Rico. The resemblance was startling, borderline unnerving.

When Teri removed the smock from around Victoria's neck and helped her down from the chair, the young woman wrapped her arms around Teri's waist and gave her a fervent hug. She released Teri and did the same to Nicole. "Thank you both *so* much," she said, with an innocent joy that couldn't be contained.

"Glad to, honey," Teri said with her silky Southern accent. She grabbed a small, zippered pouch from the counter, filled with basic cosmetics. She presented it to Victoria, who accepted it as if it contained the Crown Jewels. "Now then, when you get home, make sure you use a good makeup mirror."

"Makeup mirror?" Victoria asked. She looked over at Drew. "I'm not exactly sure what that is."

"It's a mirror with bright lights around it," explained Nicole. "It helps you apply your makeup evenly."

"Oh." Victoria frowned and spoke with a hint of dejection in her voice. She certainly didn't own one of those.

Drew could immediately read her adolescent mind. She was no doubt imagining that her makeup would never look as good as it did at this very moment without this magical mirror that was required to do the job correctly.

"I think I might have one in the storage unit," he quickly chimed in. "I'll look for it tonight. If not, we can always go get one. No worries."

The broad smile returned to Victoria's face. All she needed was a makeup mirror and all would be well with the world. She turned back to the large salon mirror to catch her reflection, even pursing her lips slightly like a *Harper's Bazaar* fashion model.

The three adults flashed spontaneous smiles as they celebrated the birth of a young woman.

"You going straight back to Oak Island?" Drew asked Nicole as they stood next to her car in the parking lot of the Fieldstone Salon.

Her response was slightly hesitant. "Not right away. Lee

Wayne is out of town tonight, so I'm going back to Belville to pack up some things."

"Good enough," he said, allowing her vagueness to go unchallenged. "Be safe." He gave her a brief hug, suitable for public display, then ambled back to his vehicle.

Victoria had been watching from the passenger seat of Drew's Jeep and her interest was growing. "What were you talking about?" she asked when he climbed into the driver's seat.

"Nothing. Grownup stuff."

"You have that sad look again."

He squinted in confusion as he started the engine and backed out. "What do you mean by that?"

"Your face gets sad sometimes. Like you're thinking about something that makes you unhappy."

"Perhaps it does," he admitted. "I'll work on it."

"Do I make you sad?" she asked.

"What? No! Why would you even ask that?"

"I know you miss your little girl. I don't want to bring up bad memories."

Drew sighed and shook his head. He made a hard right into a parking lot and shut off the ignition. He turned to face her. "Listen to me... yes, I miss my daughter. Terribly. But when I'm around you, it's about the only time I'm *not* sad. Don't ever forget that."

A sense of relief spread across Victoria's face. "I won't. I promise."

Drew started the Jeep and pulled back into traffic. They'd gone a few blocks in silence before Victoria spoke. "Does *she* make you happy?"

"Who?"

"Nicole."

"I enjoy her company, yes."

"Do you like her?"

Drew shot a wary glance at Victoria. "She's very nice."

"That means you like her."

"Maybe it does, maybe it doesn't."

"Oh, it does. It definitely does."

"Suddenly you're the expert on relationships?"

Victoria ignored the comment and pressed forward. "Is she the reason you go to the beach so much?"

"One of them."

"What are the others?" she asked.

"Like I said, grownup stuff. Nothing you need to worry about."

"Does it have to do with why you get so sad sometimes?"

Unsure about the answer himself, Drew considered his response for nearly half a minute before finally replying. "It's complicated."

She let it remain there.

Instead of driving off, Nicole had returned to Teri's salon. She was trying to calm herself, knowing the conversation she was about to have was going to be difficult. She was going to ask Teri for a job. Answering phones, sweeping floors, anything. She hated to do it, but she was desperate to make ends meet.

Teri looked up from folding a pile of freshly laundered white towels when Nicole walked back inside. "Hey, hon! Forget somethin'?"

Nicole took a few more steps toward Teri before speaking. "I wanted to—" Pride and humiliation suddenly prevented Nicole from completing the sentence. It was just too much to ask.

"What is it?" Teri asked, confused as to why Nicole had paused.

"I just—" Nicole began again, her emotions rising. "I just wanted to thank you for helping out my friends today. That was exceptionally nice of you."

"Aww, honey, that was my pleasure."

Nicole could only purse her lips and bob her head. Tears that seemed to begin in the middle of her throat were rising to the surface.

Teri immediately wrapped her arms around Nicole and squeezed her tightly. She could sense there was more on Nicole's mind than just "thank you." She pulled away slightly and gently placed her palms on Nicole's cheeks. "I would do anything to help you, hon. Anything. All you have to do is ask. You know that, don't you?"

Nicole nodded and forced a smile.

Nicole sat in her car and stared down at the phone in her hand. The embarrassment that had been preventing her from asking for a job from Teri an hour earlier had slowly been overridden by economic fear. She had less than seventy dollars in her purse.

It might last a week if she were frugal, but then what? Sell what few possessions she had with her at Oak Island? Sell her sewing machine?

Shaking her head as if still unsure she was making the right decision, Nicole began typing a text message to Teri. As succinctly as possible, she explained her situation and emphasized that she needed a job just until she could get her financial feet under her again. She made it clear she didn't want a loan, and certainly not a gift. She just wanted to earn some money to get through a rough patch.

Nicole read over the message but made no changes. She sent it and hoped for the best. Nicole waited a few minutes for a response, but none came. She prayed it was because Teri was busy and not angry. Nicole thought back to the advice Vera had given her in the NICU. She would go do something that brought her joy.

Nicole's favorite fabric store on the west side of Wilmington was a banquet for her senses. The rainbow of colors, grouped by similarity of shade and pattern, made her eyes dance with excitement. The aroma of whole cloth was as pleasurable to her as the scent of a lavender candle. The sound of bolts being flipped over on the cutting table and scissors shearing through the fabric was like music. Best of all, she loved feeling the myriad of textures. She could spend hours slowly running her fingers across the fuzzy corduroys, the coarse burlaps, the delicate linens, the dense tweeds.

She always gravitated toward the remnant section to see what bargains might still be clinging to the cardboard tubes, the leftovers just begging for someone to take them home as if they were colorful puppies at the pound. She immediately found the fabric she'd envisioned for a summer dress. It was a Japanese block print, Indigo blue that warmed the eyes and poplin material that would keep her cool in the evening sun. Nicole pulled the remaining three yards of fabric from the roll and clutched it in her arms, breathing in the smell like a bouquet of freshly cut flowers. Yes, this would definitely bring her joy.

She glanced around the checkout counter to see if there were any 'Help Wanted' signs posted. Seeing none, she didn't dare ask if they were hiring. Enough rejection for one week.

The euphoria Nicole was feeling when she exited the fabric store was immediately dashed when she stepped into the parking lot. What she saw was nearly impossible to process. A large black tow truck was backed up to the rear of her Mercedes. Two scruffy men were moving quickly around her car, neither of whom appeared as though they'd ever set eyes on a dentist's chair.

One of the men, dressed in a tank top and a greasy baseball cap that professed his allegiance to some race car driver, pulled on one of five knobbed levers on the side of his tow truck. With a whirr of a motor and a hydraulic hiss, a large metal arm resembling a giant tuning fork slowly extended from the back of his truck. The man at the controls expertly guided the mechanism down to the pavement and under the back wheels of Nicole's car.

Nicole rushed up to the man, her eyes flaring with confusion. "What are you doing? You're stealing my car!"

"Not stealin', ma'am. Repossessin'." He continued to guide the lifting mechanism into place.

"What? Repossessing? That's not possible!" she yelled. The two men ignored her and continued their mission. "Stop!" she pleaded. "Please stop! There's been a mistake!"

The man at the controls shook his head. "Sorry, ma'am, but ain't no mistake."

She fumbled through her purse, desperately searching for her phone. "You don't understand! This is *my* car! I'm calling the police!"

The repo man let go of the lever. He reached inside the open window of his tow truck and pulled out a clipboard. He flipped over a few pages and then dragged his finger down the printed sheet in front of him. "You Nicole Shepherd?"

"Yes." Nicole tilted her head back, slightly surprised the man knew her name.

"Then there ain't no mistake. Paperwork says you haven't made a payment on this vehicle in three months."

Nicole shook her addled head. Her voice was getting louder and higher pitched. "But I don't make the payments. My husband does."

"Apparently he doesn't." He held up the clipboard and tapped the paperwork with his index finger.

"But . . . but I had no idea! Nobody gave me any notice!"

"Don't have to in North Carolina, ma'am. You miss one

payment and legally we can repo your car. Like I said, you done missed three."

The repo man set the clipboard aside and went back to his controls. The wheel lift clamped snugly around the tires of the Mercedes. He pulled on another lever and the back of the car slowly lifted two feet off the ground.

The second repo man busied himself by attaching dirty yellow transport straps around the tires. The harsh ratcheting sound as he tightened the straps further added to Nicole's anxiety.

"This is insane!" she yelled frantically. "Please stop! We can sort this out! I can make a payment right now!" She knew she couldn't, but she'd say anything at this point to keep these men from loading up her car.

The man operating the levers ignored her plea. "That's between you and the bank, ma'am. I'm just doin' my job."

"But I need my car!"

"Then start makin' payments." With the Mercedes lifted and secured, the two repo men calmly got inside their tow truck, slammed their doors, and drove away with her car.

Nicole closed her eyes and raised her head heavenward, feeling beyond helpless. She sat down on the curb and clutched her bag of fabric to her chest like a security blanket. She fought back tears.

Nicole's stomach was churning as she sat alone in the back booth of a coffee shop, a short walk from the fabric store. She was motionless, transfixed by the heart design the barista had artfully crafted into the brown foam of her hazelnut latte. The coffee had cost her roughly ten percent of her current bankroll but she didn't care. Emotional paralysis had gripped her. She didn't know what to do next. Where to go, who to call, nothing. In truth, she didn't want to call anyone, not even Teri and especially not Drew. Today felt like the zenith of her mortification for having lived a life where others were always in control of her. It had been a journey that was predestined. Nicole felt like from the very first day she was born, she'd been foreordained to be a surrogate and enabler to everyone else's dreams and whims. She felt like Daisy Buchanan in *The Great Gatsby*, a dominated trophy wife with no opportunity to realize her own ambitions. Nicole wallowed in regret as she continued to stare into the steaming cup of coffee she held tightly in her hands. She finally raised the coffee mug to her lips and took a sip, destroying the foam art in an instant like someone throwing a pebble into the still waters of a reflecting pool. She closed her eyes and tried to pinpoint where it had all gone so wrong.

"Hello, Nicole," came a low voice. Nicole jumped like someone being awakened from a catnap. She snapped her head up and saw Lee Wayne lording over her table, holding a small shopping bag in one hand. He was unshaven, his clothes were wrinkled, and his hair uncombed. He gestured to the other side of the booth. "Mind if I sit down?"

Nicole shrugged. "Like I have a choice." She sipped her coffee and shook her head in dismay as Lee Wayne slid into the booth across from her. "What are you *doing* here?" she asked.

Lee Wayne ignored the question "Can we talk?"

"About what?" she snapped.

"Our future."

Nicole shook her head. "We don't have one."

"Will you please just listen? I've been lost without you. I can't eat, I can't sleep, can't focus on my work. I'm a wreck." He gestured to himself with both thumbs. "I mean, look at me!"

Nicole sipped her coffee with dismissive nonchalance. "I don't have the energy for this. My car just got repossessed. Don't suppose you know anything about that?"

Her question went unanswered. "Oh, before I forget," he said. He reached down on the seat of the booth and retrieved a book from the shopping bag. It was a hardcover copy of *Where the Crawdads Sing* by Delia Owens. He slid it across the table. "I got this for you. The lady at the bookstore said it was good. I think they made it into a movie."

Nicole held the book in her hand and opened it. Like any lover of books, she so enjoyed the sound of the spine crackling on a new hardcover. Never mind that she'd already read the book more than three years ago and it was prominently displayed on her shelf at home.

Lee Wayne leaned forward and placed his clasped hands on the table. "Will you please give me just five minutes? That's all I ask. Hear me out and then I'll go. Five minutes? Please?"

Nicole exhaled through tightened lips and shook her head in surrender. "Okay, okay. Five minutes."

Like an attorney laying out a closing argument in front of

a jury, Lee Wayne spent the next ten minutes stating his case for why Nicole should come back to him. It was organized, passionate, and compelling. More than anything, it was apologetic. *I've quit drinking. I'll get counseling. I realize the error of my ways. I know I'm not perfect. We all make mistakes. We all deserve a second chance. I can change. I've already changed. I love you.*

Frequently intermingled among all his pronouncements and confessions were the words *please, I'm begging you*, and *I promise*. His eyes had a thin film of tears. She'd never seen him look so defeated or so contrite

"Come home, Nicole," Lee Wayne summarized in a low, earnest voice. "Let me take care of you. Give me another chance to be the husband you want me to be."

Nicole stared into the swirl of her coffee as she absorbed Lee Wayne's oral argument. She felt as though she were at a fork in the road, with two very different paths in front of her and neither of them optimal. Her first instinct was to jump up and flee, but for some reason, she didn't.

Maybe it was the muted tone of his voice or the wistful look in his eyes, she didn't know, but as she turned her head and stared out the front window at the people and cars passing by, Nicole's mind drifted back to a time when she and Lee Wayne were first dating. They were taking an evening horse-drawn carriage ride through historic Charleston, South Carolina. There was a chill in the air and he'd wrapped his arm across her shoulders and pulled her closer to him, keeping her warm. More than anything, she'd felt safe. In a life where she'd been abandoned at birth and ferried from one foster home to the next like a borrowed casserole dish, it was the first time in her life she'd ever felt a genuine sense of belonging. Here was someone who actually *wanted* her in his world. It was also the first time Lee Wayne had told Nicole that he loved her. She remembered pushing even closer into his body and laying her head on his shoulder, soaking up a euphoric feeling of contentment she'd never realized was possible. She couldn't recall a single landmark the tour guide had pointed out on their ride through Charleston that evening, but the memory of that moment was like a postcard she carried in her heart.

The flashback to that blissful carriage ride triggered other nostalgic recollections of their early days together. Rooftop cocktails, sunset picnics next to a lake, slow dancing to a street musician. Ah, yes. Those early days together had all been like delicious and irresistible chocolate ice cream. But just like anyone who eats too much chocolate ice cream, you eventually come to despise the taste, even the sight.

Nicole drew in a deep breath and vigorously shook her head. "I'm sorry, but I can't do it." She turned back to face him. "I just don't believe we belong together anymore. In fact, I don't think we ever did. It's time to move on."

Lee Wayne nodded. He leaned back in the booth and crossed his arms. He chewed on his bottom lip and waited a good fifteen seconds before speaking. "Well, I hate to tell you this, but that's unacceptable."

Her eyes widened and her shoulders stiffened. "Unacceptable? What do you mean by *that*?"

"It means I'm not goin' to let you go."

She scoffed. "I'm sorry, but you don't have a choice. I'm going. I'm already gone."

Lee Wayne smirked and smacked his tongue against his teeth. "See, that's where you're mistaken, Nicole. *You* are the one who doesn't have a choice."

"You're not making sense."

"Let me explain it to you. That fancy car that just got repossessed? Guess who was behind that? I put it in your name, didn't make the payments, then told them where they could find you. And now are you not only without a car, but your credit rating is also shot to hell."

"I'll find another car."

"Good luck with that. I also canceled your insurance. Next thing I'll do is cut off your phone."

Nicole jutted out her chin in defiance. "Go ahead. Do anything you want. I'll figure out a way. I'm leaving you, Lee Wayne. The sooner you get that through your head, the better off we'll both be. Goodbye." She stood to leave, gathering up her purse and her bag of fabric.

"This little babysittin' thing that you do at the hospital. You still doin' that?"

Nicole had only taken one step toward the door when she turned back. "It's called cuddling and it's not little. Don't call it that."

"Whatever. Anyway, it's important to you, isn't it?"

"It is, yes. What about it?" she answered tersely.

Lee Wayne drummed his fingers on the table. "What if the hospital got a letter from an anonymous source and it went somethin' like this." Lee Wayne reached into his pocket and removed a sheet of paper, folded down the middle. He smoothed out the center crease and cleared his throat before reading the printed words. "To whom it may concern . . . I'm a prominent lawyer in town and I need to remain nameless so I won't get into trouble for violating attorney-client privilege, but I would be remiss in my duties as a human being if I didn't bring to your attention the checkered past of one of your volunteers, a Ms. Nicole Shepherd. A few years ago, Ms. Shepherd was accused in several instances of sexually abusing children in her care as a nanny. As her attorney, I was able to negotiate a quiet settlement and charges were never brought. However, the case against Ms. Shepherd was extremely strong and therefore, I feel it's my duty as a citizen to let you know that this is an unsavory part of her past." Lee Wayne looked up and grinned. "It goes on, but I reckon you get the gist."

Nicole's mouth was gaping. The blood was visibly rising in her cheeks. "None of that is true! You made all of that up!"

"Doesn't matter if it's not true. Perception is everything. All your folks at the hospital need to do is get a whiff of some inappropriate behavior involvin' children and you'll never darken their door again. They're not about to risk gettin' sued over some meaningless little unpaid volunteer. Oh, and there's another thing. I have the sneakin' suspicion that you've been seeing someone behind my back. I would hate to have to hire a private investigator and find out more. That could get *very* messy."

"You can't do this!" She spoke loudly enough for other customers to turn their heads.

"Oh, I can, and I will. You see, I have a reputation in this town I need to uphold. If the public finds out I have a wife who's left me, well, let's just say that's bad for business. On top of that, the partners at the law firm might start wonderin' what's going on in my personal life and that doesn't help my chances of movin' up in the firm. The optics are bad. You understand?"

Nicole sat back down and lowered her voice. "Optics? You think I care about *optics*? Have you lost your mind?"

"Here are your choices, Nicole." Lee Wayne started counting by holding up his fingers, one by one. "You come home to me and you get your nice car back, you get your insurance restored, you get your credit cards and your bank account back, and your cell phone stays on. You have a place to live and don't have to worry about where your next meal is comin' from. All your money problems are instantly gone." He snapped his fingers like a magician. "And best of all, I rip up this letter. On the other hand, if you *don't* come home, then you have to face all of those problems and anything else that might come your way. Now, I think that's a fair offer, don't you?"

Nicole was seething. If she'd had a gun in her purse, she would have pulled it out right then and there and shot that smarmy look right off of Lee Wayne's hateful face. But she didn't have a gun. All she had in her purse were some worthless credit cards, car keys that were now useless, and a cell phone that was on the brink of being rendered inoperable. She closed her eyes and let her shoulders slump. She felt nauseated. Her head was swimming as she tried to make sense of anything that had happened in the last thirty minutes.

Her phone *dinged*. She took it out of her purse and glanced at the screen. It was a message from Teri.

CHAPTER THIRTY-TWO

"If there's a book that you want to read, but it
hasn't been written yet, then you must write it."

— Toni Morrison

O f all the books that had shaped Drew's life, it was the
one he was about to open that would provide the most
seismic change. He discovered it inside a duffel bag in
the back of his storage unit as he searched for a makeup mirror
he vaguely recalled packing away.

The cylindrical duffel bag held much of Emilie's diving
equipment and was scratched and scarred from her numerous
underwater adventures. Her wetsuit, buoyancy-control vest, mask,
regulator, fins, and waterproof camera, all neatly packed away
after being rinsed with fresh water. As Drew picked up the bag to
move it, his hand felt a rectangular bulge in the storage pocket on
one end. He unzipped it and slowly removed the contents as if it
were some precious treasure he was recovering from a shipwreck.

He held in his hand the *Ultimate Diver's Log Book,* approximately eight inches by five inches and less than half an inch thick.
The photo on the cover was an eerie bluish-gray with the focal
point being a scuba diver suspended in the deep sea, floating
between the walls of an underwater crevasse. The image could
have been interpreted as either peaceful or haunting, depending
on the person viewing it. For Drew, it was decidedly the latter.

This had been Emilie's treasured record of every dive she'd
made. Location, time, depth, diving buddies, conditions, and

problems encountered and overcome. A detailed diary of diving that would bring memories rushing back of thrilling plunges into the blue waters of the Caribbean, Polynesia, and the Great Barrier Reef, and the rare shells that she brought to the surface to add to her collection. Drew had thumbed through the log book on occasion but was never able to fully comprehend its content of Visibility Scales and complex calculations of breathing rates and gas consumption. He still couldn't. But as he flipped to the last page for the first time, his breathing stopped momentarily, then rapidly increased along with his heart rate. On the lined note pages was a note penned in Emilie's elegant handwriting.

Dear Drew,

If you're reading this, it means something went terribly wrong with my last dive. Although we've always known a day like this might come, I never actually thought it would. I'm so sorry for the pain I know you're going through. When the time is right, please explain to our precious girl that her mother left this world doing what she loved, and despite what has happened, I want her to always explore new worlds and follow her dreams. I also want you to know that I have long considered the dangers of my passion, and what might happen if I were to leave you to raise a daughter by yourself. I am giving you my blessing to find another partner, one who will love you and Maddie as much as I do. You may not choose this path, but if you do, I want you to know that I am at peace with your decision, and I hope you can be too. You have to move forward, for your sake and for Maddie's. I'm sorry to leave you, my dear Drew. I hope you never have to read these words, but if you do, I want you to know how much I love you, and how much I cherished our days together. I will miss you and Maddie more than you know, but I'll always be watching over you as I ascend from the ocean to the clouds.

All my love, your devoted wife,

Emilie

Drew could barely read her final words through the rising tide of tears that covered his eyes. He pressed the heel of his palm against his forehead and bent over in anguish. His chest convulsed and his shoulders lurched as he sobbed. She'd clearly intended for him to read her note soon after her death and would have had no way of knowing that over two years would pass before her words reached him, like a message in a bottle that finally washed ashore after a storm.

Though it certainly wasn't Emilie's intent, it was like reliving the trauma all over again, as if he'd just received the awful phone call for the first time.

After more than five minutes of powerful weeping, Drew gathered himself and forced in a series of deep breaths. He first noted the irony of the tragedy. A woman who had so much skill in the water, who took every conceivable precaution to mitigate the risks of exploring the ocean, had nonetheless been a victim of its turbulent, unmatched power. He was also amazed at how prescient Emilie had been. Although it wasn't a diving accident that took her away, somehow, she'd known she might be the first to depart their union and had taken the rare measure of saying goodbye in the best way she knew how.

As for Emilie's blessing to find a suitable mate to help with the rearing of Maddie, that point was moot. He was hopelessly alone, and despite written permission from the afterlife, he knew he was destined to remain that way. Or perhaps not. A dozen images of Nicole flashed through his mind, so vivid that it almost seemed as though she were actually standing there. *Move forward,* an inner voice whispered.

Drew tucked the dive log under his arm as he exited the storage unit, having forgotten all about his original intent to retrieve a mirror. He pulled down the corrugated metal door, shrouding the contents in darkness. He locked the door and left it all behind.

CHAPTER THIRTY-THREE

"The world of literature has everything in it, and it refuses to leave anything out. I have read like a man on fire my whole life because the genius of English teachers touched me with the dazzling beauty of language."

— Pat Conroy

Drew's three texts and two phone calls to Nicole the next day had all gone unanswered. Her warning that Lee Wayne would *come after me* was now his worry. Dangerous is the man who has everything to lose.

Drew wanted to do something proactive but didn't have any idea what that might be. For no cogent reason other than it felt like he was moving forward, he'd driven to Southport and checked into the Riverside Motel, just hoping that Nicole might be coming down to Oak Island.

The rain from a summer storm fell bruisingly outside, keeping him penned in his room. He'd gone back and forth, back and forth, between trying to finish the last few chapters of *The Nightingale* and checking his phone for a message from Nicole. One moment he was transported back in time to Carriveau, France, in the middle of World War Two; a minute later he was projecting himself into the future and imagining all the things he wanted to say to Nicole the next time he saw her. He wanted her to know that she was one of the most amazing women he'd ever met. He wanted her to know he thought she was bright and talented and funny and beautiful. He wanted to tell her how much he admired her inner strength. For selfish reasons, he wanted to tell her that he was glad she'd left her husband.

Drew was forcing himself to read *The Nightingale* to rein in his wandering mind when a passage from the book jumped off the page. It was like someone had abruptly grabbed him by the lapels and slammed him against a wall, compelling him to listen. It was page 400. Isabelle Rossignol had been taken prisoner by the Germans for her activities with the French Resistance. She was strapped to a steel wheel, being forced to drag it across a field to create a road on the snow-covered ground. She was frostbitten, hungry, and exhausted. *And still, they marched.* She was sick from pneumonia and typhus. *Step. Just think about moving.* Nazis beat her with truncheons and whipped her if she stumbled or stopped. *Gritting her teeth, she took another pain-filled step. And then another.*

Drew read the passage again. If a teenage girl could continue to move forward under those circumstances, then why couldn't he? He could think of no good reason. He marked his place in *The Nightingale* and felt energized by a new resolve he didn't think was possible.

He stood and paced. It was nearly midnight. He still hadn't heard from Nicole. He called her number, something he rarely did, but again was greeted by the disappointment of voicemail. Worry creased his face. Something wasn't right. He took inventory of the possible reasons for her silence. Her phone was inoperable. There was something wrong with the cellular network. She'd fallen asleep. Or, God forbid, the likelihood that Lee Wayne had returned home early to Belville while she was still packing up her belongings and she was in serious trouble.

His mind swimming with uncertainty, Drew realized part of the problem was that he hadn't eaten in ten hours. There were no restaurants in Southport serving this time of night, but there was a convenience store up the road that might still be open. At any rate, escaping the motel room and breathing in some salt air might clear his head and steady his nerves.

The rain had finally stopped by the time Drew left the convenience store with a large bottle of water, a banana, a blueberry muffin, and two small bags of cashews.

He didn't want to immediately return to the motel, so he drove across the marshlands on Barbee Bridge onto Oak Island.

Mist rose from the murky waters like haunting spirits escaping into the night air.

Within ten minutes he was parked along Ocean Drive. He took his meager snacks with him as he walked the winding path of heavy sand through fluttering sea oats that led out to the beach.

The lighthouse from Caswell Beach pulsed its white beam across the water every few seconds, the only light on a starless night. Drew kept his distance from the waterline as he meandered barefoot across the sand with no purpose or destination. The hovering darkness enhanced the preternatural power of the ocean, giving it greater mystery and danger. The same sea creatures that swam in the blue waves of daylight now lurked beneath the black water and increased the sense of vulnerability. Even wading in the shallow foam seemed unwise.

The distant clanging of a bell from a buoy was the only sound other than the rhythmic crashing of the waves. Drew was distinctly aware that they never stopped moving forward. Tides ebbed and flowed, but the waves just kept pushing their way onto the sand, relentlessly reaching as far inland as possible until lunar forces finally reined them back.

Drew finished off his second bag of cashews and tilted his head back to take a sip of water when he noticed one house along the shore ablaze with lights. He couldn't be sure from a distance, but it seemed to be about where Teri's beach house sat. *Odd*, Drew thought. *She told me she's in Belville tonight. Must be a different house. Or maybe it's Teri and her husband?*

His curiosity overcame him, and within minutes he was back in his car and driving toward the beach house. He was stunned to see Nicole's car in the driveway. He turned off the ignition and sat in the darkness as he tried to figure out what was going on and what he was going to do next. He couldn't come up with a rational explanation as to why she had come to Oak Island without telling him. Not that she was obligated. If Nicole simply wanted to be alone, he didn't want to intrude, but if something was troubling her, he wanted to help. And, if he were being honest with himself, he desperately wanted to see her.

It was that selfish motive that propelled him out of his car and up the wooden staircase to her front porch. He had to knock several times before the door finally opened halfway.

"Hi, Drew," Nicole said meekly. She only revealed her head and one shoulder from behind the door, as if embarrassed that he'd found her there. "What are you doing here?"

He hadn't thought through what he was going to say. "I'm . . . I'm surprised to see you here."

"I know. I'm sorry."

"Why didn't you tell me you were back at Oak Island? I've been trying to reach you all day."

"I honestly didn't plan on coming tonight. That's the truth."

"So why did you?"

"Teri called me late this afternoon. Her husband's temporary job in Ohio just became permanent, so they're moving and need to sell the beach house. I have to get all my stuff out so they can start showing it. Clothes, my sewing machine, some books. I didn't know when else I could get away to do it, so I jumped in the car and came down."

Drew absorbed the information but it didn't answer all of his questions. "But why didn't you tell me? We could have had dinner together. I could have helped you pack up."

Nicole didn't answer. She bit down on her bottom lip and looked up at the top of the door frame, inhaling deeply and exhaling loudly. She stepped out onto the porch and closed the door behind her. She sat down on the top step of the staircase and patted the boards next to her, beckoning him to sit down.

Worry covered Drew's face. "If I need to sit down for this, I can already tell it's not good."

"It's not," Nicole said, swallowing hard. She took a moment to collect her thoughts, then began. "I can't see you anymore."

Drew hesitated before responding, not wanting to overreact to the one sentence he never wanted to hear. "Why not?" he asked, in a hushed tone.

"I'm going back to Lee Wayne."

"*What?*" he barked, slamming his eyes shut and shaking his head. "You're *kidding* me! Why?"

"He's begging me to come back. He says he's lost without me."

"After all he's done to you? I can't believe you'd even *consider* going back!"

"He says he wants to be a better husband."

"But he's not actually your husband!"

"He's going to be. He says he's going to make it legal."

"I don't believe that. Even if he did, why would you go

back to him? He beats you! And you *hate* him for it! Your word, not mine."

"He says he's changed. He's sorry for the way he's treated me and promises he can do better. He loves me and he wants to make it up to me."

Drew leaped to his feet and paced the creaking boards of the porch, nervously rubbing his hand through his hair to stem his anger. "He *loves* you? Are you *serious*? No, he doesn't! He just doesn't want you to press charges! Which is exactly what you *should* do!"

"I have to at least give him a chance. I need to try harder."

"Why? *Why* would you do this, Nicole? There's got to be more to this than he apologized and you're willing to accept that. Is it money? Is it something else?" She turned away without responding. Drew ran both hands across the top of his scalp. "What is it, Nicole? Why would you go back to a man who's been so cruel to you when there's somebody out there who would adore you? Someone who would treat you with kindness and respect!" He paused and honed in on one more thought. "Someone who would genuinely *love* you."

"Who, Drew?" she asked pointedly, her voice rising. "Who's out there who would care for me like that?"

There was an extended moment of silence as they stared at each other.

Nicole's voice quieted. "I can't leave him just on the fanciful hope that Prince Charming is out there, waiting for me on his white horse. I have to be practical. I have no money, no savings. At my age, and with no experience, I'd be hard-pressed to find a decent job. I've tried."

"I'll lend you the money until you get on your feet. No, I'll *give* you the money! You just *can't* go back to him! It'll *kill* you!"

"Do you not understand? I don't have any other path," Nicole said.

"Yes you do! You can make it on your own!"

She shook her head. "I have to go back. I *have* to. I just don't have a choice. Simple as that."

Drew shook his head in disbelief. None of it made sense. And it all made him furious. "Fine. Go back to him. Lock yourself back inside that cage, Nicole. Good luck with that. I think you're nuts." Drew started to descend the staircase but turned around for a parting shot. "There's a book by Christi

Paul called *Love Isn't Supposed to Hurt*. Maybe that should be our book club's next selection. Or maybe our last."

Nicole snapped her neck back in dismay. "That's not a very nice thing to say. Little out of character, isn't it?"

"Yeah, well, remember when I told you I don't have a temper?"

"Yes."

"I'm rethinking that. Goodbye, Nicole." He quickly covered the final few steps and moved briskly toward his car.

A nerve had been touched in Nicole. She clamped her lips and her breathing accelerated. She called out after him. "You know, Endicott, you're a fine one to talk about dealing with adversity."

Drew stopped and spun around. "What's *that* supposed to mean?"

She took a step forward, fearless. "What did *you* do when the universe came at you sideways? You dropped out of life and crawled inside a bottle."

"That's different, and you know it."

"Is it? Is it really that different, Drew? Aren't we *both* giving up?"

Drew stood silently and motionless except for the heaving of his chest from anguished breathing. He didn't offer a rebuttal, mostly because on some deep level, he knew she was right. But not entirely. "That may have been true at some point, but not now."

"Oh? And when did that change?"

Drew raised his chin and held her gaze. "When I joined a book club." He let his words linger on the hot night air. "And I can promise you, the *last* thing I want to do right now is give up." He bobbed his head once for emphasis.

He jangled his keys and stepped into his car, calmly closing the door behind him. He backed out and drove off into the night.

Nicole sat motionless on the top step, except to close her eyes and cover her forehead with her open palms and wonder how her life had wandered so insanely astray.

Drew had quickly checked out of the Riverside Motel and driven straight home to Wilmington that night, exceeding the speed limit much of the way.

Nicole had been right about one thing: his escape route from turmoil had been through a bottle, and that's where he'd immediately fled the moment he walked into his kitchen. It had taken three stiff doses of warm bourbon to finally send him off to sleep.

The alcohol from the night before only exacerbated the pain enveloping Drew's skull when he was awakened by relentless pounding on his door at eight o'clock in the morning.

Still in his wrinkled clothes from the night before, including his shoes, he shuffled out into the hallway, occasionally bracing himself against the wall to correct his balance. The pounding on the back door continued and the more the fog in his brain cleared, the more Drew understood it wasn't just an overzealous salesperson. He quickened his pace through the kitchen and swept back his tousled hair with both hands as if that would drastically improve his disheveled appearance. He flung open the door and found Victoria on the back deck, choking away tears.

"Hurry!" she cried, her chest heaving with anxiety. She raced back down the staircase and ran toward her backyard.

Drew stepped quickly out onto his back deck and squinted in the morning sun. He immediately saw the limp figure of Húdié face down on the ground in her garden. "Oh no! No no no! Dammit!" he cursed as he bolted down the steps and sprinted across the lawn.

Within seconds, Drew had hopped the fence and was kneeling at Húdié's side in the middle of the garden. He turned her over and saw that all the color had drained from her weathered face. He pressed his index finger against her neck to check her pulse. He slammed his eyes shut and shook his head, swallowing hard.

"What's wrong with her?" Victoria clutched her trembling hands together and pressed them against her mouth. She convulsed to keep her sobs from escaping.

"Run in the house and call 9-1-1," Drew said as calmly as he could manage. His intention was more to spare her the trauma of seeing her grandmother than to summon medical help he already knew was futile. She didn't move. Her lower lip quivered and tears filled her panicked eyes. "Go!" he ordered, jerking his head toward her house. She finally snapped out of her mild trance and ran off.

Drew pulled Húdié's tiny, lifeless body to his chest and gently slipped off her frayed straw gardening hat. He fought back tears as he gently rocked her in his arms. They sat alone in her beautiful garden with the sun beating down, surrounded by the orange peppers thriving in the soil she'd so painstakingly cultivated. "Oh, Húdié. Dear, sweet Húdié. We aren't ready for this." He picked up a handful of dirt, held it in his open palm for a few seconds, then angrily tossed it aside. He used the same hand to massage his aching forehead, leaving a trail of sweaty mud.

Drew slid his arms underneath Húdié's small frame and with minimal effort lifted her up and slowly carried her toward the house. One heart no longer beating, the other one now breaking.

It was just over thirty minutes later when a paramedic closed the rear doors of the ambulance that had backed into the driveway of Húdié's house. Drew held tightly to Victoria's hand as they stood and watched the emergency vehicle slowly pull away. Its red lights were flashing but the siren was silent as it drove off. The man and woman inside the ambulance had no doubt witnessed this scene hundreds of times, and though professionally respectful of the current situation, they were impervious to the pain they were leaving behind. Just another day.

For the man and young girl they left standing in the front yard, the fresh pain was crippling. Not just another day. They both felt numb. Confused. Helpless. Shock had not yet made room for grief. Drew let go of Victoria's hand and wrapped his arm around her shoulder. He pulled her closer. The little girl turned her face into his chest and cried uncontrollably. Her tiny shoulders bobbed up and down as she released a torrent of tears. He understood the anguish of losing a loved one and the bitter irony of how the one person you need more than anyone else in the world to console you at that moment is the same person who just left you. He thought of Emilie and Maddie and the aching gap in his heart grew wider. Drew dropped to one knee and wrapped Victoria in his strong arms. She buried her head in his shoulder and they both wept as much as they needed.

CHAPTER THIRTY-FOUR

"To acquire the habit of reading is to construct for
yourself a refuge from almost all the miseries of life."

— W. Somerset Maugham

It had only been two days, but Nicole's life back under the
same roof with Lee Wayne was noticeably different than
before. She still slept on the living room couch and an
uneasy air of tension constantly floated through the hallways,
but she no longer felt like she was incessantly on the brink of a
physical beating. He seemed to be genuinely trying to treat her
better. Nothing dramatic or over the top like a dozen roses, but
little things, like only having one cocktail when he got home
from work. He'd let her sew in peace and even asked on one
occasion what she was working on.

They were sitting across the table from each other at dinner,
something they hadn't done in her recent memory. Nicole
fidgeted with her utensils and uneasily pushed her food around
her plate. She wanted to start a conversation but for the life of
her, couldn't find a jumping-off point.

Her husband ate quickly without looking up. He scraped
the last morsel off the plate and slid it into his mouth. "That
was really good, Nicole. Thank you. I need to finish up some
work before bedtime."

Nicole was astonished. It was the first time he'd ever complimented her cooking, even during their early days together. On
top of that, Lee Wayne had taken his dishes to the sink after

eating. He still hadn't made the leap to rinse them and put them in the dishwasher, but she didn't want to push it. It signaled effort. Had he really changed? Was his contrition authentic? It was too early to tell, but at least the situation was tolerable.

During their truce, there was certainly no attempt on his part at intimate contact, either forced or consensual. He could sense her boundaries and kept his distance. However, there *was* something new. Last night, before heading down the hallway to bed, Lee Wayne had gently rubbed Nicole's right shoulder and whispered a soft goodnight. It was the first thing he'd done in years that actually made her smile, even if only briefly. Because there was so much ugly history between them, Nicole fully understood that it was going to take a long time to get back to any semblance of a trusting, healthy relationship and that they might never get there. She had to keep reminding herself that he had essentially blackmailed her into returning home. But if he was truly willing to try, then she felt an obligation to do the same.

Other than an aging minister in an ill-fitting suit and a few employees of the funeral home, there were only two other people in attendance at Húdié's memorial service. Victoria sat next to Drew, trembling. She squeezed his hand tightly. Drew had put on the same black suit he'd worn to the services for his wife and daughter. It was a little tighter on him but not terribly.

The minister recited a few lines of New Testament scripture without regard to Húdié's actual religion. Buddhist, Drew surmised. The pastor offered up as many comforting words as possible about someone he'd never met, to an audience that had never met him. Nonetheless, the brief homily seemed to have a calming effect on Victoria as her trembling subsided with each mention of the word "heaven." The little girl had been through a traumatic event, discovering her grandmother dead. She'd been staying at Drew's house for safekeeping but had hardly slept and was exhausted in every way. Perhaps the memorial service was the beginning of some healing for a young heart that had already known too much pain.

When the brief service concluded, Drew and Victoria slowly rose to their feet and began their exit from the small chapel. A somber recording of organ music crackled over the speaker system. As they made their way down the center aisle that cut between empty rows of stark white folding chairs, Victoria leaned against Drew for both stability and comfort. The young girl walked bravely out of the funeral home and into a world of uncertainty.

Over the last three days, in addition to making funeral arrangements, Drew had spent much of his time moving many of Victoria's belongings into his house. Together, they'd decorated his spare bedroom after a visit to Target and converted the empty space into something suitable for a thirteen-year-old girl. The transformation sparked the occasional smile for Victoria during a time when she really didn't feel like smiling. It would be her home until Social Services decided what to do with her.

During one of his trips to the grocery store, Drew made a quick detour to Old Books on Front Street and found a used hardcover copy of *A Gentleman in Moscow*. He had no idea if Nicole was reading it as well, but in the absence of talking to her, he still wanted to feel a connection.

He'd bought another book that day, but it was one he didn't intend to read.

Victoria pulled the covers up to her chin on the twin bed in Drew's guest room. She lowered the back of her head onto the pillow and settled in for the night.

"I brought you a present," Drew said as he entered her room with his hands behind his back. "Actually, two of them."

Victoria sat up but without the normal excitement of a child expecting a gift. "What is it?"

Drew revealed a small, hardcover book with a picture of a young girl with a flashlight about to ascend a dark flight of stairs. He handed it to Victoria as he sat on the edge of the bed. "It's a classic. Required reading for anyone who wants to become a member of the literati. That girl on the cover is Nancy Drew."

"Who's Nancy Drew?" Victoria held the book closer to her face to inspect the front cover in the dim light of the nightstand lamp.

"Only the greatest girl detective of all time! You're gonna love her. She's daring, caring, and she uses her brain to solve mysteries. Plus, you gotta love anyone named Drew, am I right?"

Victoria nodded without really agreeing as she quietly thumbed through the well-worn pages. She held it up to her nose to drink in the slightly musty smell that comes with vintage books that have been anxiously waiting for someone to pull them off the shelf.

"And if you like that one, there's about fifty-five more waiting in the wings," Drew said. "It might be a little young for you, but let's consider it an appetizer until you're ready to take a bite out of Agatha Christie and Sherlock Holmes."

Drew's intentions with the book were twofold. He wanted Victoria to step inside a classic series of books that had launched millions of avid readers over nearly a century, just as Harry Potter had done for an entire generation. He also wanted to take her mind off her deep sadness. Victoria stopped looking at her book and angled her eyes up to Drew. "You said you had *two* presents for me."

He laughed. "Nancy Drew's got nothin' on you." Drew reached around to his back pocket but waited before revealing what was in his hand. "I'm going to give you my most prized possession. Not *loan*, mind you, but *give*."

Her eyes grew wider over the mystery about to unfold. "What is it?"

"Close your eyes and hold out your hands," he told her.

She eagerly obeyed. "I'm ready," she told him with a nod.

Drew placed in her tiny hands a book light, royal blue with a clip on one end and an adjustable neck. "Okay, you can open them now."

Victoria unclamped her eyes and cast them over the sleek device in her hands. Her mouth went slightly agape as she clicked the bright LED light on and off.

"Now you can read as late as you want."

She leaned forward and hugged him. "Thank you," she whispered. "I love it."

He expected her to clip the light onto her Nancy Drew mystery and immediately dive into the story, but instead, she placed both the book and the light on her nightstand. She flopped her head back onto her pillow and stared straight up at the ceiling.

"Remember that palm tree that we bought? The one in your living room?" she asked.

"Of course. What about it?"

"It's called an Areca palm, but it's also known as the butterfly palm. So grandmother will live in your house forever."

Drew swallowed hard and nodded in understanding as he reached over and stroked Victoria's forehead. She was remarkable in every way.

Drew stood and clipped the book light onto *The Hidden Staircase* and turned it on. He switched off the lamp on her nightstand, leaving only the glare of the LED light to illuminate the bedroom. "Goodnight, Victoria. Nancy Drew awaits."

"Night," she said softly. She opened *The Hidden Staircase* to the best part of any book: page one.

Drew closed her bedroom door and walked down the hallway. He had his own reading appointment with *A Gentleman in Moscow*.

He stopped and glanced back at her room, a faint sliver of light creeping out from under the bottom of the door. Maybe Nancy Drew would help yet another little girl forget about the harsh realities of life for at least a few hours.

Hours later, as Drew sank lower into his chair in the living room, a shard of a sentence fragment from the Towles novel cut into him. "Hiding behind books," the author had written about Count Rostov, the titular character. *Hiding behind books*, Drew thought. Simple, yet profound. Hiding behind books was something Drew had done most of his life. He'd done it first as a writer, expressing opinions, leveling complaints, sending up sharp criticisms, and otherwise telling people how he thinks the world and its inhabitants ought to be organized and fixed, all through hiding behind the voices of characters he'd invented.

He'd gone into hiding as a reader, running with Hemingway's bulls in *The Sun Also Rises* or storming the beaches on D-Day in Stephen E. Ambrose's *Band of Brothers*, all without having to face the actual dangers himself.

And for the last two years, as an aspiring recluse, he was hiding behind books again. Sitting in his darkened living room with a book in hand, he could escape to another dimension and visit with new friends created through daydreams and ink and thus avoid the potential pain that comes with interacting with real humans. By hiding behind books, he never had to go out on a limb. He just sat at the base of the tree and flipped through the pages, never exposing the fears of his heart, never challenging the frailties of his soul.

He took a long look at the laptop computer sitting idly on

the side table in his living room, dustier than ever. Against his better judgment, Drew picked up his phone and texted Nicole.

Are you reading anything good?

There was no reply. Not that he'd expected one. After an hour of waiting and hoping, he gave up and trudged to bed. He missed his best friend.

Her head propped against the arm of the living room couch, Nicole was also reading *A Gentleman in Moscow*.

If they'd been able to discuss it, they would have realized that the book was a perfect metaphor for both their lives. Count Alexander Rostov had been sentenced to house arrest at Moscow's famed Hotel Metropol, for the mere crime of being an erudite aristocrat during the Russian Revolution. He was comfortable, yet still a prisoner.

Drew easily made a connection with the Count's fatherly friendship with the precocious child, Sofia, while Nicole could identify with Sofia's friendship with the hotel seamstress, Marina.

Prisoner, captive, confinement. Those were the words that kept swirling through Nicole's head as she read. *Trapped.* Despite her best efforts to give Lee Wayne another chance, there was still a nagging feeling deep in her soul that perhaps she'd taken the wrong fork in the road. It was the same sense of impending doom she'd felt as a teenager when walking through a haunted house at Halloween, always on edge, bracing for the unseen danger lurking around the next corner.

Nicole rested her open book across her breastbone. She saw the text from Drew but didn't respond. She missed her book club.

CHAPTER THIRTY-FIVE

"Books may well be the only true magic."

— Alice Hoffman

It was perhaps the most glorious summer sunset he'd ever witnessed, or at least the best one since he'd started looking upward again.

Drew leaned against the fence in his backyard and gazed out over Húdié's garden. The five-color Chinese peppers were just days away from maturity, their red skin matching the crimson glow of the evening sky.

In his moments of quiet introspection, he considered, marveled even, how much his own life had transformed from the day that Húdié had first married the tender pepper plants with the rich soil he'd churned up for her. He'd lost weight, he'd nearly given up alcohol, and ate more green food than he knew existed. He'd rediscovered his love of running. And now he had a teenager living in his house, complete with cosmetics on the bathroom countertop and terrible music coming out of the clock radio he'd bought her. And he loved it. All of it. He felt a joy inside that he thought had disappeared two years ago with the deadly pull of a riptide. All of that, however, was tempered by the nagging feeling of how much he missed Nicole. How he missed talking to her about books. How he missed everything about them.

The bright colors of the sunset were slipping away as the evening stars appeared. He tapped his fingers on the top of the fence, trying to discern whether forgetting about her was the best way to move forward, or perhaps the worst.

At bedtime, Drew knocked gently on Victoria's door.

"Come in," came her tiny voice.

Drew pushed open the door and stood in the doorway. "How's Nancy Drew coming along?"

The Hidden Staircase was by her side, bookmarked near the end. "Where am I going to live?" she asked him, staring at the blank ceiling.

Her question caught him off guard, but he tried not to show it. "I don't know," he replied softly. "But you don't need to worry about that tonight."

"But I *am* worried. I know I can't stay here forever. What's going to happen to me?" She looked squarely at him. "And tell me the truth."

Drew measured his words carefully, wanting to be both honest and reassuring. "Well, I imagine Social Services will track down your nearest relatives. You can live with them."

"But I don't have any relatives here. They're all in China. What happens then?"

"I don't know," Drew said with an uneasiness growing in the pit of his stomach. "Let me look into it. Not to worry." He forced a smile that was meant to look reassuring. "It'll be okay. I promise."

Victoria nodded and looked up at him with more trust than he felt he deserved.

It was taking Nicole longer than usual to read *A Gentleman in Moscow*. Every sentence was so exquisitely crafted, each word so carefully chosen. She wanted to drink in Towles's brilliance like someone with no time constraints strolling through an art gallery filled with Renaissance masterpieces.

She'd even made notes on lines she wanted to commit to memory. Page 20 . . . *imagining what might happen if one's circumstances were different was the only sure route to madness.* The top of 298 . . . *brush the past aside instead of bowing to it.* Sometimes she felt as though the author had penned those words exclusively for her, and that they might not be in anyone else's edition.

But it was a passage on page 441 that spoke the loudest to

Nicole. As Count Rostov gave guidance to young Sofia, Towles wrote, *"our lives are steered by uncertainties, many of which are disruptive or even daunting; but that if we persevere and remain generous of heart, we may be granted a moment of supreme lucidity—a moment in which all that has happened to us suddenly comes into focus as a necessary course of events, even as we find ourselves on the threshold of a bold new life that we had been meant to lead all along."*

Nicole replayed the chain of events after her fateful wrong turn down a one-way street years ago. The car accident that followed, then meeting Lee Wayne in his law offices, their courtship, and ultimately her imprisonment in a dangerous relationship. Had it all been part of a grand life lesson? And now that she was back under the same roof as her tormentor, had she really learned anything?

She escaped from her thoughts and misgivings by returning to the pages of her book.

Drew re-read the passage on page 420, which examined why certain people show up in your life at critical moments. Towles expressed Count Rostov's thoughts, at the age of forty-eight and set in his ways, on taking in six-year-old Sofia and raising her to adulthood as if she were his own daughter. He wrote, *"there are people who play an essential role at every turn . . . as if Life itself has summoned them once again to help fulfill its purpose."*

The single word that kept reverberating in Drew's mind was *purpose*. It clanged like a ship's warning bell, forcing him to take stock of his course and alter it if necessary. The Count, while imprisoned within the walls of a Russian hotel, had still found purpose in his life by devoting himself to the rearing of a little girl. As she blossomed and matured, he'd transitioned from babysitter to guardian to uncle and finally to father. The relationship eventually defined him.

Drew's exchange with Victoria earlier that night was still roiling through his head. *What's going to happen to me? Where am I going to live? What happens then?*

I don't know. I don't know. I don't know. But perhaps he did.

Drew pulled out his phone and dialed Nicole's number, knowing full well his message was heading directly to voicemail.

His voice was animated, nearly breathless, as he unleashed his thoughts in a barrage of words.

"Nicole? It's Drew. You probably guessed that. Do you know how we're always asking each other, why do we read? I've been thinking all this time that it was to give our lives meaning. To help us understand our place in the universe by comparing ourselves to the lives of fictional characters. But I've suddenly figured out it's more than that. Much more. I think we read to give our lives *purpose*. From the Bible to *The New York Times* Best Sellers list, we scour the pages of good books looking for words that will inspire us to a greater purpose. We're like . . . we're like prospectors panning for gold, sifting through all the sand and rock of meaningless chatter in search of those tiny nuggets of truth that we can apply to our own lives. It's not just entertainment or escape or edification... it's to find *purpose*. Why have I never thought of this before? Just wanted to tell someone, and you're the only person I know who would understand. Thanks for listening. I hope you're doing well. I miss you. Take care. Bye."

He hung up, feeling good that he'd reached out, but tinged with sadness that he hadn't spoken to her directly.

A minute later, in the darkness of her living room, Nicole listened to Drew's voicemail. More than what he'd shared, it made her happy just to hear his voice.

CHAPTER THIRTY-SIX

"Reading was my escape and my comfort, my
consolation, my stimulant of choice: reading for
the pure pleasure of it, for the beautiful stillness
that surrounds you when you hear an author's words
reverberating in your head."

— Paul Auster, *The Brooklyn Follies*

Drew tried to read a magazine in the anteroom of the
law office of Parnell and Draper but his mind couldn't
focus on the glossy pages in front of him. He tapped
his feet and fingers nervously as he waited to meet with his
lawyer, Lawton Parnell. His anxious state was a combination
of little sleep the night before, and increasing worry about the
life-changing discussion he was about to have.

Lawton Parnell was considered one of the sharpest legal
minds in the Wilmington area, but Drew hadn't initially sought
out his services because of his legal reputation. He'd met him
several years earlier at a fundraiser for the local library where
J. Andrew Endicott had been brought in as the keynote speaker.
Minutes into their first conversation over cocktails, Drew was
impressed by how well-read he was. Parnell was intrigued by
the publishing world and asked extensive and astute questions
about Drew's writing process. Drew felt certain that Lawton
had a legal thriller of his own in his future if he ever stopped
working eighty hours a week. He also figured that anyone with
the word *law* in their first name must be a good attorney.

When Drew had needed legal counsel a year ago, he asked around for some names. He simply wanted the most honest lawyer in town, not necessarily the best. As it turned out, he got both with Lawton Parnell. During the course of their business relationship, Lawton had also become a trusted friend, which is why he'd agreed to squeeze in a meeting with Drew between other pressing appointments.

"He can see you now," called out the receptionist, startling Drew out of his worried thinking.

"Thanks." He rose slowly from the couch and showed himself down the corridor to Lawton's office.

Lawton was a sturdy six feet one inch, and even though he was in his mid-sixties and had lost much of his hair, he still looked like he could play baseball for Wake Forest, where he'd starred as a third baseman in his undergraduate years. His congenial smile and avuncular demeanor belied how dogged he could be in the courtroom on behalf of his clients. He always wore a suit with a starched white shirt and plaid tie, fitting attire that matched his folksy Eastern North Carolina accent.

"Hey, buddy," he said in greeting, as he came around to the front of his desk to shake Drew's hand. He quickly checked his watch, perhaps to send a subtle message that he was pressed for time.

"Thanks for working me in. I wouldn't have bothered you if it wasn't important."

Lawton studied Drew's ashen face and the purplish bags under his eyes. "I can see that. Have a seat. Let's talk."

Minutes later they were deep into the discussion of what to do about Victoria. Lawton quietly took notes as Drew explained his situation.

"If I don't get custody of her, what happens?" Drew asked.

Lawton leaned back in his chair. "She falls under the auspices of Child Protective Services. First thing CPS will do is look for relatives. If they can't find any, she goes into foster care and gets put up for adoption."

Drew stared down at the carpet and shook his head with resolve. "I just can't let that happen."

"I admire your optimism, Drew, I really do, but it's not up to you. It's up to the county."

"So what do you think? Can we do this? Can I apply for custody with the aim of adoption?"

"Absolutely."

"And can you use your considerable influence at the court-house to get this expedited? The thought of Victoria spending even one night in a foster home makes me ill."

"I'll do what I can," Lawton said with a slight hedge in his voice, "but I gotta be honest . . . it's a tough row to hoe."

Drew nodded in understanding. "Whatever you can do. And make sure you bill me. Money's no object."

"Don't worry, I'll go easy on you. Just enough to buy a small yacht. Nothin' too fancy."

Drew smiled for the first time all morning as the two men stood to shake hands. As they walked to the door, Lawton scratched the back of his head.

"Drew, can I ask you something, not as your attorney, but as your friend?"

"Of course."

"You sure you know what you're doin' here? This seems a little like an emotional decision. Like maybe you're tryin' to make up for something."

Drew bobbed his head. His eyes darted from side to side as he formulated his response. "That's *exactly* what I'm doing. I'm *supposed* to make up for everything I didn't do the first time around. This girl needs me, Lawton. And frankly, I need her. It just might save us both."

"All right. Just makin' sure. I'll get the ball rollin' as fast as the wheels of justice will allow."

When Drew returned home, he saw Victoria working in Húdié's garden, wearing her grandmother's favorite straw hat. He parked in the driveway and ambled over, formulating the right words for the delicate discussion he was about to have with her.

"Hi," he called out from a distance so as not to startle her.

She answered without looking up. "I know you told me to stay indoors while you were gone, but these peppers are ripe and I needed to pick them. It's up to me now to take care of the garden."

"Your grandmother would be very proud." Drew moved closer while she continued to carefully pluck the bright red peppers from their stems and place them in her basket. He took a deep breath, unsure as to why he was so nervous. "Victoria...

what would you say if I could arrange it so you could stay here permanently? With me. I'd be your guardian."

Victoria didn't say anything. As if she'd been hoping he'd utter those words, she dropped her basket and slammed into him. She wrapped her arms around Drew with more strength than he knew she had. He gently patted her shoulders, just as a father does to his happy daughter.

CHAPTER THIRTY-SEVEN

"A house that has a library in it has a soul."

— Plato

A week had passed since Drew's last obligatory visit to see his mother. The walk from the parking lot and down the long corridor of her nursing home always felt like the last mile. How he envied the other visitors he saw in the hallways who always seemed to be delighted to be spending time with their aging parents. They often had grandchildren in tow and were perpetually loaded down with baked goods or a wreath of some sort. How had they managed to heal the scars of childhood? Or perhaps avoided them altogether? It just didn't seem possible.

Gloria was sleeping when Drew entered her room. He stared at his mother for a few moments before waking her, wondering how much more time she had before moving on to the next realm. He pulled up a chair and softly jostled her elbow. "Mother? It's Drew."

Gloria lurched awake but quickly realized who was at her bedside. "Hello, son. I didn't know you were coming today." She rolled over onto one elbow and looked beyond his shoulder. "Did you bring Nicole?"

Drew's reply was uncertain and slow. "Uh, no. She's not here."

"I like her."

"I do too." *More than I should admit,* Drew thought.

"Is that her natural hair color?" Gloria asked.

"I'm . . . not sure. I would assume so." He leaned closer and smiled. "I have some good news. You're going to be a grandmother again."

Gloria's eyes widened. Not with delight, but with suspicion. "How? Is your brother having another baby? He's too old for that."

"I'm adopting a little girl. She lives next door, but her grandmother died. Actually, she *lived* next door. She lives with me right now, and I plan to make it permanent."

"You've never mentioned her before. What's her name?"

"Victoria."

"Victoria," she repeated. "Victoria. Is she British?"

"No. She's of Chinese descent."

"Chinese?" Gloria said with a small degree of alarm. "You're adopting a Chinese baby?"

"She's a teenager. And yes."

Gloria's eyes darted agitatedly back and forth, not focused on anything in particular, as she tried to absorb the news. "Have you thought this through? Children are a *lot* of work."

Drew had to take a breath to measure his words and avoid blurting out what he truly thought. His sarcastic voice wanted to reply *why no, Mother, I haven't thought one bit about the responsibilities associated with adopting a teenager. I'm so glad you brought that up.* His annoyed voice also wanted to say *and thank you for referring to my upbringing as "work."* Instead, he deflected. "I'm looking forward to being a dad again. I hope I do a better job this time around."

There was a long pause as Gloria rolled onto her back and stared at the ceiling, reflecting. She broke her silence in a whisper that was tinged with regret. "It's not easy being a parent. All parents make mistakes. Hopefully, they're forgiven."

She closed her eyes and drifted back into sleep.

Drew leaned forward, forearms between his knees, and simply watched her. He remembered how beautiful she'd looked as a young woman in old scrapbook photos and silent 8mm films. How she used to laugh while enjoying a Manhattan, or smoking a cigarette. How she had made more of a fuss of him getting his first library card than over his driver's license. He tried his best to think about happier times. They appeared in bits and flashes, becoming more focused when he closed his eyes and sought out distant memories. Drew felt the first trickle of something rare moving inside him. Nostalgia.

◆ ◆ ◆

Drew knew that lawyers don't generally make house calls unless it's something imminent and serious. When he opened his front door that evening and saw the knocking had come from the knuckles of Lawton Parnell, he knew his attorney wasn't the bearer of good news.

"What's wrong?" Drew said.

"I'm afraid there's been a snag."

Drew's chin dropped to his chest. He stood aside and motioned with his head for Lawton to come inside.

Moments later, Lawton had broken the news that distant relatives had come forward to claim custody of Victoria. "They're from Naperville, Illinois, outside of Chicago. It's apparently a cousin of Húdié's. Last name of Huang. I'm not sure of the direct relation."

"How'd they even find out about it?"

"Who knows. Something popped up on the internet, I'm guessing."

Drew looked down at the floor as if the answer to his next question might be there. "So . . . how's this going to impact me?"

Lawton scratched the nape of his neck, careful to answer. "I gotta be honest. If there's no overridin' concern for the child's safety and well-being, courts usually give preference to blood relatives, no matter how distant the connection might be."

"But she's never even *met* them!" Drew argued. "I would be *such* a better fit."

"I don't disagree, but in the eyes of the law, you don't have much standing."

"Standing? What does that mean?"

"Standing is the legal term for how close your connection is to the child. How long have you known her, how long has she lived with you, anything along those lines."

Drew's face tightened. He exhaled through the side of his mouth. How in the *world* was he going to break the news to Victoria?

On the day she returned home to live with Lee Wayne, Nicole had promised herself she wouldn't contact Drew. If she were truly going to make a go of her marriage, she would need to keep J. Andrew Endicott completely out of mind. As much as she'd wanted to respond to his texts, she'd intentionally ignored his messages to uphold the puritan pact she'd made with herself.

However, she was still checking for his messages on her secret phone, so her vow of communication chastity wasn't entirely pure. She'd rationalized her actions by reminding herself that she *still* wasn't legally married. It was one of several promises Lee Wayne had thus far failed to keep in his self-described rebirth.

Nicole would check her secret phone for a message again tonight, feeling both fearful and hopeful: fear that Drew might be in a dark place because of her return to her old life, and hope that he was still thinking about her.

The text that popped up on her screen startled her enough that she put her hand to her mouth to prevent an audible gasp.

> N... Sorry to drop this in a text, but I wanted you to know that I'm trying to adopt Victoria. I'm not sure if you knew that her grandmother passed away. If it works out, I may need some advice. Don't know if you're open to that, but it would help me out. Hope all is well D

Glancing over her shoulder to make sure Lee Wayne was still fast asleep in his bedroom, Nicole texted back.

> What a lucky little girl! My ability to help you is obviously limited, but if you have any questions you think I might be able to answer, I'll of course do my best. I'm really happy for you. Take care. N.

They both shut off their phones, the electronic equivalent of turning off the lamp on the nightstand and rolling over. Miles apart, they were both still reading the same book, and both thinking about the other member of their exclusive book club more than ever before.

CHAPTER THIRTY-EIGHT

"In order to write about life first you must live it."

— Ernest Hemingway

It had been close to a year since the last time Drew was seated next to Lawton Parnell in a courtroom. During that proceeding, they'd been trying to get restitution from Drew's former business manager, who'd drained most of his accounts and fled the country. Lawton had secured the legal victory, but it was impossible to collect a dime when the defendant was presumably living somewhere on a beach in the Caribbean under an assumed name. All of the proceeds from Drew's literary genius were no doubt being spent on tanned women and tropical drinks. At least someone was enjoying it.

Seated at the table to their right, barely arm's length away, was the plaintiff in this case, Li Huang. Close to a dozen of his family members were seated in the gallery, all having made the trip down from greater Chicago to support his bid to take custody of Victoria.

Victoria was not present for the proceeding. An unadorned, middle-aged woman from Child Protective Services had picked her up at Drew's house earlier that day. According to Lawton Parnell, "That's because the judge doesn't want kids to hear all of the crap people sling at each other in a custody battle."

The only supporter on Drew's side was Nicole, who had quietly slipped inside the courtroom and taken a seat in the back row. He had hoped she would be there but hadn't expected her to make the trip. He patted his heart in silent thanks when he spotted her in the gallery. She blew him a small kiss which brought a much-needed smile.

The Huang's lawyer, most likely hired after a Google search, clearly seemed like someone who'd untangled hundreds of family matters prior to this case. She was late thirties and close to six feet tall, even in short heels. She was stylishly dressed with diamond earrings and a Movado watch that indicated to Drew that she was very good at her job. She bounced her large designer purse onto the counsel table in front of her, whispered something to Mr. Huang, then took her seat and spread open a thin file. She gave all the outward appearance that she was ready to do battle.

As they patiently waited for the custody hearing to begin, the courtroom was choked in an oppressive quiet. All sound was dampened by the circa-1970 charcoal-gray acoustic panels and striped olive-green carpeting that covered the front and rear walls. The echoes of bickering lawyers, pounding gavels, and weeping parents were smothered and swallowed up before they could bounce off the wooden benches in the gallery and brown oak paneling on the side walls.

The only splash of color that interrupted the monotonous earth tones were the American and North Carolina flags posted in stands on either side of the judge's bench, and the portrait of some revered judge from ages past hanging in the middle of the acoustic baffling.

"All rise!" called out the bailiff, a female deputy in black pants and a black shirt adorned only by a diamond-shaped patch on one shoulder. "This court is now in session. The honorable Leslie Harkin presiding."

The handful of people in the courtroom rose to their feet as the judge entered from a side door. Judge Harkin was in her late forties with stylish shoulder-length brunette hair and split eyeglasses with ruby red frames dangling from a chain around her neck. She wore a traditional black robe, but it was unbuttoned slightly down the front to reveal a modest dress with a lavender-and-white Damask print. She carried four or five pale blue file folders in the crook of her wrist as she ascended the three steps to her bench. She snapped the two magnetic halves of her glasses into place on the tip of her nose as she sat down in a swiveling office chair.

"Thank you," she told the courtroom. "Please be seated."

The court reporter eased into the chair to the right side of the bench. She seemed detached and unemotional, undoubtedly having already documented the rancorous 'he said/she said' testimony of thousands of custody cases before this one.

Even though Judge Harkin moved quickly and with purpose, as if this was an exceedingly busy day on the docket, she had a genial aura about her, unlike the stern and taciturn jurists portrayed in courtroom dramas. She had soft, hazel eyes, and it seemed to Drew that she was accustomed to listening intently to both sides before rendering a decision. He hoped that might work in his favor.

"Case number 12-CVD-646, Huang versus Endicott," the judge said into a thin gooseneck microphone, shattering the crushing silence.

Mr. Huang was called to the witness stand and sworn in by the bailiff simply by raising his right hand and promising to be truthful. No Bible involved.

His attorney began with a series of mundane questions: *your name, your occupation, where do you reside and for how long?* Huang's command of the English language was uncertain at best, and his responses were so timid and muted that they were barely audible. More than once, the bailiff had to adjust the gooseneck microphone in front of him to amplify his answers.

The next ten minutes were filled with leading questions by Huang's attorney about the home into which Victoria might be placed. *Financial situation, living arrangements, mental and physical health, schools.* All questions and answers were carefully orchestrated to make the Huang residence appear idyllic. The overriding question was saved for last: *why do you believe you should have custody?* Li Huang's coached response contained the word *family* at least a dozen times.

Just as his attorney had finished her rehearsed laundry list of questions, and thanked Mr. Huang, Judge Harkin interjected. She was flipping through the pages of her files as if she were missing some information. "Mr. Huang, do you happen to know the child's current age and her date of birth? I don't see it in any of my notes."

Huang couldn't answer either question.

"We will locate that information and get it to you right away, your honor," chimed in Huang's attorney.

"Thank you," replied the judge, still riffling through the pages in her files.

As Li Huang shifted uncomfortably on the witness stand, Drew leaned over and whispered into his attorney's ear. Lawton nodded.

"Your honor, if I may streamline the process?" Lawton said.

"Yes, Mr. Parnell?" the judge asked.

"My client informs me that for the record, the child's birthday is April the twenty-second. She's thirteen."

"Thank you, Mr. Parnell." Judge Harkin made a quick notation, then peered over the top of her glasses at Li Huang's attorney with a look that said *you probably should have known that.*

It was Lawton's turn to ask Mr. Huang a few questions. His inquiries were primarily about amenities and living conditions in his neighborhood. Schools, parks, recreational activities. And then, in his disarming avuncular way, Lawton tossed this spear. "Mr. Huang, not to question your motives for wanting to adopt Victoria, but did you know she inherited her grandmother's house? By my best guess, it's worth about $150,000."

"Objection!" called out Huang's lawyer. "Irrelevant."

Judge Harkin shook her head. "I'll allow it."

"Were you aware of that, Mr. Huang?" Lawton pressed.

"Yes," he answered meekly. "But that has nothing to do with anything."

Lawton smiled at Mr. Huang. "That's good to know. No further questions."

Lawton returned casually to his chair. Li Huang looked rattled as he exited the witness stand and couldn't take his eyes off of Judge Harkin who was quickly jotting notes after the uneasy exchange.

Drew couldn't believe how his nerves jangled at him as he took the witness stand and was sworn in. No matter how he situated himself, he couldn't get comfortable.

Huang's attorney, and then Lawton, went through the same battery of questions covering Drew's background and ability to care for a teenager. There was certainly nothing on his life's resumé that would preclude him from being a qualified custodian, that is if they didn't know about his bouts of depression, no steady job or income, and his occasional proclivity for excessive alcohol consumption.

With the dramatic timing and posture of a good Southern lawyer, Lawton leaned closer and posed the overarching question. "Mr. Endicott . . . please tell this court why you believe you would be the better choice to receive custody of this child."

Drew gathered his thoughts and pulled in a few breaths of steadying air. His nerves were jumping worse than ever. He had mentally outlined his speech, but the words poured from his heart. "With all due respect to the Huang family, and I'm sure they're fine people, but they haven't been in her life. They never even knew she existed until a few weeks ago. They never came to visit. They don't know what she likes to do for fun, or what vegetables she likes to eat, or what books she likes to read." He was getting more agitated with every new thought. "Christ, they didn't even know her birthday!" Drew looked directly at the Huang family. "Did you know she has a beautiful singing voice? Did you know she can run like the wind? Did you know she's already thinking about boys? No, of course not! You couldn't possibly! But *I* do. I know *all* those things because I've been there! I'm the one who taught her how to shoot a basketball and ride a bike and to read Louisa May Alcott." His voice was on the verge of cracking. He paused to collect himself. "And I know that she wants to stay with me. If you ask her, that's what she'd tell you. Simple as that. She wants to stay with *me*. And she should. If you truly want to do what's best for this child, you'll let her stay right here." After he spoke, he turned back to face the judge, silently pleading his case.

"Mr. Endicott," Judge Harkin said softly, "as an avid reader myself, I am somewhat familiar with your personal history. I am sorry for the losses you have suffered in your life." Drew nodded his thanks. "May I ask, is there any female presence in your home at this time? A sister, grandmother, aunt? Anyone who could provide you with some help with the nurturing of a thirteen-year-old girl?"

Drew shook his head. "No, your honor." His eyes met Nicole's. "Not at this time."

"Thank you," the judge replied. "You may step down."

Drew returned to the counsel table and took a seat next to Lawton. The last exchange with the judge notwithstanding, it seemed to have gone well. Drew twisted around to exchange a glance with Nicole, but upon seeing the tears glistening in her eyes, turned back before he began weeping as well.

It may have only been a few minutes, but the wait seemed interminable while Judge Harkin carefully made notes at her bench as if there were nobody else in the courtroom. Drew labored to breathe, wringing his hands and staring into the grain of the table. His stomach felt the same excruciating churning as when he'd buried his wife and daughter.

Judge Harkin pulled her microphone closer to her face. "This has been a difficult case for me. I see merits on both sides. Both homes are more than suitable when it comes to stability, primary caretakers, environment... all factors to which I give considerable weight. I have also spoken to Victoria in chambers, and she has made her wishes known that she would prefer to remain here.

"Even so, when there is no clear difference, and I can find nothing detrimental to the child's welfare in either situation, I am always inclined to rule in favor of immediate family, particularly when there is a strong female presence in the home. Therefore, I am granting sole custody to the Huang family."

Judge Harkin made brief but intentional eye contact with Drew as if trying to convey that she understood the pain she was inflicting on him with her ruling, as carefully considered as it was. He got the sense that at this moment, even she wasn't sure she'd made the right decision.

Drew's head slumped, his worst fear realized. Lawton Parnell put his hand on his client's shoulder, but Drew couldn't feel his touch through the sudden numbness overtaking his entire body.

To their credit, the members of the Huang family were embracing one another, but in a subdued manner out of respect for the raw feelings on the other side.

"However," Judge Harkin said, regaining everyone's attention as she let that single, powerful word dangle in the air. "The net proceeds from the sale of the house in which Victoria Hai now resides will be put into a trust fund. She can access it at age eighteen for her education. If she doesn't want to pursue higher education, then she can access the money at age twenty-five to do with it what she chooses." The judge looked over the tip of her glasses directly at Lawton. "That provision should eliminate any questions as to the motivation for taking custody of the child." She turned her attention to Huang's attorney. "Is that amenable to the Huang family?"

In Drew's mind, what should have been a quick nod in the affirmative was instead a lengthy exchange of whispers between Mr. Huang and his attorney. Huang didn't seem too happy with the judge's addendum but was resigned to accept it.

"That would be fine, your honor," answered Huang's attorney.

"Good. Is there any other matter that needs to come before this court as to this proceeding?"

"No, your honor," replied both attorneys in near unison.

"Thank you," Judge Harkin said. "That concludes this matter. I will entertain a motion for visitation at a later time if Mr. Endicott chooses to pursue that. This court is adjourned." She tapped her gavel lightly and descended from the bench.

"All rise!" called out the bailiff. It was all Drew could do to get to his feet. His heart had been ripped out. He felt as though he was collapsing inside himself, like a dying star.

Nicole dabbed her watery eyes with the shreds of her only tissue. She understood both the stinging emotions Drew must be feeling, that of giving up a child, and also the fear and uncertainty Victoria was certain to experience as she entered into the world of a stranger's family.

Head down, Drew steadied himself on the table, pressing his weight onto his clenched fists. In less than twenty minutes the course of Victoria's life had been decided. She would live in Naperville, Illinois, a town she'd never heard of until this week, with people she'd never met.

"I'm sorry," Lawton said somberly as he gathered up his files and slid them into his briefcase. "I'll follow up on visitation."

Drew nodded and patted Lawton on the forearm, a silent *thank you* for all of his earnest legal efforts.

Nicole made her way to the front of the courtroom and flung her arms around Drew. He held on tightly. The pain they were feeling was palpable and agonizing, even to those in the courtroom who had witnessed similar events innumerable times. They both released a fresh ocean of tears. Enough to drown in.

Less than two hours after he'd left the courthouse, Drew was standing in his driveway helping the Huangs pack up all of Victoria's belongings into their three cars. He felt like he was building the gallows for his own hanging. Victoria's basketball was the last item he squeezed into the overflowing trunk before Li Huang slammed it shut.

Right on cue, the woman from Child Protective Services pulled into the driveway with Victoria in the front seat. Victoria burst out of the car and ran to Drew's arms, clinging to him in the midst of the storm. She sobbed, convulsing at first, then going limp in his strong embrace.

"I'm sorry," he was finally able to whisper. "I let you down."

Victoria shook her head. "You did your best."

He stroked the back of her head. "I'll come visit," he told her.

"I hope so. And promise that you'll take care of grandmother's garden. And water our butterfly palm."

He nodded his vow, then gently pulled away. "You have to go now. Your family is waiting."

She fervently hugged him one final time, choking her final tears into his midsection, then slowly turned away and joined the Huangs. Two of the female members of the family put their arms around Victoria's shoulders and gently escorted her into a second car. Three engines roared to life, and they all backed out of the driveway. Their caravan disappeared down the street. Just like that, Victoria had been swept away.

For the next three hours, long after light had faded and exhaustion had set in, Drew picked vegetables.

Drew pulled the door closed on the spare bedroom where Victoria had slept the last few weeks, happily reading another installment of Nancy Drew each night before she drifted off. The sound of the door latching echoed off the empty walls. He didn't know if he could ever go back in there.

He reached high into the back of the kitchen cabinet and found a bottle of bourbon that hadn't been touched in weeks. He poured three fingers' worth into a short crystal glass. The first sip burned his tongue as the flavors of anise, caramel, and clove awakened and aroused his taste buds. He'd forgotten that feeling of fine alcohol provoking his senses even as it numbed his body. He held up the glass to the light and studied the honey-brown liquid, swirling it in slow circles. He placed the glass back on the counter and let it settle until it was perfectly still. The motionless bourbon now reminded him of the dark days when he'd stopped moving forward and wallowed in his grief and suffering. He'd lost so much. His wife and daughter, his career, a substantial sum of money, and now a child he'd grown to love. It would be so easy, so understandable, to seek solace in a glass of bourbon. So very easy. He picked up the glass and swirled it again, bringing the liquid back to life. He knew the next taste would be even better than the first. He breathed through his nose, pulling in more of the aromas from its bittersweet flavor wheel.

With an abruptness that surprised even himself, Drew tossed the remainder of the bourbon down the drain. He threw the half-empty bottle of liquor into the trashcan under the sink and kicked the cupboard door closed. He exhaled loudly, then snatched a bag of ground coffee from the pantry.

Minutes later, with a steaming cup of coffee on his desk, Drew's computer screen was filled with a blank page. He laced his fingers together and cracked them, then placed them on the keyboard. He began typing the first of the 90,000 words that would follow.

The Garden of the Butterfly
A novel by J. Andrew Endicott

The phone number for Holly Hedrick's New York literary agency was scribbled on a notepad next to his coffee mug.

For the next six days and nights, Drew would write as fast as he could type, the story pouring out of him.

CHAPTER THIRTY-NINE

"Books are good company, in sad times and happy
times, for books are people – people who have
managed to stay alive by hiding between the covers
of a book."

— E.B. White

The raspy snoring began quickly. Lee Wayne had only turned off the bedroom lights ten minutes prior to his clogged nasal passages trumpeting that he was fast asleep.

Nicole tiptoed across the floor in the darkened living room. She pulled the thick volume of *Crime and Punishment* off the bookshelf and carried it back to the couch, brimming with anticipation over any messages from Drew she hoped the hidden phone might bring. In the few texts they'd exchanged since they'd last seen each other in the courtroom the week before, he'd told her he was writing again but offered no details.

She sat down and flipped open the cover of the book. Her heart stopped. It was empty. Nothing in her secret hideaway. Alarmed, she leaped to her feet and retraced her steps to the bookshelf, searching along the way to see if she'd unknowingly dropped the forbidden phone.

The overhead light flipped on.

"Lookin' for this?"

Nicole spun around and saw Lee Wayne emerging from the shadows, holding her cell phone high in his right hand as he slowly approached. She couldn't even begin to think what to say. "You startled me!" she finally blurted, slinking away from the bookshelf and back toward the couch.

Lee Wayne moved closer. "I'll ask you again, Nicole. Are you lookin' for this?" He shoved his arm forward, pushing the cell phone up to her face.

She was in a total panic now, trembling with fear as he stood just inches away.

"Who've you been talkin' to?" he demanded.

"Nobody. I store my music on that."

"Don't lie to me, Nicole. You're ugly when you lie." He clamped his free hand onto her bicep like a shark. "Who is he?"

"Nobody."

"Stop lyin'!" he snarled through gritted teeth. He squeezed harder.

"Please let go. You're hurting me."

"And you think it doesn't hurt me when you go sneakin' behind my back, talkin' to who knows who in the middle of the night? How long has this been goin' on?"

"Nothing is going on."

"I don't believe you." He picked up the hollow book on the coffee table. "I think we both know what the crime was... but the question now becomes, what's the punishment?" He gripped her arm harder and pushed her toward the wall, pinning her against it. He grabbed a handful of her hair and held it in his closed fist.

She cowered, begging. "Please don't. I can explain."

Lee Wayne shook his head, his malevolent eyes riveted on hers. "I don't think you can. I don't think I'm goin' to even let you try." He slammed the cell phone against her temple, instantly drawing blood. "Who ya gonna call *now*, Nicole? Huh?" Lee Wayne struck her repeatedly on her head, the edge of the phone digging into her scalp. She was determined not to cry, which only made her assailant angrier and more forceful in his blows.

Sweating and short of breath, Lee Wayne finally relented. He smashed the phone on the floor then raked back his hair with his fingers and broke into a lurid smile. He started to untie the drawstring on his pajamas. "Now then... let's see what you can do to make it up to me."

Her back against the wall, Nicole pressed her palm against the top of her head and felt blood seeping into her hair. "You promised me that if I came back you wouldn't do this."

He snorted. "That was before you cheated on me."

As Lee Wayne looked down to finish untying the knot in his sleep shorts, Nicole sent a swift knee into his groin. He winced but quickly recovered. With the reflexes of a boxer, Lee Wayne backhanded his wife across the face, sending her crashing downward. She remained slumped on the floor in the fetal position as he lorded over her, dizzy with pain and breathing hard. If he wanted to beat her again, if he wanted to defile her, she could offer no more defense.

Mercifully, for no other reason than fatigue, Lee Wayne tied the drawstring above his aching testicles and derisively shook his head at the woman balled up in front of him. "You're pathetic," he spit out. "Why did I ever think I could turn you into somethin' decent?"

He started back toward his bedroom but suddenly stopped before entering the shadows of the hallway. On the side table in the living room was St. Nicholas, his eyes still twinkling despite what he'd just witnessed. Lee Wayne studied the doll for a moment, then looked back at Nicole, still in a broken heap. With no warning, he picked up Father Christmas and slammed him into the hardwood. Keeping his eyes riveted on Nicole, Lee Wayne stomped on the doll again and again and again and again, as if transferring the pain from St. Nicholas to the woman on the floor. "Pathetic," he barked again, then turned and retreated to his bedroom.

After waiting several minutes, Nicole crawled over to the other side of the room and held the fractured pieces of her doll in her hands. Bits of velvet and fur, twigs and berries. His delicate wire-rimmed glasses were a crumpled mess. His limbs were scattered across the floor. She tried to fit the pieces together as if there were some chance he could be made new. It was futile. Beyond repair. Beyond hope. Beyond her limits to endure.

Nicole fell into a fit of sobs. The dam of suffering had finally broken. She crawled to the couch and buried her head face down in the cushions that had been her bed for so long. She cried until the tears soaked through the fabric, until her knees were rubbed sore from the hardwood floor, until she had no more tears to give.

Within minutes, Lee Wayne's awful snoring croaked from the bedroom, real this time. Nicole raised her head and stifled her cries. A look of grim resolve seeped into her face. She turned her head toward the bedroom and listened. She decided she would never have to suffer another night under the same roof and under the thumb of Lee Wayne Shepherd.

Nicole sat on the edge of the couch, staring into the darkness. Thinking. Planning. Scheming.

An hour later, certain he was dead asleep, Nicole rose slowly to her feet and set about doing three seemingly random things.

She charged her cell phone, the one Lee Wayne hadn't smashed to bits.

She pulled two empty suitcases from the closet and placed them in the foyer next to the front door, like someone waiting for a cab that was arriving at any moment.

She threw Lee Wayne's terry cloth bathrobe into the garbage.

She sat back down on the couch in the living room and again stared into the emptiness of the dark night. A wry smile, borderline wicked, crept into her face. It would all be over soon.

CHAPTER FORTY

"Fairy tales are more than true: not because they tell us
that dragons exist, but because they tell us that
dragons can be beaten."

— Neil Gaiman, *Coraline*

Nicole Shepherd was going to push buttons today. Five
of them, to be exact.

The morning sun, just bleeding in through the blinds,
cast layers of light across the living room. Nicole slid her feet
off the couch and looked at her watch on the coffee table. It was
a few minutes after six o'clock.

While Lee Wayne was still sleeping, she unlocked the dead-
bolt on the front door and opened it slightly so the next person
to arrive wouldn't even have to knock.

She stepped into the hall closet, squeezing herself amongst
the winter coats hanging limply from the rack. She pulled the
closet door nearly closed, then took out her phone and let
the light from the screen fill the tiny space. She dialed 9-1-1
without the normal haste of a true emergency. Three buttons
that would change her life. Several lives, actually. She took one
more deep breath.

"9-1-1," answered a woman in a calm voice. "What's your
emergency?"

"Help me!" Nicole whispered as loudly as she dared into
the phone. "Please help me!" She truly sounded vulnerable and
afraid.

"What's your location, ma'am?"

"Rosebend Way. Fourteen thirty-one. Hurry! He's going to kill me!"

"Who's going to kill you?" the dispatcher asked.

"My husband! Please hurry!"

"I have someone on the way. Is your husband armed?"

Nicole hung up, not waiting for the rest of the questions. She stepped out of the closet and moved silently across the living room. She stopped briefly at the end of the hallway to listen for any signs of movement from Lee Wayne's bedroom. Nothing. Nothing except the usual relentless snoring. She calmly walked to the antique curio cabinet against the far wall and unlatched the glass door. She put the camera on her cell phone into video mode and pressed the red button at the bottom of the screen. She leaned her phone against a white porcelain angel inside the cabinet that had the tip of one wing chipped off, positioning the camera lens to make certain it would capture everything in the room.

Nicole quietly closed the door to the curio cabinet and eased away. The tiny red light on the phone continued to blink, a silent witness hidden amongst the curios. She pulled on a pair of dress boots with two-inch heels and exceptionally sharp points at the toe. She picked up a small backpack that had been sitting in the chair and put an arm through each strap to attach it to her shoulders and back. She threw on a light jacket to hide the backpack as much as possible. Ready.

Nicole calmly marched down the hallway with an echo reverberating from each footfall of her leather heels. She yanked open Lee Wayne's bedroom door and flicked on the overhead light, then pushed the biggest button of them all.

"Lee Wayne? I'm leaving you. This time for good."

The man in the bed lifted his groggy head. He propped himself up on one elbow and rubbed his bleary eyes with the thumb and forefinger of his free hand. Lee Wayne glanced at Nicole, framed by the doorway, then looked quickly at the clock on the nightstand, then back at Nicole. He looked terrible. Hungover and haggard. Disheveled and disoriented. "What did you say?" he finally blurted.

"I said I'm leaving you. Right now. Right this minute."

Lee Wayne violently tossed back the covers and kicked his feet over the side of the bed. He ran his hand through his hair as he stood up. "You're doing *what*?" he barked.

"I'm walking out the door," she said. "For good. Something I should have done years ago. Something I should have done the very second I met you. Goodbye, Lee Wayne."

As she vanished from the doorway, he reached for his bathrobe which was normally hanging on a hook on the back of the closet door. It was gone. Thick, black hair covered his shirtless chest, back, and protruding gut.

He burst through the bedroom door wearing nothing but pajama bottoms. On unsteady legs, he stormed down the hallway into the living room.

Nicole was standing calmly in the foyer next to her two suitcases with a hand on each handle as if about to pick them up and embark on her journey. The sight of her impending departure enraged Lee Wayne, stoking his splenetic ire like bellows pumping air into a blacksmith's furnace. He did what he always did when his fury overtook reason, which was often. He lunged at Nicole, clamping his sweaty hands around her throat and choking her until she reddened in the face.

She let loose of the suitcase handles as she reached up and grabbed at his fingers to relieve the pressure on her windpipe. She gasped for air, kicking him as hard as she could in his bare shins and unprotected groin with the sharp points of her leather boots. Yelping in pain, he shoved her hard against the wall, his normal move whenever he felt it necessary to punish her. Her back slammed against the wallboard, rattling the curios in the nearby cabinet. She recovered enough to scramble closer to the front door as if desperately reaching for the door knob. Lee Wayne wrestled her to the ground and sat on top of her. Nicole covered her face with her hands, doing her best to fend off his bare knuckles with her forearms and elbows. Hitting him with her knees, Nicole managed to loosen his grip and flip over onto her stomach. She balled up on the floor and succumbed. He beat her mercilessly across the back with his closed fists, as if it were *his* life that depended on it.

"Stop!" she whimpered, barely able to breathe. "Please stop! I'm begging you!"

"I'll stop when I'm good and ready to stop!"

Blow after blow rained down on Nicole. "Nobody makes a fool out of Lee Wayne Shepherd! Ya hear me? Nobody!" She just curled up and took it, like so many other times. But this time it was easier because she knew it would be the last time.

The last of the boilovers, the last of the beatings, the last of the bruises.

So all-consuming was Lee Wayne's blind rage that he never heard the distant wail of police sirens as he continued to pummel her. "You'll *never* leave me, Nicole!" The sirens grew louder as Lee Wayne continued his assault. Nicole knew it would be over soon. She'd taken it before and she could take it again. It had never been this brutal, this savage, but she knew she could survive it.

She heard tires squeal to an abrupt stop. Two car doors slammed. Heavy boots clambered up the walkway to a front door that had intentionally been left open.

Two uniformed police officers, one man, one woman, burst inside. Lee Wayne didn't see them at first, too intent on delivering more blows to Nicole's scalp and back as she absorbed all his raw venom. By the time he realized there were other people in the room, it was too late. The two officers tackled him and sent them all sprawling across the hard tile of the foyer.

Whatever was said next, Nicole didn't hear. Her ears were ringing from the thudding blows to her head. Within seconds, Lee Wayne was handcuffed and standing on his feet as the female officer was reading him his Miranda rights. He looked pitiful. Rivulets of sweat flowed from his temples as his hairy chest heaved for breath. He hung out of his pajama shorts in all the wrong places.

The female officer led him out the front door to the waiting patrol car. This was exactly how Nicole wanted to remember Lee Wayne Shepherd. Not only impotent but also powerless. She spoke not a word, resisting the temptation to taunt him. His immediate future was going to be bad enough. He'd lose his law license, his reputation, and his livelihood. Hopefully, he'd serve jail time. She didn't care.

"You okay, ma'am?" the male officer asked gently.

She nodded and smoothed back her hair as if that would compensate for the welts on her face and arms. "I'll be fine," she said in a calm, resolute voice.

"Do you need any medical assistance, ma'am?" the officer asked.

Nicole shook her head and walked slowly to the front window. She watched the female officer shove down the top of Lee Wayne's head as she steered him into the backseat of the police car. With the tip of her tongue, she wiped away a droplet of blood from the corner of her mouth. She allowed herself a thin but triumphant smile as she saw Lee Wayne with his head hung low in the back of the cruiser. Defeated. Humiliated. Pathetic.

As curious neighbors began to appear in doorways and driveways, trying to figure out what was going on, she imagined Lee Wayne was doing the same. He was undoubtedly wondering how his life had been turned upside down in just a matter of moments. He'd been fast asleep not ten minutes ago, and now he was heading downtown to have his mug shot taken. But it had not been minutes in the making. It had been years. Years of abuse. Years of excuses, years of living in fear and loathing. It had all ended with the touch of a few buttons. And for the first time in a long time, the fantastical murder plots were no longer formulating in Nicole's brain.

"Good day, ma'am," the officer told her. He nodded again as if to provide some signal that their conversation was over. He backed out of the front door and quietly closed it.

The police cruiser pulled away with a punctuating roar of the engine. It was over. Lee Wayne Shepherd's grimy hands would never touch her again, in any manner. The next thing his fingers would press against with any force would be an ink pad. Attorney Lee Wayne Shepherd was going to be on television for personal injury, but this time from a very different perspective.

Nicole slipped off her jacket and removed the backpack she'd been wearing underneath it, setting it upright on the ottoman. She unzipped the top compartment. She pulled out handfuls of cloth remnants she'd stuffed inside, then tossed them onto the couch. Leftover scraps of fabric from baby blankets and a turquoise cocktail dress that had yet to be worn. They had done their job, absorbing most of the battering from the pernicious but utterly predictable Lee Wayne Shepherd.

Nicole stepped into the shower. The pulsating water stung in places where bare fists had landed on unprotected skin. Purplish knots were rising on her arms. Both temples throbbed. She could feel her left eye swelling. A cut on the corner of her mouth and a small gash along her hairline had finally stopped bleeding. She wiped away the dried blood with a white washcloth.

The warm water was not only cleansing, it was cathartic. The cascade on her hair and the soap on her skin felt like a fresh start. She had turned the page and couldn't wait for the next chapter.

Dried off and dressed, Nicole sat with her phone on the edge of the bed and watched the video she'd recorded from the curio cabinet. It was all there. She smiled at the thought that it would eventually be shown in a court of law.

She dialed Drew's number and only had to wait a few seconds for him to answer.

"Hello?" he answered in a voice that indicated he didn't recognize the number.

"It's me," Nicole said. "The caged bird is free."

Drew burst through the open door of Nicole's house. He was stunned to see her bruised face and opened his mouth to speak, but she shook her head and held her index finger to her lips to quiet him. Nicole melted into his arms and clasped her hands around the back of his neck. They kissed for the first time, as if it was their *very* first time having kissed anyone. Even though the anticipation of this moment had been simmering for months, their kisses were long and unhurried, as if they both knew there was an endless supply in their future.

Drew left Nicole's house with the promise to have her over to his house that evening for a candlelight dinner. As he pulled up to his own home, he saw a car with Illinois license plates parked in his driveway. He immediately realized it was a car he'd seen before.

Puzzled, Drew parked on the street and quickly exited his vehicle. As he walked with long strides across the front lawn toward the car, Li Huang quickly emerged from the driver's side.

"I have been waiting for you," Huang said in a thick accent that was also heavily laced with annoyance.

"I can see that. What's wrong? What are you doing here?"

Huang opened the backseat of his car and motioned for Victoria to step out. "We are returning her," he proclaimed in a manner intended to make it clear there was no room for discussion.

"What?" Drew cocked his head and looked at Victoria. "What's he talking about?"

Li Huang shook his head vigorously. "This arrangement is not working out. The girl is very poorly behaved."

Drew narrowed his eyes as he studied Victoria, then looked back at Huang, who was growing more agitated. "What do you mean, she's poorly behaved? I find that hard to believe."

Huang pointed angrily at the young girl. "She bounces a basketball all day and all night. Nonstop. Bounce, bounce, bounce! It is ruining our lives. We tell her to quit, but she does not listen."

Drew looked directly at Victoria as she looked at the ground. Drew bobbed his head as he frowned. "Doesn't listen, huh? Kinda like bok choy?"

"What?" asked Li Huang.

Drew waved him off. "Never mind."

Huang stepped closer to Drew. "She is yours if you still want her. I will sign whatever papers you need."

Victoria looked up at Drew, her eyes filling with tears.

"Of *course* I want her," he answered, never taking his eyes off Victoria. "Who *wouldn't* want a kid like that?"

Victoria sprinted to Drew and flung her arms around his waist.

"I can think of several people," muttered Li Huang, as he removed Victoria's belongings from the trunk of his car, including the offending basketball. "This goes too," he declared as he tossed it on the ground. Li Huang slammed the trunk. "I will have my attorney call yours. Good day." He climbed quickly into his car and shut the door with more force than was necessary. He backed out and sped away.

Victoria pressed her head sideways against Drew's stomach and sobbed tears of relief. He kissed the top of her head as a broad smile swept across his face. "So… you couldn't behave for *one* week? I just have one question, young lady. What took you so long?"

CHAPTER FORTY-ONE

"The problem with books is that they end."

— Caroline Kepnes, *You*

Victoria splashed in the lively blue-green waters of the Atlantic off of Oak Island. Her orange life vest made her easy to spot in the choppy surf. Although it was the first time she'd seen the ocean, she instinctively knew what to do. It all seemed so miraculous to her. The push and pull of the waves, the salty taste of the water, the sheer enormity of it all. And thankfully she knew only of its pleasures and none of its dangers.

Drew watched her closely as he sat on the edge of the dry sand, just out of reach of the foamy fingers of the crashing surf. He appeared to be relaxed, but through his sunglasses, he wouldn't take his eyes off Victoria as she frolicked in the sand and sea.

"This seat taken?"

Drew spun his head to see Nicole standing behind him. He sprang to his feet to embrace her and exchange a soft kiss. He took her arm and helped her ease down to the sand. They both watched the young girl tumbling and momentarily disappearing in the small waves, again and again, delighted beyond measure.

Nicole glanced briefly at Drew, then back to the ocean. "She'll be okay, you know."

"I know," he answered, still watching her. "It's just hard." She nodded in understanding, reaching over to weave his hand into hers. He knew that Nicole was talking about much more than just this moment, more than just the immediate safety of a young girl in an ocean that harbored sudden dangers. He knew the days would come when he would have to let her go on overnight field trips and drive a car by herself and go on dates with immature boys and go off to college and move away for a job and on and on, and he wouldn't be there to protect her. Letting her expand her horizons, even in small ways, wasn't going to be easy. But he also knew that over time, despite his painful memories of Emilie and Maddie, he would eventually be able to do it. Birds and butterflies are meant to fly, and sometimes fly away. When the time came, he knew he would have to find the strength to let her out of his sight. Just not today.

He pulled himself out of his mild trance and squeezed Nicole's hand. "So here we are. Back where it all started, huh?"

She smiled. "Ground zero for the Oak Island Book Club. Maybe one day the state will erect a historical marker, like the one for the Wright Brothers at Kitty Hawk."

Drew laughed and pulled his hand across the air as if he were reading a plaque. "This is where it all took off!"

She leaned over and kissed his cheek. "I'm afraid my visit to this hallowed ground is a little bittersweet today."

"Oh? How so?"

"I won't get to come here anymore. At least not in the same way."

Drew responded without taking his eyes off the water. "And why's that?" he asked calmly.

"Teri sold her beach house. It was only on the market for one day."

Drew barely reacted to the news. "I know," he finally said.

"You knew it sold?"

"I did."

Nicole popped back her neck and wrinkled her brow. "How did you know that?"

Drew slowly turned to Nicole and slid his sunglasses off of his face. "Because I bought it."

Nicole was having trouble comprehending what she was hearing. "What? *You* bought it?"

"Yep. And most of the furnishings. I made Teri promise not to say anything." He bobbed his head in Victoria's direction. "We wanted to be the ones to tell you."

Nicole scrambled to her feet. "You're making that up."

"Nope. My old agent, Holly Hedrick, got me a fairly sizable advance on the new novel I'm writing. It was enough for a healthy down payment and I couldn't think of a better way to spend it. I've already started moving in." He got to his feet and dusted off a layer of sand from his shorts. "Come on. I'll show you." He cupped his hands around his mouth and yelled out to the water. "Victoria! Let's go in!"

She waved in acknowledgment and high-stepped over the last few waves as she bounded toward the shore.

Drew looked at Nicole and pointed his thumb toward Victoria. "See? She listens."

The interior of the beach house was essentially the same as when Teri had owned it. She'd come and removed her personal belongings and a few wall decorations, but the changes were minimal. A few dozen books were already neatly in place on the built-in shelves. A healthy Areca palm was standing in a place of honor in a corner of the living room.

Victoria was halfway up the staircase. "Do you want to see my room?" she asked Nicole.

"Sure, I'll be up in a minute." Nicole looked at Drew and spread open her palms. "I just need a little more time to let all of this sink in."

"Okay! I'll go change." Victoria skipped up the stairs and disappeared.

The most noticeable additions to the décor had been carefully placed on the fireplace mantel. Inside a picture frame fashioned from driftwood was the photograph of the three of them, taken the day they'd gone to Teri's salon to have Victoria's hair styled. Next to the framed photo was a large doll with wire-rimmed glasses and a black velvet robe. Father Christmas.

As she slowly approached the mantel, Nicole covered her mouth with her hand in disbelief. She looked at the doll, then at Drew, then back to the doll. She lifted St. Nicholas off his perch and held him reverently in her hands, stroking his soft robe with the side of her thumbs.

Drew stepped beside her. "It's not exactly like the one you lost, but I'm hoping it's pretty close."

She clasped her hand around Drew's arm just above the elbow. "He's perfect." She studied every detail, beaming. "Where did you find him?"

Drew winked. "The Christmas House in Southport is a wonderful place."

Nicole returned the doll to the mantel, turning him just slightly to face the window with the ocean view. She wrapped her arms around Drew and kissed him softly on the lips. "I can't even," she told him.

"It was a big part of your past. Now I'm hoping it's part of your future. *Our* future. The three of us. And one day, maybe more."

She kissed him again and pressed the side of her head against his chest. "When can we start?"

Drew stepped back and reached into his pocket. He pulled out a diamond ring and held it up. "As soon as you say I will."

With misty eyes, Nicole pressed her fingers against her mouth and nodded. "I will."

Drew brushed his hand across her cheek and kissed her lips. She wrapped her arms around him and reveled in their safe embrace. "I will," she whispered.

Cameron Kent has published five previous novels: *The Road to Devotion, When the Ravens Die, The Sea is Silent, Make Me Disappear*, and *Mayor Molly*. His historical novel, *The Road to Devotion*, was selected for Winston-Salem's "On the Same Page" community reading event in 2011, and *The Sea is Silent* was selected for the 2019 "Blue Ridge Read" by the Alleghany County Arts Council. His other writing credits include four films, which have aired on NBC, HBO, Lifetime, and at the American Film Institute. He's also written a Christmas musical, *Welcome to Virginia*, which has been performed at community theatres across the country. He's an Emmy-award winner and a member of the North Carolina Broadcasters Hall of Fame for his thirty-two years in television news. Cameron splits time between his home in Winston-Salem, North Carolina, and a cabin in the Blue Ridge Mountains.